Praise for *Every Secret Thing*

"Mesmerizing. . . . This is a standout. . . . Lippman shows a deft storytelling hand."
—*Orlando Sentinel*

"Powerful . . . incisive. . . . Lippman examines her disturbing subject with grave intelligence and sensitivity."
—*New York Times Book Review*

"Suspenseful. . . . A disturbing but seductive thriller. . . . With a deft, delicate touch, Lippman slowly reveals what actually happened then and what is happening now."
—*Milwaukee Journal Sentinel*

"This may be the best book I've read all year. . . . So pitch-perfect I couldn't put it down. . . . You're in for a treat."
—*Charlotte Observer*

"Lippman writes fiction that convinces. There's not a false note or a clunker here, and the book's tone brilliantly conveys its mounting gravity. . . . *Every Secret Thing* plays with our expectations, constantly pulling us in surprising directions. . . . Lippman has great sympathy for her characters, and she refuses to condescend to her readers."
—*Seattle Times*

"Absorbing. . . . Palpable tension. . . . Lippman boldly marches into stand-alone territory with a novel that is full of social relevance with wry comments on contemporary society, a plot that doesn't let go of the reader, and excellent character studies. . . . With *Every Secret Thing*, she has explored a disturbing subject with depth, compassion, and a heartfelt sincerity."
—*Sun-Sentinel* (Fort Lauderdale)

"Lucid, tight, and compelling. . . . A chilling study of mothers, daughters, love, and murder."
—*Kirkus Reviews*

EVERY SECRET THING

Also by Laura Lippman

LAURA
LIPPMAN

EVERY
SECRET
THING

wm

WILLIAM MORROW
An Imprint of HarperCollinsPublishers

EVERY SECRET THING. Copyright © 2003 by Laura Lippman. Excerpt from *The Most Dangerous Thing* copyright © 2011 by Laura Lippman. All rights reserved. Printed in the United States of America. No part of this book may be used or reproduced in any manner whatsoever without written permission except in the case of brief quotations embodied in critical articles and reviews. For information, address HarperCollins Publishers, 195 Broadway, New York, NY 10007.

HarperCollins books may be purchased for educational, business, or sales promotional use. For information, please e-mail the Special Markets Department at SPsales@harpercollins.com.

A hardcover edition of this book was published in 2003 by William Morrow and a mass market edition in 2004 by Avon Books, both imprints of HarperCollins Publishers.

FIRST WILLIAM MORROW PAPERBACK EDITION PUBLISHED 2011.

Library of Congress Cataloging-in-Publication Data has been applied for.

ISBN 978-0-06-207489-8

15   OV/RRD   10 9 8 7 6 5

For Vicky Bijur and Carrie Feron

The end of the matter; all has been heard. Fear God, and keep his commandments; for this is the whole duty of man.

For God will bring every deed into judgment, with every secret thing, whether good or evil.

—ECCLESIASTES 12: 13–14

Acknowledgments

This is a work of fiction. I am grateful to Bill Toohey, Gary Childs, and David Simon for helping me with the technical aspects of police work. Joan Jacobson and Lisa Respers told me what I was getting right (and what I was getting wrong) about our hometown and its inhabitants. Susan P. Leviton, director of Maryland Advocates for Children and Youth, provided a key piece of information about the state's juvenile system. But I have used all this research for my own ends to write a work of fiction. If there has ever been a case like this in the history of Maryland, I am wholly ignorant of it.

Special thanks to Sally Fellows and, by extension, the virtual clan to which we belong, for encouraging me to write this book.

July 17, seven
JULY 17, SEVEN
years ago
YEARS AGO

Prologue

They were barefoot when they were sent home, their drip-
ping feet leaving prints that evaporated almost instantly, as if
they had never been there at all. Had it been possible to re-
trace their literal steps, as so many would try to do in the
days that followed, the trail would have led from the wading
pool area, where the party tables had been staked out with
aqua Mylar balloons, past the snack bar, up the stairs, and to
the edge of the parking lot. And each print would have been
smaller than the last—losing first the toes, then the narrow
connector along the arch, the heels, and finally the baby-fat
balls of their feet—until there was nothing left.

At the curb, they sat to put on their shoes—sneakers for
Ronnie, brand-new jellies for Alice, who used whatever
money came her way to stay current with the fifth-grade
fashion trends at St. William of York. Jellies were *the* thing
to have that summer, on July 17, seven years ago.

The parking lot's macadam shone black, reminding Alice
of a bubbling, boiling sea in a fairy tale, of a landscape that
could vaporize upon touch.

"It's like the desert in Oz," she said, thinking of the hand-
me-down books rescued from her mother's childhood.

"There's no desert in Oz," Ronnie said.

"Yes, there is, later, in the other books, there's this desert
that burns you up—"

"It's not a book," Ronnie said. "It's a movie."

Alice decided not to contradict her, although Ronnie usually ceded to Alice when it came to matters of books and facts and school. These were the things that Alice thought of as *knowledge,* a word that she saw in blazing blue letters, for it had stared at her all year from the bulletin board in their fifth-grade classroom. *"A wise man is strong; yea, a man of knowledge increases strength."* The A papers of the week were posted beneath that proverb, and Alice had grieved, privately, any week she failed to make the board. Ronnie, who never made it, always said she didn't care.

But Ronnie was in one of her dark moods today, long past the point where anyone could tell her anything.

"I should call your mothers," Maddy's mom had fretted, even as she banished them from the party, from the pool. "You shouldn't cross Edmondson Avenue alone."

"I'm *allowed,*" Ronnie said. "I have an aunt on Stamford, I go to her house when my parents are working. She's this side of Edmondson."

Then, with a defiant look around at the other girls, their faces still stricken and shocked, Ronnie added: "My aunt has Doublestuf Oreos and Rice Krispie treats and all the cable channels, and I can watch anything I want, even if it's higher than PG-13."

Ronnie did have an aunt somewhere nearby, Alice knew, although Stamford didn't sound right. Neither did the Oreos and Rice Krispies—there was never anything that good to eat in the Fuller house. There was all the soda you could drink, because Mr. Fuller drove a truck for Coca-Cola. And Ronnie was telling the truth about what she watched. The Fullers didn't seem to care what Ronnie saw. Or did, or said. The only thing that seemed to bother Mr. Fuller was the noise from the television, because the only thing he ever said to Ronnie and her three older brothers was *Turn it down, turn it down.* Or, for good measure: *Turn it down, for Christ's sake.* Just last week, on a rainy afternoon, Ronnie had been watching one of those movies in which teenagers kept getting killed in ever more interesting ways, their screams echoing forever. Alice had buried her head beneath the sofa cushions, indifferent to the stale smells, the crumbs and litter pressing into her cheek. For once, she was almost glad when Mr. Fuller came through the door at the end of his shift. "Jesus, Ronnie," he had said on a grunt. "Turn it down. I swear there's just no living with you."

"You're blocking the set, Dad" was Ronnie's only reply. But she must have found the remote, for the screams faded away a few seconds later, and Alice popped her head out again.

Maddy's mother didn't believe the story about Ronnie's aunt. Alice could see the skepticism in her parted lips, painted a glossy pink, and in her squinty, tired eyes. Maddy's mother seemed torn between wanting to challenge Ronnie's lie, and wanting to get away from Ronnie—away from *them,* although Alice had done nothing, nothing at all, except get a ride to the party from Ronnie's brother.

Maddy's mother licked her lips once, twice, removing some of the pink and most of the gloss, and finally said: "Very well." Later she told everyone Ronnie had lied to her, that she never would have let two little girls leave if she had known they were going to be unsupervised, if she had known they were going to cross Edmondson Avenue alone. That was the worst thing anyone in Southwest Baltimore could imagine at 2 P.M., on July 17, seven years ago—crossing Edmondson Avenue alone.

The hill to Edmondson was long and gradual. Alice did not know if there were really ten hills in this neighborhood called Ten Hills, but there were enough slopes to punish short legs. The two girls did not have cover-ups, so they knotted their towels high on their bodies, at the spot where breasts were supposed to hold them. But they had no breasts, only puffy bumps, which they had started keeping in bras just this year. So the towels kept slipping to the ground, tangling at their ankles. Ronnie's was a plain, no-longer-white bath towel, and she cursed it every time it fell until finally, after tripping over it for the fourth time, she slung it around her neck, not caring if people saw her body. Alice could never walk down the street like that, and she wore a one-piece. Ronnie had a red-and-white bikini, yet she was so thin that the skimpy bottoms seemed to bag on her. The only curve on Ronnie's body was her stomach, which bowed out slightly. "Like a Biafran baby," Alice's mother, Helen, had said. "Oops—I'm dating myself." Alice had no idea what she was talking about, whether it was good or bad, or even how someone went about dating herself. She just knew that her mother never said Alice looked like a Biafran baby.

Alice's navy one-piece had a cutout of a daisy on her belly. Ronnie told her this was queer, and had said this every time she saw Alice in the suit this summer, which was exactly three times—a day-trip to Sandy Point, another poolside birthday party, and today. "Who wants to see a brown daisy on your fat white belly?" she had said when Alice's mom dropped her this morning at the Fullers' house before going to work.

"Vintage," Alice's mother had said. "It's vintage."

Ronnie didn't know what that meant, so she had to shut up. Ronnie liked Alice's mother and tried to be at her best when she was around. Alice didn't know what *vintage* meant, either, but she knew it was good. Her mother had a whole vocabulary of good words that Alice didn't quite understand. Vintage. Classic. Retro. New-Vo. When all else failed, when Alice was balking at wearing something because the other girls might tease her, Helen Manning would meet her eyes in the mirror and say: "Well, I think it's exquisite." This was the word that ended everything, her mom's way of saying, in her gentle way, Not-Another-Word, I'm-at-the-End-of-My-Patience. Ex-qui-site. The one time Alice had tried to use it, Ronnie had said: "Who wants zits?"

Yet it was Helen Manning who insisted that Alice play with Ronnie. Ronnie was a summertime-only friend, an in-the-neighborhood friend, the only other didn't-go-to-camp, didn't-have-a-pool-membership girl. During the school year, Alice had better friends, friends more like her, who read books and kept their hair neat and tried to wear the right things. Come fall, she was so happy for school to start because it meant a reunion with these real friends.

Only not this fall. Now that it was time for middle school, a lot of the girls in their class were going to private places. "Real private school," Wendy had said—not meanly, but a little carelessly, forgetting that Alice wasn't going with them. Alice thought St. William of York was a real private school. It was real enough that Alice's mother couldn't afford it anymore. Next year, Alice would have to go to West Baltimore Middle. Ronnie would, too. Alice's mother said it wasn't about the money, that Alice needed to meet All Kinds of People, to be exposed to New Experiences, and, besides, if she stayed in Catholic school much longer, she Might Become a Catholic, God Forbid.

But Alice knew: It was about the money. In the end, everything was about money—in her house, in the Fuller house, even in the rich kids' houses. Parents just had different vocabulary words for it—some fancy, some plain—and different ways of talking about it. Or not talking about it, as the case may be.

In the Fuller family, they screamed and yelled about money, even stole from each other. Earlier this summer, Ronnie had caught her youngest older brother going into her bank and tried to bite him. He had just pushed her down, then taken a hammer and smashed the bank, a Belle from *Beauty and the Beast,* even though she had a little plug beneath her feet. He didn't have to break her to get what was inside. And even when the money was freed—mostly pennies and nickels but also quarters, a few of those dollar coins, from when they put the woman on the coin and nobody wanted her—Matthew had kept pounding and pounding on Belle until she was nothing but yellow powder.

Alice and her mother did not fight about money, did not even speak about it directly, not even when her grandparents visited from Connecticut and said things like: "Well, this is the life you made for yourself." Once, Alice's grandfather, Da, had given her a five-dollar bill when she told him she didn't have the kind of scrunchie that all the other girls had. It was the only time her mother had ever spanked Alice, and they both cried afterward and agreed it would never happen again. Her mother would not spank, and Alice would not make up stories to get money from Da.

That had been back in the third grade, though, when neon scrunchies were important and Alice hadn't yet learned to be good. Now the thing to have was jellies, which is why Alice saved her allowance and bought her own, at Target. She had shown them to her school-year-best-friend Wendy, when it was time to open the presents, and Wendy must have approved, for she made room for Alice on the bench she was sharing with two other girls from their class.

Maddy's birthday party had been set up near the baby pool, not because they were babies, but because it was behind a fence, and they needed the fence to tie the balloons. Alice found herself counting the gifts. She was always counting. Steps on the stair, lines on the highway, birds flying south for the winter. There were fourteen presents on the table, but only thirteen girls at the party. Did Maddy's mom bring a present, too? Or did one of the girls away at camp send a gift? Fourteen presents, thirteen girls. Hers was one of the prettiest on the outside—Alice's mother had wrapped it in blue paper that shimmered—but the shape gave it away. The present was a book, just a book, and Maddy was not the kind of girl who would be happy to get a book. Maddy wanted one of those new T-shirts, the kind that leave your belly showing, and rubber bracelets, and the nail polish you could peel right off. Maddy was the youngest girl in the class, but she knew the most about makeup. She was always sneaking gloss, and green mascara, until the nuns caught her and sent her to the bathroom to wash it off.

Alice had expected Maddy's mother to be pretty, too, just so. Yet Maddy's mother was sort of plain—slender enough to wear a two-piece, but tired-looking, as if being so thin and tanned had worn her out. Even her hair looked tired, like the "before" picture in a conditioner ad. There were mainly two kinds of mothers at St. William of York, mothers who worked and mothers who didn't. But Maddy's mom was the Mother Who Used to Work. That's how she had introduced herself to Alice's mom, when she called the other day to ask a few questions about Ronnie. Alice knew what was said because she listened in on the extension. Just sometimes.

"I'm Maddy's mother. I used to work—at Piper, Marbury?" Alice's mother made an "ah" sound, as if this were a good thing. She approved of Anything Creative, as she was always telling Alice. But Alice was surprised to find out that Maddy's mom was a piper. She thought she had been a lawyer. She imagined Maddy's mother in a green hat with a feather, leading the children out of Hamlin, along with the rats. No, the rats came first, the piper took the children later. Besides, Maddy's mother must have been a piper in an

orchestra to draw such an "ah" sound from Helen, not someone who just played on the street or in circuses. A mother
who made music must be fun.

But Maddy's Mother Who Used to Work had looked as if
she had a headache from the moment the party started. Her
forehead had four creases, like two equals signs, and there
was a tiny set of parentheses at the bridge of her nose. These
seemed to get deeper and deeper as the day wore on, and by
the time it was time to open the presents, her face looked
like a very hard math problem, maybe even algebra. St.
William of York didn't have a gifted program, but Sister
Elizabeth had started giving Alice extra-credit homework in
math. This was a secret. Alice wasn't sure why. She thought
it might be because she didn't have a lot of secrets from her
mother, who always seemed to know exactly what she was
thinking. Other times, she thought her mom would be disappointed in her for liking math, which wasn't creative and led
to making money, which Helen Manning always said really
was the root of all evil—not making money, but caring about
it, counting it. When she first heard about the Root of All
Evil, Alice had asked: "Is that near Route 40?" And her
mother had laughed until she cried, then hugged her and
said: "It's not far, I'll grant you that." Later, Alice had tried
to make her mother laugh that same way again, telling the
same joke over and over, until Helen had snapped: "Don't be
such a pleaser, Alice. You weren't put on this planet to make
other people happy. Not even me. Especially me."

Ronnie's present was the next-to-last to be opened. The
paper was red and there were creases in the wrong places, so
everyone knew it had been taken off some other present,
folded into a square, and reused. It wasn't obviously Christmas paper—no Santas, no holly, no candy canes, just red—
but still, everyone knew. The girl next to Wendy whispered
something, who turned to tell Alice. Wendy's mouth was tick-

ling Alice's ear when the present emerged, and then everyone fell silent, so the secret was never shared.

"Isn't that nice," Maddy's mother said, as she had said twelve times already, with just the same inflection.

Ronnie's gift was a Barbie, and no one in the fifth grade at St. William of York had played with a Barbie, not in public, for at least a year. When they did play Barbie, they played Soap Opera Barbie, in which Ken gets Barbie pregnant and they then have lots of serious talks about what to do, and whether it was wrong to have so much sex, and how they would never do it again if God would just take the baby away. The whole point of Soap Opera Barbie was the beginning, where you put Ken on top of Barbie and had them make funny noises. But that was a secret game, played in twos. In public, the only proper response to a Barbie was polite boredom, as if you couldn't quite remember what she was for. As if you'd never seen her under Ken, going Oh! Oh! Oh!

So a Barbie was bad enough. But this was a black Barbie, which was weird, because black Barbies were for black girls, they just were, and not because of prejudice, which the St. William of York girls knew was wrong. Maybe if a girl had, say, ten Barbies, one of them would be black, because then a girl could really branch out, have an apartment house full of Barbies. Maddy, in fact, was just the kind of girl who might have her own Barbie town. Her parents were that rich. So, although she was too old and the Barbie was black, that wasn't the worst thing.

No, the worst thing was that it was a Holiday Barbie. In July.

She wore a red gown and a fur-trimmed cape, and even Alice, who was sometimes slow to understand what other girls seemed born knowing, realized the doll was some Toys for Tots leftover. Ronnie's father was always bringing home stuff like this—heart-shaped boxes of candy in late February, chocolate bunnies in May, new lawn furniture in October. Alice had heard her mother say that Mr. Fuller's Coca-Cola truck came home fuller than it went out. She wasn't sure what that meant exactly, but she had figured out it wasn't good, much less exquisite.

"Very pretty," Maddy's mother said, as if she meant it. "Say, 'Thank you.'"

"Thank you, Ronnie." Maddy was the kind of girl who could make "That's a pretty dress" or "I like your hair that way" sound more evil than anything heard in an R-rated movie. In school, she had a habit of saying, "Yes, sister," so it sounded like a curse word. Alice, who sometimes got in trouble for saying the right thing, had studied Maddy and tried to figure out how to get away with being so rude. It had to do with getting your mouth and your eyes not matching, so one—the mouth—looked pretty and right, and the other—the eyes—had this hard glitter, but nothing extra. No wink, no raised eyebrow. Ronnie, on the other hand, did it backward. Her eyes were always wide and confused-looking, while her mouth was twisted and sneering.

Ronnie knew Maddy was making fun of her.

"It's a stupid nigger doll," Ronnie said, grabbing it from Maddy and throwing it into the baby pool. "My mom picked it out."

"Ronnie." Maddy's mom had to search for Ronnie's name, or so it seemed to Alice. "Please go get your gift out of the pool."

"I'm not going into the baby pool," Ronnie said. "There's so much pee in there it will take your toenails off."

Twelve little girls looked at their toenails beneath the table, for almost all of them had walked through the water at least once that day. Alice's toenails were robin's egg blue, which matched her blue jellies. Wendy had pink polish. Ronnie didn't wear polish, not since the time she had tried to paint her fingernails and come to school with red streaks all the way to her knuckles.

"Ronnie, please." Maddy's mother put a hand on Ronnie's wrist. Instinctively, Ronnie yanked her arm away and up, hard. Alice knew it was an accident, nothing more—an accident that Ronnie's hand was clenched in a fist when she pulled away, an accident that the fist hit Maddy's mom on the underside of her chin.

But Maddy's mother cried out, louder than any kindergarten baby, as if the blow really stung, and the girls screamed as if they had just seen a car come crashing over the fence of the wading pool area.

"You hit my mom," Maddy said. "Ohmigod, she hit my mom."

"I'm sorry," Ronnie said. "I'm sorry, I'm sorry, I'm really sorry. I didn't mean to."

"You hit my mom. You hit a *grown-up*." The other girls' voices bubbled up, shrill and shocked, but a little excited, too.

When Maddy's mother spoke, it was in that quiet, scary tone that adults use so effectively: "I think we should call someone to take you home."

"I said I was sorry. I didn't mean to fight. It was an accident. You touched me first."

"You must be tired from all the sun and excitement. Is there someone at your house I can call to come get you?" Cell phone out, at the ready.

"I came with Alice," Ronnie said, grabbing her arm. "We have to go home together."

Alice was caught off guard, unprepared to wiggle out of this. Yes, technically she was supposed to go home with Ronnie, but not if Ronnie misbehaved. Why should she have to leave just because Ronnie was bad? She hesitated, and that was when Ronnie told her story, about the aunt and the Oreos and everything else.

"Very well," Maddy's mother said. "Actually, I feel better about two of you walking. Now, you are going to your aunt's house, right? On this side of Edmondson? Good."

It wasn't good and it wasn't well and it wasn't *fair*. Alice peeled herself away from the bench, grabbed her towel and her shoes. Wendy's sympathetic glance only made it worse. Ronnie walked into the pool and grabbed the doll, dropping it twice on the way back. Water had seeped through the cardboard. The doll's dress clung to her hard little body, drops of moisture beaded on her brown limbs. Alice wished she could dip her feet in the wading pool, rinsing them, because she knew what Ronnie said was only half true. The little kids did pee in it, but that wouldn't take your toenails off. In fact, Alice's mom said pee was good for athlete's foot and jellyfish stings.

And so they went, leaving those two sets of wet footprints, one slightly ahead of the other, together yet apart, linked by the sheer unfairness of things, the usual daily accidents. Up the stairs, across the vast black parking lot, up the long hill to Edmondson, where Ronnie beat on the silver button for the Walk sign, even though everyone knew it would change in its own good time and the button was just for show.

"I thought we were going to your aunt's house," Alice dared to say, and Ronnie simply stared, her lie forgotten.

"My aunt works," she said. "In the summer she works at the crab house on Route 40. Besides, she doesn't like me to come around right now. She and my dad are in a fight about something."

Crossing Edmondson was easy, as it turned out, the Walk sign staying white their entire way across the broad, busy street. Alice knew they were breaking a rule, but it was exhilarating, a reminder of the new things that would come with leaving St. William and going to middle school. Her mother had promised she could wear makeup—well, lipstick—and get her hair cut at a salon, instead of trims in the kitchen. Even though school was a long way away, Alice began to think longingly of the trip to Office Depot to buy supplies. And clothes—she would need clothes if she wasn't wearing a uniform every day.

Once safely across Edmondson, Alice had assumed they would walk west to the jagged leg of Nottingham, where they both lived. But Ronnie wanted to take what she called a shortcut, which was really more of a long cut—past the bigger houses, the ones that sat back on large green lawns with little yellow signs warning dogs and children to stay away because of the chemicals.

They were halfway down Hillside, the grandest of all the big-house streets, when Ronnie stopped. "Look," she said.

It was a baby carriage, sun sparking off its silver handles, perched at the top of the stairs.

"The metal must be hot, sitting in the sun like that."

She seemed to expect an answer, so Alice said: "And it's too close to the stairs. It could tumble right down."

"Just roll right down."

"Unless the brake is on," Alice pointed out.

"Even if the brake is on, that's not right," Ronnie said. "You're not supposed to leave a baby like that."

"Her mother is probably right inside."

Ronnie grabbed Alice's elbow and gave it a wrenching pinch on the tip. Alice glanced at the bruise from an earlier pinch, remembered the clink of Maddy's mother's teeth as Ronnie's fist struck her jaw. No, this was not a day to contradict Ronnie.

"Not even for a minute," Ronnie said. "Anything could happen. Someone has to look after that baby."

They crept up to the door. The screen was heavy metal mesh, so dense that it was hard to see much in the cool dark house beyond. But they heard nothing. No footsteps, no voices. *Did you call out?* Later, they would be asked that question so many times, in so many ways. *Did you knock? Did you ring the bell?* Sometimes Alice said yes, and sometimes she said no, and whatever she said was true at the moment she said it. In her mind, there were a dozen, hundred, thousand versions of that day. They called out. They rang the bell. They knocked. They tried the door and, finding it unlocked, marched inside and used the phone to call 911. The mother was so happy that she gave them twenty dollars and called the newspaper and the television stations, and they were the heroes on TV.

Most of the time, Alice was sure of two things—they knocked on the door, the screen door, with its mesh so tight and small that it was almost impossible to see anything in the shadowy house. It was a screen over the screen, an intricate metal design, like something on a castle. It ended in tall thin spikes, higher than their heads. They said: "Hello? Hello?" Maybe not very loudly, but they said it.

"This baby is alone," Ronnie said. "We have to take care of this baby."

"We're too little to baby-sit," said Alice, who had asked her mother about this at the beginning of summer, when she was trying to figure out a way to make enough money to buy her jellies and other things she wanted. "You have to be in high school."

Ronnie shook her head.

"We have to take care of this baby."

The baby in question was asleep, slumped sideways in her carriage, so her full cheeks were flat on one side, full and puffy on the other, like a water balloon whose weight had shifted. She wore a pink gingham jumper with matching pink socks, and a pink cap of the same gingham.

"Baby Gap," Alice said. She loved Baby Gap.

"We have to take care of this baby."

Later, alone with her mother and the woman with the spotted face—exquizits, Alice finally got Ronnie's joke—they would ask her again and again just how Ronnie said this. WE have to take care of this baby. We have to TAKE CARE of this baby. We have to take care of THIS BABY. But Alice could not, in good faith, remember any emphasis. Eight words, requiring no more than five seconds to utter. We have to take care of this baby. We have to take care of this baby. We have to take care of this baby. Wehavetotakecareofthisbaby. They were being good, they were being helpful. People like children who are good and helpful. That's what Alice kept explaining. They were trying to be good.

What did Ronnie tell *her* grown-ups—her parents, the handsome man with the shiny blond hair and the suit with the funny name? *Seersucker,* Alice's mom had said, looking at the blond man in the hallway. Seersucker. Alice knew, from her mother's tone, that this was a good thing, as good as classic or vintage, even exquisite. What did Ronnie tell Mr. Seersucker, what did he believe when it was all over?

But that was the one thing that Alice never knew, never could know, and still did not know almost seven years later when she was released by the State of Maryland for her part in the death of Olivia Barnes.

PART I

The
Usual Daily
Accidents

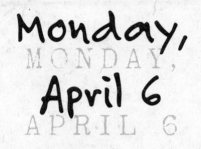

Monday,
April 6

1.

"Interesting," the ophthalmologist said, rolling away from Cynthia Barnes in his wheeled chair, like a water bug skittering for cover when the lights went on in the middle of the night.

"Not exactly my favorite word in a doctor's office." Cynthia tried to sound lighthearted. The metal apparatus was cold and heavy on her face, and although it wasn't literally attached, she couldn't help feeling as if she were in a vise. Each flick of the doctor's wrist—*Better here? Or here? Here? Or here?*—seemed to tighten the machine's grip on her.

"*Good* interesting," he said, rolling back to her. "Now, is it clearer with the first one or"—he flipped something, inserted something, she had never been sure what he was doing—"or this one."

"Could I see those again?" She sounded tentative, even to her ears, which shamed her. Cynthia still remembered what she was like back when she was always sure about things.

"Absolutely. This one"—the letter *O,* bold but a little wavy around the edges, as if it were underwater—"or this one." This *O* was not quite as bright, yet it was clearer.

"The second one?"

"There are no right answers here, Cynthia. An eye exam isn't a *test*." He chuckled at his own wit.

"The second one."

"Good. Now is it better with this one or"—another flip—
"this one."

"The first one. Definitely the first one."

"Good."

She felt a little glow of pride, then embarrassment for caring at all. She had arrived at the doctor's office on a wave of apologies, having skipped her annual exam for the last three years, despite the friendly little postcards that arrived every spring. She was AWOL from the dentist, too. And she might have passed on this eye exam, if it weren't for her younger sister's sly observation that Cynthia was squinting more often these days. "You keep straining like that, you're going to have one of those little dents," said Sylvia, who had never forgiven Cynthia for getting the one pair of green eyes in their generation. "Better reading glasses than Botox."

Cynthia had almost snapped: *Get off my damn back, I've earned that dent.* Instead she had made this appointment with Dr. Silverstein, who had moved to the northern suburbs since she saw him last.

Satisfied, Dr. Silverstein swung the machine off her face, returned her contact lenses to her, along with a tissue to catch the saline tears that flowed from the corners of her eyes. He was younger than she, it dawned on her. He must have just been starting out when she first went to him thirteen years ago. She wondered how those years had treated him, if his life had gone according to his expectations and plans.

"Well, I've seen this before," Dr. Silverstein said, smiling so broadly that his dimples showed, "but I've seen few cases as pronounced as this."

Cynthia was not comforted by the smile. She had known too many people whose expressions had nothing to do with what they were about to say.

"What? *What?" I'm going blind, I have a tumor behind*

one of my eyes, which explains the headaches. But she
hadn't told Dr. Silverstein about the headaches. Should she?

"Your eyes are getting *better,* Cynthia. We see this sometimes in people who have worn contact lenses for a long time.
Nearsightedness improves. You've been having trouble focusing on things because your contacts are old and pocked by
protein deposits, not because you need a new prescription."

"What about reading glasses?"

"Not yet."

"Good. I've heard that if you get reading glasses, your
close-up vision gets worse and worse."

"Ah, yes, that old wives' tale. It doesn't quite work that
way." Dr. Silverstein picked up a model of the human eye,
which Cynthia found disgusting. She hated to visualize what
lay beneath the fragile veneer of skin, always had. She was
nauseated at the sight of flattened squirrels and cats in her
neighborhood, and a passing glimpse of one of those surgery
shows on cable could send her into a near faint.

"There's a muscle that controls the lens of your eye, if you
will. It gets rigid with age. . . ." His voice trailed off when he
realized Cynthia was staring over his shoulder, refusing to
make eye contact with him or his plastic model. "Anyway,
no reading glasses yet, just a new contact lens prescription.
These should be ready in a week. Should the nurse call you
at home or at work?"

"Home. I haven't worked in years."

Dr. Silverstein blinked, suddenly awkward. He was one of
the people who had never had a chance to say, "I'm sorry,"
because the tragedy was almost a year in the past by the time
he saw her at her annual exam. Cynthia's life was full of
such acquaintances, well-meaning types who had been left
stranded by the tenuousness of their connection. Doctors,
mechanics, accountants. She remembered the April immediately following, when Warren asked the accountant how one

calculated for a dependent who had not survived the calendar year. Did they take the full credit, or did Olivia's death mean they had to prorate the deduction? For Warren and Cynthia, who had already asked a thousand questions they had never planned to ask—questions about burials and caskets and plots and the scars left by autopsies—it was just another dreary postscript. The accountant had looked so stricken she had wanted to comfort *him*.

She was beyond that now.

Cynthia went blinking out into the bright day, remembering, as she always did upon leaving the eye doctor, that first pair of glasses when she was ten. The wonder of finally seeing the world in sharp, clear focus had been dwarfed by the fear of her classmates' taunts. The other girls at Dickey Hill Elementary, even her friends, were always looking for a way to prick the self-importance of Judge Poole's oldest daughter. Another girl might have begged her mother to let her carry her glasses in a case, putting them on only as necessary. But to take them on and off would be an admission of weakness. So Cynthia wore those tortoiseshell frames wherever she went, holding her head high.

"Four-eyes," one girl had tried. "Four is better than two," Cynthia had said. And that was that.

She climbed into her car, the BMW X-25, a sports utility vehicle chosen not for its status but its heft. At 4,665 pounds it was heavier than the Lexus, even heavier than the Mercedes, and easier to maneuver than the Lincoln Navigator, which was a bit ghetto, anyway. Cynthia had actually wanted something a little less glamorous, because high-end SUVs were big with local carjackers. But the BMW had the best safety rating, so she bought the BMW and withstood the usual teasing about her love of luxury. Yes, she had once cared about things like expensive shoes and fine jewelry, had deserved her family's fond observation that Cynthia believed herself to be, if not at the center of the universe, just a few inches to the left. But that Cynthia was long gone, even if no one else could bear to acknowledge this fact.

Her cell phone rang. Headsets weren't the law in Maryland, but Cynthia had opted for one anyway. It amazed her to think of how she had once driven one-handed through the city behind the wheel of a smaller, sportier BMW, heedless of her heedlessness.

"Cynthia?"

"Yes?" She recognized the voice, but she would be damned if she would grant this caller any intimacy.

"It's Sharon Kerpelman."

Cynthia didn't say anything, just concentrated on passing the cars that were entering the Beltway from the tricky exit off I-83. The *Beacon-Light* had recently run a list of the most dangerous highway intersections in the city, and this spot was in the top five. Cynthia had memorized them without realizing it.

"From the public defender's office?"

"Right," Cynthia said.

"I guess this is a courtesy call."

As if Sharon Kerpelman were even on speaking terms with courtesy.

"I guess," Cynthia said, "that if you don't know what it is, I don't either."

"Yes. Well. How have you been?" Sharon asked, as if reading from a script. Maybe she had finally gotten a copy of Dale Carnegie, which she sorely needed. But Sharon, being Sharon, would go straight past the part about winning friends and skip ahead to trying to influence people.

"Why, just fine," Cynthia drawled. Not that Sharon would ever notice anything as subtle as a tone. "But I'm driving and I don't like to talk on the Beltway unless it's urgent. So—"

"This is—well, not urgent, but important."

"Yes?" Spit it out, Sharon.

"Alice Manning is coming home Thursday."

"For a visit?"

"For . . . ever. She's being released."

"How can that be?"

"She's eighteen now. After all, it will be seven years in July—"

"I think I remember," Cynthia said, "when it happened."

The headset was suddenly tight on her temples, squeezing so hard she felt as if those soon-to-be-rigid muscles behind her eyes might fly out of her head. How unfair. How *unfair*. The juvenile lament was her instinctive retort whenever this subject came up. Her father, who usually snapped at such idiocy, who had devoted his professional and personal life to establishing Solomon-like standards of fairness, had agreed with her. "Yes, it is," he said on that not-long-enough-ago day when the deal had been struck. "We have bent the law as far as we can, but we can't go further without breaking it. They are children in the eyes of the law."

"And in the eyes of God?" she had asked her father.

"I suppose they are children still. For God has to shoulder responsibility for all of us, even the monsters among us."

Today, her rage found its outlet in childlike cruelty. "Was Alice the fat one or the crazy one?" She could never forget their names, or their faces, yet she always had trouble matching them up. It was a kind of selective dyslexia, like her tendency to confuse surnames such as Thomas and Thompson, Murray and Murphy. Cynthia thought of the two as grotesque Siamese twins, connected at the waist, tripping over their four legs as they came down her street, up her porch, into her life.

Sharon's voice was prim, intended to be a reproof, as if Cynthia could ever be shamed on this topic. "Alice was the one with blond hair, worn straight back with a band. Here's a tip: think *Alice in Wonderland*."

"What?"

"As a mnemonic device, I mean. Or Ronnie-Aran, if you prefer, as in Isle of Aran, for she had dark hair and light eyes. The look they sometimes call Black Irish." An embarrassed laugh. "I mean, *I* don't call it Black Irish, but you hear that sometimes, among people of a certain generation—I mean—"

"I know what you mean." Sharon had said so much worse to Cynthia, so blithely and unknowingly, that it was hilarious she would fret over this minor gaffe. The last time they had spoken, in a chance meeting outside a shopping mall, Cynthia had yearned to box her ears. But Judge Poole's daughters didn't fight with their fists.

"Anyway, I just wanted you to know. So if you saw her. Alice, I mean."

Everything made sense now. Her eyesight was getting better because she needed to see. Come to think of it, her hearing was sharper, too, so intense that the softest sound jarred her from her dreamless sleep. She didn't exercise, it seemed idiotic now, going around and around on a treadmill or a stair-stepper, yet she had never been stronger, leaner, had more stamina. Maybe she should write a book, *The Black Coffee and Cigarette Diet: How to Mourn Your Way to a Better Body.* Good line, she would save that one up, throw it out to her sister, Sylvia, the next time they talked. Sylvia was the one person in Cynthia's life who didn't flinch at her sarcasm.

The significance of Sharon's call finally worked its way into the center of her brain. "She . . . is . . . coming . . . *home*. To my neighborhood."

"Technically, I don't think the Mannings live in Hunting Ridge. They're a few blocks outside the boundary."

Technically. How Sharon loved technicalities, legal and otherwise.

"She is coming home," Cynthia repeated. "To a house that is no more than six blocks from my house."

"Helen Manning's a city schoolteacher and a single mother. She doesn't have the resources to pick up and move." How quickly Sharon always switched from contrite to self-righteous. The defensive public defender, Warren had called her. *You must understand, Cynthia . . . What purpose can be achieved, Cynthia . . . They are little girls, Cynthia . . . Your tragedy, great as it is, Cynthia . . . There will always be some ambiguity, Cynthia. You, of all people, must value justice, Cynthia.* Cynthia, Cynthia, Cynthia.

As if what Cynthia wanted was anything less than justice. She had let them talk her out of justice.

"Can't you make it a rule that she has to live someplace else?"

"Of course not." Sharon's voice was huffy now, hurt. It was the paradoxical mark of the offensive, in Cynthia's experience, that they were offended so easily. The only feelings Sharon safeguarded were her own.

"When that man on North Avenue got pardoned, they made it a condition that he couldn't go back to the neighborhood where he had shot that child."

"It's not the same."

"No, he killed a thirteen-year-old boy. This was a nine-month-old child. Oh, and he was *pardoned.*" Cynthia did not add: *He was a black man who killed a black child. These were white girls who killed a black baby.* She let her silence say that part, let what was unsaid make Sharon squirm, in her little cubbyhole in that sad-ass state office building. *All your scheming, all your planning, and you sit today where you sat seven years ago. What was the point?*

"You live in two different worlds," Sharon said. "You'll probably never see either one of them again."

"We lived in two different worlds seven years ago, too."

"You know, I've always felt that the only way to understand what happened was to think of it as a natural disaster, almost like a tornado, or lightning." Sharon's voice was so reasonable, so sure of itself, the voice of a girl who had been on her high school debate team and still considered this a notable achievement. "A series of events came together and formed something horrible, something destructive. Wouldn't it make you feel better to see it in that light?"

Answers crowded Cynthia's tongue, backed up into her throat, until she thought she might choke on them. *It would make you feel better. You always try to have it both ways, and you won't even let me have it one way.*

Brake lights flashed ahead of her, traffic coming to a stop for no discernible reason, and her reflexes were off because of the phone call, so the 4,665 pounds of BMW squealed and shimmied, coming within inches of the rusty little Escort in front of her, a ready-to-disintegrate heap with a Kings Dominion bumper sticker and a Confederate flag decal. Cynthia didn't mind Confederate flags. She'd like to see a law that required every white trash hillbilly to have one tattooed on his or her forehead. You would see them coming that way.

"Can I have a restraining order?"

"I don't think Alice is inclined—"

"I didn't ask what anyone *wanted* to do. I asked what I could *have*. What the law will give *me*."

Sharon sighed, put-upon. "The courts can't write you a blank check for things that haven't happened yet. But I can tell you that Alice will be counseled to stay away from Ronnie Fuller and your family."

"My family? You mean she knows? You told her? Why would you tell her anything about me?" Cynthia's voice rose, in spite of herself, frantic and out of control, and she realized someone in the adjacent lane was staring at her.

"I haven't told her anything. I meant family in the most general way possible."

Family in the most general way possible. Only a single woman, a childless woman, could speak of family in the most general way possible. Cynthia hung up on Sharon Kerpelman, as she had so many times before.

It took her forty-five minutes to crawl around the Beltway. That meant the end of Dr. Silverstein, Cynthia was afraid. No doctor was worth that kind of time. Between the drive and the wait in his office, she had been gone four hours, which was much too long. She parked behind the house and let herself into the back door, where she was welcomed by the security system's polite beep.

"Hey, Momma."

"What's wrong with you?" Cynthia's eyes could keep improving for ten, twenty years, and they would never be as sharp as her mother's. Paulette Poole could see the future with her green eyes. Paulette Poole had predicted trouble when Cynthia and Warren bought this house. "Why do you want to live over there? Who are you trying to impress?" And Paulette Poole had seen from the first how the justice system, which had given the Poole family so much, would fail them when they needed it most. Paulette Poole was a witch, in the best sense of the word.

"Just traffic, Momma. Rush hour starts earlier and earlier in this city."

"Well, you go all the way to Towson to get your eyes checked . . ." Paulette Poole didn't bother to finish her sentence. Her daughter knew where she stood. Paulette Poole thought it was ridiculous for Cynthia to quit Dr. Hepple, their neighbor in Forest Park, in order to go to some white Jewish doctor just because his office was convenient to her job at City Hall.

"Where is—"

"Upstairs. With a video."

Because her mother was there, Cynthia walked with deliberate slowness, taking the front stairs instead of the back. She heard a tinny sound from the street, the *plink-plink* tones of an ice cream truck, although the ditty faded so quickly that she wondered if she had imagined it. *All around the carpenter's bench / The monkey chased the weasel / The monkey thought it was a joke.* She remembered a smile, a horrible, inappropriate smile, and the way her hand had ached to jump out, smack it from the child's face.

The alcove off the master bedroom was intended to be a dressing room, but Cynthia had renovated it three years ago, insisting it was large enough. Now that it had made the transition from nursery to bedroom, it clearly wasn't. Still, she resisted Warren's gentle nudging on the matter, pretending she didn't understand why he wanted their bedroom just for them again.

Rosalind sat on the floor, eyes locked on *Sleeping Beauty,* singing along in a breathy baby voice. *La-la-la. La-la-la.* She was such an easy baby, had been from the first, and had passed through the so-called terrible twos with barely a tantrum. She had never known colic, which had troubled Olivia so, and she was seldom stricken with so much as a cold. Well, a child breast-fed until the age of two had advantages when it came to immunities.

Rosalind had also come out shockingly light and stayed that way, a trick of the blood that Cynthia's mother claimed for her family tree, although Cynthia knew there wasn't a fair-skinned ancestor in the bunch. No one knew what to make of the amazing hair, which hung in amber ringlets. Her eyes, however, were brown, like almost everyone else in the Poole and Barnes clans. Olivia had gotten the green eyes of this generation, and family legend held that only one child would have green eyes.

"Who dat baby?" Rosalind had asked a few weeks ago, noticing for the first time the photograph in a small oval frame on Cynthia's dressing table. "Who dat?"

Who dat indeed? She and Warren had known they would have to tell Rosalind one day. But it had never occurred to them that a toddler would initiate the conversation with such a basic existential question: Who dat? She was your sister. Except—she wasn't, because you and she never existed in the same plane. She is nothing to you, and never will be. And if she had not died, you might not exist, because your mother had specific plans for her life, and having a baby at age forty-one was not one of them.

Rosalind was satisfied with the simplest truth: "Olivia." She repeated the name, patted the photo, and promptly forgot about it. All Rosalind wanted was a way to categorize and identify. That is a cow and that is a dog and that is Olivia. The cow goes moo and the dog goes bow-wow and Olivia goes . . . "Livvy." Her first word, her only word, uttered a few days before she was taken. They had joked about it at the time, how the daughter was just like her mother, so sure of her place at the center of the universe, or only a few inches to the left.

Now Cynthia couldn't help thinking it was as if Olivia knew she might never get to say her name otherwise.

On the video, the bad fairy was throwing a fit over her missing invitation. Uninvited, sent home early—it all ends the same way, doesn't it? The bad fairy reminded Cynthia not of Alice and Ronnie but of Sharon, and their last face-to-face meeting outside Columbia Mall summer before last.

Cynthia had been struggling with Rosalind's carriage, a European model that was a pain in the ass—so heavy, so not-portable, so impossible for any eleven-year-old to roll away. Sharon had stood, hands empty, chattering away, never offering to help. Did Cynthia miss City Hall? What did she think of the new mayor? Sharon had finally given up, moved to the suburbs, just to have the security of knowing she had a place to park after a long day. Was that so much to ask? Did that make her a hypocrite?

Then that obtuse woman had leaned into the carriage and uttered her own form of a curse: "Why, Cynthia, I didn't know you had a baby to replace Olivia."

The minute the words were out, even insensitive Sharon realized she had gone too far. Her cheeks burned red in a rush of blood so bright that it washed out the odd markings on the left side of her face. She scurried away, making excuses.

Not a week later, a reporter called, her voice round with fake empathy, asking Cynthia if she wanted to tell the *Beacon-Light*'s readers about this bittersweet happy ending, about her triumphant second act—those had been the reporter's words—to let Baltimoreans know how she and Warren had recovered from their horrible, horrible tragedy. Those had been her exact words, too, *horrible, horrible,* as if repeating the word would prove that she really understood Cynthia's plight. That was the reporter's term as well. *Plight.*

Cynthia wasn't fooled. She was a freak, the mother of the replacement baby, the idiot who had moved back into the same trailer park after a tornado tossed her first mobile home. They wanted to put her on parade so the paper's readers would feel safe and secure. Their babies would never be stolen, their babies would never be killed, because Cynthia Barnes had taken the fall for all of them.

Tuesday,
April 7
TUESDAY,
APRIL 7

2.

The grease smell hanging in the air behind the New York Fried Chicken on Route 40 was at least six hours old, but it still juiced Nancy Porter's appetite as she walked back and forth between the restaurant's rear door and the Dumpster, studying blood spatters. She had started a new diet yesterday and she was already having severe cravings, especially for anything deep-fried. To her way of thinking, there was nothing on earth—no vegetable, no meat, no piece of bread—that could not be improved by being dipped in a basket of hot oil.

Here on the part of Route 40 near where the state park began, the scent of frying oil bumped right into the generic green smells of an April morning. Cut grass, an undercurrent of lilacs, something else wild and sweet. Combined, the fried and the floral odors managed to trump the other smell on the breeze, the decadent, protein-laden fast food debris, mixed with the ferrous hangover of a young man's death.

"What is New York Fried Chicken, anyway?" she asked her partner, Kevin Infante. "I mean, I've heard of southern fried chicken and Kentucky Fried Chicken and even Maryland fried chicken, but what's New York Fried Chicken?"

"It's a way of saying it's better," the Bronx-born Infante said with a lopsided grin. His chauvinism was a running gag with them, whether the topic was food or baseball, a way of bridging the ten-year gap in their ages while defusing any boy-girl stuff. Not that he was her type, under any circumstances. Infante had glossy black hair and wet-looking brown eyes, and if Nancy's Polish grandfather were alive, nothing in the world could have stopped him from leaning in, pretending to run a finger across the top of Infante's head, and announcing: "Quart low." Josef Potrcurzski may have learned to live alongside Italians and Greeks in Highlandtown most of his adult life, but he had never learned to like it much.

"I don't know," Nancy said, playing along. "I like the Chicago style with the thick crust that they serve over on Pennsylvania Avenue. You know, the place we go to eat on our court days."

"That's not pizza," Infante said. "That's, like, a quiche with pepperoni. New York pizza is the best, and New York hot dogs, and New York deli and New York bagels and New York taxi drivers and New York baseball—"

The last was undeniably true, so all Nancy could say was "Oh, fuck you."

"If the sergeant knew how much you cursed when he wasn't around, he'd be so disappointed in his sweet little Nancy."

"Double-fuck you."

"Is that like Doublestuf Oreos?"

Nancy felt her color rising. That was the drawback to working with a partner, even for just a few months: they learned your weaknesses awfully fast, down to the brand names. Kevin Infante knew some things about Nancy that her husband didn't know, and Andy had been part of her life off and on since high school.

Then again, she was learning Infante's weaknesses, too: J&B, Merit Lights, the Mets, real redheads.

"Stop talking about food, okay?"

"You started it."

"I know. God, I hate stabbings. Give me a shooting every time."

Infante gave her a funny look, but didn't say anything. Nancy knew it would never occur to him to have a preference about methods. To Infante, in Homicide for five years now, there were only two types of cases, gimmes and what he called career-enders, although they never did. Not his, anyway.

And this one was clearly a gimme. The scene screamed stupidity—an absence of coolness, the telltale signs of a plan gone awry, and so much trace evidence that they could clone the whole gang of them, not that anyone but a mad scientist would want to replicate this group.

Infante crouched down next to a particularly large stain. "The blood patterns are weird, don't you think? Were they chasing him? Was he trying to get away? Then why didn't he run toward Route 40? No one was going to help him back here."

"He fought," Nancy said. "It's instinctive, to fight back when someone comes at you with a knife."

"Women don't fight."

"He wasn't a woman. He was the New York Fried Chicken Employee of the Month seven out of the last twelve months. Maybe he even got the weapon away from them. Maybe he pulled the knife on them, and they took it away from him."

"Them?"

"Definitely a them. One-on-one, I think this guy had a shot."

Franklin Morris had been found in the Dumpster by the morning crew, lying on top of the previous day's garbage. He would have looked peaceful if it weren't for the multiple stab wounds and the fluids that had leaked out of him throughout the early morning hours. He was, by his boss's account, a model worker in every respect. Perhaps a little humorless, but not a hard-ass, not a guy whose attitude might invite what looked to be a truly sadistic death, even by stabbing standards. Later, the medical examiner would catalog the number of stab wounds, calculate the eerily exact numbers in which his science specialized. He would note which wounds were defensive in nature, specify which cuts were superficial and which were lethal. He would take out the organs, examine and weigh them. The need for this precision was sometimes lost on Nancy. Eyeballing the scene, all she could think of was a magician passing a sword through a wicker basket again and again.

The victim's boss, a sixty-something white man, had fallen to his knees in the parking lot and started to cry after making the ID. "He's been with me three years," he said. "He's the best worker I ever had." Nancy, conscious of the camera crews arrayed along the perimeter of the yellow crime scene tape, had hustled the boss into his restaurant, seating him at a table where he wouldn't get in the way of the lab techs. The reporters kept trying to get her attention, flag her over, elicit a tidbit or quote, but she ignored them. That was the unofficial protocol in the county department. No one talked to the media. Not on the record, not off the record, not on background, or whatever term reporters used when wheedling. Nancy wouldn't be caught dead talking to a reporter.

It was going on eleven o'clock now and the television trucks were in place, ready to go live at noon. The *Beacon-Light* reporter had come and gone, was probably already stalking the dead boy's mama. Nancy saw the tall young corporal who handled media, Bonnie something. Nancy and Bonnie were about the same age, although Nancy had started in city PD and Bonnie had always been out here in the county. She was said to be good police, fairly solid, and an excellent marksman, not that county cops drew their weapons very often. Yet she had asked for the communications office when the number two job had opened up. Nancy couldn't imagine wanting a job in which you did nothing but talk to the press. She especially couldn't imagine being smug about it, as Bonnie seemed to be. "Corporal of communications," Infante liked to say. "Corporal of crap."

Nancy's stomach growled. She had been sitting down to her breakfast, a sorry little mess of sunflower seeds and carrot juice, when the call had come in. It had almost been a relief, getting an excuse to flee that breakfast. But now she was hollow.

"Cast-iron Connie rides again," Infante said with a twisted grin. She accepted the gibe for the compliment he thought it was. Actually, it worried her that she never got nauseous on the job, never had, not even the first time she had seen a dead body. And if that didn't make her sick, what could?

"I didn't have any breakfast," she said.

"Well, we could get you some biscuits to go," Infante taunted. He knew she was on a diet, because she had munched her way through a green salad, dressing on the side, at Applebee's yesterday. "I'm sure the staff wouldn't mind whipping up something for you. Let's walk through this again. I feel like we're missing something."

They were. On their next trip across the parking lot, Nancy spied a shell casing. This was her trademark, her gift—and sometimes her failing as well, according to her sergeant, who called her the Goddess of Small Things, which Nancy didn't get, but the sergeant said it had something to do with a book his wife once read for her book club. Nancy always did have an eye for details. Back in the city, where she had started, she had been credited with psychic, almost otherworldly powers. In the county, it was understood as a skill, no different from Infante's ability to break people down in interrogation, or Lenhardt's amazing hunches. But it was understood as a weakness, too. A detective could get lost in details. Or so her sergeant kept telling her.

"Could be from another time, another robbery," Infante said.

"Could be," Nancy agreed.

"Who brings a gun, fires it once, and then ends up cutting the guy?"

"Morons," she said. "Really mean morons."

The dead boy had owned a four-year-old Nissan Sentra, a year from being paid off, according to the records at the MVA. That was pretty much all the registration records told, but Nancy could fill in the rest, just from what the manager had told her about his employee. It would be spotless, with a pine-tree deodorizer hanging from the rearview mirror, a folded road map in the seat pocket, and a decal of some sort on the back window—a sticker for the college he had been attending part-time, Coppin, or his fraternity, if he belonged to one. Nancy had a hunch he did and that initiation had been one of the happiest days of his life.

A Ford Taurus pulled up and their sergeant, Harold Lenhardt, got out. Nancy wondered if she should take that personally. She couldn't recall him showing up when Infante was the primary. Baltimore County averaged about thirty homicides a year, and this was only her fourth in eight months in Homicide, so it was hard to establish a statistically accurate sample. Still, it irked her, seeing Lenhardt here. He was checking up on her.

"City cops found the car," he said by way of a greeting. "They didn't dump and run, but parked it in a shopping center lot over near Walbrook Junction. I guess they were trying to make it hard for us. Only the Laundromat owner noticed it hadn't moved for six hours, got pissed, and called to have it towed."

"Does the other kid, the one who worked here last night, happen to live within walking distance of where the car was found?" Nancy asked.

"No. But—go figure—he's been truant four days out of five at Southwestern High School most of this semester. So I checked with the principal's office and he was present and accounted for at roll this morning for the first time in a week."

"What time do city high schools get out?"

"Two-thirty," Lenhardt said. "But I don't think we can wait. We're going to have to deprive Junior of his day of book-larning."

"Yeah," Nancy said, seeing it. The kid thought he was smart, showing up for school today. He was counting on them to check attendance and be complacent, wait for the end of classes to talk to him. Then he'd try to cut out by lunch, find a place to lie low for a while, avoiding the cops for as long as possible. They would find him eventually, but it would still slow them down, screw up their momentum if they didn't get him today.

"The goddess found a casing," Infante said, and she shot him a look. She would take that from the sergeant, but not from her partner. "But I don't think the ME is going to find a bullet in that kid. I think it's all slices."

"Nasty," Lenhardt said. "These are some nasty mother—" He remembered Nancy was there and stopped himself. He would not curse in front of Nancy, in front of any woman, under any circumstances. Nancy tried to accept this as the simple courtesy it was. But she worried there were other things Lenhardt wouldn't say in front of her because some things could not be expressed without profanity. And these might be things she needed to know if she was ever going to be a good homicide police.

"Stabbing takes time," Lenhardt said. "You've got to have a taste for what you're doing, you stab a guy to death."

Even Nancy knew that. That was Homicide 101.

Her cell phone rang, which was weird because hardly anyone had her cell number, only Andy and her mom. The detectives still used pagers for official work and didn't give those numbers out to anyone if they could help it. She pulled the phone out of her purse—there was no getting around it, she had to carry a purse because she couldn't fit her life in her back pockets and breast pockets like the guys did. Her skirts didn't even have pockets, and the blazers she bought were hit-and-miss when it came to breast pockets. She tried to answer the call, but there was no one on the line. Then she noticed she had a small text message on the screen:

I'M COMING HOME

So what, she thought. Of course Andy was coming home. It was his day off and he had been heading out to the gym when she left for work this morning. Why would he call and tell her that? Then she thought: *he wouldn't.* And her mother wouldn't know how to text-message if you gave her a year-long course. Her parents' VCR had been flashing 12:00 for about a decade now.

Still, she had been getting a lot of wrong numbers of late, for some girl at Kenwood High whose number was one digit off from hers. They hadn't text-messaged before now, but it was probably inevitable. Nancy was only twenty-eight, but she already had the habit of shaking her head and thinking, "Those kids." She couldn't understand their desire for access, for 24/7 connectedness, their need to always be hooked up to something, anything.

Her stomach growled again, making a noise like a squeaky yawn. Lenhardt and Infante shared a smile at her expense, but didn't invoke the nickname.

"Do we have time for a pit stop?" Nancy asked.

"Depends on where," Lenhardt said. "We've got city uniforms standing by waiting to escort us into Southwestern. So we can't dally long."

"Something fast. Dunkin' Donuts. Burger King."

"Is that on the blood-type diet?" Infante asked, brow furrowed. "Or is it cabbage soup this time? Do they have cabbage doughnuts?"

Nancy waited until Lenhardt's back was turned, then mouthed at her partner "Fuck you." Infante shot her the finger. It was all harmless. They were kids, squabbling behind Daddy's back, which made the job bearable for some reason. Especially when they knew it was going to be a long day, a long week. The case may have been a gimme, but even gimmes extracted their price. Nancy had still been in the academy when she learned that it wasn't the clever perps who kept you up at night, it was the indifferent types who didn't bother to cover their tracks, literally or figuratively. The ones who were too stupid, or too young, or maybe both.

She shook the memory off, tried to concentrate on what kind of doughnut was going to have the honor of wrecking her diet in the thirty-sixth hour.

"So," Lenhardt said, his tone supercasual, "you let Bonnie handle the press?"

"Yeah," Nancy said. "Absolutely."

"Good girl."

She loved those words. Lord help her, she loved those words.

Thursday,
April 9

3.

There are no seasons in the basement of the Clarence Mitchell Courthouse, and Sharon Kerpelman sometimes had to glance at her clothes to remind herself what kind of weather she had passed through on the way to work that morning. No seasons, no weather, no sense of time passing. Today's date was vivid in her mind because of the arrangements she had made to free her afternoon, but the day had no reality beyond her schedule; it was not connected to spring or even the day of the week, which also had a way of slipping her mind. She'd hate for anyone to know how many Saturdays she had schlepped into the shower and been half dressed before she realized the masculine voice on her radio was saying *Weekend* Edition, not *Morning* Edition.

Today—a Thursday, definitely a Thursday, a fact ascertained by a quick look at the date book in her lap—she was meeting with a family in the hallway when she saw a secretary walking past with a basket of colored eggs and chocolates, and thought, *Oh, yeah, Easter*. Had it come and gone, or was it about to happen? And didn't that mean Passover was somewhere around here as well? Had she missed it? But no, her mother would never allow that to happen. Passover must be late this year, for Sharon had not yet received the annual phone call about the Seder and whether she was going to bring a date, and what would she think if her mother invited the Kutchners' son, who had just moved back to Baltimore and was very nice.

Her client's little sister, no more than five or six, followed the basket with a gaze full of longing and guilt, as if she knew better than to yearn for anything. The client himself, twelve years old and facing his second charge for selling drugs, was staring at the ground, bored by his own fate. His mother stood over Sharon, hands on her hips, jittery from want of a cigarette.

"Cullen," the mother was wailing. "How'm I gonna see him if he's all that way out there? I got no car. I thought he was going to Hickey, if he went at all. You said probation, maybe home detention. You *promised*."

"I promised I'd try. It's his second offense. Didn't help that it was on the school grounds."

"So why not Hickey?"

"Cullen has a bed in its unit for kids with addiction problems. Gordon's not going to stop selling drugs until he stops using them. Besides, it's smaller. He'd get eaten alive at Hickey."

"Cullen won't do," the mother said, as if she had a say in the matter. She was furious, with the kind of fury peculiar to the nonpaying client. Those who can't afford private attorneys, Sharon had learned in her decade as a public defender, assumed legal aid was incompetent. Do-gooders were simply losers in disguise.

"Hit's only his second offense," the mother hissed in the strange mountain accent that had somehow survived for decades in Baltimore, the legacy of the West Virginians who flooded into the city during World War II. Sharon secretly thought of their descendants as the fish-white people, evolutionary holdouts holed up in the city's last white precincts. She knew these people better than she wanted to, for she had tried living in some of the neighborhoods they favored, be-

guiled by the old stone mill houses in one, the cheap loft
spaces in the other. In the end, her hillbilly neighbors had
driven her out, all the way to the suburbs, to a sterile condo
behind a gate. At least she had tried.

"Look, your son started sniffing spray paint when he
was eight. He has been smoking marijuana since he was
ten. It's only a matter of time before he moves on to speed
or OxyContin."

"I don't use. I just sell a little," Gordon said, primed to tell
the lie over and over. *His idea or his mother's?* Sharon wondered. His mother couldn't honestly believe that her son
didn't use. Every time Sharon saw him, he had watery,
bloodshot eyes and this spacey can't-give-a-shit demeanor.
Not that she blamed him. Hell, she'd use, too, if this were
her mother, her life.

Sharon ignored his rote excuses. "I know it's hard for you,
Mrs. Beamer, him being so far away. But it's the best thing.
There's something to be said for getting him out of the city.
Kids at Hickey don't get that same culture shock, that sense
of displacement. Besides, Hickey's too . . . too . . ."

The bailiff called them to court. Sharon stood, finishing
the thought for herself. More and more, Hickey seemed to
her an internment camp for teenagers, the place where
Maryland was holding its potential enemies until some un-
declared war finally ended. She hated to send anyone under
fifteen to Hickey. Boys Village, near D.C., was worse still,
Middlebrook the worst of all.

She shook out the folds of her dress, creased from sitting
for so long. The saffron-colored dress was high waisted,
with a long, voluminous skirt falling to her ankles. Heavy
cotton, more of a winter dress than a spring one. The forecast for today must have been unseasonably cool for her to
have chosen this dress. Or was it because she wanted to look
nice, for later, and this was her best dress?

Gordon's mother studied the way Sharon smoothed her skirt, the self-satisfied pats to the rich fabric.

"You pregnant?"

The question was supposed to hurt, and it did. The woman was punishing Sharon, getting back at her the only way she could. *Send my kid to Cullen? Fine, then I'll make you feel fat.* Sharon actually had a good figure. She just preferred to keep it to herself, enjoying the glad surprise on her dates' faces when she finally disrobed.

"No—no," she stammered. "It's just a very loose dress."

"Oh. I thought you was, but more because of your face."

One insult withdrawn, another offered. If Sharon hadn't picked up her briefcase and Gordon's file, her hand might have flown up to her cheek. But there was no texture to the mark, nothing to feel there, other than the rush of blood.

"I thought it was, you know, that mask of pregnancy women sometimes get. I hear birth control pills can cause it, too."

"No, it's just . . . my skin."

"Like a birthmark."

"Well, I was born with it, so yes, I guess you could call it a birthmark."

She herself barely noticed it, any more than she would notice how her eyes were spaced, or how closely her ears pressed to her head. She almost liked the lacy pattern on the left side of her jaw and cheek, and had convinced herself that others might, too. It was a delicate spotting, as if a grid of freckles had slipped. No one had mentioned it for years.

Almost seven years, come to think of it. Here, in this very hallway, after the juvenile master had passed sentence on Alice Manning and Ronnie Fuller.

Sharon didn't have to close her eyes to recapture the day. After all, they had stood just here, in this same hallway, moving quickly because the reporters who had been banned from the hearing had been bearing down on them, and everyone was intent on getting the girls out and away, into the vans that waited on the north side of the courthouse. They were also trying to provide some cover for the parents, whose images had been used repeatedly in the media accounts, given that the girls themselves were off-limits.

Alice had looked shocked, too scared and numb to cry. But Ronnie, who had been almost catatonic throughout the whole ordeal, erupted as the girls were led away. She had actually fought her own lawyer, raking her fingernails down his cheek, kicking one of the bailiffs in the chest when her lawyer turned her around and caught her in a bear hug that was meant to still her. She bit and clawed as if she wanted to be in handcuffs, wanted them to confront the inherent lie in the proceedings. No one, not even Ronnie Fuller's earnest young lawyer, believed she was anything but a stone-cold killer. But the state had agreed to treat her like a child. Like a human, when all those who met her couldn't help wondering why she was so inhuman. She smiled at the wrong time, laughed at the wrong things, said whatever came into her head.

Still, she was literally a little girl, no more than eighty pounds. They couldn't strike back or use the usual methods to control her. Ronnie seemed to sense the adults' tentativeness, their confusion, and her flailing limbs appeared to multiply, so it was as if she had four arms, four legs, then eight, then sixteen. She was like the cartoon Tasmanian Devil, a whirlwind of motion, and everyone else was struck dumb and motionless. Photographers, trying to find positions that would allow them to capture the moment without showing Ronnie's grinning face, ended up tripping the lawyer, and Ronnie was suddenly free, running down the corridor. In her blind fury, she chose a dead end, and two policewomen finally managed to subdue her.

Watching the whole episode, her hand on Alice's shoulder, Sharon had known a horrible moment of gratitude that she had not drawn the assignment to defend Ronnie—and then such overwhelming guilt for her revulsion that she felt obligated to comfort her.

She whispered encouragement as the policewomen rushed the girl through the corridors, Ronnie's feet barely touching the floor. She murmured things more important in tone than content, the way one speaks to a dog. *It will be okay, don't be scared, we're trying to help you.* They were almost to the door, the sunlight creating a glare around the edges, like a passageway in a fairy tale or a science fiction film, a door leading to another world. As the policewomen carried Ronnie over the threshold, the girl turned her head and fairly spat in Sharon's face: "Get away from me, you ugly spotted bitch. This is all your fault."

Ronnie's lawyer was in private practice within a year, defending "real criminals," as he explained the next time Sharon saw him in Au Bon Pain, where their salad tongs crossed over the stainless steel bowl of string beans.

"I mean, you know, grown-ups," he said.

"They're less scary," he added, and they had laughed, pretending he hadn't spoken the truth.

Sharon looked at the client of the moment, Gordon Beamer, twelve years old and, unless a miracle happened at Victor Cullen, pretty permanently fucked. Not even ten years into her job, she was beginning to see the second generation, the children of the children she had defended when she started working for the PD's office. The only thing that really changed was the drugs. Crack cocaine had ebbed, and now it was more heroin and OxyContin, a little Ecstasy for the suburbanites who came to the city to cop. How soon before she saw the third generation, the grandchildren of her original clients? If Sharon were really successful at her job, wouldn't it cease to exist?

Funny, her first and last homicide case had proved to be Alice's. The state routinely "promoted" violent offenders to the adult system now—fifteen and up was virtually automatic, and it was rare to see anyone, boy or girl, charged with homicide at a younger age. So the young killers passed her by, and her expertise was of little use.

"Let's roll this rock up the hill," she said on a sigh.

"What rock?" Wanda Beamer demanded. "They got rocks at Cullen?"

She didn't wait for the answer to her own question, for she noticed her daughter had wandered off to stare at the children's paintings that were supposed to add some joy to this grim corridor. She shrieked the little girl's name—*Amber*—grabbed her, and paddled her hard. The girl cried without making a sound. Gordon Beamer stared at the ceiling. So did Sharon, thinking about how it was only a few hours until she finally got to see Alice again.

4.

Helen Manning took her lunch outside, thinking she might find a bench, or at least a ledge on which she could sit. But the day was chilly, as only early spring could be, and she ended up in her car, barely tasting her carefully assembled meal—chicken salad, which she had enlivened with tarragon and pecans and spread on a whole wheat baguette, cold asparagus in a vinaigrette sauce, a small bottle of sparkling water.

A floater rotating among several city elementary schools, Helen usually made a point of eating and mingling with the other teachers. So much was projected onto a pretty woman if she was the least bit self-contained. Helen had accepted long ago that she had to work hard to convince others that she wasn't remote or snobbish.

Today, however, Helen was too depressed to summon the energy for the polite, super-interested persona she had cultivated. Instead, she sat in her car and chewed on her sandwich, staring blindly through the windshield. It was a good neighborhood, a yuppie enclave with long rows of white-flowering fruit trees that made the streets look like a lane from a fairy tale. And yet Helen had detected a dark, Grimm-like aspect, although it had taken her a while to diagnose exactly what was wrong, what was missing. Children. The yuppies all moved as soon as they had kids. The students in the public school came from the tougher, less desirable neighborhoods that fringed the area.

Helen, who had grown up in Connecticut before coming to Baltimore for college, had never gotten used to the springs here. She had no nostalgia for the wind-whipped house on the Sound, or for her mother's prissy formal garden, which was barren much of the year. But spring came on so *fast* in Baltimore. It might be cold today, but within a week the city would be lush as a jungle, riotous with azaleas, the leaves on the trees fat and swollen. It was a gaudy time, almost obscene, like the burst of hormones that surged through some of her students. This change was particularly striking to Helen because she saw the children at seven-day intervals. One week, a sixth-grade girl would be gawky and careless, skipping across the playground. The next, she would be round and juicy, hunched over with self-consciousness.

Helen had no scientific evidence, but she was sure that girls had not developed so early in her day. She wouldn't be surprised to find out it was linked to fast food or that bovine growth hormone in milk. She had heard stories about seven-year-olds with breasts and periods. The doctors at Hopkins were trying to figure out how to arrest their puberty without turning them into midgets.

Now Helen always had very good eating habits. She wasn't a zealot, but she had always chosen whole grains and vegetables and fresh fruits, hopeful that Alice would follow her example. Of course Alice had ended up yearning for the junkiest of junk foods, and Helen had capitulated, taking her to McDonald's or Arby's at least once a week, in the belief that small indulgences would keep Alice from becoming obsessive. Hunger had been the one uncontrollable urge in her otherwise obedient daughter.

Where would Alice ask to go to lunch today, after Sharon

picked her up down at Middlebrook? Alice would probably want something fast and greasy, while Sharon would feel compelled to make an event out of it, a celebration—more like high school graduation than what it was.

"I know you can't get off in the middle of the week," Sharon had said when she called Helen about Alice's release date. "But I could meet her at the hearing in your place, and bring her home. Really, it's no trouble."

Would Helen have lied if Sharon hadn't all but offered this out to her? She wasn't sure. But given the assumption that she couldn't be there, she was glad to take advantage of it. She understood, however, that she would be in Sharon's debt. For when Sharon said something wasn't any trouble— *really*—she meant it was a lot of trouble, but she would do it anyway. Sharon had never quite let go of the Mannings, much to Helen's dismay. Everyone else wanted to forget, move on, bury the past. Only Sharon Kerpelman seemed to glory in the memory of that summer, as if it were something of which she was proud. True, she had been aggressive in Alice's defense, shrewd even. But Helen couldn't help wondering if she should have taken her parents' offer and hired an expensive criminal attorney who might have saved Alice in spite of everything.

But no, that would have been wrong. She had decided early on that she could not rationalize away Alice's role by saying she was the accessory, the dupe, the unwitting follower. There was a principle at stake. Alice had to be held accountable along with Ronnie.

Alice had understood. Alice always understood. She was Helen's confidante, her one-girl fan club, her best audience. Even when she saw through one of Helen's white lies—and Alice, unlike Sharon, would know that Helen could have gotten today off if she really wanted to—she forgave her. She was a considerate child.

A woman, Helen reminded herself. Alice had left home a child, but she was a woman now under the law, free to vote, if not to drink. Helen remembered a song from her own grade-school days: *Girl, you're a woman now*. Sung, Helen suddenly realized, by the same pop star who had told the young girl to get out of his mind. Yes, the songs of Gary Puckett and the Union Gap had a lovely progression. "Young Girl." "Girl, You're a Woman Now." "Lady Willpower." And then finally, inevitably, simply: "Woman Woman (Have you got cheatin' on your mind?)." Why, it had the arc of a novel. It was goddamn Madame Bovary. Good line. She wished she knew someone who would appreciate it.

Helen had been a pretty juicy teenager herself, although she had waited until college to explore those options. The joke among her faster high school friends was that Helen couldn't have sex in the same state as her parents. And the joke behind the joke was that it was absolutely true. She had come to Baltimore's Maryland Institute College of Art as an eighteen-year-old virgin and, within weeks, was the Whore of MICA. Not that anyone called her a whore, because everyone who could was doing the same thing, and people weren't so judgmental about sex back then, especially at art school.

God, her generation had caught the wave just right. That was the golden time, the post-herpes-but-not-yet-AIDS era, when everyone had given up on free love, but sex was cheap and plentiful, like the marijuana of the day. All changed, changed utterly. People in the marijuana trade killed one another now, according to a "special report" Helen had seen on television just this past winter. Astonishing to Helen, more astonishing than any act of terror. Almost as astonishing as her own life.

She was twenty-four, halfway toward her master's, when

she got pregnant. It was like hitting a reverse lottery, a 1-in-100 shot. But even pregnancy wasn't a big deal in those days. Abortion was an acceptable choice among her friends, backup birth control, almost a rite of passage. It didn't even require much thought. If the stick turned blue, and it wasn't love and wasn't going to be, you took care of it. The noble thing was not even to mention it to the guy, unless he was a live-in, because it was a lose-lose. He either tried to eel out of the situation, in which case you had to face up to the fact that the guy you were dating was a jerk. Or, worse, he made a halfhearted proposal and there it sat between you, like a jury summons—your civic duty, sure, but everyone still tried to get out of it.

So having a baby was kind of cool. Brave, even. Especially when the father was some BG&E meter reader, Roy Durske, met at a friend's apartment pool. They dated all summer. "Dated" being Roy's insistent euphemism. Helen had no problems classifying their meetings as screwing. Good the first few times, but the novelty of the whole adventure had worn off fast. Sheer enthusiasm could take a man only so far.

The bell at the Catholic church began to toll the noon hour. Helen glanced at her dashboard clock. She had used up her allotted twenty-five minutes for lunch. The early and short lunch hour was one of the antiperks that served to remind Helen how little valued her chosen profession was. She balled up the foil from her sandwich, capped her empty bottle, snapped her Tupperware, and put everything in the old metal workman's lunchbox she'd found at a yard sale last year. People were always knocked out by Helen's taste—"By what you get away with," as one coworker once put it. But Helen was bored by her own originality, her irreverence. What had it gained her in the end? Twenty years of teaching art to nonartists, a life alone, and a daughter who called her bluff. *Want to be daring, Mom? Want to be a true icono-clast? Try being the mother of an eleven-year-old who kills another child.* And not just another child, but the grand-daughter of a beloved black judge.

Then leave your mother to face the world's judgment.

They couldn't use Helen's name, for that would have been the same as identifying Alice, but the local television stations had somehow rationalized showing Helen's face as she ducked in and out of various government buildings that sum-mer. She wore dark glasses, her hair pulled up in a way she had never worn it before and never wore it again. But people knew, of course. They knew which girls had been sent home from the pool party after what was reported as a "racial incident," knew which children disappeared from the neighborhood, as if they had never existed. But no one ever said anything, because what would they say? *Saw you on the news. Sorry your kid killed that baby. What are you doing this weekend?*

Helen went inside and began setting up her next class, taping newspaper to the desks, straightening the little chairs, the style of which had not changed since she was in fifth grade. For all she knew, these chairs could have been in ser-vice during her fifth-grade year. The city system was pretty poor. She definitely remembered colors like these, seventies colors, colors that embodied the promises of the modern age. Aqua blue. Mod orange. Now these were the ironic, self-conscious shades of iMacs and junior high school fash-ions. She remembered an outfit, purchased for her first plane trip—an orange-, blue-, and brown-striped dress with a matching scarf, from the old Best & Co. Her mother had saved all Helen's clothes, and Helen had taken it out of a box when Alice was the same age. But she was too big for it. Hormones. It had to be hormones.

Thank God the afternoon classes would be fourth-graders. They were still baby sweet, unlike the middle-school-bound fifth-graders. The fourth-graders reminded her of Alice, the lost Alice. In remembering her daughter, Helen always imagined her from the back—the part in her hair, two tails of yellow hanging down on either side of her head, tied with bows that Helen fashioned from fabric remnants and Christmas ribbon. She conjured up her smell, which was sharpest at the back of her neck, varying with the day and the weather. Chalk, soap, grass, suntan lotion, chlorine, peanut butter, pickles. She saw that neck bent over the kitchen table, intent on a project—a Christmas gift, homemade Valentines—saying to herself, as she must have heard Helen say: "Homemade is nicer." She was so *good,* there was no other word for it.

But Alice's goodness, her very lack of reproach, became a reproach. "I did something bad," she would say to Helen in their last days together, tentative, hopeful of contradiction. "When you do something bad, you have to be punished."

"Yes, baby," Helen had said. *Show them how strong you are, and then one day they'll realize you're really a good girl, that it was just a mistake. It was a mistake, wasn't it, baby? A mistake, an accident? Whose idea was it, baby? You can tell me. Tell Mama what happened. I know the truth is sad, but it's important to tell the truth. Always, always. It's better if we know everything. Maybe it will change things. Nothing's really done, nothing's really decided, not yet. Just tell the truth, Alice.*

But Alice had shaken her head, refusing to tell Helen anything. "Everything's decided now," she had said. "I have to go away."

That was the night before the final hearing, the formal sentencing. On top of everything else, Alice had just gotten her period for the first time, and they were in the bathroom, fixing her up, soaking her underpants in cold water. Menstruating at eleven, not even in sixth grade. Helen had started at thirteen, and her mother thought *that* was young.

Helen had given Alice the sex talk in bits and pieces over the years, so Alice wasn't scared. She was so placid, so composed, that Helen couldn't help trying to shake her up, make her treat the moment as more of a milestone.

"In my day, we didn't have these adhesive-backed pads. We had to wear little belts," she said. "With teeth."

The image startled Alice, sitting on the toilet with a sanitary napkin in her hand.

"Did the teeth bite?" she had asked, eyes round, and Helen regretted mentioning it.

"No, they weren't teeth-teeth. Just little holders, for the napkin's tabs. You're lucky. But remember, you have to be responsible now. You're still a little girl, but your body thinks it's a woman. Don't forget that, okay?"

That damn song popped up again, lodged in Helen's brain the way only an unwelcome melody can burrow in. Girl—you're a woman now. Strangely, it brought a memory with it, but not of when Helen first heard it. Instead, she saw herself sitting on the edge of that useless kidney-shaped pool at the apartment complex off I-83, the summer after her first year of graduate school. Suddenly, anachronistically, she could remember everything—the seat of her suit pulling at the rough-textured concrete, the sun on her back, the baby oil cupped in her palm, ready to anoint her lovely freckled shoulders. And then Roy surfaced, shaking his hair, so long by today's standards, water streaming down his well-formed chest, looking almost as good as he thought he did.

"You live around here?" he asked, and she smiled at the sheer stupidity of his come-on, delighted that he was dumb, because then she wouldn't fall in love with him, she could just fuck him for the summer and move on, happy and carefree. She had been right about that much, at least. She hadn't fallen in love with him. For all she knew, he could have come and read her meter over the past decade, and she wouldn't have recognized him.

Had he recognized Helen, in her sunglasses and piled-up hair seven years ago, racing across his television set? Had he realized his daughter was one of the "pair of eleven-year-old killers" mentioned incessantly on the news, in the paper, until the phrase lost its ability to shock? Even if he had, Helen couldn't fault him for not coming forward and confessing to Alice's paternity.

She probably wouldn't have either, given the choice.

5.

"Don't you want dessert? They make great sundaes here."

Alice looked up from her plate, where half of her cheese-burger and most of her french fries still sat. She wasn't try-ing to impress Sharon with her willpower—she never worried about impressing Sharon—and she wasn't self-conscious about her appetite. She plain didn't *like* this cheeseburger, which had come with Cheddar instead of American cheese, or these fries, which were too *real* to Al-ice's way of thinking, with the skins still attached, and soft, lumpy insides, damp with oil.

"I bet you didn't have anything like this at Middlebrook," Sharon had said when their meals arrived, clasping her hands together as if she might say grace.

No, Alice thought. *What we had was better*. Thin, crispy fries, which went straight from the freezer to the fryer. Not as good as McDonald's fries, which were the best, but better than these flabby things. Actually, the food at Middlebrook had been pretty good all-around. It may have had the worst reputation in the state, but it had the best food.

"Really," Sharon said, "have a sundae." Sharon loved that word: *really. Really, Alice, you have to trust me. Really, Al-ice, this is for the best. Really, Alice, I believe you*. But what did *really* really mean when Sharon said it? Did it indicate that everything else Sharon said was fake? Or was it supposed to show that what followed was extra-real, really-real, super-size real?

"I don't need a sundae," Alice said. *"Really."*

"Today's not a day to worry about calories. Treat yourself."

Oh, so she should worry about calories, just not today. "I guess I have to go on a diet," Alice said, head lowered over her plate, maintaining contact with Sharon's puppy-brown eyes through the fringe of her pale lashes.

"No, no, that's not what I meant at all," Sharon said. "Everyone has to worry about calories. Just not every day. It's important to build a treat day into your schedule."

"But I'm fat," Alice said. "Didn't you notice? I got really fat while I was in Middlebrook."

She loved this word, adored making cruel pronouncements about herself. *I'm fat. I'm ugly. I'm clumsy.* She wasn't looking for automatic contradictions. In fact, she didn't actually hold herself in such low esteem. No, she just liked the way adults panicked when she spoke this way, enjoyed their frantic reassurances. Sticks and stones, grown-ups said when you were little. Turned out they were the ones who feared words.

"Oh, no, honey, you shouldn't talk that way. You're just . . . big-boned, like I am. And the diet was so starchy there, and you didn't get enough exercise, and, well, what with everything, you put on what some people call the 'freshman fifteen.' "

"Only I'm not a freshman," Alice said. "I'm a graduate. I got my GED."

"Freshman year of college," Sharon said. "Because that's when most kids are away from home for the first time, making their own choices. . . ." Her voice trailed off miserably.

"So I'm precocious," Alice said.

"Yes," Sharon said, clearly not getting it. "Yes, you are."

"I've got the freshman *fifty*—and I won't start college until the fall."

"You're going to go to college, then?" Sharon bobbed her head. She was so easy to please, there was no joy in it. "Where? What do you plan to study?"

"Community college. I have to get a part-time job and help pay my way." She gave Sharon a sly look. "It's hard to get scholarships, coming out of Middlebrook."

Sharon took this as a rebuke. Alice knew she would. No one had ever wanted Alice's approval as much as Sharon Kerpelman did. The slightest suggestion that Alice's life was less than it might be was wounding to this woman, who seemed to feel Alice owed her gratitude and affection, if not downright love. Sharon *cared* about Alice, she announced often, a note of pride in her voice. Sharon's pride was what kept Alice from returning her affection. Sharon could not think so well of herself for sticking by Alice unless sticking by Alice was a weird thing to do.

"You know what you should do?" Sharon asked, changing the subject.

Alice was interested in spite of herself. She was quite keen to know what she should do. She always had been. She liked those magazine articles with rules and checklists. She tore them out and tried to follow them, but it was never as easy as it looked. There was always something—an ingredient, an assumption—that kept her from completing everything as prescribed. Kosher salt, for example, for homemade pedicures. She wasn't sure what that was, and how it was different from other salt. Not that she would have been allowed to give herself any kind of spa treatment at Middlebrook, but she had been looking ahead to a day when she could.

Sharon leaned forward. "You should *walk,*" she said triumphantly. "You'd be surprised what it does for the body. Just lots and lots of walking. Whenever I go visit friends in New York, I can eat whatever I want because I walk everywhere."

Sharon beamed at her own brilliance, nodding and smiling, looking for some kind of response. Alice felt stranded, the way she often did in conversations, as if she were standing on an ice floe and needed to leap to another one. The whole sequence mystified her: Walking. Friends. So Sharon had friends? Friends in New York, no less. Why did she have friends in New York? Wasn't she from Baltimore? Hadn't she told Alice that a hundred times, how she had grown up less than a mile from Alice, on the other side of the park, in that place with the stupid name?

"My grandparents live in Connecticut," Alice said at last. Connecticut was right next to New York. It was all she had to offer, conversationally. She had never been there herself, but she had heard her mother speak of it. It was known as the Nutmeg State. To spell it, you have to Connect *i* to Cut. Connecticut.

"Yes, I remember your grandparents. Have you talked to them lately?"

"No." Sharon frowned, full of pity. "But then, I never did. Talk to them much. I only saw them once a year, before. They came down a couple of times, at first, but my grandmother said it was too hard."

"How *selfish*." Sharon almost yelped the last word, and people nearby jumped, as if a glass had tumbled to the floor.

Alice thought about the word *selfish*, turned it over and over in her mind. Certain words had an almost hypnotic effect. Always candid Helen had told Alice about her own "youthful experiments"—Helen's phrase—with marijuana and other drugs, and how a single word could become the funniest thing in the world for no reason. But you didn't have to be high to latch onto a word. *Selfish.* Related to the self, of course. But *ish* was usually reserved for those things that were inexact—oneish, warmish, newish—or kind of gross. Oh, *ish,* her friend Wendy would squeal when something offended her. It was cute, even the boys thought so, but only Wendy, who was petite, could get away with that kind of baby talk. Alice would have been mocked for lisping.

"Alice?" Sharon prompted.

"They're not really selfish," she said, now that she had worked the word out for herself. "They just live so far away."

Which was, of course, what Helen had said to Alice, as if she were trying to convince herself. They were old, older than most parents, and Da hated to fly, and Ma-Ma hated Da to drive, and it was such a pain taking the commuter train into Grand Central, then getting on Amtrak over at Penn Station, so they just couldn't visit that often. Alice understood.

"Well, I'm sure they love you very much," Sharon said.

"They do."

"That's what I just said."

"Not as if you believed it."

Alice stared hard at Sharon until the woman finally looked away, pretending to study the toy airplanes hung from the ceiling of the restaurant. Her lawyer had changed very little over the seven years. Of course, Alice had changed so much that everyone else's changes seemed inconsequential. But she had noticed the subtle differences in her mother's face, even though she saw her far more often than Sharon. Helen had kept herself up. That was her term, another phrase that had stuck in Alice's brain, for it suggested an image of her mother in scaffolding, men working away with paint and brushes. *She kept herself up.*

But over the past two years, Helen had begun to look her

age, no more, no less. She knew it, too, and claimed to be complacent about it. "The French actress Catherine Deneuve said a woman over forty has to choose her face or her fanny," Helen had said to Alice on her last visit to Middlebrook. "I'm going the fanny route." And she had patted her slender hip—her "yoga butt," as she had taken to calling it—and laughed. Alice had laughed, too, for it was her favorite version of Helen. Breezy, a little silly, talking about things that no one else on Nottingham Road could make sense of.

And as long as Helen worried about her own looks, she didn't worry too much about Alice's. She was philosophical when Alice started putting on weight two years ago, said the body knew what it needed and that Alice's body was probably reacting instinctively to needs Alice didn't even realize she had.

"It's like your body thinks you're a bear, in hibernation. Maybe it's because they have you on this rigid eating schedule. You don't get to eat when you're hungry, you have to eat when they say you do, so your metabolism slows, in case they start starving you."

Alice had a different theory. She believed she had a tumor. Someone had left behind a newspaper—a real newspaper, not one of those shameful things from the supermarket racks—with a story about a woman at Johns Hopkins who had a 180-pound tumor in her stomach. No one could figure out why she was gaining weight. Then they took the tumor out, and she was normal again.

The local newspaper did not have a photograph of the tumor, but the writer described it as—the words were burned into Alice's memory—"an onion-shaped growth the color of a brown egg and covered with fine, silky hair." Alice took to pressing her fists into her abdomen, looking for signs of a growth. The skin was soft, yielding, yet she thought there might be something unwanted beneath its folds. Finally, she went to the infirmary and asked if there was a tumor test. The doctor was kind, listening intently with no expression on her tired face. She took notes, prodded Alice all over, asked her questions.

"I'm afraid that it's just, uh, a fairly normal weight gain, given your circumstances," she had said apologetically, as if she, too, had wanted to find a tumor. "It comes down to arithmetic—calories expended subtracted from calories consumed."

"I'm good at math," Alice told the doctor. "I always was. I'm doing Algebra II, but if I were in a regular school, I'd probably do Trig and even Calculus."

"I bet you are. So here's what you do—keep a little notebook, jotting down what you eat. You'll see that you're taking in more calories than you think. Don't try to change the way you eat at first. Just observe yourself."

"Like the woman who watches the monkeys?" Alice had seen a special about a famous anthropologist, although she couldn't remember when, or what the woman learned from all her notes.

"Yes. No. I mean—take notes for a week or two, and include how you feel when you eat. Learn your own patterns, and then adjust accordingly. Portion control is half the battle. It's not what we eat so much, but the fact that we eat so much of it."

Disappointed that she did not have a tumor inside her, with or without fine, silky hair, Alice had never even started the notebook. But now, sitting in this too-cheery diner with Sharon, she considered the idea. Girls in books were always keeping notebooks, or diaries. She could do that, she supposed. But she knew she wouldn't. Not because she lacked discipline. She had plenty of discipline. But she wouldn't want to tell anyone, even a book, everything about herself.

Before a day passed, she knew she would be hiding things. Because someone else would read it. She had never heard of anyone keeping a diary that someone didn't read.

"So what's the first thing you're going to do when you get home?" Sharon asked out of the blue.

"Open the door?"

Sharon threw back her head and laughed her startling thunderclap of a laugh, although Alice had not meant to make a joke.

"Very good. One point for Alice. No, I mean are you going to look for a job, or enroll in summer school? Have you learned how to drive? I could teach you, if you like. You'll need to know."

"Why? We only have one car, and my mom uses it for work. She teaches art in a summer program, you know."

"Well, you may have a job one day, and you'll need to drive to work."

Alice thought about this. "I can take the bus."

"Sure, for now. Depending on where the job is. But don't you want to learn to drive?"

She should say yes. Yes would be the normal answer, and Alice was so keen to do and say the normal things, the expected things. Which were not, of course, always the truthful things, or the things she really wanted to do. She was back on her ice floe, looking for a place to jump. Or maybe a conversation was more like a game of Twister, which Helen sometimes played with Alice and Ronnie on rainy summer weekends. Right arm—red. Left leg—blue. You had to figure out how to keep your balance, how not to fall over, while still following directions. You could twist yourself up some, but not too much.

"I like those new Volkswagen Beetles," she offered.

This pleased Sharon for some reason. She squealed with delight, bobbed her head. "Me, too." Then her gaze shifted

and her eyes widened, a sign that Sharon was about to become Very Serious. "What are you *not* going to do, Alice?"

It was true, Alice thought. Almost no one's eyes are the
same size. And Sharon's right eye was a lot bigger than her
left.

"Alice?"

"I'm not going to do anything . . . bad. Never again."

"I know you won't. But specifically, what's the one thing
you should *not* do?"

Not kill anyone? But not even Sharon would ask Alice
such a question. Sharon believed in Alice, always had. You
didn't have to understand a person in order to believe in her.

"I'm not going to"—she struggled, trying to figure out
what would be the worst thing she could do—"be idle."

"That's a good idea. Idle hands . . ." Sharon laughed, an
apologetic bark, although Alice couldn't see what was
funny. "I think the key thing is that you shouldn't see, or talk
to, Ronnie."

Alice looked up, amazed. How could anyone think she
wanted to see Ronnie?

"Her family moved. My mom said."

"Yes, but they're not that far away. They're just off Route
40 now, in those row houses near the old Korvette's."

"Korvette's?"

"It's a Metro now. But when I was a kid, it was a discount
department store, like Kmart or Target. I bought my first
record album there." Sharon seemed on the verge of going
off into one of her long stories about her childhood, stories
that mystified Alice, for they seemed to be told to show how
much alike Sharon and Alice were. Yet they always ended up
proving the opposite.

Luckily, Sharon didn't succumb to one of her odd reveries
this time. "Look—Ronnie had really serious problems.
That's why she went to a different place than you did."

"Harkness."

"What?"

"She went to Harkness, right? The one near D.C." The old grievance still gnawed. Ronnie had gone to Harkness. Alice had been stuck in Middlebrook.

"She started out at Harkness. She finished somewhere else. Anyway, all I'm saying is that she deserves a new start as much as you do. But I don't think you two can be friends again."

"We *weren't* friends," Alice said. After all these years, she couldn't let this pass. She didn't always mind when people got it wrong and said she killed Olivia Barnes, but she wasn't going to be known as Ronnie Fuller's friend.

"Right," Sharon said, with a bright, placating smile. "Now, are you sure you don't want a sundae?"

"I guess I will. After all, starting tomorrow, I'm going to be walking a lot."

"You are? Oh, that's great, Alice, just great. Really."

Was it great because walking was good for her, or great because it was Sharon's advice? Alice had learned long ago not to ask such questions out loud. But she had never stopped thinking them. Sometimes, she felt her fat was like a cave, and she lived far inside it, watching the world with glowing eyes.

Saturday,
April 11

6.

Ronnie Fuller was used to waking in the morning with strange yearnings. She just kept forgetting she was now in a position to do something about them. Some of them, at least.

She had been home for almost a month, for her birthday was in March, a few weeks before Alice's, a fact that almost no one ever remembered: Ronnie had a birthday, too, and it came first. Still, even after a month at home, she had to think for a moment when she opened her eyes before she could place herself in the world. Her new room, a middle bedroom with no windows, was dark as a submarine and somewhat plain. Her mother had said Ronnie could do whatever she wanted with it, but Ronnie couldn't think of what to do.

On this particular Saturday morning, she awoke with a desire for honeysuckle, but it would be another two months before the first blossoms appeared, longer still before they could be sucked. She decided to look for a substitute at the convenience store at the foot of the long, winding hill where her parents now lived. She had the day off, so she walked straight there as soon as she was dressed. After surveying her choices through the fogged glass, she selected a Mountain Dew. She knew it wouldn't taste like honeysuckle, but the color was close.

The dark-skinned, turbaned man at the counter took her money without comment. "Terrorist," she said, intending it to be a question inside her head, but somehow it slipped out. That happened to Ronnie a lot. She tried to keep her thoughts to herself, but they made themselves known, which usually got her in trouble. It didn't seem fair.

"Seek," he said angrily, pointing to his forehead. *"Seek."* Seek what, Ronnie wondered. Sick? Was he saying he was sick? Her mind was so busy turning over those questions that she turned the wrong way leaving the store, walking toward the old house by force of habit. Or so she told herself.

Ronnie had arrived on her parents' new-to-her doorstep on a March day of record-breaking heat, a black nylon overnight bag weighing down her right shoulder. The house had been empty, for both her parents were still at work, and the last brother had moved out months ago. She found the promised key under a flat rock in the front flowerbed, and let herself in.

Familiar furnishings marked the new place as "home," whatever that was, and it was clearly nicer than the old one. Her father used to say the town house on Nottingham was built of cereal boxes—it was damp and frail, the walls yielding easily if someone happened to bump them hard, or even throw a punch. And with three boys around, those things happened. Bumps. Punches.

On that hot March day, it hadn't occurred to Ronnie to be disappointed that no one was there to welcome her. Her parents worked, that was a fact of life, the acceptable answer to all sorts of requests—back-to-school night, cupcakes for the holiday party, field trips. Besides, Ronnie had gotten a nice send-off on the other end—not a ceremony, which would have been queer, but a handshake from her doctor and hugs from some of the staff. One of the counselors had given her a gift-wrapped box, which Ronnie had tucked away in her overnight bag, automatically saving it for later. She hadn't been able to give a lot of presents over the past few years, so she didn't realize people liked to see their gifts opened. And if someone had tried to tell her as much, she would have been puzzled by this information. Better to give than to receive, right? The giving should be enough.

"Try not to jostle it too much," the counselor had said.

"Is it fragile?"

"Not exactly. But—well, you'll see. When you get home."

The counselor liked Ronnie. All the staff did, for she had been one of the better-behaved kids in the unit. Most of the juvenile offenders assigned to the Shechter unit were sullen teenagers whose borderline felonies, things like robbery and car theft, had been compounded by addiction problems. But Ronnie had all but auditioned to get her bed there, trying to convince the necessary people that she was just crazy enough, no more, no less.

The campaign had begun by accident, around the time of her fourteenth birthday. Ronnie had taken to poking her body with a ballpoint pen, inoculating herself wherever the skin was softest—crooks of elbows, tops of thighs, backs of knees. The pinpricks began to itch; she scratched. The infection got so bad that she ended up running a high fever, which meant a trip to a hospital emergency room. The attending doctor sent her to Shechter for observation. Once observed, she was sent back to Poolesville. But Ronnie had made her own observations. Shechter was clearly the place to be.

She couldn't have said why she liked it. After all, it was a program for crazy kids, and her family had fought hard against the assumption that she must be crazy, or confused about right and wrong, perhaps even retarded. The buildings at Poolesville were new and clean, and Ronnie usually preferred new to old. Yet the onetime school turned juvenile detention center was where she wanted to be. Maybe it was the lack of fences, or the rolling farmland that surrounded it. Maybe it was the dormitories of the nearby college, which provided a vision of a life that seemed as glamorous to Ronnie as any television show. From the front lawn, she could watch the college girls—what they wore, what they carried.

But she understood that she could not say she wanted to go to Shechter, quite the opposite; she had to pretend to be going along with the rules and structure of Poolesville, had to deny the evidence of her own made-up craziness.

Patiently, she began to cut herself with any implement she could find, nicking her body with pop-tops and pencils, nibbling herself with her own teeth, and when all else failed, scratching herself raw, until her calves were lined with long red tracks. What could they do? No matter how closely they trimmed her nails, they always grew back. They could cover the tips with Band-Aids, put her hands in restraints at night, but unless they were willing to rip out her nails all the way to the beds and extract her teeth, they could not disarm her.

"You're smarter than Yossarian," her doctor said when she finally got her permanent bed at Shechter.

"Who?"

"*Catch-22*? 'I am not the bombardier'?" Ronnie shook her head. "It's not important," he assured her.

She liked the doctor, as much as she could like anyone who got to tell her what to do, who decided when she was right and when she was wrong. He seemed to be on her side. But she couldn't be too forthcoming with him because he might turn on her, too. Ronnie had thought lying was something children were forced to do because they lived by others' rules. She had thought growing up would mean lying less, but it hadn't worked out that way so far. Yes, Shechter had been pretty good. But she would have been truly crazy if she hadn't been happy to leave.

Home. She had tried out the word on the new place the day she first saw it. So this was home. It was set up in the usual rowhouse floor plan. Good, there was a dishwasher.

One less chore for her. And a microwave, too. She imagined her father bringing it into the house, imagined her mother asking, with equal parts pleasure and irritation: "What truck did that fall off of?" Ronnie hadn't understood the question when she was younger, but she did now.

Ronnie had climbed the stairs, knowing what layout to expect—a master bedroom across the front, which would get the light, one dark interior room, a small bedroom in the back, and one bathroom for all.

Her room, the dark room in the middle, had a bed, a dresser, a small lamp—and nothing else. She pulled two bills from her back pocket and looked for a place to hide them. It was hard to hide things in an all-but-empty room. She took the clothes she had packed in her overnight bag and placed them in one of the drawers, then hid the money in the folds of a T-shirt. No, her mother might go there. The bed was made with a new spread, white with little raised dots. When she left home, her bed had been covered with a Scooby-Doo spread, which would be pretty stupid now, but Ronnie wasn't sure she liked the white one. She lifted the thin, bumpy cotton and slid the bills, a ten and a twenty, between the mattress and box spring, as far as her arm could go.

The money had been intended for cab fare and it had started out as two tens and a twenty, old bills almost reproachful in their limpness, as if her parents wanted Ronnie to remember that their money was scrounged from pockets and purses and wallets, not snapped up from an ATM or a bank teller. From the moment she saw the money emerge from the envelope, Ronnie had known she would find a way to pocket it. She would take a bus home or hitch, but she would keep as much of that forty dollars as possible.

Of course, the staff never would have allowed such a thing, so she had gone through the pretense of summoning a cab to the top of the hill, of waving to them all as she climbed in. It was then that the counselor had given her the small gift-wrapped box, the one still in her bag. She had felt grand, a bit like a girl in a movie—perhaps the one about the girl who learned she was a princess—riding down the hill.

Then, as soon as the cab was off the grounds of the hospital and a few blocks down the street, she tapped on the Plexiglas and asked the cabdriver to let her out.

"What?" he barked. He was white but foreign, with a strange accent and an acrid body odor. "You call for ride to Saint Agnes Lane, over by Route 40. You can't get out here."

"Why not?"

"Is illegal."

She was pretty sure he was lying, but she made the mistake of sounding weak: "You have to let me out if I ask?"

"No, is dangerous. I get ticket if I discharge you here."

"So pull into that 7-Eleven parking lot."

"No. You call for long ride. You must go or pay."

She knew from the way his story shifted that he was making this all up. He was a cheater. Ronnie had never been much good at arguing with anyone, but cheaters were the worst.

"Please pull over."

"You will pay."

"Pull over."

With a sigh so forceful it might as well have been a shout, he did just that. The meter said $3.50. Ronnie offered him one of the tens and waited for her change. The man took the bill and put it away.

"You can't take ten dollars for a three-fifty fare," she said.

"Extra dollar for call," he said, pointing to a red light on the meter box.

"That's still only four-fifty."

He was ripping her off. Because she was a girl, because she was young. Such encounters had once made Ronnie fierce, with the focused rage of a small dog. But now she was supposed to work toward solutions. Unfortunately, the lessons of the hospital had assumed there was always some nice neutral person who could step in, a doctor or a principal, a teacher or a parent. *Use your happy tones, Ronnie. Anger is just a letter away from danger.*

Here, in the parking lot at the 7-Eleven, there was no one to sort things out between Ronnie and the cabdriver.

"I came for big fare, not little fare. Plus, you owe me tip."

She got out of the cab, frightened of her own feelings, frightened by the fix she was in. Now she had only thirty dollars, and thirty dollars might not be enough to take a cab all the way home. She could take a bus, but it would have to be at least two buses, and which two buses? Plus, she needed change for the bus, and no one would give her change unless she bought something, which would mean losing another dollar or two out of the thirty. Aware of the cabdriver's eyes on her, she walked into the 7-Eleven with her head high, as if this had been her destination all along. Then she hid in the chip aisle until she was sure he was gone.

Back on the street, she knew her only choice was to find a ride. She had never done this before, but her older brothers had. And there had been a girl at Shechter who had bragged about getting rides all the time. "I never had to do anything, either," the girl, Victoria, had said.

"But how do you keep them from, you know?"

"You've got to be picky about who you ride with." Victoria enjoyed having Ronnie seek her out, ask her advice. No one knew exactly what Ronnie had done, but rumors were rampant at Shechter because she wasn't required to attend AA or NA. Which, at Shechter, usually meant someone was really nuts, scary nuts. Some people said authoritatively that Ronnie had killed her entire family, despite the fact that her mom visited regularly. Others said Ronnie had been part of a thrill-kill, that her boyfriend had talked her into murdering someone just for fun.

Ronnie liked the idea of being credited with a boyfriend. She also felt a strange, sour pride in the fact that no one ever came close to guessing why she was really there. Anyone who was alive in Baltimore that summer would probably remember the story of the missing baby and how she had been found dead, and then the constant mention of two eleven-year-old girls, two eleven-year-old girls, two eleven-year-old girls, can you believe it, the baby was killed by two eleven-year-old girls. Now she and the event floated free from each other, disconnected. Victoria had no idea who she was or what she had done.

Ronnie persisted, not afraid for once to show her ignorance. "Picky *how*?"

"Go for guys in ties."

"Guys in ties?"

"Yeah, and boring cars like your dad drives."

Ronnie's father still drove a Coca-Cola truck, and the family car was an old AMC Hornet—at least, that's what it was when Ronnie went away. But she knew what Victoria meant.

"You want a businessman, like. A guy who will freak if you scream, or say you're going to tell or go to the police. With a young guy, a guy closer to your age, he's not scared of getting in trouble, so you got no—what's the word?"

"What word?"

"That word for when you have control over another person?"

Ronnie shrugged. She had no idea what Victoria was talking about.

"Anyway, don't go with anyone under thirty. Oh, and don't stick your thumb out."

"But I thought that's what hitchhikers did."

"It's not your *thumb* that gets you the ride," Victoria said. "Turn your back to the traffic, and walk as if you mean to be walking. But twitch."

She demonstrated. Victoria was a large, fleshy girl who wore tight jeans. Her bottom did shift a bit as she walked, but it just looked uncomfortable, as if it wished it weren't packed so tight.

Out on the street, Ronnie turned her back, as Victoria had advised, and walked as if she had a destination. She didn't try to twitch. There was a golf course to her right, with lots of men playing, even though it was a weekday. Were they rich, or did they call in sick to their jobs? Her dad had been known to go missing from his job, as he put it, but he said it was bad luck to lie about being sick. He said the trick was to come up with a story that couldn't be checked, a story that couldn't hurt anyone. He had never told her what those stories were.

She was almost past the golf course when she got the first offer. The boy was cute on first glance, and he drove one of those little Jeep-like cars, the sort of thing Ronnie would have liked for herself, if she ever learned how to drive. But there was something off about his face, the longer she looked at him, and Victoria's advice carried the weight of a rule. *No, thank you, no, really. I'm fine, I'm fine, I'm fine.*

The next guy was older, behind the wheel of a van with the name of a painting company stenciled on the side, and he was freckled with paint. Not a van, Ronnie knew, although Victoria had not thought to tell her this. Never a van. She felt as if she were trudging along one of the board games she had played as a kid, Candy Land, or the one with the ladders. She had to pick carefully if she was going to get home with her thirty dollars.

The third one was just right, everything Victoria said. A tie and a four-door black car, not new, but not old. His face was shiny and red, although the interior of his car felt cool through the window he lowered to talk to Ronnie.

"You need a ride?"

"Well—I was just going up to the bus stop."

"How far are you going?"

"Pretty far," Ronnie admitted. "Saint Agnes Lane, over near Route 40."

"Outside the Beltway?"

"No, in. Near—" What was it near? It wasn't just that her parents had moved, it was that Ronnie was no longer sure what milestones had survived along the Route 40 corridor. Arby's? High's Dairy Shop? The Crab King? "Do you know that sign, the one that says you're entering Baltimore City?"

"So it's on the city-county line?"

"Just over, in the county." Her mother had been so proud about crossing that line.

"That's not so far, if you know the right shortcuts. Hop in."

She did, arranging her black nylon overnight bag so it filled her lap.

"You can put that in the back."

"I'm okay."

"Or in the trunk."

"I'm okay."

"You sure?"

"Yeah."

It was only once they were under way that Ronnie saw the problem she hadn't anticipated: she had no idea how to answer the man's questions, innocuous as they were. School? She had actually finished in January, because of summer school credits, but where was her diploma from? She couldn't say she had graduated from Shechter Unit. Plus, if she said she was finished, she couldn't say she was fourteen later, which Victoria said was the deal-breaker for most guys, being fourteen.

"I go to . . . Towson," she said, hoping it was the name of a high school.

"Yeah? My cousin goes there." He said a name, but of course she didn't know it. He named more names. She just kept shaking her head and shrugging her shoulders. Maybe it was good for him to think she was stupid and didn't know anyone at high school.

"How is it," he said at last, "that you go to Towson High, but your parents live over in Southwest Baltimore?"

She thought of the answer her doctor had told her she could use, when asked about her past. "It's really complicated."

"Oh, yeah, I know how that works. Use a fake address to get into a better school. I went to Calvert Hall myself." He seemed pleased with himself, but it meant nothing to Ronnie.

They had been driving west—she could tell by the sun— and the landscape of houses had been shifting constantly, from very rich to very poor. They had passed a hospital, and the racetrack. She was keeping tabs because you never knew, Victoria said, where you might get put out. Now it looked like the neighborhood where Ronnie had grown up, except everyone on the street was black.

The driver—he had said his name was Bill—took several quick turns and they ended up on a narrow road along a stream. The car slowed, and Ronnie made sure she was holding the door handle, but there was no shoulder and he kept going. He passed through a neighborhood where all the houses were white, and Ronnie realized she knew it, that she was close to home. The houses began to peter out, and they were in a dense corridor of trees that were just beginning to bud. Somehow, the stream was now on the left side. When had they crossed it? Ronnie had not noticed a bridge. And then there was a barrier, a big sign saying the road was closed until further notice.

"Well, I'll be," her driver said. "I forgot they closed this off."

But he didn't try to turn around, just put the car in park and reached across her to the glove compartment, opening it and taking out a small bottle of clear liquid. If it had not been for the black bag on her lap, he would have rubbed his arm against Ronnie's breasts. Instead, he had to settle for brushing against nylon.

"This is Leakin Park," she said. "My house is just on the other side of these hills."

"Right. But we'll have to backtrack, go the long way around via Forest Park."

"Why is the road closed?"

His hand was in his lap, the tip of his tongue protruded between his lips, but he was otherwise the same shiny-faced man who had picked her up, the man named Bill who had gone to Calvert Hall, whose cousin had gone to Towson High.

"They're building some kind of walkway. They call it a nature trail, but Jungle Land would be more like it. Or Baltimore Safari. Walk through Leakin Park, see if you come out alive. They could make one of those reality TV shows about it."

"Why is it unsafe?" Ronnie had played along the edges of Leakin Park when she was as little as seven, and ventured farther and farther inside as she got older. Of course, she didn't have permission, but she had never felt scared there.

"Because that's a bad neighborhood up on that hill."

"Oh. I thought it was because—well, I heard something really bad happened here once."

"Like a ghost story? You want to tell me a ghost story,

honey? Come sit on my lap and tell me your story. Tell Uncle Bill your story."

She hugged her bag tighter to her chest.

"Show me your titties, Alice." For that was the name she had given him, when he asked about high school. Alice Manning. Alice Manning, Alice Manning, Alice Manning. It was the first time Ronnie had to make up a name for herself, and she automatically said, Alice Manning.

"Show me your titties, and I'll take you the rest of the way home. Just pull up your shirt, show me those pretty little things. I won't touch 'em. I promise I won't touch 'em."

"I'm fourteen," she said.

"Oh, I don't think so. You walk like you've been fucked a time or two. You've been a bad girl, haven't you? Tell Uncle Bill. Tell Uncle Bill what you let the boys do to you."

His hand was beginning to move in his lap, but his voice was still dreamy and pleasant.

"You're a bad, bad girl," he crooned. "I know all about you."

"I'm *not.*"

Her voice was shrill and hard, the angriest voice she had allowed herself in quite some time. She tried to rein it in. "But I know someone who was—who is. I'll tell you what she did."

"Tell Uncle Bill, baby. Tell Uncle Bill."

"There were two little girls—"

"Oh, that's a good story, Alice."

"And they found a baby. A baby whose mother didn't love her, who left her all alone on the front porch. They took her away from her mother and they made a . . . safe place for her. But the baby was sick, all along, she was going to die anyway. And the girls—well, one of the girls—got scared and said they had to take her back. But the other girl said no, that they couldn't, that they had to kill the baby because no one would believe them anyway."

His hand had stopped moving.

"It really happened," Ronnie said. "Right here, seven years ago. I know the girls who did it. They went to my school."

"I thought you went to Towson."

"My school before," Ronnie said, staring him straight in the eye. "Middle school."

The man's face was now gray-white instead of red, although still quite sweaty. He wiped his hand on his pants leg, turned the key in the ignition, and said to Ronnie: "Tell me again where you live."

And so she had arrived home on the hottest March day in history, thirty dollars richer, and she hadn't had to do a thing. She had sat on her bed, thinking about her choices. She could have gone downstairs and seen what was in the refrigerator. She could have turned on the television in her parents' room, flopped across the bed on her stomach. She could have taken a walk, headed down the street to the convenience store. The store stood where her old street and her new street met, a hinge between the old life and the new.

Instead, she had decided to take the gift-wrapped box from her bag and open it. The square box had a sticker on it: *Port Discovery: The Kids' Museum*. Ronnie didn't remember such a place from when she was a kid. Back then, all the museums had been boring adult ones, full of vases.

The box yielded, from layers and layers of spun cotton, a collection of key rings, all with little toys attached. A tiny replica of the old Operation game, the board from Life, the bald man with magnetic hair to be arranged and rearranged. The final ring held a miniature Etch-a-Sketch. The counselor had painstakingly written on its tiny surface: "Good luck, Ronnie."

She had also enclosed a note: "I wasn't sure which one you'd like best, so I got you all of them." Nice, she was nice.

But why a key ring? It seemed a weird gift. And then Ronnie had understood. For the first time in seven years, she would have keys. She would open her own doors, and close them behind her.

It was April now, and that Etch-a-Sketch, long wiped clean, was in her hand, clenched so her keys—just two, to the front door lock and the dead bolt—dug into her palms. She was in the old block, walking past the Mannings' house. She could not risk slowing down, or even staring openly. It was early, anyway, and Helen often slept until noon on Saturdays. But if their paths did cross, if she saw Ronnie and said hello, then Ronnie could ask, as if it had just occurred to her, as if she had not thought about it almost every day for the last seven years: *Do you remember the honeysuckle?*

She knew Helen would.

7.

Wagner's Tavern had become the county homicide detectives' bar of choice by way of becoming a police scene. An SUV crammed with five screaming teenagers took the curve outside the bar at 100 miles per hour one night before Christmas. At least, that was the speed estimate after the fact, when traffic investigators began to crawl around the three steaming pieces of the bright-red Isuzu Rodeo that had come to rest inside Wagner's, a few feet short of the pool table. The top speed could have been 90 or 95, but 100 made for a nice round number, and the television reporters always used the biggest numbers they could get away with, whether it was speed or snowfall.

"Except in the case of windchill," said Lenhardt, interrupting his own story. "Then they use the lowest number. You know—the temperature will be thirty-seven degrees today, *but it will feel like twenty below*! Tune back in at five and it may be thirty below! Our twenty-four-hour Doppler Radar Storm Center Hoo-Haw guarantees the most dire weather forecast in Baltimore, or your money back."

Lenhardt had happened to be on his way home the night of the crash when he saw patrol cars and uniforms swarming. The human toll was miraculously light—the only Shock Trauma transports were two of the kids in the car, and as

Lenhardt said later in his Lenhardt way, "Hard to get choked up about *that*." The redheaded barmaid had a broken leg, and a couple of people caught broken glass, some of it flung from the ornaments on the demolished Christmas tree, which was the first thing the Isuzu hit after coming through the wall.

But the bar had lived to tell the tale, and the only visible change was the guardrail on the curve. On late nights, Lenhardt could be found at the curve of the reconstituted bar, or sitting at a plastic-covered table, buying rounds for his detectives.

"So that's why you come here." It was Nancy's first time at Wagner's, because she usually said no and hurried home to Andy. But she needed to be one of the guys tonight, even at the risk of pissing Andy off.

"What?" Lenhardt said, playing dumb, no small play for him. "You trying to imply something about my choice of drinking establishments?"

"You picked this as your hangout because you figure it can't happen again. Which is really superstitious."

"I'd call it playing the odds."

"Only the odds haven't changed because the curve hasn't changed."

"Huh?" Infante said, truly lost. But Lenhardt grinned knowingly.

"It's not like there's a standard probability for a bar getting hit by a car," Nancy said. "A bar on this kind of curve is going to get hit more often than a bar that's not on the curve, guardrail or no."

"Standard probability." The sergeant turned to the other detective. "Listen to that, Infante. We're wasting our time here. Let's go to Atlantic City, let Miss Nancy demonstrate her knowledge of standard probability at the blackjack tables."

"So why *do* you come here?" Nancy was already bored

with the topic, but she had to stick to her guns, show Lenhardt she had the stamina to stay with an argument.

"I come here because the beer is cheap, they'll open the kitchen for a public servant working late, and it's on the way home. Don't overanalyze things, Nancy. How many times I gotta tell you that?"

Infante laughed in his hand, and Nancy could feel a blush spreading across her face like a stain. Sometimes she hated being so fair, so blond.

Lenhardt took pity on her. "You got your own stuff to work on, Infante."

She bit into a popper, the closest thing to a vegetable she had eaten in three days. "Hey, how come he's Infante and I'm always Nancy, or Miss Nancy?"

"Fer Chri—" But Lenhardt wouldn't even take the lord's name in front of Nancy, so he ended up saying nothing more than "Fer cry." Most times he didn't even get halfway into the word, but the day had taken its toll.

"You're not going to get all feminist on me, are you?" Lenhardt asked now. "I mean, he"—he stopped himself again—"heck, you want me to call you Porter, I'll call you Porter. I'll even try to call you that mouthful of consonants you were born with—Padrewski, Portrotsky. But cra"—another deft catch—"c'mon, it's just, it's just a way of talking, Nancy. I mean Potter. I mean Porterchinski."

"Potrcurzski. That's okay, sergeant. I got a special name for you, too."

"Yeah? What?"

"The Double-L."

"How you get a double *l* out of Harold Lenhardt?"

"It's not for Lenhardt." Nancy grinned. "For Living Legend. Because that's what everyone tells me I'm working for. My uncles, Andy—they remind me at least once a week that my sergeant is a genuine goddamn livin' legend."

She thought this would make him laugh, but Lenhardt just shook his head. "There are no living legends, Nancy. Only dead ones."

They had cleared the New York Fried Chicken case that evening. Now it was the prosecutor's to lose. It had taken twelve hours of interviews with four different kids, but when the day was done, they had booked all four, three on homicide, one on a lesser charge, because that was the deal he had struck. In some ways, Nancy thought the deal-maker the finkiest of the four, but wasn't that the way? They were always the ones who turned.

Lenhardt misread her mournful expression, seemed to think she was feeling sorry for herself. "You'll be a good murder police."

Good, but not great, Nancy thought, then wondered why she was so defensive. No one had criticized her over the past four days, or suggested she was inadequate in any way. She had been praised for some of her work. Yet she felt rebuked, stupid, exposed. A kid had seen through her. A jumpy killer, with the impulse control of a mouse on Ritalin, had gotten to her.

Her Nokia cell phone chirped. Andy typed his good night:

LONG DAY. GOING TO BED.

Even his text message sounded angry. Beneath the table, Nancy typed back:

SUIT YOURSELF.

Then she wanted to take it back, but she couldn't.

They had been together since high school, one way or another, but it was only lately they had fallen into the habit of sniping at each other. Her mother said it would pass, and her mother had a thirty-five-year marriage on which to stake her expertise. But what did her mother know about twelve-hour days that left you feeling at once victorious and ashamed? You couldn't go straight home after a day like that. If anyone could understand, it should be Andy, who had been a police and was now working for the feds while attending law school at night.

"I feel like we know what happened," Nancy said, "but not *why*. It was supposed to be a robbery, with a gun."

"*Why* isn't our problem," Lenhardt said. "Forget about it."

She couldn't. "According to the inside kid they were going to wear masks, put the manager and their accomplice in the freezer to throw detectives off. The gun was supposed to be for show, to get the money."

The inside kid, the coworker, had been almost grateful to be found. After all, he knew better than anyone the potential vindictiveness of his buddies, all former employees at New York Fried Chicken. The inside kid had pled to a lesser charge of manslaughter, but his main crime in Nancy's opinion was being dumb enough to think that if you unlock the door at a Route 40 chicken shack and admit three unmasked guys with a gun, they're going to be content to take the money and depart, doffing their caps as they go. *Doffing their caps* was another Lenhardt-ism, of course: "Tally-ho, good day, thank you for these tens and twenties, and may I have some of the Cajun extra-crispy to go? It ain't Cary Grant on the Riviera, Nancy. If it were, robbery would be working it. People don't kill people sometimes, we're out of work."

"Yeah, I know," Nancy said. She suspected that Lenhardt wanted to let it go, put the day behind him, but she couldn't. She had to learn. It had been so easy to catch them, so hard to break them down. They had an insolence that left her breathless. Her Polish grandfather had escaped from Europe

with nothing but the clothes on his back, survived the sink-
ing of an ocean liner, and refused the easy names pressed on
him when he arrived at the Port of Baltimore in 1916. Josef
Potrcurzski had carried his own knife, and later a gun,
guarding his block like a sheriff in the Old West. Yet even he
would have been terrified by this trio.

"The killing *was* the point," Lenhardt said. "More than the
money, which would have lasted maybe forty-eight hours,
and that's if they got some financial planner from Merrill
Lynch to help them invest it. They didn't kill someone in a
robbery. They had a robbery so they could kill someone."

"So why bring a gun," Nancy said, "and use one of the
kitchen knives?"

Lenhardt pressed his palms into his eyes and rubbed,
hard, the way the redheaded barmaid had twisted Nancy's
limed-up margarita glass when Nancy asked for extra salt.

"I don't know, Miss Nancy. I just don't know. You found
the casing in the parking lot. Maybe the kid with the gun
fired it and was scared by the noise. Maybe they shot and
missed, what with the vic swinging that knife around, assuming they were telling the truth about that. Poor bastard
died defending the honor of New York Fried Chicken."

"Okay, so they wanted to kill someone. But why someone
they'd be connected to so easily?"

"They're not thinking this through, Nancy. *They* don't
know from standard probability."

"Seriously."

"Maybe they killed him because he was their boss once.
Because he told them to clean out the fryer, and put those
napkins out, and make sure the tables are wiped down. Because he enforced the hair net rule. They killed him—"
Lenhardt paused. He knew how to tell a story, how to get his
audience hanging on his every word. "Because he cared, because he thought it mattered that the New York Fried

Chicken on Route 40 had clean bathrooms and fresh oil and low absenteeism. The fast-food true believer met the West Side Existentialist Club, and the existentialists won."

Lenhardt rolled his eyes—*Did I say that?*—and Infante laughed, repeating *existentialist* in a slightly drunken slur, as if it were funny, maybe even a little dirty.

"You know, five miles east, and it's not even a county case," Infante said. "I don't think it's where the crime occurs that should establish jurisdiction. I think it's where the mope lives. Their bum, their tax dollars, their detectives."

"Shit, you play by those rules, the only thing we're catching is domestics in Dundalk. Besides, we represent the victims, remember? We work for the citizens of Baltimore County."

Lenhardt's mood had been rising and falling since they arrived at Wagner's. He always plunged after the initial high of getting the work done. "Homicide hypoglycemia," he called it. Nancy experienced the same thing, if to a lesser degree. It felt good to get the clearance, but the process exacted a price. She found that she listened to the confessions the way she watched a scary movie, basically wishing it all undone, urging the actors to do the things that would make the movie end in five uneventful minutes. *Don't open that door. Don't confide in that man. Don't pick up that phone.*

"Cheer up, Sarge," Infante said. "We won this round."

"Campbell died last week," Lenhardt said.

"Campbell?" Nancy asked, even as Infante nodded.

"H. Grayson Campbell. H. Grayson Campbell the Third, or maybe it was the Fourth. Died in a nursing home. Last time I stopped to talk to him, he thought I was his stepson. Guy's got no control of his bowels or his bladder or his brain, he's facing down death—and he still won't tell me where she is."

"Do I know Campbell?" Nancy asked. The name was familiar. Maybe she had seen the file on Lenhardt's desk. He pulled old files all the time. The sergeant never stopped learning, never stopped studying. And she never stopped watching him.

"Just a rich guy who had a habit of bouncing his wife off the walls every now and then, even after they split up. One night, she doesn't bounce back."

"You *allege*," Infante said, aping a defense lawyer's prissy voice.

"Yeah, I allege. Her kids from her first marriage allege. Her family alleges. We're all alligators, heaping our suspicions on this poor, misunderstood citizen because his ex-wife happened to go over there to talk about her Visa bill, and she's never seen again, dead or alive. Now that the bastard is dead, I can say it out loud, say it to the world, and it doesn't do a damn thing. It was her husband. And he left this planet without telling me where he left her."

"Where do you think he put the body?" Nancy asked.

"I don't know. Where do county guys go to dump their bodies? If he was a city mutt, I'd check Leakin Park. But he ain't no city mutt, and even after ten years out here, I never have figured out where county guys dump their bodies. Too much acreage."

Nancy looked down at her plate, an assortment of deep-fried things—mushrooms, zucchini, the cheese-filled poppers. She needed to go back on her diet. She hadn't tried, not with a case working, which meant life was all carryout. She calculated calories and carbs, pondered buying a stationary bike. She thought about anything and everything to block out the memories that surged whenever anyone said "Leakin Park."

Lenhardt looked in his lap and Nancy understood that his beeper must have gone off.

"Wife time," Infante said, laughing.

"Hey, at least Nancy and I are still on our first spouses," he said, getting up and going to the phone, leaving Infante and Nancy alone.

An awkward silence fell. Although the two had spent plenty of time alone together, they seldom socialized. "I had a case once," Infante said, "where I thought the guy put his wife in a wood-chipper. Guy was really big on gardening. I've never seen so much mulch. Everything was mulched."

"That's ridiculous," Nancy said, with an inappropriate heat.

"What?"

"I mean, if there was a wood-chipper, you could check it for blood. You can't mulch a person without a trace, much less scour all the trace evidence out of a wood-chipper."

Infante looked at her as if to say: "The fuck did I do?" Nancy couldn't tell him, because he hadn't done anything. But picking on Infante would somehow even up the day, make up for what happened when the last of the quartet was being maneuvered into handcuffs for transport to the county jail.

This was the one who had done it, the one who had taken the knife and driven it into the victim again and again and again. He was slight, weighed less than Nancy. But there was something menacing in the very fineness of his bones, as if a bigger boy had been boiled down until all that remained was this concentrated bit of rage and bile.

He had bugged Lenhardt, too, although he didn't realize it. That was a mistake, not knowing when Lenhardt was mad at you.

"We got you, you know?" Lenhardt couldn't help telling the little one after he signed on the dotted line. "Your friends gave you up. They told us plenty, by the way. Your buddies, your pals, your confederates."

Confederates—another Lenhardt-ism. He had told Nancy he used it for the very associations it raised. Confederate–

Confederacy–Civil War–slavery. For the young black men of Baltimore, the wrongs done to their ancestors brought them nothing but shame. To have been a slave was to have been weak. To be descended from slaves was just as bad. But only Lenhardt would think it through this way.

For a fleeting second, the young man had looked surprised, then his face closed up again. Nancy guessed his emotions had flowed much the same way at the chicken place. He had been caught off guard by his former boss's bravery—and punished him for it. He had chased the night manager from the kitchen to the parking lot, increasingly desperate, worried not about being caught, but about being disgraced by the other boy's futile courage. He had killed him to show the others the price of such valor.

Now he lunged at Nancy, grabbing a handful of her ass.

"Nice," he said, "for a white girl."

Lenhardt had punched him so hard in the stomach that the kid had doubled over and fallen to his knees. The sergeant smiled at Nancy over the boy's prostrate body, happy for the opportunity, inviting her to land a kick or a punch if she wanted. When she passed, he gave her a curious look, then helped himself, distributing the punishment he thought fair. The kid had to lie there and take it.

He had touched a cop. Nancy couldn't help feeling that she had failed, that a better cop wouldn't have been grabbed in the first place. And Lenhardt had let her mistake slide because he was so happy for a chance to smack that kid before the day was over.

"The wood-chipper—" Nancy began again, and she knew she was going to off-load to Infante the anger she had caught from the kid. Life was just a long game of emotional tag, one bad mood passing from person to person. But before she could finish, her Nokia chirped and the text message scrolled by in plain view.

I ' M   H O M E

The words seemed to shiver on the screen, but that was probably just some disturbance in the cell. The Kenwood Homecoming Queen again. Why didn't she just get her own public access channel on Baltimore County cable, keep her friends up-to-date with a 24/7 crawl.

"Your hubby?" Infante asked.

"I don't think so," she said. "He's pissed at me. Besides, I already know where he is."

The message stared insistently back at her. Was it for her? No way. She wouldn't even try to make a connection if it weren't for Lenhardt, the sheer coincidence of tonight's conversation: *If he was a city mutt, I'd know to check Leakin Park.*

Leakin Park. Even a near homonym, such as Lincoln or leaking, could make her jump. Leakin Park. The name always brought back the little lean-to in the woods, or the silhouette of her classmate from the academy, Cyrus Hickory, standing in the door. He told her to stay back, but Nancy had to prove she could do whatever he did, so she crossed the stream, walked up to the falling-down house—

No. Over the past seven years, Nancy had learned she could choose, that she had the power not to cross the threshold if she wasn't up to seeing what was on the other side. So tonight, she did what she didn't do then. She backed away, so she was moving away from the little house in the woods, splashing backward through the polluted stream, edging up the hill, her gloved hands empty, blessedly empty.

Lenhardt came back to the table, threw his money down, and waved off the bills that Nancy and Infante tried to add. "I'm one drink away from a divorce," he said. "Marcia is more lenient than .08, but not by much. You should go home, too, Nancy."

"What about me?" Infante asked.

"Not even Dr. Joyce Brothers herself could save your relationships, Kevin."

"True enough," the detective said amiably, more amused than anyone at the string of Mrs. Infantes that had come and gone in the last twenty years. He got up and headed to the bar. The barmaid had a trace of a limp, but she was still redheaded and still pretty, in that hard, shellacked-hair way of a county barmaid.

Out of nowhere, Lenhardt asked: "You ever think about a baby?"

"Baby?" *He knows,* she thought. *All this time, he's known and he's never asked.* Of course he would know. Cops gossip like Polish grandmothers. *You know the background on Porter, right? The Kolchaks' niece? A shame, but she brought it on herself. You'd think she'da known better, with her background.*

"Having a baby. You think about it?"

"Oh." She was so relieved that she didn't mind Lenhardt getting personal with her. "Doesn't everybody? But Andy has one semester of law school left, and I just made Homicide."

"Babies are more important than any of that."

"Yeah. How many kids you got?"

"Three," Lenhardt said. "That I know of." He popped his eyes and let his mouth gape, but he was too tired to pull off his own shtick.

"Be good," he said abruptly and ambled off.

Be good? Where had that come from? But she took his advice, took it across the board. Drove straight home, woke up her sleeping husband, and made love to him, which he assumed was her way of apologizing, and maybe it was, although she didn't think she had anything to apologize for. Life was so short, and she didn't want to be at odds with the person who knew her best. The person who loved her before, the person who loved her after, the person who swore he would love her always.

Andy went back to sleep, but Nancy never did, not that night. She stared at the ceiling, adding seven to eleven, then subtracting it.

The call had to be a wrong number.

Thursday,
April 16

8.

The first child disappeared from the Rite Aid at Ingleside
Shopping Center. She was strapped into a cart on aisle 11—
Baby Needs, Foot Care, Feminine Hygiene—when her
mother, Mary Jo Herndon, remembered a new kind of hair
gel she had seen advertised just that morning. The gel promised to get rid of the frizz while adding shine. She saw herself with straight, glossy hair, tossing it around as she
laughed with some man. Maybe Bobby, maybe not. The actual man was less important than the shiny banner of hair,
flying around the way it did in commercials, warm as sunlight on her shoulders.

Hair care was one aisle over, but there was a woman between Mary Jo and the end of the aisle, a big-butted woman
who was studying the Dr. Scholl's products with fierce concentration, her basket placed at an angle that made it impossible for another cart to get by. And Mary Jo didn't want to
ask her to move because there was something obstinate in
that big behind, the sense of a woman spoiling for a fight. It
was easier to leave the cart, step around the woman, and jog
to the hair care aisle. After all, she was just going to grab the
gel and then go to the cash register. The trip was already out
of control. Mary Jo had come for toilet paper and charcoal,
and now her cart was almost full.

Rite Aid didn't carry the brand she remembered from the

commercial, but it had a dizzying array of alternatives and Mary Jo paused to consider her options. There was a whole line of products in sleek lavender bottles, but the manufacturer called it a *system,* suggesting it was all-or-nothing. Part of her mind knew this was a gyp, a bluff. There was no way you had to buy the whole set to get the benefits of the gel.

But Mary Jo also believed an expensive purchase could be transforming. The product might not be any better, but choosing to pay extra was a way of saying you deserved a little luxury in this world and that mind-set could make it so. Didn't she deserve the best, or at least something better? That's what everyone said: You deserve better. Of course, her friends and family were talking about Bobby and her living situation, but there was no product on the earth that could fix Bobby. She grabbed a bottle of the lavender stuff and trotted back to aisle 11.

Aisle 11 was empty. No Jordan, no cart, no big-butted woman staring down at the Dr. Scholl's products. Mary Jo must have gone the wrong way, turned right when she should have turned left. No problem. She retraced her steps, heading to aisle 9.

That was empty, too.

The first empty aisle had made her nervous, but it had been a safe, contained nervousness, for she assumed she had taken a wrong turn, that Jordan was waiting for her around the next corner. Mary Jo had felt the way she did on the long, cranking climb of the roller coaster at Adventure World— scared for the sake of it, yet secure, knowing the climb was just part of the suspense, that the fine print on the ticket was just for show.

When she reached the second aisle, she no longer knew what was happening or how it would end, and then all bets were off, all promises voided. She started trotting the long, diagonal corridor that bisected the store, shouting out Jordan's name and trying to imagine the worst. Because if she could imagine a thing, it couldn't happen.

A child cried, sharp and scared, and Mary Jo ran toward the sound with gratitude and relief. But the child she found on aisle 3 was a boy, his face red from where a hand had just lashed out, his mother glaring at Mary Jo, ready to defend herself. Mary Jo left them, thinking: *You are so lucky to have a child to slap.* No, that wasn't quite right. She promised God she would never slap Jordan again, never raise a hand to her in any way if he would just give her back. She didn't, not often, and she knew it was wrong. Never again, she promised. *Never again. You hear me, God?*

Other promises followed as she ran a serpentine path through the store, up and down the aisles, calling Jordan's name at intervals. She would be a better mother overall, patient and kind, not even yelling. She would be nicer to her sister, although Mimi did have a way of lording over her, making Mary Jo feel like a fuck-up because Bobby had proved to be so unreliable. What else? Oh God, she would be so perfect in every way if Jordan turned up.

"Ma'am. Ma'am." The pharmacist's voice was insistent, chiding, a voice of authority. He was going to tell her to stop shouting, stop running. Who was he to say she couldn't yell, when her baby was missing? "Ma'am—please, ma'am."

"I'm looking for my little girl, my Jordan. She's three? Has long curly hair like mine, only kinkier and darker?" She didn't understand why everything was coming out like a question, as if she needed this strange man to confirm what she was saying. "She was wearing—she was wearing—"

Oh, God, what was she wearing? A dress. Jordan was going through this stubborn phase where she insisted on wearing dresses every day. Green? Blue? A hand-me-down from Mimi's three girls, something with smocking or embroidery at the top. In the car, Jordan had pulled the top off her Sippee

Cup, leaving a dark red stain on the front. Mary Jo had screamed at her because Jordan knew better, she had taken the cup apart to be contrary. But Mary Jo wouldn't do that, never again. Stains came out if you treated them right. Stains weren't important.

"Ma'am." The pharmacist grabbed Mary Jo's arm and pulled her down a corridor leading to a rest room. There was her cart, with all her things—the toothpaste and the toilet paper and the potato chips and the charcoal and the two plastic lawn chairs in case they cooked out tonight, if Bobby stopped by for dinner. And there was Jordan in the booster seat. Her dress was blue. Right, she knew that. Her daughter's dress was blue.

Jordan looked scared, and Mary Jo, who could not see her own face, didn't realize her expression was not much different from when the Sippee Cup had come apart in the car. She grabbed the girl from the cart and covered her with kisses, asking what had happened, demanding to know who had moved the cart, but giving Jordan no chance to answer. She started sobbing, thinking of all the possible bad endings. Only then did Jordan begin to cry and babble. But her three-year-old vocabulary was not up to the task of telling her story.

"Did you see anyone?" Mary Jo asked the pharmacist. "Who would have pushed my cart here? Was she in the way? Who would do a thing like that? What kind of store is this?"

In her mind, she was seeing some employee push the cart aside because it was blocking the aisle. She would sue, she would raise a fuss. What kind of person pushed a cart with a baby into this little corridor by the bathrooms?

The pharmacist shrugged. At dinner that night, he would tell his wife the story, putting all the blame on Mary Jo. His own children were grown. He could afford to be smug, all the near misses his family had known over the years long forgotten.

As for Mary Jo, she never told the story to anyone—not to Mimi, who would have found a way to blame her, or Bobby, who was in a sour mood when he finally dropped by that evening, long after Jordan had gone to bed. He brought a few dollars, but when Mary Jo asked when she was going to start getting a check regular, now that he was working, he said he'd quit if she tried to garnish his wages, that a man couldn't get ahead in this world if women were always going to be at them. She said he wasn't much of a man if he couldn't support his daughter.

It was a familiar argument from start to finish. Bobby slammed out, leaving her to clean up after their cookout. Bobby was always careful to get a meal before he let a fight begin. Mary Jo went to bed alone. He hadn't even noticed her hair, which she had washed and styled with the new gel. If he had commented on her hair, she might have told him the story of what happened in Rite Aid. Or not. Bobby might have used it against her, and even Mimi would have found a way to blame Mary Jo.

It would be two months before the next child disappeared.

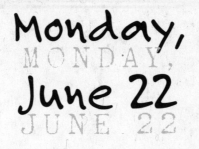

Monday,
June 22

9.

Summer finally began. It began over and over again. It began in mid-May, with a disturbingly early heat wave. It began again on Memorial Day, when the private swim clubs opened for business, even though the heat wave had receded and the weather had reverted to the cold and dreary days of April. It began with each last day of school, district by district, with the city of Baltimore always the last to release its children. It began with the first Code Red day, an index of air, not terror, issued when the heat held the smog too close to the city. It began every Friday about 4 P.M., when the local radio stations reported that the back-ups at the toll plazas for the Bay Bridge were now three miles, four miles, five miles long. It began when the fireflies appeared and a new generation of children tested the folklore that the insects could not fly if one walked with them balanced on a fingertip.

A new summer ritual was also under way that year—the disappearance of children, little girls. They went missing from parks and stores, from yards and porches. But no one noticed, because the girls reappeared minutes later, before their absence had been logged. Even the girls themselves did not seem to recognize the extraordinary thing that had happened to them. Even if they had, they couldn't have told anyone, for they were toddlers, too young to speak, much less compare notes.

By the time the vernal equinox actually arrived, summer already seemed careworn and used. This happened to be the day that Nancy put on her best suit and went to the courthouse, perhaps the ugliest public building in all of Baltimore County, no small distinction. There, she testified before the grand jury, which needed little encouragement to hand up capital murder indictments against three of the four boys in the New York Fried Chicken killing. The fourth would be tried on robbery and manslaughter charges, which was the deal he had cut for himself. He chose to risk the near-sure death sentence of being a witness, to the guaranteed death sentence given to anyone convicted of a capital crime in Baltimore County.

Duty done, Nancy and Infante met their sergeant at the Italian place on Washington, the chain restaurant that she liked so much. Lenhardt always insisted on treating, claiming the county would pick up the tab, but Nancy suspected these lunches came out of his pocket.

"She going for death?" Infante asked Lenhardt, the *she* in question being the Baltimore County prosecutor.

"She always does," Lenhardt said, slathering a bread stick with the restaurant's trademark tapenade. Nancy was pretending to enjoy a small house salad.

"Good," Infante said.

"But the victim's mother might not want it," Nancy said. She was remembering the woman she had met back in April, a woman whose life had tested her faith yet never weakened it. The walls of the woman's rowhouse had featured a riotous competition between God's only son and her only son, with Jesus edging out Franklin Morris. "She's Christian."

"So?" Infante said. "Aren't we all?"

"I mean a real one. Very devout. And you know the state's attorney won't go for the death penalty if the relatives don't want it."

"Christian?" Lenhardt pretended to be indignant. "Well, eye for an eye *is* the oldest Christian rule of all."

"I guess she's more New Testament, turn the other cheek, like."

"The New Testament," Lenhardt said, wagging his bread-stick, "is the New Coke of religion. They need to throw that sucker out and go back to the original recipe."

Nancy gasped so hard, trying not to laugh, that she almost swallowed a cherry tomato from her salad. She was no more religious than the average lapsed Catholic, but it was not a subject about which she could joke. She felt too guilty, being AWOL from St. Casimir's all these years.

"Anyway, you let that nice Christian lady sit through a little testimony, see a few crime scene photos, and she'll be ready to give those guys the injection her own self."

Infante nodded sagely. It was one of his few moves that got under Nancy's skin, that wise nod, as if there were things that only he and Lenhardt could understand.

Lenhardt was on a roll, the topic of religion having struck his fancy for some reason. "Vengeance is mine, saith the Lord. And that's the New Testament, by the way."

Nancy didn't know the Bible that well, but she was determined to argue the point: "Is *mine*. His, not ours. So isn't God saying we're not supposed to be in the vengeance business?"

"He's saying we do it for him, so we better do it right." But Lenhardt was guessing at the meaning, too. Not a one of them at the table—two Catholics and a Lutheran—at least she thought Lenhardt was a Lutheran—had the credentials to play even half-assed theologians.

"I'll tell you what I know about revenge," Infante piped up. He pronounced the word REE-venge, as if it were an act of repetition, not reaction. "It feels *good*. That's why God wants it for himself. He knows how much fun it is."

"I feel a reminiscence coming on," Lenhardt said. "Wife number one or two?"

"Two."

"Didn't you cheat on Two?" Nancy asked, knowing he had.

"Yeah, but I felt bad about it. You know, adultery isn't what kills a marriage, it's just—"

"A symptom," Nancy said, winning a big laugh from Lenhardt, which made her feel good. Infante's marital history and the accompanying litany of excuses were well known to them.

"Fuck you," he said, but without bite. This, too, was part of the litany, the beginning of Infante's marital beatitudes. "Yes, I slipped up, and she caught me, but I wanted to get back with her so bad, I was willing to do anything. Only she didn't want me anymore. She wanted my house and my furniture, though. And all our money, not that there was so much of it, but her lawyer told her to drain every penny out of our joint accounts. The one thing she didn't get from me was my key."

"Really?" Nancy had been working on raising one eyebrow—she thought it was an expression that might have its uses in interrogations—and she tried it now. She caught a glimpse of her face in the metal napkin holder and the effect was far from what she intended. Even allowing for the distortion of the napkin holder, she looked silly, like a cartoon character trying to be menacing. "Calculating as she was, and she didn't get the key from you, or change the locks?"

"Well"—Infante's grin belied the hangdog dip of his head—"maybe I had a copy made one day, for emergencies, and she forgot about that. At any rate, one night when she was out, I let myself in."

"To what purpose?" Lenhardt asked.

"That was the funny thing. I didn't really have a plan when I went in. It was one A.M.—"

"Was this an alcohol-related crime, Mr. Infante?" Lenhardt pulled out his pad, pretended to take notes.

Again, his grin confessed all. "So I'm there, in my old living room, and I can already see how she's, like, eliminating me from our life. I had this picture of a boat, kind of a painting, and I just really liked it. It's not over the mantel, so she's put it away somewhere. She doesn't want it, but she won't let me have it. That's what she was like. The cat comes in and sniffs at my ankles and my feet, and I start thinking about what she loved most in the world—"

"*Not* the cat." Nancy was remembering a famous bit of Baltimore lore about a lobbyist who had put his ex's cat in the microwave.

"No. What kind of pervert do you think I am? But I look at the cat, twisting around my feet, and when I look at my feet, I see my shoes and I remember—Lorraine loved shoes. So I find a hacksaw in the basement—*my* hacksaw, by the way, from *my* toolbox—and I go upstairs and saw the heel off every right shoe in her closet."

"Why every right heel?" The detail fascinated Nancy, an insight into Infante, maybe into all men.

"Because you don't have to take both to ruin the shoes, you know? And she has, like, ten, twenty pairs of shoes. Half of 'em black, by the way. So when I'm done there's just like this little pile of—" He gestured, incapable of defining what he had created.

"Dismembered shoes," Lenhardt supplied.

"Yeah. I just left 'em in the middle of the rug."

"She ever say anything?" Lenhardt again, the consummate cop, intent on getting the facts while the suspect was feeling voluble and expansive. Nancy was too dumbfounded to comment.

"Naw. I kept checking the precinct, too, but she never filed a report. So she knew it was me."

Nancy finally thought of what she wanted to ask, the question she wanted to ask every mutt, but seldom got a chance. "Did it feel good, sitting on the floor of your old bedroom, sawing shoes?"

"Yeah. Well, actually, I cut my hand up a little, but I enjoyed every bit of it, absolutely."

"You left trace evidence," Lenhardt said, only half joking. "You could have fucked up your career over something like that."

"Naw. I had a key, my name was still on the deed. And I bought those fuckin' shoes, so I was just taking my half."

"I wonder," Nancy said, "what she did with all those left-over shoes. You think there's a charity that specializes in giving shoes to one-legged women? Like, you might see a woman come hopping at you one day, and she'll be wearing a pump from your ex-wife's closet?"

"I tell you what," Infante said. "That is the day I take a one-legged woman dancing."

Their main courses arrived—cream-rich pasta dishes for the men, penne arrabbiata for Nancy, who had signed up for an online diet service that helped to track one's daily calorie intake. It had a whole list of what you were supposed to eat in different kinds of restaurants, and it swore by penne arrabbiata in Italian places. She watched wistfully as the waiter grated fresh Parmesan on the others' dishes, but shook him off with a noble little nod.

"There are about a million calories in that green stuff," she said wistfully of the tapenade. Lenhardt and Infante, used to such non sequiturs from her, dug into their food, their chins hanging low enough to catch the steam from the hot bowls of pasta.

"What about you, Nancy?" Lenhardt asked. "You ever gotten back at anyone?"

"No one's ever done anything to me. I mean, not like that."

"Really?" For a moment, she thought Lenhardt knew she was lying. He was a good homicide police and being a good police meant knowing how to listen to everything, how to keep secrets and retain them for years, in the hopes they might be useful some day.

No, she told herself, trying to remember to chew her food with the careful "savoring" bites recommended by her e-Diet program, she was giving her sergeant too much credit. He didn't know everything. The knowledge felt blasphemous, but good. It was not unlike the way she felt when she realized the priest at her cousin's wedding was drunk, or that Father Mike couldn't know if you didn't tell him absolutely everything at confession. Even her computer wouldn't know if she was lying, at day's end, when she dutifully logged her meals. There was only one God and only He—she couldn't help herself, she still thought of him as He in raised gilt letters—only He really knew what He wanted. Everybody else was just making it up as they went along.

Friday,
June 26

10.

It was at the Catonsville branch of the Baltimore County Public Library that someone finally thought to call the police. The always busy branch was particularly antic on the third Friday in June, with children selling band candy and a community group gathering signatures on a petition for plantings along the Frederick Road median strip. Inside, the talk—loud, insistent talk, not at all library-like—was about the Fourth of July celebration, and whether there would be fireworks, given last year's unfortunate incident. (A small fire, no injuries, but still it raised the question of whether the local Elks Lodge should be entrusted with this task again.)

Miriam Rosen, a patron at Catonsville for more than thirty years, always felt a surge of nostalgia for its more formal past. The reconfigured branch was so crowded, so overwhelmed by all the services that libraries were now expected to provide—not just books and periodicals, but compact discs and videos and DVDs and computers with Internet access—that it seemed more flea market than library. *No wonder Starbucks had become so popular,* Miriam thought. In Starbucks, a person could find a place to sit.

She parked Sascha, Jake, and Adrien in the children's section, reminding Sascha to keep an eye on the baby, as Adrien was still known at age three. Twelve-year-old Sascha rolled her eyes, irritated, but that was as far as her adolescent moodiness had progressed. Miriam's friends envied her this polite, solemn daughter, but Miriam considered Sascha almost too passive. She wanted her children to be fighters, quick to challenge authority, even hers.

Now, Jake was a toss-up—at age eight, he was a cipher, polite but secretive, with a con man's charm, and Miriam sensed that his underwear drawer would yield all manner of contraband as he got older. Then there was Adrien, her late-in-life blessing, her favorite mistake, the Disney World souvenir, just like in the commercial. "You went to Disney World with an eight-year-old and a four-year-old, and still found a way to have sex?" her friends had marveled. Really, Adrien was a bit of a boast all the way around. Everyone in the Rosen family doted on Adrien, yet she was impossible to spoil. She soaked up love the way a napping cat absorbed sunshine. Look at her, sitting Indian-style at Sascha's feet, paging through a picture book, absolutely contented. She was obedient without being a goody-goody, sweet but not saccharine.

"Sascha?"

"What?" The teenager gave the word two syllables, almost three.

"Keep an eye on Adrien," Miriam repeated. She headed to the CD section to see what operas were available. The Baltimore Public Library was a bit populist for Miriam's taste, skewing its collections to what people really wanted, as opposed to what they should want, so the classical music selection was thin. But Miriam never complained, perhaps because she felt a bit guilty about checking out CDs so she could download them onto her computer at home and, with Jake's help, burn her own CDs. It wasn't wrong, exactly, but it also wasn't right—one of those middle-class everyone-does-it crimes, like speeding or rounding down on income taxes.

Miriam had been pregnant with Adrien when she began playing opera CDs on her endless bouts of chauffeuring the older two, hoping appreciation would come with repeated exposure. When she first left her job at the Homeless Persons Representation Project, she had tried listening to Italian language tapes, but her thoughts ended up drifting. She decided music might require less concentration, permitting her to check in and out. Like a baby in a womb, stereo speakers blasting Mozart at mother's convex belly, she drove around in her Volvo, willing the music and foreign words to wash over her.

But so far, the only thing she had learned was how many little bits of opera had entered everyday life, like common foreign phrases so familiar they were no longer regarded as foreign. Miriam recognized melodies from *Carmen* because they had been incorporated into an episode of *Gilligan's Island,* and she could hum Pagliacci's lament only because it had been used to tout the wonders of Rice Krispies when she was a child. No, it was Adrien who sang along to *Madame Butterfly,* whose face brightened when a car commercial included that famous strand of notes from *Lakmé.*

Oh, to have the spongelike mind of a child again, to soak up knowledge as easily as you popped a Flintstone vitamin. Jake was at that stage where he wanted to know everything, *everything,* and he used his knowledge with an almost unattractive aggression, correcting Miriam until she got a bit sharp with him. Sascha was beginning to seek forbidden information in secret. Sascha being Sascha, this meant a copy of *God's Little Acre* under her bed. Really, the girl was almost quaint in her attempts to rebel.

Blessed Adrien remained incurious about the world, content that it would reveal its mysteries to her soon enough. Which was fine with Miriam. Childlike wonder was a bit wearying the third time around.

Her CDs chosen—*La Traviata* and *Manon Lescaut*—

Miriam checked out the new acquisitions, best-sellers all, and a table of for-sale items, last year's best-sellers. Back in the children's section, Sascha was lost in *The Red Fairy Tales,* the world forgotten as she leaned against the shelf, a piece of hair drawn between her lips. It was a lovely tableau, even with the hair-chewing bit. An incomprehensible teenage habit, yet Miriam had done it, too. Tasted her hair, split the split ends, plucked out one strand at a time, just because she could, because it was her hair to do with as she wished, and because this drove her mother crazy. For a moment, Miriam saw Sascha as a perceptive stranger might, a girl poised between childhood and adolescence. *You rushed so hard to grow up,* Miriam remembered—*until you realized you had no choice.* Then you wanted to slow down, draw childhood out, go back to simpler stories and simpler games.

It took her a second to register the fact that Adrien was nowhere to be seen.

"Sascha," she said, feeling a mild irritation at the girl's thoughtlessness, "where's your sister?"

Sascha looked up, needing a moment to surface from her imaginary world. "Adrien? She's right here. I mean, she *was* right here. Maybe she went off with Jake."

Perhaps because it was a library, and perhaps because Miriam, too, loved fairy tales, it still didn't occur to her to feel anything more than impatient.

But when she found Jake alone at one of the library's computers—trying to hack his way past the filters, just to see if it could be done—a slight panic began a skipping beat somewhere between Miriam's stomach and heart. *Where had the baby gone?* The three Rosens split up, looking everywhere. Adrien was not in the children's section, or in the rest rooms, or curled up in an aisle's cozy dead end. Miriam's hands began to shake, and she had to exert enormous control not to yell at someone, anyone. Sascha and

Jake, for their carelessness. The library staff, for running such a chaotic bazaar instead of a hushed, serious place for study. The other families, for daring to be whole.

The children's librarian, who knew the Rosens well, made an announcement on the seldom-used PA system. *If anyone sees a little girl with long curly hair in a green T-shirt and pink plaid pants, please bring her to the Information Desk.* Yet the amplified voice could barely be heard over the buzz of the library. Ten minutes passed, fifteen, twenty. Miriam, hands shaking ever harder, insisted on calling the police despite the staff's assurances that this happened every now and then, and the children always—always—turned up.

"Not always," an old man muttered. "In California last week . . ." But no one wanted to listen to him.

The police took their time getting there. They still had not arrived when Jake had the idea of searching the lower level, used primarily for storage and the board's monthly meetings. "There's nothing scheduled down there today," the children's librarian said, "and the room is usually locked when it's not in use." But it was something to do, a way to keep moving forward, a way to still the doleful voices in Miriam's head, the ones predicting the end of life as she knew it.

The three Rosens descended the stairs together, mother in the center, hand in hand. In the time it took to walk to the lower floor, Miriam saw every assumption she had made about her life torn from her. Twenty minutes ago, asked what she feared, she might have said that she hoped her children stayed away from drugs, that they would be spared cruelty, that they would go to good colleges and make happy marriages. Pressed to the outer limits of her imagination, she could have envisioned the horror of a sick child, or an injured one. But not a missing one and certainly not—but she couldn't say it, even to herself. *Don't do this to me,* she instructed God. *Don't you dare.* Her nonobservant life—her so-so Seders, her refusal to fast on Yom Kippur—came back to haunt her. But even in utter despair, she could not vow to change, to love God more if he would bring her daughter back. She didn't want to make a promise she knew she would forget to keep.

"Mom—" It was Jake, his voice careful. "You're muttering."

At the bottom of the stairs, they found themselves in a small foyer. Miriam reached out and placed a palm on the double doors that faced them, the way you were supposed to do in a fire. The doors were cool to the touch. She pulled and they balked, seemingly locked. But she yanked on them again, and the sticky lock disengaged, opening to reveal an empty meeting space.

Adrien was sitting quietly on the floor in a corner of the room, a picture book in her lap, other books scattered around her in a haphazard semicircle.

"Baby," Miriam said, running toward her, arms outstretched.

Adrien frowned and sat where she was. "*Not* baby," she corrected.

"Why are you down here? How did you get here?" Miriam had pressed the girl so hard to her shoulder that she couldn't answer until she wiggled around, freeing her mouth.

"Lady said."

"What lady? One of the librarians?" Miriam indicated the staff members who had crept down the stairs behind her.

Adrien studied them gravely, then shook her head. Because of her long amber curls and green eyes, she was used to admiring glances, but she had never had so many people watching her at once. She seemed to like it.

"Gone," she said, with a dramatic sweep of her chubby little arm. "Lady gone."

The police arrived as the Rosens were gathering their things. Miriam made a report only because she felt so sheepish. If she didn't make a report, then she was a silly hysteric who had acted on groundless fears. A report made it true. She told the officer that she had left the baby under Sascha's supervision—not to blame Sascha, she told herself, but to establish a record, in case it happened again. Someone had lured her daughter to that basement room, probably some dotty old lady. Still, she wouldn't want another family to experience the panic she had just known. And there was the question of how the room had come to be unlocked, which seemed to bother the library staff even more than Adrien's disappearance.

"It hasn't been used since the library board met there yesterday," the children's librarian kept saying, "and the library board is not inclined to be careless about such things."

"All's well that ends well," Miriam said, unashamed of the cliché. "I just want it on the record in case anything like this happens again."

The young officer studied Adrien for a few seconds.

"Her shirt," he said, "was it always on inside out?"

It was only then that Miriam noticed the seams, visible on the shoulders of the long-sleeved T-shirt that Adrien had insisted on wearing despite the day's heat. Yes, there were the grass-green machine stitches, which looked like little surgical scars. The pink plaid pants were on right side out, though, and the shoes were still tied in Miriam's distinctive rabbit ear. She was glad, looking at those shoes, that she had developed this silly way of tying shoes. If her daughter's shoes had not been removed, then her pants had not come off. If the pants had not come off . . . then Miriam never had to think of this again.

Only she did. And when she did, she thought of the day as the knot on a piece of embroidery thread. The needle had poked through the muslin and was anchored in place by a strong knot, tight as a fist. But until it poked back through, creating that first small stitch, there could be no pattern. There was only a knot, a beginning, hidden on the other side of the cloth.

Saturday,
SATURDAY,
June 27
JUNE 27

11.

"Where's the baby, Mom?" Alice asked Helen at breakfast. She had the "Lifestyles" section of the *Beacon-Light* propped up on the sugar dispenser, turned to the comics and horoscope.

"What?" Helen's voice was sharp, her morning tone. "What baby? What are you talking about?"

"The doll's head, the one that used to sit in the middle of your cut-glass saltcellars. I just noticed it's not on the shelf anymore." Alice pointed her forkful of fried egg at the wall next to the kitchen window, where painted shelves held the things Helen had started and stopped collecting over the years—saltcellars, vintage salt and pepper shakers, cobalt blue glassware.

"Oh." Helen had a habit of touching her own face, her hair, her neck—not the usual pats and rubs that people used to put things back in place, but lingering strokes with her fingertips. She drew the skin of her forehead up and into her hairline, smoothing the furrows in her brow. "I got tired of it. It was too . . . precious. Like the time I nailed the old wedding dress to the wall. Remember that? The wedding dress on one wall, the black cocktail dress on the other."

Alice did remember. She had an even clearer memory of

the shoes that Helen had nailed below the dresses, the white and black pumps. The white ones had been attached to the wall sole down, side by side, prim and proper. The black spike heels had been driven into the wall through the vamps, so the phantom wearer appeared to be spread-eagled. There had been a pair of long black gloves as well, thrown wide, as if a singer were finishing a song. Helen had told people it was an artwork titled *Madonna versus Whore, Part I*. Young as Alice must have been at the time—seven, maybe eight— she had understood there would never be a Part II.

"Now that everyone else is doing stuff like that, it's not so much fun," Helen said on a yawn. She had slept late, as was her habit on Saturdays and Sundays, coming down at noon in her yellow silk robe, uncovered at the Dreamland vintage store years ago, back when most people were a little afraid to go down to that part of Baltimore. "I can't run with the herd, you know."

Alice knew, for it was the type of thing her mother often said of herself, in different ways. Helen Manning's interest in her own personality was inexhaustible. *I am not a morning person,* she might announce, almost startled by the insight. *I have never liked sweet potatoes. I simply cannot wear that shade of off-green.* But then, most people were like that. Alice was odd because she didn't find her quirks interesting. She wasn't even sure she had any.

Still, she missed that doll's head. It had been so unexpected, sitting there among Helen's saltcellars. It was the old kind of baby doll, with lashed eyes and a rosebud mouth with a little hole, where a child could stick a bottle. Then, depending on how you held the doll, Helen had explained to Alice and her friends, the water-formula would flow out through the doll's eyes or bottom. For a long time, Alice had assumed the head was one of the toys Helen had salvaged from her youth. Their house was full of Helen's old play-things. But it turned out it was another flea market find, purchased because Helen found it interesting.

"Anything in the paper?" Helen asked.

"My horoscope says all eyes will be on me today—and that I'll find something I misplaced."

Helen's hand knocked her cup, and although it didn't turn over, it sent a great slosh of coffee over the Formica table. Automatically Alice got up and grabbed a sponge from the sink, wiping up before the spill could lap the edges of the newspaper. As a child, Alice had found this table embarrassing, although her friend Wendy had insisted she considered it, and the entire kitchen, extremely cool. "It's like the Silver Diner," she had said approvingly, inspecting the old-fashioned sugar container, the tin signs advertising various ice creams, forgotten flavors such as Heavenly Hash and Holiday Pudding. "Or TGI Friday's."

Wendy had not liked the living room, but then—neither had Alice. The furniture was fussy and uncomfortable, her grandparents' castoffs. The walls had been kept a boring and now somewhat dingy white in order to showcase Helen's *real* artwork, as she called it. These were bright oil paintings of animals doing housework. A dog making breakfast, a fox vacuuming, a duck changing a baby duck's diaper. When visitors asked about the paintings, Helen always said they were ideas for a children's book she had never gotten around to doing. Alice was glad the book never happened, because the paintings scared her. It was hard to explain why. Perhaps it was because the animals did not look happy as they went about their chores, and there were no human touches—no clothes, no bonnets. Alice thought the fox, for example, should be wearing an apron, a frilly one, and the dog should have a chef's hat.

"No, you don't get it," Helen had said when Alice tried to explain why the paintings disturbed her. "I don't want to *celebrate* housework. I don't want to make it pretty. If I put clothes on them, the paintings would become too cozy, too safe."

Yet the baby duck was wearing a diaper, Alice noticed, although she didn't point this out, for she knew her mother would say she was too literal. That was her mother's primary complaint about Alice. She was too factual, too fond of numbers. "You're a concrete thinker," Helen had said once. Alice knew what this meant, more or less, but she couldn't help imagining herself as a big blockhead, her head as square and hard as a rectangle of sidewalk.

"If you're going to read the newspaper," Helen said now, inspecting her sleeve for coffee stains, "you might consider the want ads. You've been home for more than two months and you still don't have a job."

"I've been going to places in person. I went to Westview Mall looking for a job. You told me I had to find a job, remember?"

"What kind of job were you looking for at Westview?"

"Clothing stores."

"Those are hard to get."

Hard for a fat girl, Alice thought, but said nothing.

"I don't understand why you don't try the fast-food places. There are a dozen of those places on Route 40 alone, and you could walk to most of them, or take the bus."

"I said, I'm *looking*."

"But they're always hiring."

"I'd rather not work at a fast-food place if I can find something else."

"Why?"

Alice tried to think of a reason her mother might find acceptable.

"I don't approve of what they're doing."

"What's that?"

"Destroying the rain forest."

"And I don't care for what Baltimore city schools do half the time, but a person has to work, baby."

"You won't even *eat* at those places."

"Yes, that's true." Helen reached for her bony hip, gave it a squeeze. "But you do. And if you eat it, you can't then draw the line at working there for the rain forest's sake. There's nothing wrong with working at McDonald's until you find something better."

"But when will I have time to find something better if I'm behind a fryer every day?"

Helen didn't answer. She had drifted back into her morning silence, her private thoughts. Alice's words often seemed to reach Helen on a delay, like some of those talk radio shows whose callers misbehaved. Minutes would pass, and Helen would suddenly respond to a question that Alice no longer remembered asking.

But when Helen spoke again this morning, it was all too clear she had heard every word Alice had spoken.

"I ran into Ronnie Fuller's mother at the Giant. She said Ronnie had gotten a job."

Ronnie Fuller's mother. Alice tried to remember the woman, but she had been such a ghostly presence in the Fullers' household, tiny and wan. She remembered the father and the brothers much better. She had always thought Matthew, Ronnie's youngest oldest brother, liked her. He teased her a lot, pulling her braids and punching her.

"Yes?"

"At the Bagel Barn."

"I wouldn't want to work there."

"No one wants you to work there. But the Bagel Barn happens to be next to Westview. Alice—what were you really doing over at Westview?"

"Looking for work."

"Tell me the name of one place where you've put in an application."

"The Safeway."

"The Safeway's at Ingleside."

"I started at Ingleside and then went to Westview. It's right across the street."

"The Safeway's union. They wouldn't even let you apply."

"I know. I *asked*. I asked to put an application in and they said no, but it still counts."

"Alice—"

"I did. CVS and Rite Aid, too. I've got no experience, and no one's hiring. Except the convenience stores, and you said I couldn't work there because they might put me on a night shift."

"*Alice.*" Helen grabbed her by the wrist. No lingering fingertip strokes for Alice, not in this situation.

"I'm not doing *anything*." But that sounded defensive, so she altered it. "I mean, I'm not doing anything I shouldn't be doing."

"Alice, baby. Baby, baby, baby."

The old endearment felt ludicrous now that Alice was almost as tall as her mother and outweighed her by at least fifty pounds.

"You've got to let things go, baby."

"I know."

"You can't undo what's done, baby."

"I know."

"The past is the past, baby."

"I know."

"I'm sorry I ever said anything. You ask me things, and I answer, I tell you the truth. I always did. Maybe that makes me a bad parent. But you've got to put *everything* behind you."

"I know."

"I *love* you, baby."

"I know."

Alice began to feel as if they were singing a song to each other, like one of the old R&B songs her mother used to put on the stereo late at night, sitting in the dark with a glass and a cigarette. Alice wasn't supposed to know about the cigarette, but she did because the music always woke her up and she crept to the top of the stairs, listening, too. She knew that smoking was bad, really bad. They taught this in school every year, beginning in first grade. But she couldn't begrudge her mother those middle-of-the-night cigarettes, not even when she finally figured out her mother was smoking dope, which was even worse than tobacco. The nuns said you should call the police if your parents used drugs, or talk to the priest. But Alice wasn't falling for that.

"I am really, truly looking for work, maybe not as hard as I could, but I am looking. It's just—this is my first summer, my first real summer in so long. I want to have a little fun."

She felt guilty, guilt-tripping her mother. It was too easy. Besides, she didn't want to dribble her power away, didn't want to squander it on small things. She had always been a saver—Helen called it "hoarding"—the type of child who put away her Christmas and birthday checks until the small amounts became medium ones. She had saved for things her mother found ridiculous, items that Helen would not buy for Alice no matter how inexpensive. "I'd rather have one pair of well-made Italian shoes than twenty pairs of shoddy, so-called stylish ones." Actually, Helen had been known to treat herself to both. "But I'm a grown-up," she would remind Alice. "My feet have stopped growing."

Alice needed money to buy the things she knew would transform her. All she wanted was to be popular, and—slowly, surely—she had been inventing that girl. A girl who lived in a strange house, yes, with a strange mother, sure, but also a girl who was still cool enough to be friends with someone like Wendy. Helen's approach to life, her preemptive disdain for the things that she could never have, was not Alice's way. She would rather be a minor star in a major constellation than to be a lonely, mediocre sun in an inferior solar system. That was the only thing she remembered from the high school astronomy unit taught at Middlebrook. Their sun was average, mediocre.

But it made her feel horrible, thinking such thoughts about Helen. Helen, who hadn't had to be a mother, who truly chose to bring Alice into the world. She had been very candid with Alice about this, explaining how she had fallen in love with a man and they had rushed into things and the next thing Helen knew, she was pregnant and he was dead in a car crash. "Just like the president's father," she said, referring to the old president, the one who had been in charge when Alice went away. His father had died, too, before he was born. And his father was kind of a bum, too. Helen hadn't made that connection, but Alice had figured it out. A good father didn't die in a car crash before his baby was born. That only happened to a father who was out doing something he wasn't supposed to do.

"Do you know what your horoscope says, Mom? 'Aquarius: It's time to see the world through fresh eyes. Be a friend to get a friend. Virgo, Pisces predominate.'"

"Lots of eyes in the horoscope today."

"Do you know where that baby is?"

"What?"

"The doll's head. Did you put it away in the basement or attic?"

"Oh, gee, I don't know, baby. Why do you want that old thing?"

"I don't know," Alice said. "I miss it. I like things to stay the same."

"Well, they don't, baby. That's the one thing I can guarantee you. Nothing ever stays the same."

12.

The last customer of the day at the Bagel Barn was a tapper. She leaned forward from the waist, so she was eye level with the wire baskets of bagels, and hit the glass with her index finger the way a kid *plink-plink-plinks* the same key on a piano. Her nails were manicured—a tapper's nails tended to be manicured—but relatively short, with clear polish, and Ronnie wondered why anyone would pay to get her nails filed straight across.

"Two sesame—no, three sesame, two poppies." *Tap, tap, tap.* "Are the sunflower seed good? No? Yes? Okay, four plain, two sun-dried tomato." *Tap, tap, tap.* "How many is that?"

"Eleven," Ronnie said.

"Do you do thirteen for the price of a dozen?"

"No, ma'am."

"Everyone else does."

Ronnie shrugged, at a loss. Clarice, the Saturday manager, caught Ronnie's eye and tried to share a smile with her, but Ronnie was scared to do anything with her face. O'lene, the kitchen worker, brushed her hip against Ronnie's as she edged by, already starting her part of the closing routine, and Ronnie allowed herself a small bump back.

"It's the end of the day," the tapper wheedled. "You're just going to end up throwing these away."

"I'm not allowed, ma'am. I'm sorry."

The woman continued to tap. It was almost as if the sound were part of her thinking process, as if she needed the *tick-tick* noise of her finger to get her brain to work.

Such end-of-the-shift customers were common on Saturdays, when people always seemed surprised by the 3 P.M. closing. The rest of the week, Ronnie's shift ended without complaint, but Saturdays always saw some last-minute person, usually a woman, harried and disorganized.

For all that, and despite the crummy pay and early morning hours, Ronnie liked the Bagel Barn. On weekdays, once the morning rush ended, it was a gentle place that ran to solitary, undemanding folks who seemed to have a lot of time to sit and stare out the window while their coffee cooled. She worked the cash register, which paid less than the prep jobs, but she preferred it. She didn't like the idea of touching other people's food, because she didn't want anyone handling hers. Sometimes, glancing over her shoulder, she would see Clarice place her broad hands on the back of the serrated bread knife and press it down through a fully loaded bagel. The tomatoes, so juicy this time of year, would spurt out the sides, leaving smears of red and small seeds on the cutting board. The sight made Ronnie queasy. Not the juice so much as Clarice's black-and-white hands bearing down on the bagel, squeezing the life out of it. When Ronnie got hungry, she ate one of the sweet bagels, whole, like a cookie.

The best thing, in Ronnie's opinion, was the limited menu. The Bagel Barn knew it was a place that sold bagels, and didn't try to be anything else. After 11 A.M., you could get sandwiches—or sandwishes, as Clarice called them in her lisp, which came and went depending on the fit of her dentures—but they came on a bagel. You could get an open-faced pizza, even, with tomato sauce and cheese, but you still had to have it on a bagel.

Yet there were always a few people who expected to be the exceptions, who asked for things they couldn't have. *Can I get that on whole wheat?* No. *Do you have French bread?* No. *Do you have focaccia?* Ronnie didn't even know what that was. *Do you have lattes?* No, no, no, she would say politely, trying not to show how much she enjoyed saying no. She did not understand where people got off, thinking they could have stuff that wasn't on the menu. The menu was a kind of law, she thought, and people should obey it. Like a speed limit, or cleaning up after your dog. If they had allergies, they could go somewhere else. The menu should be—what was the word? The one printed on those fake checks that came in the mail, showing her parents what it would be like if they won a million dollars in a sweepstakes. *Nonnegotiable,* that was it. "Am I asking you?" Ronnie's father had bellowed when his children expressed a preference for something other than the meal that sat in front of them. "Am I asking you?"

Ronnie could never yell at a customer, of course. The owners, who dropped in unexpectedly, would have fired her on the spot if they heard her being rude or disrespectful. But she had an ally in Clarice, who also disliked people who expected special treatment. Especially white people, suburban mothers like this one, who stopped by on their way to somewhere, forever in a hurry, always making special requests. Clarice hated white people, period.

Which was funny, because Clarice was more white than black. She was a black woman whose color had ebbed away, leaving splotches of brown and dark brown on her ghostly face and neck. Apparently she had whatever disease Michael Jackson was always pretending to have. Clarice hated Michael Jackson, too. She had confessed to Ronnie that she disliked white people in general, whereas she hated black people on an individual basis. She said everyone was this way, so it wasn't really prejudice. You hated the people who were different from you as a group, but you hated people like you one by one.

"But I'm talking only on the other side of the counter," she told Ronnie. "And mainly the women. The men are okay, at least around here. I used to work at the North Side Bagel Barn, near the big collitches, and *everybody* up there was bad. Saturdays were hell."

Saturdays were slow at this Bagel Barn. On weekends, Ronnie had figured out, people could drive a little out of their way, go to fancier places with more choices. But that was good, too, because Clarice let her and O'lene, the kitchen prep girl, start close-up early so they could scoot as soon as the door was locked. She also let them take bags of bagels, although the Fuller family wasn't much on bagels. Still, Ronnie liked bringing home that plastic bag of bagels for the freezer. It made her feel like her father, carting in cartons of sodas at week's end, incomplete six-packs and forgotten-about flavors, like Mr. PiBB.

Ronnie had been assembling that day's bag of bagels when the tapper had banged through the front door, pushing through with such authority that the bell seemed to ring a few more notes than usual. The woman wore workout clothes, almost always a bad sign, and she had her keys in her fist, another bad sign. Ronnie, stooped down behind the cases in order to make her selections, looked back at Clarice, who nodded. This was definitely someone who would want special treatment, who would berate them for being out of some bagels, even if it was fifteen minutes to closing. It had been agonizing, getting her to choose two dozen, but Ronnie finally had them bagged when the tapper straightened up as if startled by her own thoughts.

"I won't have time to go to the grocery store," the woman said. "So I might as well get some cream cheese here."

"The spreads are in the refrigerator case on the far wall," Ronnie said, carrying the two bags to the cash register. "Self-serve."

The woman looked confused and glanced around, as if the refrigerator case were hard to find. Once she located it, she ran to it as if every moment counted. She pushed the prepacks around, disrupting the careful order that Ronnie had just established, knocking one or two to the floor and putting them back in the wrong places.

"But I need that—oh, the whatchamacallit, the special one."

"Salmon spread?" Ronnie guessed.

"No, no, that's not it."

"Sun-dried tomato?"

"No," the woman said, growing impatient, as if Ronnie should be able to name what she wanted, even if she herself couldn't.

"Artichoke-parmesan?"

"Yes, that's it." She came back to the counter, carrying a plain and a veggie-lite. "Do you have any?"

"I can scoop some out for you," Clarice said, using the sweet-as-pie voice that Ronnie knew she reserved for people she especially loathed. "Why don't you make sure there's nothing else you need while I do that?"

Clarice weighed and priced the artichoke-parmesan spread. The woman resumed tapping, deciding that she wanted yet another dozen. When Ronnie had peered at her through the glass, she had looked to be about thirty, in her leggings and clingy top. Close up, it was a different story. Her face, while surprisingly smooth, was tired and droopy. Her gaunt neck was beaded with lines. And with her head bent forward, Ronnie could see the gray roots in the chocolate-brown hair. She had to be forty-five, maybe even fifty.

Her order finally assembled, the woman began searching through her bag, looking for her billfold. It seemed to take forever for her to find it in the bulging canvas tote she carried, and when she did, she had no cash.

"Oh, my God," she said. "I forgot I left the house without a cent. Can I write a check?"

Ronnie glanced at Clarice. This was one of the few areas where the manager had some say-so. The Bagel Barn did not accept checks as a rule, but Clarice had the authority to make exceptions.

"What's the big deal?" the woman asked when Ronnie didn't answer right away. "I'm good for it."

What's the big deal? That's what everyone said when they wanted special treatment. What's the big deal, what's it to you? The big deal, Ronnie wanted to tell them, was that rules were rules and you had to follow them, or else the world got crazy, and you went crazy with it. She and her doctor had worked on this back at Shechter. "You can sometimes break rules for a *reason*," her doctor had said. "But the reason can't be 'Because I feel like it.' That's what we call ethics, Ronnie. In certain situations, ignoring a rule because you realize that following it would do harm is the ethical thing to do. Everything else is just an excuse, a rationalization."

"You got an ATM card?" Clarice asked. The woman nodded. "There's a machine, right behind you. You can get cash out of that."

"Oh, but the fee is so high. Two dollars on a twenty-dollar order. It's a rip-off. Just on principle, I'd prefer to write a check."

Ronnie looked at the woman's canvas bag, which had leather handles and trim, at the rings on her thin hands, the tennis bracelet on her wrist. She knew Clarice had caught the same details. The woman wouldn't miss two dollars. But the thing was, the tapper was the kind of person who would

complain, who might call the owners and make trouble for
Clarice. No more than three seconds passed as Clarice considered what to do, but the woman pushed her billfold impa-
tiently at Ronnie, flipping it open to her driver's license.

"I have ID. You can see I have ID. What, do you think I
spend my Saturday afternoons kiting twenty-dollar checks?"

The photo on the ID showed the woman with a different
hairstyle. A familiar hairstyle to Ronnie, and a familiar
name. Sandra Hess. Maddy's mom. Even the address was familiar to Ronnie, although she had never once been to
Maddy's house. But she knew the streets where the better-
off St. William girls had lived. Maddy's mom. She should
have known her by her squinty eyes, her put-upon voice.

"You're such a liar," she said, not meaning to say it out
loud.

"What? *What?*"

Clarice stepped forward. "Of course we'll take your
check, ma'am. Just make it out to the Bagel Barn and make
sure you put a phone number on it."

"Can I make it out for a little over?" Sandra Hess wheedled, and Ronnie knew she was pressing her advantage because of what Ronnie had said. She had the upper hand now.
She probably didn't even need the cash, but she was going to
make them treat her special because that's what women like
Maddy's mom did. Clarice nodded, and she wrote it for
twenty dollars above the total.

Ronnie handed over the bagels. "Can I have extra freezer
bags?" Of course she could. "Do you have a bigger bag than
this, one with handles?" They did. When she was finally satisfied and had turned to go, Ronnie called to her.

"Say hello to Maddy for me."

The woman turned back, instinctively gracious, clearly
pleased by the very mention of her daughter. But her mouth
ended up hanging open as she looked long and hard at Ron-

nie's face. She then edged out the door backward. Once in the parking lot, she walked-ran to her car, a gleaming silver sedan, and drove away in the herky-jerky panic of someone who thought she might be pursued.

"What was that about?" Clarice asked, locking the door behind the fleeing tapper, although it was only 1:55.

"I went to grade school with her daughter. The girl was a jerk, and her mom was a bitch. I guess nothing changes."

"But why did you call her a liar?"

Ronnie hated how smoothly her own lie came, how easy it was to deceive Clarice. "I could see the edge of some bills in her wallet. She had plenty of money, she was just saving it for something else. I'm sorry. I won't do it again."

"You got to keep those thoughts close," Clarice said, worried for her. "I was thinking some much worse things, but you notice I didn't say them out loud."

Ronnie wished she could tell Clarice the true story, the whole story. How Maddy's mother had gone on television giving interviews after Alice and Ronnie were arrested and charged. How she had told all sorts of lies about what had happened that day, so no one would think it was her fault. She said the girls had left the party without permission, that they had assured her they had a ride. Lie, lie, lie. But no one came after Maddy's mother for anything. No one locked her up for not telling the truth. At least Alice didn't get away with her lies. The world was full of liars.

Yet Ronnie had to lie, too, just to get along. Her doctor had said it was okay, that she did not owe the world the story of her life, that there were lies of omission and lies of commission, and the first kind was okay. But how she ached to tell the whole story. She wanted someone, anyone to take her side. She could not tell Clarice the truth about Maddy's mother without telling Clarice everything, and then Clarice would never take her side again, in anything.

13.

Cynthia Barnes was on Nottingham Road, heading home. She found herself on Nottingham almost every day. She rationalized that it was an excellent shortcut, although she had managed to live in the neighborhood for years without using this secondary street. Now it seemed the perfect route to everywhere, and places that could be reached via Nottingham became preferable to those that could not. If Warren wanted Chinese food, for example, then the run-down carry-out on Ingleside was clearly superior to their old favorite on Route 40. Cynthia told Warren she preferred the shrimp fried rice at Wung Fong, which she slathered with hot mustard until it was almost painful to eat. She really did like the fortune cookies, whose messages had a retro glumness missing in more modern ones.

On this particular day, she was driving home from visiting her sister, Sylvia, out in the suburbs. She had followed the odd stretch of highway that dead-ended at the edge of Leakin Park, where construction was halted years ago by environmentalists. A highway-to-nowhere, one of two in Baltimore. She tried to remember what had stopped this one. Opponents had argued that the park was a valuable ecosystem, a refuge for deer and other wildlife in the heart of the city. Leakin Park's reputation as a place to dump dead bodies was temporarily forgotten and it became a sylvan glade in the heart of the city. Funny, what people could come to believe, so quickly and so fiercely.

Be careful what you wish for, as a Wung Fong fortune cookie might warn. The deer population, all those little Bambis whose photos had helped to block the highway, was out of control, raiding gardens in the nearby neighborhoods. Cause and effect, Cynthia thought, cause and effect. Very few people had the patience or rigor to think things through. Save the park, save the deer, and now the deer rampaged through the local gardens and there was still no effective east-west route through the city. Happy now? Was everybody happy now?

Even if her life had adhered to the smooth, easy path that she and everyone else had assumed was her birthright, Cynthia would have been cynical about the passions that direct public policy. Her tenure in city government had left her with little respect for anyone. She could see all sides of an issue, she liked to tell Warren—and the primary thing she could see was that no one was ever right, about anything.

Take taxes. The public was so easily duped on this issue. Property and income taxes were sacred cows in Maryland government. Politicians didn't touch them in bad times and only pretended to cut them in good, spreading the pain around in invisible ways—enabling legislation that allowed jurisdictions to muscle in on everything from videotape rentals to building permits to junk food. When she sat in the back of the city council chamber listening to the gored ox of the day—that was her term for the constituents—drone about the pain exacted by some tax hike and urge the city to tighten its belt, it was all she could do not to laugh. She wanted to follow them into the street, ask them what they would do if someone decided to cut their household budget by 10, 20 percent for a year. No one ever wanted less in this life. Everyone wanted as much as they had yesterday, plus a little more.

Cynthia had been able to leave her eighty-thousand-dollar-a-year job without a pang because Warren's income was spiraling up, up, up. A plaintiff's attorney, he took on the black clients who had missed various legal bandwagons—lead paint, tobacco, asbestos. He was now part of the cell phone litigation. The money just kept rolling in, and Cynthia no longer had any idea what to do with it, except watch it accumulate.

The city had moved on, elected a new mayor. Even if Cynthia wanted to work, there was no job for her now, or so she told herself. And in this way, her thoughts took her one, two miles, from the looping exit of the dead-end highway onto Security Boulevard and then to Cook's Lane and up Nottingham, past the house where Alice Manning lived with her mother.

Cynthia noticed the woman in the bikini first. Thin and youthful looking at first glance, she betrayed her age on Cynthia's second glance, which picked up on the telltale signs of a woman trying too hard—the little ruche of flesh at the midsection that seemed to affect almost every middle-aged woman, the sarong knotted at the waist, possibly in hopes of hiding less-than-perfect legs. Then there was the slack in the upper arms as the woman lifted her arm to shield her eyes, looking into the distance, toward the corner, where a heavyset blond woman was trudging along.

A heavyset blond woman. It took a beat to reconcile this figure with the image Cynthia carried in her head—a milk-bland little girl, her eyes wide and her mouth set, looking more amazed than anything else. Cynthia made a sudden right turn, glancing into the backseat to see if the abrupt movement had awakened the sleeping Rosalind, then turned back onto Nottingham.

So this was Alice Manning at eighteen. Fat, listless-looking, and paler than ever, although her arms had a pinkish hue, the beginning or the end of a bad sunburn. These things should have pleased Cynthia, but they just made her angrier. Because fat was a sign of life, proof of something that continued to live and grow and even thrive, however unattractively.

I could kill her, she thought. *I could turn the wheel to the left and kill them both.* Sure, it would be suspicious, but let the authorities try to prove it was anything other than an accident. Make them prove intent. After all, the ambiguity of intent had been so crucial in Olivia's death. Warren would make sure she had the best criminal defense attorney in the city, assuming it went that far. Cynthia was willing to bet that a grand jury would no-bill her.

But Rosalind was in the backseat, so Cynthia drove sedately by, her gaze fixed on Helen Manning. What was it like for an attractive woman to have an unattractive child? Did a good-looking woman ever reconcile herself to having a child whose face did not invite loving coos and fond glances? Of course, Cynthia knew the answer to those questions.

The thought came and went so quickly, she could have pretended never to have had it. But something akin to heartburn fanned out in her upper chest and throat. Cynthia drove miserably home, where she tried to be a little cool to Rosalind for the rest of the afternoon, as if that could compensate for the momentary betrayal of Olivia.

Alice noticed the BMW, but only because it was shiny and big, moving so slowly up the street, and then doing the curious turn and circling back, like someone who was lost. Helen didn't notice the SUV at all because she was staring with dismay at Alice's sunburn—pressing her fingertips into the soft flesh of her daughter's upper arms, shaking her head at the white marks that appeared.

"A girl with skin like yours should never go out without putting on something with an SPF of 15 or higher," Helen said. "Now, I have a little olive undercoat to my complexion, even though my hair has so much red in it. In my day, I could lie out with nothing but baby oil on and not get burned. But you have your father's skin."

In my day was another Helen-ism, her day being defined, whether she realized it or not, as the months between college graduation and Alice's birth. But she almost never mentioned Alice's father, in any context, and it gave Alice a rare opportunity.

"What was he like? My father?"

"Handsome. Big—broad-shouldered, very tall. Hair a shade darker than yours."

This was how Helen always described Alice's father, in physical terms, and Alice seldom pressed her for more information.

"I mean, what kind of person was he?"

"Well, very . . . capable. He was all alone in the world, had been since he was seventeen. An orphan, with no brothers and sisters." Her mother was always adamant on this point. Her father had no relatives, not even a cousin, that Alice could hope to find. "Strong. If he had gone to college, he might have been an architect. As it was, he built houses, from the ground up."

"I'd like to be an architect," Alice said, then realized she was saying this only to test the idea. Once she gave voice to the desire, she knew she'd like nothing less.

Helen continued to press on Alice's arms, ghostly fingerprints appearing only to disappear again. Her touch felt unexpectedly good on Alice's scorched skin, for her mother's hands were cool and greasy with the lotion she had applied for her late-afternoon sunbath, a habit of long standing. She would spread her towel in the backyard, near the fence overhung with honeysuckle, between the hours of four and five—never any earlier, and never for a second more than an hour—and always with an exotic drink at her side. Over the years, Helen had fixed herself piña coladas and Mudslides and daiquiris, Cosmopolitans and Appletinis. This summer's drink was a julep, made with mint that grew wild in the yard. Helen prepared her juleps with a sterling silver muddler, and the preparation of the drink took almost as long as the sunbath.

"Speaking of what you'd like to be," Helen said, "have you found a job yet?"

"No, but that's what I'm doing. Looking for a job."

"I know the economy isn't as flush as it was, but you sure are having a hard time of it."

"Yes, I am," Alice agreed.

She had no intention of finding a job, and had not been looking for one on this hot Saturday. A few weeks back, she had made inquiries at the county's social services department, which had a job placement program. But she didn't hear what she wanted to hear, so she left. Alice was, however, following Sharon's advice. She walked up to six, seven miles a day, yet she didn't appear to be losing any weight. She walked morning and night, usually west, until her feet were sore and cracked at the heels. She walked along Frederick Road and ended up at the community college, where she took home course information for the fall semester. She detoured through the pretty old neighborhoods along Frederick Road—Ten Hills, North Bend, Catonsville—and made up stories about the families she saw in the old Victorian houses, with their big porches and cupolas.

Today, she had walked to Westview Mall, drawn by the memory of the G. C. Murphy's. Alice had loved the old dime store, with its smells of fresh-popped popcorn and wooden floors. She used to buy chocolate-covered peanuts there, and she had never found ones that tasted quite the same, even as her mother brought her Brach's and Russell Stover's, Fannie

Farmer and See's on visiting days at Middlebrook. Exasper-
ated, Helen finally told Alice that her memory was playing
tricks on her, but Alice trusted her mouth's insistent recall.
G. C. Murphy was long gone, but she had a theory that the
dollar store that had taken its place might be the best place to
find a similar treat, that the flavor had been captured in the
walls, in the floorboards.

She had not headed out with the plan of seeing Ronnie.
But she couldn't forget Helen's mention of Ronnie's job, at
the bagel place over by Westview. The Ronnie she had
known had no talent for routine. The most basic require-
ments at school—bringing permission slips, milk money—
had defeated her. She wondered what Ronnie looked like,
how she had changed, if at all. If she saw Ronnie, she might
understand what people felt when they looked at Alice. Her
mother and Sharon had seen her pretty regularly over the
past seven years, so it wasn't as if they had to adjust to a
whole new Alice when she came home. But they acted as if
they had, as if they expected a little girl, and didn't know
what to do with this heavyset eighteen-year-old who looked
so much older than she was. It wasn't Alice's shape that
made her look old so much as the way she moved, dragging
her feet as if her legs were swollen. Store clerks called her
"ma'am," and she probably could have gotten served in a bar
if she were so inclined. She wasn't. But seeing Ronnie—yes,
seeing Ronnie had a definite allure.

She wasn't sure what feelings might surge up if she saw
Ronnie again. Hatred, of course. Time had dulled that emotion somewhat—Alice's stomach no longer twisted at the
mere thought of Ronnie, and the girl was largely gone from
her dreams—but hatred was still there, along with the desire
to see her punished, really and truly.

Once, just once, Sharon had come close to saying what
Alice needed to hear, but she had said it in the odd round-

about way she used with Alice. This was just a few years ago, when Alice was forced to go back to the chaos of Middlebrook after a year in a smaller, much more pleasant juvenile home. She was upset about leaving the old stone building where she thought she would get to stay until she was eighteen, and in her hurt she had lashed out at Sharon. Why had the law treated Alice and Ronnie as if they were the same kind of girl, guilty of the same things, when everyone should know they were not?

"Well, imagine Ronnie was someone who went swimming and got a cramp," Sharon began.

"In her stomach or her leg?" Alice asked.

The question seemed to catch Sharon off guard, although it seemed reasonable to Alice. It would make a big difference, where the cramp was. "In her stomach, I guess. And she begins to drown, and you're swimming nearby, so you go over and try to help her. But sometimes drowning people get panicky and they grab the people who are trying to save them and drag them down, and they both end up drowning."

"Does it happen a lot?"

"Um, no. Because lifeguards are trained to handle panicky swimmers. I was a Water Safety Instructor." Alice was used to Sharon's tendency to bring every subject back to herself, so she barely noticed this stray bit of information. Besides, Water Safety Instructor didn't sound very cool, not like being a lifeguard, on a high chair with a white-creamed nose. "But if you're just another swimmer passing by, you might not know what to do when someone grabs you."

Alice thought about this. It still sounded as if it was her fault, then.

"If you're not a lifeguard and the person grabs you, are you allowed to push them off you? Is it okay to leave them to drown?"

The question left Sharon uncharacteristically silent. She

placed her hand on her left cheek, rubbing her spots. Alice
had noticed that Sharon reached for that part of her face
whenever they came close to discussing how unfair everything was. Perhaps it was unfair that Sharon Kerpelman, a
not unpretty woman, had been born with those spots on her
face. But that was nothing compared to Alice's life. Besides,
Sharon's story made Ronnie sound almost normal, doing
what anyone might do, in order to survive.

Alice could have told Sharon the story of how Helen had
taken her and Ronnie out to the Baskin-Robbins on Route 40
one summer night and bought them both double-scoop
cones. This would have been the summer between third and
fourth grade, when Ronnie had attached herself to the Mannings like a stray cat they had made the mistake of feeding.
Helen didn't seem to mind that she was always around, but
Alice did. After all, she was the one who would have to distance herself from Ronnie when school began again in the
fall, peeling her off like a piece of gum on her shoe.

At the Baskin-Robbins, Alice had gotten vanilla and
chocolate, despite Helen's urging to be more original, while
Ronnie had opted for chocolate chip and orange sherbet, a
truly gross combination that she copied from Helen. Only
Ronnie's top scoop, the chocolate chip, rolled to the floor
with her first lick.

"Oh, baby," Helen began. But before anyone could say
anything else, Ronnie turned around and knocked Alice's
cone to the floor. "Don't laugh at me," she had shrieked at
Alice, who had not made a sound. She had smiled, perhaps
just a little bit. But Ronnie's back was to her, so how could
she know that? Helen had wheedled the counterman into
giving both girls new cones, but the evening's happy promise was gone. A second cone simply made Alice aware of
losing the first one, which meant this one could be lost, too.

She ate her ice cream with such tiny, cautious licks that more melted down her arm than ended up in her mouth.

All these memories had crowded into Alice's head as she sat on a curb with her just-purchased bag of chocolate-covered peanuts, studying the Bagel Barn. The restaurant sat off by itself on the edge of the parking lot, not quite part of the mall, not completely on its own. The Bagel Barn had been many things, even in Alice's short memory of what she thought of as the before time. It had been a White Castle, a Fotomat, then a taco stand. At some point, while she was gone, it had been expanded from its original little hut shape, so it now had a seating area, and the roof had been painted red. But it didn't have a lot of customers, and Alice bet it would be something else within a year or two. That was the kind of place that would hire Ronnie Fuller, a place on its way down.

She couldn't go in, of course. It was one thing to see Ronnie, another thing to let Ronnie see her. And the restaurant's placement made it hard to get too close to it. So she sat back on the curb near the mall. She should give up, go about her day. Her horoscope for this morning had said "Finding the right answers depends on knowing the right questions," which had sounded promising, but also demanding.

Even as she told herself to leave, Alice sat for five more minutes, then ten, then twenty. The day was hot, and she was tired from all her walking. Shortly before 2 P.M., she saw two girls come out of the Bagel Barn and light up cigarettes. One was a short girl in an apron, one of those people who could be anything—black, Spanish, Italian. The other was a thin girl with dark hair. Ronnie.

She was taller, but not by much, and although she had a bust, she still had a way of carrying herself as if she just didn't care about her body. Her posture was bad, a little stooped, and she folded her arms across her breasts as if they annoyed her. Her dark hair was worn in the same way—a bang across the front, the rest hanging to her shoulders. If she had tried to style it in any way, it didn't show. Alice reached for her own hair, which had remained pale blond and stick straight. It was quite the prettiest thing about her. Helen had said so, years ago, in just those words, and it remained true. "Your hair is beautiful, baby. Quite the prettiest thing about you." Alice thought her blue eyes were a nice color, but Helen said blue eyes were even more striking on a brunette. Like Ronnie.

Ronnie stared across the parking lot, straight at where Alice was sitting. But Alice didn't panic or try to run away. People couldn't see what they weren't looking for. She had the advantage of knowing that Ronnie worked here. But Ronnie had no expectation of seeing Alice on the edge of the Westview Mall parking lot. It was almost as good as being invisible.

The aproned girl said something and Ronnie appeared to laugh. She hunched up her shoulders and bobbed her head, looking as if she was enjoying herself. She dragged hard on her cigarette, throwing back her head on the exhales. When had she learned to smoke? You couldn't smoke at any of the places Alice had been. Not even adult prisoners were allowed to smoke these days. Had Ronnie smoked when they were little? Alice had no memory of it. But she had always suspected that Ronnie knew all sorts of things she didn't tell. That was what Alice had been trying to get the grown-ups to understand back then: Ronnie had secrets. Ronnie knew things she wasn't supposed to know, which was what made her so dangerous.

Ronnie took the cigarette from her mouth and dropped it into a low ceramic pot, what Helen called a "butt beach," one of those little containers of sand outside restaurants and movie theaters. Helen hated these fixtures, not because she objected to smoking, but because they were always ugly and cheap looking. The butts sticking up in sand, some with lipstick-smeared ends, made Helen shudder.

Now Alice shuddered, too. But it wasn't the cement basin that bothered Alice, it was seeing Ronnie use it. The very neatness, the orderliness of this act was disorienting. It was natural for Ronnie to smoke. But once her break was over, she should have flicked her butt into the air in a care-less arc and let it fall where it may. Ronnie was the kind of girl who littered, dropping candy wrappers and soda cans in the gutter. At least she had been. Ronnie was the bad one. There shouldn't be any confusion about this, even now. Especially now.

Her latest attempt at chocolate-covered peanuts, forgotten while she was watching Ronnie, had melted to mush in the brown paper sack in her hand. It was just as well. They weren't going to taste like the old ones. Nothing did. Strange, when she tried to stand, her breath caught in her throat and her lungs seemed to slam shut, as if she were the one who was drowning.

14.

Daniel Kutchner eased himself out of Sharon Kerpelman with the sweet-but-sheepish air of a man who had just had sex with someone he might never see again. Sharon didn't mind. She had made a similar decision about Daniel before they ended up in bed, but the evening had a little momentum going for it. At least she would be able to tell her mother with a clear conscience that she'd really tried. She would not be explicit, of course, telling her mother that she and Evelyn Kutchner's son had—what was the hideous phrase she had heard a twenty-something toss off the other day—*landed the deal*. But her mother would figure it out, and appreciate the codes that Sharon used to convey such information. *Nice enough. No real chemistry.*

"Bathroom?" he asked.

"The first door on your right, when you go out in the hall-way," she said. *Was he a washer,* she wondered. *Or did he just need to pee?* Both, as it turned out. She listened as one stream of water followed another. She rather liked his fastidiousness.

So what was wrong with Daniel Kutchner? Some women, aware that they had dated their way into an instantaneous dead end, might have turned the question on themselves, but Sharon never would. She got up, comfortable enough in her skin so that she didn't feel the need to put on a robe or

T-shirt, and headed out into the hall, knocking on the bath-room door as she passed by.

"Do you want anything? I'm going to fix myself a drink."

This interrupted the third stream of water—probably from the faucet. Daniel Kutchner must be washing his hands now.

"You mean, like a glass of water, or a soda?"

"I have those, too," Sharon said. "But I was thinking of a drink-drink, truthfully. I like to have a glass of white wine, or Baileys on the rocks before I go to sleep. I've got a full bar."

"How not-Jewish," Kutchner said through the door and they both laughed, for it was the theme of the evening, the pleasant bond they had established over dinner, making a list of what was Jewish and what was not. "Okay. Sure. What-ever you're having."

Sharon wandered through her apartment, which would have surprised her coworkers if they had ever been invited to see it. Her apartment was the only clue to Sharon's secret: She could afford to work at the public defender's office be-cause there was family money. Not a lot, but enough to close the gap between the barely middle-class lifestyle afforded by a government wage and the upper-middle-class life to which she was accustomed. That's why it was nice, bringing home someone like Daniel, who knew about the Kerpelmans and the small foundations company that had made everyone permanently comfortable when it began catering to post-op breast cancer patients.

She returned to the bedroom with two old-fashioned glasses, aluminum Russell Wright knockoffs, on a matching tray, and set them on the bedside table.

"How civilized," Daniel said, coming back into the room. He was skinny and on the short side, and his hairline would probably start receding soon. But those things didn't matter to Sharon. The real problem with Daniel Kutchner was that her mother had picked him out for her, as his mother had picked Sharon out for him, and this could not be overcome.

He sat on the side of the bed, as if he hadn't decided whether to sleep or flee. Sharon didn't care if he left eventually. The only thing she asked of her intermittent lovers was that they talk to her afterward. Hence, the ritual of the drink. If she had smoked, that would have worked, too. But she didn't, and so few people did now. But confronted with an offer of a drink, few men could insist on going to sleep, or running out the door.

Daniel set his glass back down, knocking over a small wooden frame. As he righted it, he peered at the face in the photograph, just visible in the available light coming from the bathroom.

"Who's this? Not you with these pigtails."

"No, I was never a blond, that's for sure."

"Niece?"

"Client."

The photo was one of Alice, an old snapshot that Helen Manning had given Sharon for reasons she could no longer recall. She only knew it was a "before" photo of sorts, a picture of Alice from earlier in the summer of her eleventh year. A snapshot of a perfectly normal-looking little girl. Which was the point, of course, the thing that Sharon had never wanted anyone to forget.

"Client? Why do you have a photo of a client by your bedside?"

"Because it was probably the most amazing case I'll ever be involved with." She had meant to be a little hyperbolic, but realized the words, once spoken, were the simple truth. "You're from Baltimore, right?"

"Originally."

"Seven years ago—I'm not sure if it was in newspapers

outside the area—two little girls were accused of killing a baby."

"And that girl is—"

"One of the accused. Even now, even here, I wouldn't say her name to you. It's privileged. We kept their names private, which was no small thing, let me tell you."

"So they weren't tried as adults?"

"They were eleven!" Sharon's voice rose automatically, and she had to remember to yank it back down to a tone better suited to a postcoital chat. "There was no provision in Maryland law to try children that young as adults. Not that the parents of the victim didn't push for that. And then, when it was clear the family wouldn't get its way, the victim's mother threatened to lobby to have the law changed, so homicides could be moved into adult court no matter what the age of the accused."

"Bad cases make bad law, right?"

"Yeah. And she had the juice, her family was connected. She could have done it. That's why we were forced to compromise."

"How so?"

"At the time, the law held that juveniles couldn't serve more than three years for any one crime. The other girl's lawyer and I crafted a plea that allowed the state to give them seven years on three counts—homicide, kidnapping, and felony theft. For the baby carriage," she added, anticipating his question. "I don't remember the brand, but it was one of those things that was expensive because it was so light."

"Like a laptop," Kutchner said. "Or a cell phone. The smaller it is, the more you pay."

Sharon nodded, annoyed at the interruption. "So they went away until they were eighteen, and the victim's mother calmed down. Eventually." She swirled the Baileys in her glass, watched the creamy pale brown liquid flow over the ice. "Truthfully, I've always thought my client would have been better off if I could have taken the case into an adult court, with a jury and the public's full oversight."

"How can that be?"

"She told me she was innocent. That she wasn't there when it happened. She was with Ron—the other girl—when they took the baby, but it was a kid thing. They thought the girl had been left alone, they were trying to do the right thing. They didn't set out to be criminals, to do something violent. Something went wrong."

"How did—I mean—"

"Suffocation. That was another thing. The child's death wasn't inconsistent with SIDS. I could have argued that."

"Isn't that paradoxical? Arguing that your client wasn't there, arguing that your client might have been there but the death was due to natural causes." Daniel Kutchner was an accountant.

"A good defense doesn't have to be consistent."

No sound came from Daniel Kutchner's side of the bed, except for the ice in his glass, a small swallow, a slight creak in the springs as he shifted his weight. An accountant sitting in judgment on a lawyer. Sharon decided not to mention what accountants had wrought in recent years.

"In a way, I've always felt Alice was sacrificed." Sharon did not even notice she had given up the name she was usually so vigilant about protecting.

"Sacrificed?"

"There was so much . . . bad feeling about what happened. The victim was black, the accused girls were white. As you can see. And the media harped on the case so. People wanted to feel that something had been done. They wanted guarantees that it would never happen again. Which is impossible. Look, there are cases of young killers going back hundreds of years. And I don't mean sociopaths, or some stupid bad seed scenario. Kids kill. To me, the amazing thing is that they don't kill more often. Because they don't really get it, you know? Death, I mean."

She did not share with him her fantasy of trying Alice before a jury of her true peers, a dozen little big-eyed girls who knew what it was to make mistakes out of no larger sin than the desire to go along and get along. She imagined twelve little gamma girls—or was Alice a beta, according to the terms set out in the flurry of literature on "mean girls"— watching her solemnly as she laid out the facts, described Ronnie's sway over her client. It would have taken such a jury less than an hour to acquit Alice.

"Except—you don't think your client did kill." Daniel Kutchner had leaned against the headboard, but his left leg dangled over the side of the bed, still in contact with the floor, like an actor trying to make love according to the old Hays Code. He wasn't the type to stay overnight, which was fine with Sharon, the best of all possible worlds. As long as they didn't rush into the night or escape into sleep immediately after sex, she didn't care what they did.

"No, she didn't."

"Then why would you let her serve seven years? Why didn't she draw less time than the other girl?"

"The evidence was . . . somewhat contradictory. And the girls' statements were diametrically opposed. She said–she said. The judge who presided couldn't see any fair way to sort it out."

"Sounds like your client got screwed."

"You don't know the half of it."

The band had tried to quit at 1 A.M., but Andy—tie undone, jacket shorn—had seized the microphone and demanded that the wedding guests open their wallets and pay for another set. Nancy, filled with liquid goodwill, beamed at her

husband. This was the man she had fallen in love with, bois-
terous and confident. The feds did not encourage such per-
sonalities, and he had to keep himself so tamped down at
work that his broad shoulders had rounded a little and his
head seemed to hang at times, heavy on his neck. She hoped
the law, once he finished school and entered a practice,
would restore some of Andy's self back to him.

Now, dropped to one knee on the dance floor, bills
clenched in his fist, he was every bit the boy she had known
since junior high and loved since high school. "More," he
bellowed. "More, more, more. We will have music. And the
bar *will* stay open. A Polish wedding can't end this early. It
would be shameful."

Eventually the reception ended, and neither Nancy nor
Andy was really in any shape to drive. But neither was anyone else, so they ambled to the Double-T Diner out on Route
40, albeit on the opposite end from New York Fried Chicken.
There, her latest diet long forgotten, Nancy dragged french
fries through gravy with her left hand and held on to Andy
with her right. With his free hand, he flipped through the
tabletop jukebox, but it was a bit of a gyp, for the restaurant's
sound system was dominated by whoever had the fastest
quarter. A Bon Jovi song bounced through the night, and she
couldn't tell if it was one of their old ones or one of their new
ones that sounded like one of their old ones. She could have
been eighteen again, it could have been the night of her senior prom. Her bridesmaid's dress, a yellow horror, would
have fit right in at the Kenwood High School prom.

Nancy was one of the few people she knew who admitted
to being happy in high school. Why was that such a badge of
shame for others? She didn't see it as some *Glory Days* high
point, but it had been fun, and she had been conscious of the
fact that life wouldn't always be fun, or easy. And it was for

this very reason that she had gloried in eighteen, hadn't wasted a minute of it. True, she had worried about her weight even then, but what she wouldn't give to have back her teenage body. Even the low points—the brief breakups with Andy, the science classes that had almost sunk her completely—had made her appreciate the effortless fun, day in and day out.

Andy was trying to put a french fry in his coffee.

"I am so driving home," she told him, not minding that he was wasted. He worked hard; he had earned this.

"Let's"—it came out a little slurred, but nowhere near as bad as it might have been—"let's drive up to Gunpowder Falls."

"Now?"

"Yes, now. Why not now? Like we used to."

"Like we—" Then she got it.

Within forty-five minutes, she was on top of him in the bucket seat of his Jeep Cherokee, part of her mind grateful for the room these SUVs provided, another part thinking how funny it would be if some county patrol cop came tap, tap, tapping at their window with his flashlight, then saw Nancy astride Andy, the yellow horror pushed above her hips and below her breasts, revealing the wretched strapless bra that had been digging into her all night. Andy couldn't have gotten that off with a knife, the shape he was in.

"Evening, Officer," she imagined herself saying, holding up her badge to the window. "I'm Homicide Detective Porter and this is Federal Agent Porter, from the local ATF field office."

But they were left alone, so Nancy settled for the efficient, shuddering pleasures her husband provided. At the last minute, he asked if she wanted him to pull out, as he hadn't brought anything with him, but she just held him hard inside her, shaking her head. Later, she wondered why she hadn't minded taking the chance. Certainly it wasn't because she was worried about the dress.

Helen Manning saw the sun come up that Sunday. More accurately, she saw the light seeping into her kitchen, which faced east, while she sat in her still-dark living room. Her glass was long empty, had been for hours. She had allowed herself exactly three cigarettes, and these were long gone, too. The cigarettes had been the tobacco variety because dope was something she had only when the right man was in her life, and there were fewer and fewer men these days. Strange, but she had dated even more infrequently after Alice went away, which seemed counterintuitive. After all, it should have been easier to meet men when she was unencumbered, but she found she had little taste for it. Helen preferred the admiration of men to their companionship. And that was easy to get, as long as a woman kept herself up. Helen could go weeks on the warmth of a single glance in the supermarket. She still turned heads.

Finally she heard the sounds she had waited all night to hear—a car door slamming, footsteps on the walk, the storm door opening, the key in the unlocked lock, turning one way, then the other.

"Good morning," she said to Alice.

"You don't need to wait up for me."

"It's six A.M."

"Really, you shouldn't worry." Alice's voice, which had been husky even as a child, was a pleasant contralto, all warm concern.

"You've been out all night. Where did you go? Who were you with?"

"Nowhere. No one. I'm sorry, I just can't sleep these days. So I walk."

"It's dangerous." Her voice scaled up, unintentionally tentative, making the maternal assertion sound like a question.

"Not where I go."

"Which is—"

"You know, you should go to sleep, Mom. You're useless if you don't get your eight hours."

It was just what Helen said about herself, all the time. *I'm useless if I don't get my eight hours.* Alice had repeated it back in her usual pleasant voice, with no judgment attached. Yet Helen felt judged all the same. With or without eight hours of sleep, she was useless to her daughter now and would be until she gave her what she wanted, until she told her what she wanted to hear.

If only she could.

Friday,
July 3

15.

Brittany Little disappeared late in the afternoon on the first day of the holiday weekend, wandering away from her mother and her mother's boyfriend while they shopped for a sofa in Value City.

"One minute she was there," her mother, Maveen Little, kept telling police, "and then she wasn't." No one seemed to believe the minute part, Maveen could tell. Who could lose a child in a minute? But she was adamant: She and her boyfriend, Devlin Hatch, could not have turned their backs for more than a minute as they studied the love seats and sleepers and couches. A minute was a long, long time. "Count it out for yourself," she snapped at the young officer, who was acting sympathetic. But if they believed her, why wasn't she talking to a detective yet? Why were these officers baby-sitting her and Devlin in their own apartment, instead of searching the city for her baby?

The two patrol officers had said they needed to come to the apartment to get a photo of Brittany for the evening news. Maveen knew they also wanted to poke around her home, look for evidence that wasn't there. They seemed to suspect Devlin more than her, but that was just as infuriating.

"Look, when a child goes missing, we always find them," said the younger of the two young officers, Ben Siegel, the one who had been left to sit with her on the old sofa. This was the piece of furniture Maveen and Devlin had hoped to replace when he got his insurance check. She wanted to explain that she knew it was beat-up and old, that it had been a castoff from her mother. Maveen never would have chosen a light solid that showed the dirt, not with a child. But Officer Siegel didn't seem to notice. He sat between Maveen and Devlin as if he spent every night here, waiting for the ten o'clock news to come on.

"You always, always find them?" Maveen asked.

"Always. I can't remember a single case where a child truly went missing for more than a few hours."

She caught that *truly*. He was still accusing. Everyone was judging them all the time.

The news finally came. Maveen felt a weird burst of pride to see her baby's photo up there, the second story of the evening, and Devlin smiled in a fond way that he seldom did when Brittany was here. You didn't have to be rich or famous for your missing baby to matter. A lost child was a lost child. That's what made the U.S. of A. a great country. And Brittany was so beautiful, people couldn't help taking extra notice, Maveen thought. It had killed Maveen's parents when she had taken up with Byron, but who could argue with the result? Brittany had skin the color of a coffee that was half cream, ringlets just a shade darker, and green eyes with lashes so long you'd swear she was wearing false ones. She was delicious looking. Even other children wanted to pinch her cheeks, stroke her hair.

The telephone rang before the last notes of the newscast's theme song had bounced away. Maveen jumped on it, only to hear another officer, Donald something, tell her to put Officer Siegel on the phone. Reluctantly she turned over the phone, feeling a strange sensation, as if a moth or a bug was trapped in her throat.

"What's wrong?" she demanded when he hung up the phone. "Something's wrong, I can tell. What did he say? What's going on?"

Crazily, the thought ran through her head that she should beat on his chest with her fists, the way women do in the movies, only to have men grab their wrists and kiss them. It wasn't that she wanted to kiss this cop, who didn't appeal to her at all. But if she started acting like it was a movie, maybe it would end like a movie, with everyone safe and happy.

"Nothing's wrong, exactly," he began, licking his lips. "The thing to consider is that it's a lead, and leads are good. Assuming . . . if . . . Ms. Little, did you mention what Brittany was wearing today?"

"I told you and told you. She had on a sundress, denim with white stitching at the pockets, and white tennis."

"And she was toilet trained?"

"Sort of. She was wearing pull-ups." Officer Siegel looked confused. "For when she forgot."

Brittany had been forgetting a lot lately, ever since Devlin came to live with them, but Maveen didn't see any reason to tell the officer that.

"It's just that"—he put his hand on her shoulder, and Maveen flinched as if someone had hit her, as if a two-by-four had fallen on her—"the custodian at the mall was doing the bathrooms and he found something in the trash. It was a denim jumper—"

Maveen broke down so completely that the officer didn't finish his piece. He let her collapse, crying, into Devlin's arms, standing awkwardly to the side. It was left to the homicide detectives, who arrived within the hour, to decide if they wanted to tell the still-sobbing mother about the shorn hair at the bottom of the wastebasket and the blood-soaked T-shirt that was on its way to the lab for testing.

PART 11

The Dogs of Pompeii

Saturday,
July 4

16.

The elevators in the Baltimore County Public Safety Build-ing were famously slow, so all but the laziest workers had an informal rule known as "one floor up and two floors down." Nancy, however, always checked the elevator bays before ducking into the stairwells. You never knew when the com-missioner or a major might be waiting there, or a detective with whom she needed to compare notes. This was the kind of thing she had learned from her uncle Stan, who had been known as the thirty-three–thirty-three lieutenant, for he had attained that rank at the age of thirty-three and advanced no higher until his retirement thirty-three years later.

But there was zero expectation of a useful chance en-counter on a Saturday morning, especially over a holiday weekend, so Nancy went straight for the stairs, almost run-ning the steps from the tenth floor, home of Homicide, to the eleventh, which housed the crime lab. The eleventh was the top floor, and the lab was there for a practical reason: the placement reduced the building's exposure to damage if the lab's contents ever exploded. Nancy had found this possibil-ity ludicrous when she first joined the department, but it no longer seemed so. Everything was possible now.

"I didn't know you were working this case," said the lab tech, Holly Varitek. "Isn't it awfully fast for you to be up again?"

Nancy shrugged, determined not to bitch. Infante had thrown a tantrum when Lenhardt changed the rotation on them last night, following the sergeant into the men's room to plead his case. Infante had planned to drive out to Deep Creek Lake with the redheaded barmaid, Charlotte something. He had slammed out, and been curt to Nancy the rest of the night. Guys could get away with being bratty. Nancy had to be stoic. She even had to be stoic about being stoic.

"Well, at least your snatcher was considerate," said Holly, a chatty type inclined to fill silences. Brisk and wide-eyed, with shiny dark hair and vivid coloring, Holly was one of those people who seemed to be put together with higher quality parts than everyone else. Even her metabolism was better than the average person's, for she could eat anything she wanted and not get fat. Nancy couldn't help noticing that.

"Considerate how?"

"Well, first of all he—you're assuming a he, right, given that the stuff was found in the men's room—left the girl's hair with the jumper. It's like he wanted to make it easy for us to compare the DNA if the blood didn't match. Of course, we still needed the mother's sample, for control, because you wouldn't want to assume the pile of hair is the girl's hair. You see—"

"I know," Nancy said, trying not to let her impatience show. The people with technical expertise—the lab techs, the M.E.'s, even those who conducted ballistic analysis—were all a little in love with their knowledge, like eleven-year-old boys who had just learned some basic fact of science or math and had to bore the rest of the world with it. "Do we have a match on the blood or not?"

Holly's easygoing temperament made her impossible to offend. "The spots on the jumper are definitely blood, but it's not the missing girl's, or the mother's. No match. It does, however, match this man's T-shirt, which was balled up in the same trash can and had a lot more blood on it."

"Huh." Nancy slumped against the counter, thinking. It struck her as a backward break, the kind of information that widened the investigation for now, but could narrow it later, with luck. The blood on the jumper was probably the kidnapper's, although it wasn't 100 percent. If they made an arrest, they'd have a key piece of physical evidence.

The only problem was how were they going to make an arrest? The biggest break in the case would be the saddest one as well—the discovery of a body, which might yield more clues than the men's room at Westview Mall. Nancy had barely slept last night, wondering if the girl might still be alive. She so wanted her to be alive. The case had been given to Homicide because of the large amount of blood on the T-shirt, but now they knew it wasn't the girl's blood, so it was a not unreasonable hope.

"Does it seem weird to you," Nancy asked the lab tech, "that the blood is on the front of the jumper?"

Holly shrugged. "Not particularly. Someone was bleeding heavily. A head wound could have dripped. Then again, the bloody T-shirt could have nothing to do with the jumper, could have stained it when someone tossed it in the trash."

"But if you were standing behind a child, cutting hair—" Nancy mimed the motion more for herself than Holly, and finished the thought in her head. It would be hard to cut oneself that severely with a pair of scissors, harder still to drip just a few drops of blood on the girl's jumper while leaking blood all over a T-shirt. But if the kidnapper were standing in front—she acted out that scenario, too. No, it didn't make sense. Perhaps the blood had fallen on the jumper after it was removed. Or, worse luck, maybe Holly was right, and the blood-soaked T-shirt had landed in the trash after the jumper, staining it by accident. Nancy could imagine some homeless man reaching into the garbage can to find a rag to stanch a wound.

Had the child reached out and scratched the person who was cutting her hair? Children didn't like haircuts, or so Nancy had heard from her cousins with kids. But you could hardly call this a haircut. Based on the thick coil of hair found in the trash can, the kidnapper had sliced the hair just below the elastic band that held Brittany Little's ponytail. The act had been swift, with little attempt to shape or style the hair left on the girl's head.

Nancy carried the news, such as it was, back downstairs to Infante, who was cursing his luck at being the primary on this case. Not only was the disappearance of Brittany Little not a dunker or a gimme, it was going to attract press attention once the details began to shake loose. The department had managed to stall the press on Friday with the usual wink-wink, nudge-nudge signals. A few years back, there had been a rash of what Lenhardt called six-hour kidnappings. Teen girls in the city, girls who were apparently too impatient to take the nine months necessary to have their own babies, had started grabbing other people's children as if they were dolls left untended. But it's hard to steal a baby without drawing attention to yourself if you're a teenage girl living with your own family, so those cases were always wrapped up in a matter of hours. "Easier to hide a pregnancy than a child," Lenhardt sometimes said, usually when they were trying to track down a girl who had left her own baby in a Dumpster.

The rash of six-hour kidnappings had been during the spring, seven years ago. The city cops had thought Olivia Barnes was one of those cases, Nancy recalled, at least in the beginning. There had been a baby-sitter, a heavyset, dimwitted girl whose story hadn't tracked. Another seventy-two hours passed before they asked the academy class to search

Leakin Park. Even then, they had thought it was more of a field exercise for the cadets than a mission that would yield results.

"Stranger blood, huh?" Infante echoed when Nancy told him what she had learned on the eleventh floor. "Now, if I were a lucky guy, it would match the boyfriend."

"I thought they both came up pretty clean. No Social Services file, no neighbor complaints, no record of 911 calls to the address." When a parent—or a parent's partner—killed a child, there were usually a few practice runs.

"Yeah, other than an assault charge on her and a weapons charge on him, they're the nicest young couple since Mary and Joseph. But it's the only thing that makes *sense*. Boyfriend goes too far administering discipline, he and panicky girlfriend concoct a cover-up. Who grabs a little girl from Value City? That's not exactly the best place to find the next Lindbergh baby. You just know it ain't going to be a big payday."

"Yeah, for that you gotta go to Ethan Allen, maybe Crate & Barrel."

Infante laughed. "You're such a secret smart-ass. If Lenhardt knew half the shit you said—"

"Did you check for sex perverts in that part of the county? Could be a Peeping Tom or a groper who's worked his way up to the next level."

"No one jumped out of the computer. The most likely ones are locked up."

"Biological father?"

"He's also locked up, in Worcester, Massachusetts."

Nancy picked up the photo of the girl off Infante's desk. Such beautiful, beautiful hair, thick and shiny even under the cheap studio lights. It had been slicked back for the photo, but those baby ears could barely hold that cascading mane. Her ears were pierced, Nancy noticed, which she thought barbaric on children. "What about the scissors?"

"What do you mean?"

"You saw the hair. It was *shorn,* not hacked off with a pen knife. Do you carry scissors on you? Real scissors, not Swiss Army knife ones? Because that's what it's going to take to go through a hank of hair like that."

"So either the guy is walking around with a pair of scissors—"

"Or bought a pair after identifying his target. We should check the CVS, Jo-Ann's Fabrics, every store in the mall that sells scissors. Everybody's got computerized inventory, right? So we should know who sold scissors yesterday at what time. We also might want to see who bought clothes for a toddler at Westview yesterday. Because he didn't take her out of there naked, or just in a pair of pull-ups."

Infante wagged an approving finger. "I like you, Porter."

"That can be our secret."

Infante opened a crisscross directory and began compiling a list of stores in Westview Mall. He didn't have to tell Nancy that they would visit the stores in person. They did their job face-to-face, showing badge and ID. No one worth talking to ever volunteered anything over the telephone.

Nancy kept staring at the photo, the original they had used to make the dupes for the television stations and the newspaper. It was a Kmart special, or one of those mall photo studios, the girl backed by a field of fake flowers. Nancy should stick it in an envelope now, make sure it got back to the mother as soon as possible. How horrible it would be if the photo arrived after the fact—assuming the fact turned out to be the worst possible fact of all. That was the assumption, despite the hair and the discarded clothes. There was no getting past the blood on the T-shirt, even if it wasn't the girl's. Something had happened in that rest room.

It was funny about the photo, how it had been played in the media. As usual, the *Beacon-Light* had demanded the

most from the department and given the least. They had even
tried to persuade Nancy to drive the photo to the downtown
office last night, arguing that it would mean overtime if a reporter had to act as the courier. As if Nancy cared about *their*
overtime. The paper had ended up sending a young reporter
from the county bureau. But because the department was
noncommittal about the nature of the girl's disappearance,
the paper hadn't used the photo at all. Clearly, some *Beacon-
Light* editor had run the available information through his
formula for news and decided it didn't qualify. Because the
girl's parents were poor? Because the girl was biracial? It
was hard to understand how newspapers thought. Television
was better for this stuff, anyway. Played it high, got results.
People watched television.

Plus, television kept the missing girl in play all day long,
while the newspaper was a one-shot deal at best. Every local
station had shown the photo on the ten and eleven o'clock
newscasts and were now using it on their Saturday morning
news shows every half hour. Nancy could tell how often the
morning television shows were cycling by the pattern of the
phone calls. The girl's picture would pop up on Channel 2 or
11 or 13—just the picture, and an explanation that she had
been missing since she "wandered off" in Westview Friday
evening—and a few minutes later the phone would ring the
double staccato chime that indicated it was being forwarded
from the 911 communications center. The public didn't realize it, but the department gave out a seven-digit exchange for
the com center in such cases, which meant that everyone
who called ended up on the Caller ID log. So far, every tip-
ster had been a lunatic. But it only took one, as Lenhardt
liked to say. It only took one.

The phone rang just then, almost as if Nancy had willed it.
"Nancy Porter?"
"Yes?" This was odd. Her name wasn't out there in con-

nection with the case. Only Bonnie, the corporal, had gone on camera.

The woman on the line quickly answered the unspoken question. "I just spoke to your sergeant and he said I should speak to you. I have . . . information."

Nancy sat at her desk, working her notepad from her purse, digging out a pen. "Can I ask your name?"

The caller ignored that question, racing ahead, eager to say her piece. "There is something I think you should know about the missing girl, Detective Porter. Something you would not be expected to know, but something I cannot help knowing. When you have this piece of information, I think it will change the way you are pursuing this matter."

Jesus, Nancy thought, has this tight-ass woman ever heard of contractions?

"This is information that might not be meaningful to you, but it is meaningful to me, and it should be meaningful to you. It will be meaningful to you if you pay careful attention—"

Holy Christ. How had this one gotten past Lenhardt? She was clearly a well-intentioned wacko, some shut-in who yearned to find her place in the world by pretending to knowledge she didn't have. Was Lenhardt playing a joke on Nancy or testing her?

"If you could get to the point, ma'am," Nancy said as gently as possible.

"This is the way I get to the point," the caller snapped. "My name is Cynthia Poole Barnes. And you will listen to me. You will absolutely listen to me, and everything I have to say."

17.

Cynthia had awakened that morning to the sound of a familiar song, one she heard almost every day now, at least twice a day. "I know you. . . ." Rosalind was watching *Sleeping Beauty* again. She had watched it every day this summer until Cynthia had been forced to put her on a schedule—once in the morning, once in the afternoon, with no other television at all. She had thought that once Rosalind understood it was a choice between *Sleeping Beauty* and the rest of the television-video universe, she would choose to watch other things. But Rosalind was a monotheist straight from the womb. She wanted one toy, a stuffed bear, and one book, *Grimm's Fairy Tales*. She also needed only one parent, but given that it was Mommy, Cynthia didn't mind that so much.

And now Rosalind wanted this white-blond princess waltzing in the forest over and over again. The end of the film, which scared Cynthia to this day, did not intimidate Rosalind at all. The thorns grew over the castle, the dragon's shadow filled the screen, yet Rosalind's gaze remained locked on the set, unflinching and unwavering. She could watch without fear because she knew how it ended. She was equally blasé about the terrors in Grimm, whether it was Cinderella's stepsisters mutilating their feet, or Rumpelstiltskin tearing himself in half from fury when the Queen guessed his name.

Cynthia looked at the clock—it was seven-thirty. Warren would be up and dressed, anxious to go to his golf game, but determined not to disturb Cynthia while she slept. She slipped on her robe and went downstairs, giving him permission to escape into the summer morning. There was something about her husband in golf clothes that made her want to cry, a combination of pride and irrelevance she could never explain. It had mattered so much, once upon a time, to get into Caves Valley. Then it mattered not at all.

Warren knew it, too, felt the loss as deeply as she did. She never doubted his grief, never claimed hers was any larger than his. But only one of them could withdraw from the world, and he had granted Cynthia that privilege. Warren still worked, and part of his work meant playing golf on Saturday mornings, putting on his spikes and his cheerful-lawyer face, heading out to oil the relationships that brought a steady stream of work into the firm. Cynthia would be the first to tell anyone who dared to ask that Warren, in some ways, had it harder than she did.

The thing was, no one ever dared to ask.

Yet he always felt guilty about leaving her on Saturday mornings, always looked abashed. Which was good, for it kept him from realizing on this particular Saturday how much she wanted to be alone. Cynthia didn't want Warren around when she called the police.

But she wouldn't call for several hours. To call so early would seem hysterical, suspect. She would wait until the local news stations had shown the photo again and again. And then she would call, feigning ignorance, pretending not to know or care who was assigned to the investigation under way.

It had taken Cynthia's father less than an hour last night to put her in touch with Sergeant Lenhardt, who was still in the office at midnight, although he had sent his detectives home to prepare for the long day ahead, a day of interviews and field work, even if it was the Fourth of July. He had treated Cynthia with respect and kindness—she was the daughter of Judge Poole—and encouraged her to call the detectives directly.

"Nancy Porter," he said. "Or Kevin Infante, who's the primary on the case. But if you'd rather deal with Nancy—well, that's okay."

"And why would I rather deal with Nancy?" She knew, of course. Some things are never forgotten. But she was curious whether this sergeant knew as well. Cynthia had a weakness for wanting to know how much others knew about her, the strange attraction-repulsion that gossips, even reformed ones, often feel toward gossip. She dreaded the idea that people might be talking about her. She dreaded the idea that they weren't.

"I don't know," the cautious sergeant said, leaving a space for her to fill, if she so chose. When Cynthia volunteered nothing, he added: "Women like talking to women sometimes, in my experience. They're both good detectives, they'll hear you out. They'll want to know what you know."

"Why don't you tell them what I've told you? Why do I need to call them at all?"

Now it was his turn to be evasive, to wait out a silence. But the seconds ticked by, with neither speaking, and it was the sergeant who finally broke.

"If you call Nancy—or Detective Infante—then it's a lead they've developed. If it comes from me, they'll feel second-guessed."

Plausible, Cynthia thought. But the very fact that she found it "plausible" marked it for the half-truth it probably was. The sergeant wasn't telling her everything. Which was only fair, as she had not told him close to everything.

So she sat in her kitchen on Saturday, waiting for the morning hours to tick by, waiting for *Sleeping Beauty* to fol-

low the arc of her destiny, from privileged birth to a date
with a spindle to the deathlike sleep from which only true
love could wake her. She heard all this because the nursery
was still equipped with a baby monitor, which was on all the
time. If only Tanika, upstairs on the phone, had remembered
to turn it on *that* day, as Cynthia thought of it. That day, the
only day. If only Tanika, hearing the phone ring, had remembered there was one in the kitchen, hadn't dashed up
the stairs to grab the extension in Cynthia's room. If only
she had remembered on which side of the door she had
parked the carriage—or hadn't lied about it later, hadn't
sworn to the skies that Olivia was inside the house, behind
the latched screen door. The girl's clumsy lies, told to cover
up her mistakes, had only slowed down the investigation and
sent detectives scrambling in the wrong direction.

Cynthia made a pot of coffee, transferred it to a carafe
that sat on a ceramic trivet. *Italy,* she thought. *Our honeymoon.* Whenever she thought about Tanika—stretched out
on Cynthia's bed, chatting to her boyfriend, shoes leaving
black marks on the spread—she always ended up in Italy, on
her honeymoon.

Why are you going to Italy, people—well, her parents'
friends—had asked the young couple. Why not Hawaii?
Why not Jamaica? Go someplace you won't work so hard.
Why Italy?

"For the shoes," Cynthia drawled.

People had laughed as she knew they would. "Oh, but
you'll want to see Rome, of course, and Venice, and Tuscany
if you have time," they advised. Cynthia had put a cautionary
hand on the arm of such well-intentioned travel guides, and
repeated slowly, as if they were hard of hearing, and some of
them were: "Yes, that's all very nice. But I'm going for the
shoes."

No one had believed her, of course. That was one of the

advantages of exaggerating one's own persona. No one ever
quite believed that Cynthia was as vain or self-centered as
she insisted she was. Perhaps she wasn't. They may have
gone for the shoes, as she later told her friends, but they
ended up doing the whole damn boot, from toe to top. They
had done it on an unofficial one-for-Warren, two-for-
Cynthia basis. This was the model on which their marriage
would be based, and it had worked pretty well, up until that
day when nothing worked anymore, except inertia and this
shared grief, a grief so profound that it would defeat anyone
who tried to carry it alone.

In Italy, Cynthia had been surprised to learn that Warren
was a dutiful, earnest tourist. It was the first unexpected bit
of knowledge in her marriage, and while not unwelcome, it
made her wonder just how observant she was. She had seen
herself as a conqueror, winning an impossible prize over a
large field, yet Warren-the-tourist—guidebook in hand—had
ventured dangerously close to geeky. In hindsight, Cynthia
realized she should have known that a man as successful and
handsome as Warren should have had a little more dog in
him. But the face, the shoulders, turned out to be fairly late
developments in the life of a bookish little nerd. Growing up
in Pittsburgh, Warren had been a grade-grubber whose
asthma kept him out of sports, while his strong-willed single
mother kept him off the streets lest he be tempted into more
unsuitable extracurriculars. Egypt had caught his fancy and
led him to a more general appreciation of archaeology. His
idea for their honeymoon, broached with the tentativeness of
a man already used to his ideas being rejected out of hand,
was a dig in Central America, where you paid money for the
privilege of sifting through dirt in some maybe-temple.
Cynthia had gotten a lot of mileage out of that story.

Still, she would never have denied him his day in Pompeii. She didn't accompany him—she had stayed in the ho-

tel, writing thank-you notes to her mother's friends, who would be quick to let Judge and Mrs. Poole know if Cynthia was tardy on this task—but she had paged through the books he brought back. And wished she hadn't. There was one image she could never shake, an image that came back to her unbidden, time and again. She had seen it when her cell phone rang on July 17, seven years ago. And she saw it last night, about 10:02 P.M., when Brittany Little's image flashed on her television screen.

It was odd that she had seen the news at all, for Cynthia's family treated Cynthia like the Sleeping Beauty, trying to shield her from certain things. Only instead of spindles, it was missing children that Cynthia was not allowed to contemplate. For seven years, newspapers had been hidden and television shows muted, lest Cynthia hear about another missing or dead child.

The thing that no one understood was that she didn't care about any child but her own, and never would.

Finally, 11 A.M., her self-imposed deadline, arrived. She dialed the number the sergeant had given her, and asked to speak to Nancy Porter. She thought she heard a catch in the girl's voice when she revealed her name, an invitation to speak of their shared history. But she hurried by it, into the present. Nancy Porter was nothing to her. For reasons Cynthia could never quite fathom, she felt shamed in front of the girl, as if the detective had something on her.

"As you may recall, my own daughter was taken almost seven years ago," she told the detective.

"I remember the case," the detective said, but she didn't volunteer anything more.

"Yes. And as you probably recall, she was missing for several days before she was . . . found." Cynthia paused, wondering if she needed to add a word to that sentence. Dead. My baby was found dead. To this day, she hated to say it so plainly. It wasn't the starkness of the word that bothered Cynthia, it was its simplicity. Dead did not begin to encompass what had happened to her child. Dead ended.

"I know," the detective all but whispered.

"They're home, you know. Within the past few weeks. They're home, back in Southwest Baltimore, not even three miles from where this happened."

"Do you have any specific information that links them to this case?"

"They're home. What more do you need to know?"

"Well, but—in some ways, the two . . . disappearances are very different. Your daughter was an infant, this girl is a toddler. Your child was taken on impulse, this seems to be part of a more calculated plan, with clothes being swapped—"

"You want information? You want similarities? Well, here it is. The little girl who was taken—" She groped for the name, which had not registered.

"Brittany Little."

"Yes. Brittany Little. Well, Brittany Little has long curly hair and café-au-lait skin. Brittany Little is, in fact, a dead-ringer for my three-year-old, who's sitting upstairs right now. But I can't help wondering if that might be different, if these girls weren't so inept."

"You have another daughter?" The detective's voice was surprised, almost awed.

"Yes. And I'd like this one to live. I'd like Brittany Little to live, too." The sentiment was a split-second late. Of course she wanted the child to be found unharmed. She wouldn't volunteer anyone for what had happened to her.

But what Cynthia really wanted was for Alice Manning and Ronnie Fuller to be held accountable at last.

"Do the girls know about your new child? Have they threatened your family in any way, or made any attempts to contact you?"

"This is not a time for questions." Cynthia had lost all patience and was, for a moment, the woman she used to be—a boss, a supervisor, a political operative, a person who gave orders and saw them carried out. "Don't sit there blabbing to me. Who knows why they do what they do, then or now. Who cares anything about their *motives*? They waited, last time. Remember? They waited four days. If you arrest them now, maybe they won't do what they did last time. Maybe they won't kill another child."

"Mrs. Barnes—"

"You will talk to them." It was at once a question and a command.

"I'm not at liberty to discuss our investigation."

Cynthia did not allow any tentativeness to seep into her voice this time. *"You will talk to them."*

"Yes." The detective's voice was almost a whisper. "God, yes. Of course we'll talk to them."

Cynthia Barnes hung up the phone and poured herself another cup of coffee. The trivet took her to Italy, Italy took her to Pompeii, and Pompeii always brought her back to the place where the world ended, which happened to be on Oliver Street in East Baltimore, on July 17, seven years ago.

She had been on a corner in East Baltimore because the mayor, who loved to dress up, had put on a garbageman's uniform and gone out with a trash crew to one of those neighborhoods that was always bellyaching about how neglected it was by the mayor's administration. Normally, Cynthia wouldn't have been there at all, but there was an out-of-town reporter following the mayor, and she wanted to keep an eye on things.

While she was baby-sitting the mayor, Tanika, a nineteen-year-old Coppin student, was baby-sitting Olivia. The girl had just started with the Barnes family a month before. Dutiful and dull, she had been hired for her seeming lack of in-

terest in boys and clothes, and—more crucially—boys'
seeming lack of interest in her. Who could have known that
she already had a boyfriend, a demigangster she was forbidden to see at home, who called her at the Barnes house every
hour of the day? Who could guess that he would call just as
she pushed Olivia's carriage out on the front walk and that
she would run back inside to take the call, thinking it would
require no more than a minute of her time? And who could
guess that Tanika, terrified of her reverend father's knowing
of her disobedience, would fritter away five, ten, fifteen,
thirty, sixty, ninety precious minutes trying to find Olivia on
her own? Ninety minutes were lost by the time she dared to
call Cynthia on her cell. Ninety minutes gone, then four days
gone, and finally, a lifetime.

But at the corner of Oliver and Montford, seven years ago,
Cynthia knew none of this. She knew only that the baby-
sitter was on the phone, trying to relay the impossible news
that Olivia was missing. At that moment, Cynthia was still
fighting, still struggling, still convinced she could do something—and that's when she remembered the image from
Warren's guidebook, the one that had turned her stomach. It
had been a photo of a dog, lashed to a post, preserved in the
moment of *his* struggle. Twisted, writhing, he fought against
the molten lava and the ash, determined not to die. For some
reason, the dog seemed more conscious of his fate than all
the humans of Pompeii combined. They stood still. The dog
fought back.

"What's wrong?" asked her summer intern, a bright
young thing named Lisa Bell, who had styled herself after
her boss until she was known as Cynthia-ette, or sometimes
just Junior. "What's wrong, Cynthia?"

It happened that the photographer who was traveling with
the out-of-town reporter caught the mayor in the pose she
wanted at the exact moment Cynthia snapped her cell phone

shut. The photo captured the mayor in the foreground, grinning as he lifted a can onto the back of the truck. But if one squinted closely, there was Cynthia in the background, preserved in ash, another dog in Pompeii.

Now, on this July morning, she felt the first real stirrings of life she had known in ages. Not even Rosalind, turning somersaults on the sonogram, had made Cynthia feel this vital, this necessary. Alice Manning and Ronnie Fuller weren't through with her yet? Well, Cynthia Barnes was just getting started, too.

18.

Helen Manning had just gotten up when the detectives arrived on her doorstep. She recognized they were detectives before they announced themselves and she pulled the sash tighter on her robe, although it was already quite tight. It was not her state of dress that made her feel shy and tentative before this dark man and fair, apple-cheeked girl. It was more as if they could see right through her, to the source of whatever mistakes she had made. Yet even as the silk-slippery sash cut into her narrow waist, she realized she was not at all surprised. It had taken years, but the second shoe had finally dropped.

"I'm Kevin Infante," said the male detective, who had the kind of Mediterranean good looks to which Helen was once partial. She found herself patting her hair, running her fingertips across her neck as if she might be able to erase the beaded lines that had come to rest there, like those wispy necklaces favored by young girls. "And this is my partner, Nancy Porter."

"We were hoping to talk to your—to Alice Manning," the girl said. Although plump, she struck Helen as everything Alice had once yearned to be—unthreatening, agreeable, popular. Miss Congeniality. The class secretary but never the class president. Alice probably hadn't broken the habit of wanting those things, poor thing.

"She's not here. She's . . . out."

"Do you know where she is, or when she might be home?"

"May I ask what this is about?" Helen's voice squeaked a little.

"We just want to talk to her," the female detective repeated with a firm, unyielding tone. "Nothing more."

"I think she took a walk."

"A walk?"

"She walks a lot." God, she must look like a terrible mother, standing here with her morning hair, in this decadent silk robe, like some madam in an old Storeyville brothel. All she needed to complete the picture was a bare-chested man at her kitchen table, reeking of sex and screaming for his breakfast. But Jesus, Alice was eighteen, a grown-up under the law. Was Helen to be held to a different standard because of the past? How many women could produce their eighteen-year-old children on a Saturday afternoon? *It's 1:30 P.M., do you know where your children are?* Helen had always thought the old public service announcement was more for children than for adults, for she had never felt safer than when she was curled up on the sofa in her family's den, hearing that rhetorical question just before the nightly newscast. Her parents knew where she was. She knew where her parents were. All was right with the world.

"Does she have a cell phone? Or a job where we might find her?"

"You know, I've encouraged her to get a job." Helen felt relief at being able to tell that small truth. "She says she's looking. That's probably what she's doing today, following up on some leads."

"Do you know where?"

"Well, no." Helen tried to remember what they had discussed, specifically. "Not the grocery stores, because they're union. And not the convenience stores. They're not safe. I mean, don't you agree? You wouldn't want to have a daughter working in a convenience store, would you?"

She was flirting, she realized, setting up the male detective to tell her that, no, he didn't have a daughter, wasn't even married, in fact. Maybe he would scrawl his home number on his business card, or ask with fake nonchalance if there was a Mr. Manning.

But it was the girl who pulled out a card and handed it to Helen.

"Would you call us when she comes home? We just need to talk to her. Nothing formal. May have more to do with one of her friends than her."

"Alice has a friend?" Helen could not bear the idiocy of her own voice, this stupid, echoing, out-of-it quality, as if she were some Judy Holliday type. She never sounded this way, never. "I mean, she seems to keep to herself, as far as I know."

"When did she get home?" the female detective asked.

Until that moment, Helen had been trying to cling to the idea that this was all a coincidence, that there was no link between present and past. *Damn it, Alice,* she thought, suddenly furious with her daughter. She had been given every chance to start over—second chances, third chances, even. But she would rather keep punishing Helen than take advantage of her opportunities.

"Last night," the young woman prompted. "What time did she get home last night?"

"Do I have to talk to you?"

"No," the male detective said. "But why wouldn't you?"

"I can think," Helen said, "of no shortage of reasons. For one thing—you still haven't told me what this is about."

"Well, it's not really about anything. We're working on a case, your daughter may be able to help us. That's all."

Ah, these were the police Helen remembered, in their most unhelpful guise. They were always so maddeningly elliptical, so noncommittal. Taciturn, reserved, insisting you were on a need-to-know basis even as they began destroying your life. *Do you recognize this, Ms. Manning? Have you seen this before, Ms. Manning?* The question had come before she could focus on the *this* in question. That detective had been middle-aged, thick-middled, and reeking of tobacco. She remembered still that she had not specifically requested "Ms." and the presumption had irked her. She refused to look at the bagged object in their hands, eager to disavow it, even though she knew she could not.

After all, Alice's name was written on the bottom of the metal box in firm purple marker. Alice wrote her name on everything—toys, books, notebooks. Once, she had even scratched her initials on the back of a locket with her name engraved on the front. "Because it says Alice, not Alice Manning," she had told Helen at the time. "So another Alice could take it." Alice had worried a lot about phantom Alices, little ghost girls intent on stealing everything she had. She wrote her full name everywhere she could, including even her despised middle name to be on the safe side. Alice Lucille Manning, Alice Lucille Manning, Alice Lucille Manning, ALICE LUCILLE MANNING. "Did you name me for Lucille Ball?" she asked Helen once. "No, for my mother's mother." "Oh," Alice said. "Well, can I tell people that you named me for Lucille Ball, like she was a distant relation?"

At least these detectives were empty-handed, a reprieve of sorts. Maybe it really was an innocent coincidence, a traffic accident seen, a robbery witnessed, nothing more. "I don't know when she'll be home," Helen told them. "But she's always home for dinner. Especially Saturdays. We have pizza on Saturdays."

The female detective's parting glance was pitying. Helen didn't mind. Pity was the least she deserved.

The afternoon sun created a powerful glare on the parking lot at Westview, so Ronnie did not notice the man and woman walking purposefully toward the bagel shop until they were inside. But once she could see them, she knew they were officials of some sort, on business. Health Department? Not on a Saturday, and not with guns on their belts. Mall security? Those guys wore uniforms and didn't come in pairs. No, these were cops.

"Ronnie Fuller?" the woman asked. She looked familiar for some reason, yet Ronnie didn't know her. Maybe she just had one of those faces.

"Yeah."

"We need to talk to you, if we could."

Ronnie was aware of Clarice listening, although her back was turned. "I'm five minutes from taking a break. Could this wait until then? I'll meet you outside."

"Sure."

The police officers didn't go outside. They grabbed a pair of sodas from the case and seated themselves at one of the round tables, so they were facing Ronnie, watching her. They talked in low, casual voices, but one of them was always looking at her, sometimes both. And with Clarice now stealing looks at her, too, Ronnie couldn't help feeling nervous. It had been a long time since so many people had looked at her at once.

The five minutes passed slowly, a fact that Ronnie registered as odd. Given that she didn't want to talk to them, the minute hand on the big Coca-Cola clock should have shot forward five spaces in a matter of seconds. But the time dragged. She waited on a few more customers, teenage girls.

Wait, she was a teenage girl, too. She forgot that sometimes. She felt like she had more in common with Clarice than she did with the girls on the other side of the counter. They compared calluses, the ones they got from standing, and talked about how their legs ached at the end of the day.

"You take your break," Clarice said at last. "I can watch the cash register, slow as it is."

She seemed to be trying to say something else with her kind brown eyes, but what? Was she disappointed in Ronnie because police officers had come to talk to her? She would be even more disappointed if she knew about Ronnie's past. Would she let Ronnie continue to work here? Probably not. Even if she did, she wouldn't be Ronnie's friend anymore. She would treat her with the cold, polite reserve that she used on the customers. When the teenage girls had stood in front of the counter, giggling and changing their orders back and forth, Ronnie could feel Clarice's dislike for them. *White, silly, self-important, foolish.* She would die if Clarice treated her that way.

But if Clarice found out about Olivia Barnes, she would think Ronnie was one of those white people who hated black people. That had been another one of the lies told by Maddy's mom. Of all the things that Ronnie had done, or been accused of doing, this detail remained so sharp. She had said a horrible word, the one word you could never take back. That was why most people believed Alice over her, when it came down to it. Alice had never said the horrible word.

"I just have to go in the back," she told the detectives, "and hang up my apron. We're not allowed to wear them on break. It has something to do with the Health Department."

Clarice probably gave her an odd look at that, knowing it for the lie it was, but Ronnie didn't care. She pushed her way back into the kitchen, where O'lene was studying the ovens.

"Hey, Ronnie," she said, "do I have to put in a new batch of anything? Or can we make it to three P.M. with what we've got?"

"What we've got," Ronnie said tonelessly. She folded her apron, put it on top of one of the boxes, and opened the back door, the one used for delivery.

"Hey, what the—"

But she was already out of O'lene's earshot, running blindly toward Route 40. She didn't know where she was going to go, or what she was going to do. The only thing she knew was that when they came for you, their minds were already made up. So you might as well run, and be free for a few hours longer. You might as well run.

It was just before 6 P.M. when Alice let herself into the house, blinking violently. Helen didn't approve of air-conditioning—that was her exact word, *approve*, as if it were an idea, or a habit—and she kept the house dark and shuttered in the summertime. It worked, actually, and the living room was surprisingly pleasant. But the abrupt change in light was hard on Alice's eyes. She swore she could actually feel her irises opening, desperate to find enough light to focus in the dim room.

Then she saw Helen, sitting in an old easy chair unearthed from the Salvation Army and covered in a bright flowery print that Helen had raved about. Marimekko, Alice recalled. "I had dresses made out of this when I was your age," Helen had said. Now she sat in the chair, still in her robe, although it was almost dinnertime.

"Some people came looking for you."

"People?"

"Police detectives."

"What did they want?"

"They want to talk to you."

"Why?"

"They wouldn't tell me. Why don't *you*?"

"How can I tell you what I don't know?"

"Are you sure you don't know?"

"Of course I'm sure." Alice lowered herself onto the sofa, removed her shoes, and examined the soles of her feet. She had been using a special cream on her heels, but they were still cracked and split from her rambling, as she had come to think of her long walks. She wished she knew someone other than Helen who might ask what she was up to these days, because she would like to use that answer: "Me? Oh, I've been rambling." It sounded romantic.

"Alice—I can't go through this again."

"What?"

"You know."

Alice did, but she wanted Helen to say it. "I don't have a clue what you mean."

"Alice, baby."

"Don't call me baby."

"You are my baby. My one and only. You will always be my baby."

"Right," Alice said, with a short bark of a laugh. "Right."

"Why would the police want to talk to you?"

"I told you, I don't know. But I guess there's only one way to find out."

She held out her hand, weary in a way she hadn't been coming up the walk. Then she had felt energized, despite her long day of rambling. She had been thinking about their Saturday night pizza, which Helen insisted on ordering from one of those gourmet places that served pizza with things like shrimp and chicken fajitas and even stuffed grape leaves. Alice would have been happy with a plain cheese from Domino's. Instead, she usually ordered something called a "margherita," which was just tomato-and-cheese in disguise. So Helen. She kept giving ordinary things the most extraordinary names. A tomato-and-cheese pizza became margherita, a piece of fabric was Marimekko.

Helen stared, perplexed, at Alice's outstretched hand.

"They gave you a card, right? Well, give it to me."

Helen fished it out of her robe pocket and handed it over. Nancy Porter. Baltimore County Homicide.

"Are you going to call?" Helen asked, as if Alice were the adult, the one who got to make decisions.

"After dinner. It's pizza night, remember?"

"They might have gone home by then."

"Then I'll talk to them Monday."

"But—"

"If it's important to them, they'll come back," Alice said, going into the kitchen to grab the carryout menu from beneath the refrigerator magnet shaped like Glinda the Good. Even though she knew the menu and the phone number by heart, she liked to study it before ordering, just in case she decided to try something other than her usual. "They always come back."

19.

Nancy and Infante managed to make good use of their time that afternoon—canvassing the mall's shops, looking for anyone who might have sold scissors or a new outfit for a toddler. The people they interviewed were all helpful, too, which wasn't always the case. At least they *wished* to be helpful. A missing girl generated that kind of response. But no one really knew anything, and ignorance took longer to process and assess than pertinent information.

Still, Nancy and Infante felt almost at peace with the day they had put in. Almost. Flight was tantamount to confession. Ronnie Fuller was hiding something, and she would tell them what it was when they found her. And they would find her. A teenage girl who worked in a bagel shop and lived with her parents could hide only so long. Ronnie didn't even know how to drive—Nancy and Infante had learned that from her mother, a woman who wasn't so much pale as gray and lumpy, like a doll left outside too long. Ronnie didn't have a boyfriend, or any friends, period. That was how her mother put it, sitting at her kitchen table, head bowed in shame: "No boyfriend. No friends. Period."

But what if time mattered? Even if their client was a corpse—which was Lenhardt's private slogan for their department, "Your corpse is our client"—time was important. But if the girl was being kept alive, as Olivia Barnes had been, then time was an enemy and an ally, a tease and a cheat. Every minute that passed gave them hope. Every minute filled them with despair.

"And you know what would be the worst possible outcome?" Nancy said, speaking as if she had been airing her thoughts out loud all along.

Infante caught up with her, a ballroom dancer used to following a partner's improvisations.

"If she was alive for a while and now isn't," he said. "I mean, if she's going to be dead, it's better if she's been dead all along, since early Friday night. Otherwise, it's lose-lose. People will be second-guessing us, and whatever we did will be the wrong thing in hindsight. Solving the case won't matter."

"It won't matter as much."

"I gotta say, I think she's dead."

"I don't know what to think. It doesn't make sense. Cutting the hair and changing the clothes suggests abduction for a purpose. But then there's this T-shirt with blood on it."

"Only not her blood."

"It just doesn't sound like what they would do. The girls, I mean. It's nothing like what they did last time."

"That's right—you know them, don't you?" Infante's tone was supercasual, the kind of tone he might use in an interrogation. Nancy wondered what Lenhardt had confided in Infante last night, in the men's room. She was told he wanted them to work the case because Jeffries was up, and Jeffries wasn't much good. A year from his twenty-and-out, he was like a piece of furniture that had gone out of style and they just kept shifting him around the room, too sentimental to call bulk trash to haul him away. So it was credible that Lenhardt didn't want him to work this case. Credible, plausible—but Lenhardt would be the first to remind Nancy that those words didn't guarantee truth, just a reasonable facsimile. Credible stories were the kind they picked apart every day.

"I wouldn't say I *know* them," Nancy said, choosing her words carefully. She had never spoken to Ronnie Fuller before today, and Alice Manning was still nothing more than a face she had glimpsed at the courthouse long ago. It was their *handiwork* that had gotten tangled up in her life, the evidence of their venality, not the girls themselves. "I had a . . . minor connection to the Olivia Barnes case. So, some coincidence, huh, me working this case?"

She was giving Infante a chance to contradict her, to tell her if Lenhardt had moved them up in the rotation for any specific reason.

"I don't know. You work in law enforcement long enough, you're going to see certain people more than once, even if you change jurisdictions. Like Lenhardt and the Epstein case."

"Yeah." Nancy didn't have a clue what Infante was referencing. She didn't mind asking questions when she didn't know something, but she had also figured out that much would be revealed from context, if a person was patient. *The Epstein case.* She filed it away, knowing the story would emerge eventually.

They were on the Beltway, completing the long, sweeping loop around the city, making their way back to headquarters. The vast, inefficient expanse that was the county still amazed Nancy. Driving, just driving, accounted for a third of her overtime every year. Some people said the county was shaped like a wrench, and Baltimore was the lug. Nancy thought it looked like a piece of snot hanging from the Pennsylvania line. "So much space, so little crime," Lenhardt said, his voice almost wistful for the felony-dense precincts of the city. It had to be an easier place to hide. But then,

Ronnie didn't know the county either. She was a city girl, and the only place she had known for the last seven years was whatever juvenile facility had held her.

All Ronnie had was a five-minute head start on them, but so far it had proved to be enough. That's how long they had needed to conclude that she wasn't going to emerge from the kitchen, wasn't hanging up her apron, or going to the bathroom, or combing her hair. O'lene, the girl who worked the ovens, just shrugged her skinny shoulders and said she hadn't noticed anything. The manager, Clarice something, had been as unhelpful as she dared, her loathing for Nancy and Infante palpable. A middle-aged black woman living and working in Southwest Baltimore was not likely to be a fan of the police under any circumstances. But Clarice's antipathy had been pronounced, personal. Nancy had the impression that the woman didn't want anyone to talk to Ronnie until *she* had a chance to question her.

Yet it was Clarice who, unwittingly, told them what they needed to know: On Friday, the day Brittany Little had disappeared, Ronnie had left the store at 3:30 P.M. Clarice had told them this as a way of praising Ronnie's constancy, her excellent work habits, and they had nodded, as if they agreed. But all it meant was that Ronnie was off on her own, a few hundred yards from Value City, only a few hours before Brittany was reported missing.

"Brittany Little's mother called the police about six-thirty," Infante said. "That gives Ronnie Fuller three hours to walk across the parking lot, buy whatever she needed, then pick out her victim."

"But see, that doesn't make sense if the whole point is that the girl looks like the younger sister of the baby Ronnie killed seven years ago. If Cynthia Barnes is right, it's a case of mistaken identity. But Ronnie knows what Cynthia and her husband look like. If she saw Brittany with her real mother, she wouldn't make that mistake."

"Maybe she thought the woman was a baby-sitter or something. I will say Maveen Little was pretty convincing, stupid as she is. Her story stayed constant, late as we talked to her last night. Hey, you ever date a black man?"

Now it was Nancy's turn to follow Infante's twist of thought. "Just because her boyfriend is black, and her baby's father is black, doesn't mean she dates only black men."

"I bet she does. It's a type, you see it all the time, especially in South and Southwest Baltimore. What's that about, anyway—white girls who date only black guys? I never got that."

"I don't know."

"So did you ever date a black guy?"

"I've been with Andy since I was in high school. I barely dated *anyone*."

"Yeah, but would you? Like . . . Denzel Washington. Would you go out with him? I mean, not *him*, because hell, I'd probably bend over for him, rich and good-looking as he is. But say there's a guy in, I don't know, Auto Theft, and he's attractive and nice and treats women right. Would you go out with him?"

"I'm *married*, remember?"

"But if you weren't. C'mon, play with me, Nancy. Would you date a black guy under those circumstances?"

"Yeah, sure." Actually, she didn't think she would, although she would never rule it out. Her taste happened to run to blond men, men like the Polish boys she had known all her life, a Daddy thing.

"I'd love to go out with a black girl."

"I thought your thing was redheads."

"I'm—what's the word—inclusive."

Nancy had to laugh at that. Infante's candor about his

weaknesses made them easy to forgive. He didn't pretend to be anyone other than who he was.

She wished she could say as much about herself.

The sun was setting when they got back to the office. The longest day of the year had come and gone, but the days were still plenty long, and a case like this offered no natural stopping point. Sometimes, going home was a form of discipline, a way of admitting you were only human, needing sleep and food. But who would leave work, much less sleep, when a girl was missing? They had put out the Amber Alert this morning, and Lenhardt had told them the commissioner wanted to launch a search if they didn't have any solid leads in twenty-four hours. The only question was where would they search, how could they establish a grid? In the area around the mall, the area around Ronnie Fuller's home?

Or the site of the old crime, the place where Olivia Barnes had been killed.

Leakin Park, taunted a voice in Nancy's head, a voice she had been shouting down all day. *You're going to have to go back to Leakin Park.* It was a cool, detached voice, one she had begun hearing more and more as she advanced in the department. She thought of the voice as an older, wiser self, visiting from the future. Sometimes she wished the voice would tell her everything it knew. Other times she just wanted it to go away, leave her alone.

Besides, the Chicken Man's house surely was long gone. It had been decrepit seven years ago, and the trail project should have meant its demise. Or the Barnes family had made sure that the shack was bulldozed. That sad, broken-down place wasn't the kind of memorial anyone wanted for their child.

Infante's pager went off in the parking lot and he looked down. "Weird," he said. "It's coming from inside the building, from the switchboard."

They walked into the lobby and the desk attendant looked up, not at all surprised by the synchronicity that brought the two detectives into view seconds after they had been paged.

"These ladies," the attendant said through the perforations in the Plexiglas, "are here to see you."

Infante and Nancy turned and realized that the two women sitting in the lobby were Helen Manning, who looked different in her street clothes, and a hulking, almost obese woman in a pink T-shirt and brightly printed stretch pants that were being forced to live up to their name.

"I'm Alice," the fat woman said, "and I want to help you any way I can."

20.

Mira Jenkins sat in the downtown office of the *Beacon-Light* on another ho-hum Saturday night, trying to figure out exactly when newspapers had decided they preferred nothing to happen. She had come in for her weekly night shift determined as always, happy to spin straw into gold if that's what she needed to get a byline in the next day's paper. But the day cop reporter had been lamentably efficient, scooping up the overnight array of misdemeanor murders and fatal auto accidents and transforming them into briefs. Mira was left with nothing but condition checks on those who hadn't been considerate enough to die by 5 P.M.

Now, with 10 P.M. fast approaching, she wouldn't be allowed to leave the office for anything short of World War Whatever—defined as a multiple murder in a bad neighborhood or a single homicide in a good one—because the night editor couldn't authorize overtime or hold the pages without the managing editor's go-ahead. Plus, she had to be in the office to watch the ten o'clock and the eleven o'clock news, because the one thing the television stations did better than the paper was jump on stories from the scanner.

Even then she wasn't guaranteed a byline. Some weekends the editor might dismiss even multiples as briefs, depending on the demographics. But there had also been

Saturday nights when Mira was sent out to horrible neighborhoods for rinky-dink two-alarms with no bodies, just because some flashy image in the video had caught the
executive editor's eye.

Her one crucial responsibility, or so she was informed
when she started the Saturday shift, was the 8 P.M. dinner
run. The night editor, who otherwise kept her on a short
leash, would juggle anything to make sure she was free to do
that chore.

"You can pick," he had said, fanning the take-out menus
in front of her. "Chinese, pizza, Japanese. You go, you
pick."

"Why do I have to get your dinner at all? Because I'm the
girl?"

"Oh, settle down, Gloria Steinem," he said. He was that
out of it, he actually said Gloria Steinem. "Night cops gets
dinner. Ask anyone. Ask rewrite. Ask the *guy* who did this
job before you. This is a godforsaken neighborhood after 6
P.M. on Saturday. We have to brown-bag it or send someone
out. Wear your beeper."

The last admonition was unnecessary. Mira always wore
her beeper. She had arrived at the paper with one, an accessory not commonly needed by a neighborhood reporter in
the county bureau. It had been her expectation that the suburban assignment would last six, maybe nine months at the
most. But she was still stuck in the county seventeen months
later, watching newer and less worthy reporters get the call
downtown. All because of one mistake, a mistake that could
happen to anyone, a mistake that wasn't entirely her fault.

Yet Mira was perhaps the one person at the paper who
didn't blame her situation entirely on That Story, as it was
known in newsroom shorthand. Mira blamed her name.

"It's Mira with an *i,*" she sang into the phone almost every

day. "M-i-r-a, Mira." The confusion was entirely her own
fault, for she had been born Myra with a *y* and decided upon
entering college to revise herself by just one letter. *Myra*
was an old lady's name, whereas *Mira* had a certain glamour
to it.

The unexpected consequence was that she went through
life correcting people upon first meeting. "No, it's Mi-ra,
long *i*. Not Meer-a. Not like the actress." She should have
gone whole hog, changed the pronunciation along with the
spelling, but that had seemed like a bigger mistruth. That
was Mira's word for the white lies of which she availed herself no more often than anyone else. Mistruths.

But if she'd had it to do over, she would never have contradicted the top editor when he referred to her as Meera.
"It's Mi-ra," she had said automatically, and then realized
her mistake. Nostrildamus, as the editor of the paper was
known behind his back, had been disturbed to be in error
even on something as innocuous as the pronunciation of an
unusual name. Mira got the job, but she was left with the dis-
tinct feeling that if Nostrildamus—then known to her only
as Willard B. Norton—wanted her to be Meera, she should
have agreed to be Meera.

She had tried to make up for that early blunder by crack-
ing the code of this particular workplace culture, as she had
done in high school, college, her internships, and her previous job. By every measure, she had much of what was required for success here—she was young, hardworking, and
pretty in the right way. *The right way* being interpreted, as
everything about Nostrildamus was interpreted, by inference
and example. Judging by the women he hired, he preferred a
skinny kind of prettiness, not too flamboyant and not overtly
sexual. He also liked the females to solicit his opinion on all
matters, large and small, to treat him like a father figure. The

young women agreed it was creepy, but innocuous, the kind of gray area flirtation that had long been part of their pretty young lives.

After that disastrous first meeting, Mira had styled herself after the paper's most successful reporters. She had made appointments to "drop by," seeking his story ideas, asking for his career advice. If he had called her Meera again, she would have let it stand, but instead it seemed his gaffe was what he remembered. "Why, it's Mira with an *i*," he said when she entered his office. He said it in the hallway, if she happened to pass him by, and on his infrequent visits to the bureau. She began to wonder if he knew anything else about her.

When she asked him where she might go next, when she spoke of being ready for new challenges and bigger beats, he became vague and distant, as if she were a telemarketer he wanted to brush off politely: "It's my observation that people here don't spend enough time on their beats, don't hunker down and really learn the ins and outs of beat reporting. I predict"—he was big on predicting, which explained half his nickname; he would even hold his index finger aloft, a regular Mr. Wizard—"I predict you will have plenty of time to do other things."

"And until then?"

"Let's keep giving those neighborhoods the careful attention they deserve. Go to community meetings. Take local activists to lunch. Build up your Rolodex, develop sources. Neighborhoods are the building blocks of society, the DNA of Baltimore."

"Yes, but neighborhoods aren't as defined in the county as they are in the city," she ventured, making sure it sounded more like a question than a challenge. Speaking with Nostrildamus was a variation on *Jeopardy!* Every answer had to be in the form of a question. He simply nodded, assuming agreement in her voice. Sometimes she wasn't sure that Nostrildamus heard the actual words that came out of her mouth, or anyone's mouth. His responses didn't quite match up. Something seemed to go dark inside him when another person spoke, as if he left his body through astral projection and returned only when it was his turn to take the helm of the conversation.

"Yes, indeedie," he said, being the kind of man who said "indeedie" and "awesome be dawesome," and, most mysteriously, "Thanks for the college knowledge." "Neighborhoods are the DNA of our city, and you have to see yourself as one of the scientists trying to crack the genome."

She nodded earnestly, staring up into the black, bottomless holes of his nose, which accounted for the other half of his nickname. He had remarkably large nostrils, and because of the way he held his head while speaking, his reporters were forced to gaze into them.

"Watch out for him," an older reporter had told Mira in her early weeks. "He'll send you to the cornfields."

"What?"

"That's right, you're too young to remember *The Twilight Zone*. There's a little kid with psychic powers who holds a whole town in thrall because he punishes anyone who doesn't do exactly what he likes. What he likes is the same food day in, day out, with a birthday party at the end of every day. And no contradictions. If he even catches you thinking contrary thoughts, he'll send you to the cornfields, which means you're as good as dead."

Mira had shrugged, bored as usual by the baby boomer habit of referring to things from their youth. *The Twilight Zone*. Jesus. Why not *The Honeymooners*, why not Fibber McGee? The way she saw it, anyone who remembered black-and-white television should have the good sense to read a few magazines, keep up with what was going on now.

Nostrildamus couldn't send her to the cornfields because she was already there. But he could keep her there for her mistakes. The irony was, That Story was his fault. But only he and Mira knew this. Nostrildamus was the one who had passed the handwritten letter along to her, with his distinctive red printing: *Just a suggestion, but this looks very interesting.*

Just a suggestion was widely understood as *Do it now,* so she had knocked herself out. She had driven to the Wood-lawn neighborhood and interviewed an elderly black man about his role in desegregating a nearby amusement park, Gwynn Oak. Almost forty years after the fact, the man wanted to buy the abandoned property, which remained be-hind fences, a wild and implausible place in a once-suburban neighborhood that was going rapidly to seed. He described a vision of a public park, with statues to civil rights leaders. All he needed, he said, was start-up money. He was even willing to mortgage his own modest home to get the ball rolling. That had been his phrase—to get the ball rolling.

The story had run off the front on Martin Luther King Jr.'s birthday, and the only ball that rolled had been the one that flattened Mira's career. The calls had started at 7 A.M., over-whelming the morning cop reporter, the only person in the office early on a holiday morning. Mira's subject was a penny-ante con artist, hopelessly delusional. On the day the civil rights protesters had marched on Gwynn Oak, he had been serving time for larceny. His dream may have been true, but little else in the story was. He didn't even own the house he was willing to mortgage.

Who would lie about such a thing? What was the point? "If your mother says she loves you, check it out," one of the older reporters told her, in seeming sympathy, but Mira sus-pected he was rejoicing at her blunder. Although neither she nor her story was cited in the subsequent memos and work-shops, everyone knew why they were being reminded to run criminal record checks and pull the clips. If Mira had compared her source's stories to the original coverage, she would have seen he was wrong on several key details.

The Saturday night cop shift had been her self-selected penance. She had cut a deal with Nostrildamus and the secretary who kept the pay sheets, agreeing to work six days a week for straight-up comp time instead of overtime. Comp time the bosses knew she would never take, because she didn't even use up her two weeks of vacation time. That was another part of the culture here: no one got ahead by taking time off. If the union knew about her arrangement, they would shit, but the union took twenty-two dollars a week out of her paycheck and what did it do for her? Oh, they had been ready to defend her when she screwed up, but that was more for them than for her. The union wasn't going to get her downtown full time. If Maryland law had allowed it, she would have quit or refused to pay the dues. Then Nostrildamus would know where her true allegiance lay.

So she was downtown one night a week. Just her luck, Saturday nights went cold when she arrived. The good stories, the page-one stories, now seemed to happen every other night of the week. There was nothing to do but read the wires and other newspapers, which didn't actually interest Mira much. Mira liked the *idea* of newspapers, enjoyed telling people she was a reporter, but the daily product meant little to her. Her passion was hitting milestones, accumulating tangible proof of her advancement.

Now she was stuck. In this city, in the suburbs, on permanent Saturdays, in limbo. She was even between boyfriends, unusual for her. She no longer remembered why she had chosen journalism, but she remembered her determination to succeed in it. She was not going to slink off to PR. Thank God she hadn't jumped ship in the dot-com boom, which had lured so many of her friends away, then stranded them.

She was not a failure. She got lots of "good jobs" from Nostrildamus and the occasional fifty-dollar American Express gift cheque, largely in recognition of all that unpaid overtime. She was being reborn. It was just taking so damn long.

For some reason, this made her think of the story from one of the western states, where a mother had hired a rebirthing coach to help a troubled child, and they had ended up smothering the girl in her own vomit while simulating passage through the birth canal. Now that would be a good story. She could do something with that. What could she do in a city where it was just boom-boom-boom, one lowlife taking out another lowlife, and not even at the hours that fit her schedule?

The night editor's voice interrupted her reverie: "Call for you, Jenkins."

"Put it on 6129."

"I know the extension," the night editor said. He was quick to remind Mira of everything he knew—and everything she *didn't* know. A few months ago, on a freezing winter night, he had ordered her to go stare at a street sign on a forlorn corner five blocks north because she had misspelled it in a brief. She had gone downstairs, hidden in the ladies' room off the lobby, and come back a suitable interval later. "Centre Street," she had said, "C-E-N-T-*R*-E," pretending humility, shivering a little for effect. She had checked it on the map she kept in her purse. "I won't get it wrong again."

"Newsroom," she said on a sigh. "Mira Jenkins."

"You're a reporter?"

The very challenge in the voice, the unearned hostility, signaled trouble. The night editor must have forwarded one of the regular nuts just to play with her.

"Yes, I'm a reporter. I cover police on Saturdays, but during the week I'm out in Baltimore County."

That should scare her caller off. Nuts always wanted to

talk to the most important people, Nostrildamus or one of the metro columnists.

"How old are you?"

"I'm not sure how that's relevant. Is there something I can help you with tonight?"

"Oh, it's rel-e-vant."

The husky female voice was perplexing. The syntax was ghetto, but the pronunciation was sharp, exaggerated. It reminded Mira of the way people speak after drinking, when they're trying to convince others they aren't drunk.

"How may I help you?" Mira repeated. She must not lose her temper with any caller, no matter how rude. One unhelpful word to the wrong person, a person who knew Nostrildamus, and she was beyond rehabilitation.

"You can help by knowing a little history. You know history?"

"I like to think I do."

"You know *local* history?"

The rhythms were definitely ghetto to Mira's ear, but she had to be careful. There were some politically connected types who spoke that way.

"Is there something I can do for you tonight?"

"A baby disappeared."

"Yes, we've been following that story." Another chore done by the day cop reporter, who had thoroughly covered the absence of leads and the Baltimore County cops' refusal to say whether they thought this was a stranger kidnap, a domestic homicide, or something in between. Nostrildamus didn't like the story, Mira had heard from the night editor when she came in today. "I predict," the executive editor had said at the Friday four o'clock news meeting, "that this will prove to be a sad but small story. The media has gone overboard in its coverage of such stories, which have no true global importance. I predict"—finger held aloft—"that it is time for the pendulum to swing the other way." No one in the meeting had the heart to suggest that Nostrildamus might see the future differently if the child had been white and middle-class, instead of a biracial girl from a marginal city neighborhood. "If you want page-one treatment from the *Beacon-Light*," the night editor had told Mira, "you need to disappear from a better part of town. Preferably his."

The night editor was just trying to make her feel better for being elbowed out of a story that had actually happened in one of her duller-than-dirt neighborhoods. Mira's only contribution so far had been to ferry a photo downtown, which had earned her a 'trib line, even though the desk forgot to use the photo.

"You have been following," the voice agreed. "Now you need to lead."

"I'm not sure I—"

"You must remind people that this has happened before, that such coincidences are to be explored, not ignored."

"I'm sorry," Mira said, checking out the Caller ID log on the phone. But because the call had been forwarded by the night editor, it showed his extension, not the originating number. "But I don't know what you're talking about."

"Now, see." The voice was triumphant. "That's why I asked your age, where you were from. Nobody who lived here seven years ago could forget what happened that summer."

Seven years ago. Mira was starting her senior year at Penn, dating a boy named Bart, short for Bartholomew. He had money *and* ambition—the first sometimes precluded the second, she had later learned. She knew she didn't love him, not really, and he didn't love her, but they would use the word from time to time, to be polite. The memories came back to her, like a movie montage. The golden autumns, the tender springs, the scullers on the Schuylkill.

"Well, I didn't live here then, and I don't know."

"A girl named Olivia went missing," the voice hissed. "Judge Poole's granddaughter. Two white girls killed her but they got juvenile time because they were white. You want to think what would happen to two black girls who killed a white judge's granddaughter? You think the legislature would have said, 'Oh, no, we can't be lowering the limit, you can't send eleven-year-olds to adult prison.'"

"What does this have to do with the child who's missing now?" The very suggestion of racism put Mira off. She didn't deny its existence in the world, but talking about it every day was like discussing anything else you couldn't control—the weather, time, death, taxes. People needed to move on.

"They sent those white girls away seven years ago. Now they're home and another baby's gone. And I can guarantee you, the police are looking at those girls, trying to find out if they had anything to do with it. You call the police. You ask them if they're talking to those girls and they'll have to say yes if they're not lying to you. You tell people that another child is going to die because they wouldn't do it right the last time."

"What—"

The line was dead.

Mira stared at the phone for a good long time.

"Hey, Bolt," she called to the night editor, who probably wouldn't look up if his first name were uttered. "You notice the number on that call you forwarded?"

"Didn't know the number, didn't know the voice," he said promptly. "We got a new weirdo joining the ranks?"

"Maybe."

"Well, whoever it was asked for you by name. You got a friend out there?"

No, but she had a 'trib line on the story, she remembered, and had tried to make a few follow-up phone calls this evening.

She closed her AOL e-mail account, on which she had been sending witty, vicious letters to various college friends, and called up the paper's in-house library. She specified a date range, giving herself a three-year period—people were imperfect when it came to time—and dropped in the terms *Olivia* and *missing*. Too many files came back, including several reviews of *Twelfth Night*. She looked at the notes she had doodled as the woman spoke. She tried *Olivia* and *Poole*.

Seventeen matches in all, and not one more recent than the summer of the crime, seven years earlier. Mira read with careful, absorbed attention, breaking away only to watch the evening newscasts. All four programs carried stories about the missing girl, but not one mentioned the old case or suggested a connection. There seemed to be no developments at all.

When the end of Mira's shift arrived, the night editor had to remind her three times that she was free to go. She printed out the library stories she had been reading and tucked them away in a manila folder, taking them home.

21.

Nancy had been experimenting with several postures and stances in interrogations, not to mention various intonations and degrees of eye contact. Lately she had tried standing, her back against the door, her arms folded across her chest. She thought this pose projected the air of a stern teacher or parent. "That's the problem," Lenhardt had told her. "You do look like a teacher, and these aren't the kind of people who have fond memories of school. If these guys had listened to their teachers, they might have turned out a little differently."

He was right. The men—and so far Nancy had interviewed mostly young men, with an occasional mom and girlfriend thrown into the mix—were sullen or resentful, seldom cooperative. But Nancy couldn't intimidate the way Infante did, especially toward the end of the day, when his five o'clock shadow gave him that blue-black werewolf look. Nor did she have Lenhardt's air of mournful disappointment, which was surprisingly effective with a certain kind of mutt. Plus, if she stood, it gave her a height advantage.

One thing she was sure of: She wasn't going to go all girly. A cop couldn't flirt confessions out of people, and she would look weak if she tried.

None of these concerns, however, applied to Alice Manning, who had arrived here with the nervous shake of someone who actually respected authority. Nancy took a seat across from her in the interview room, hands folded on the table in front of her. Alice unconsciously mirrored her, the way a chimpanzee in a zoo imitated onlookers. Only she looked like someone waiting for a meal at a city mission. Nancy glanced at the girl's pale forearms, searching for fresh nicks or cuts, but saw nothing. The rest of her was too covered up to scout.

"I want to help. I really, really want to help," Alice kept repeating.

"Well, the way you can help is by telling us what you know."

"I'm not sure I know anything."

"So why are you here?"

"Because my mom said you wanted to talk to me."

"Do you know why we came to your house looking for you? Do you know why we think you may have information to share with us?"

"Because of my . . . past."

The choice of word sounded like something Alice had been taught to say. Nancy could imagine Helen Manning schooling her daughter in just this fashion, giving her this grand yet inadequate word, as if Alice were a young Bette Davis, back in her glory days, when her big wounded eyes always seemed to hold some secret.

"Sort of." It was important not to lead the girl, not to give her too much information. "A little girl disappeared Friday night. We're looking at a lot of leads."

"I'm a lead?" Alice tested the word, at once attracted and repelled.

"Well, that's what we're here to find out."

"Is *lead* another word for suspect?"

Nancy couldn't swear to it, but she thought she caught a wisp of something sly in Alice's face just then, a hard light in those wide blue eyes. Again, very Bette Davis. Like the

song, the stupid song that had been on the radio when Nancy
was in middle school. She'll tease you, the song had promised. It was the only line Nancy could remember. She will
something and something and tease you.

"Sometimes leads are suspects. And sometimes they're
just leads. Right now, you're just a lead."

Would Alice think to ask for a lawyer? It was funny how
much and how little neophytes knew about the criminal process. Repeat offenders, of course, had the drill down cold.
But first-timers didn't think they could ask for a lawyer until
they had been charged and read their Miranda rights. They
didn't realize they could just get up and walk out, say, "I'm
not talking to you until you're ready to charge me." Or that
they could lawyer up anytime.

Then again, Alice wasn't a first-timer. And she had been
cagey at eleven, Nancy recalled, almost preternaturally consistent, according to the detectives who caught the case.
*They had taken the baby because they thought she wasn't
safe. They were scared to return her after her parents made
such a big deal of her disappearance. And then the baby got
sick. But Alice didn't know why Ronnie killed her. She wasn't
even there at the time.*

"Why don't you tell me," Nancy began, her voice as bland
as possible, "where you were Friday afternoon and evening."

"I was walking."

"Walking?"

"I've been walking a lot. It's a good way to lose weight."

Nancy willed herself not to let her eyes drift down to the
indistinct bulk beneath Alice's bright pink T-shirt. The girl
had to weigh almost two hundred pounds. God help her if
she had weighed more when she came home.

"Walking? For how long?"

"Well, I don't walk every minute I'm out." Alice must
have seen where the question was going. "I walk for a while,

then take a break inside someplace air-conditioned, someplace they'll let you sit or browse."

"Like a fast-food restaurant."

"Yeah, although there you have to buy something. At least a drink. Which is a waste of money, they put so much ice in."

"Or a mall?" Keeping it generic was deliberate. No need to mention Westview yet.

"Sure."

"So where did you walk on Friday, where did you stop?"

"I started out Route 40 and I filled out an application at an Arby's—I'm looking for a job. I don't want to work in fast food, but my mom says I can't afford to be picky."

"It's not so bad. I did it for a little while."

"Yeah?" She seemed genuinely interested.

"I was a counter girl at Long John Silver's the summer I was sixteen, until I got a waitressing job at a Chili's. I was saving up for a car."

Why had she told the girl this stray bit of personal information? It was one thing Nancy never did. But there was something about Alice that made Nancy want to curry favor—something closed off, an unspoken accusation in her face, like a stoic child who had taken an unearned punishment without flinching or complaining.

"I like Chili's," Alice offered, "but my mom doesn't. Were you popular?"

"At the restaurant?"

"In high school."

"I don't know. I never thought about it." She was glad Lenhardt wasn't watching this. It was bad enough that Infante was tracking the conversation through the one-way glass. She was losing control, letting Alice direct the flow of conversation. Maybe it would loosen the girl up, lead to something she could use.

"So you must have been. Only a popular person wouldn't think about it."

"It was just high school."

"I didn't get to go to high school. Not a real one. Although I got my diploma at Middlebrook."

Suddenly Nancy knew what Alice wanted from her: pity. The girl actually expected sympathy, for missing high school and all the other normal rituals of adolescence.

"Well, Olivia Barnes didn't get to go to high school either."

Alice, chastised, bent her head so Nancy could not see her eyes when she whispered: "I know."

"There's another little girl missing, Alice."

"I know."

"How do you know?"

"I saw it on the news. My mom told me."

"Which is it? You saw it on the news or your mom told you?"

"My mom told me and then I saw it on the news for myself, this morning."

"She disappeared from Westview Mall. Is that one of the places you go, when you're walking? It's on Route 40."

Her head was still down, her voice faint. "Yes."

"Do you know anything? Anything at all about this missing little girl?"

"I know," Alice said, "something I'm not supposed to know. But I know it because, because . . . I broke a rule."

"A rule?"

"Well, more like an admonition." Alice raised her head, as if surprised she knew this word and could use it.

"An admonition?"

"I think that's right. I mean, it's not a law, or a rule, it's just something I was told I shouldn't do. My mom and my lawyer, they said there were certain things I shouldn't do. And I sorta did them."

"What did you do, Alice?"

"I *didn't* walk by the Barnes house," she said. Interesting. Asked what she had done, the girl began by citing what she had not done. If she hadn't walked by the Barnes house, would she even know there was a new little Barnes?

"There's no reason for you to. Is there?"

"It's in my neighborhood and it's a pretty street. I used to walk up and down it all the time. But I don't go there now."

"Have you seen the Barnes family at all?"

"No."

Her denial felt like the most honest thing she had said so far. Which meant that she would have no reason to grab a girl who looked like Rosalind Barnes. Nancy allowed herself a moment of despair. What if this were all a coincidence? What if Cynthia Barnes's paranoia had set them off in the wrong direction? She tried to reassure herself that she and Infante had kept all their options open. A young detective from Family Crimes was trying to stay on top of the Social Services end of it, checking out the family more thoroughly. And this, sadly enough, was the only lead Nancy and Infante had developed in twenty-four hours. If Nancy hadn't been interviewing Alice, she'd just be taking phone calls from helpful, helpless cranks, interviewing dimwitted mall employees, watching security tapes that showed nothing.

"So that's what you *didn't* do. What *did* you do? What"— she chose, quite deliberately, to echo Alice's word back to her—"admonition did you ignore?"

She whispered: "I saw Ronnie."

"Ronnie Fuller?"

Alice nodded, her face stricken, as if she had confessed to something horrible.

"You saw Ronnie . . ." She left a space for Alice to finish the thought, but the girl didn't jump in. "You saw Ronnie do what?"

Alice looked deflated, as if she had expected a more horrified reaction. "I just . . . saw her. I walked over to where she works and I watched her. She didn't see me. But I'm not supposed to see her. Sharon said."

Sharon who? Nancy let it pass. "So you saw her. When was this?"

A flash of impatience: "Yesterday. That's what we're talking about, right? Yesterday."

"You were at the Bagel Barn yesterday?"

"I didn't go in. I didn't even get close. I just sat on the curb for a while. I could see Ronnie, but she didn't see me."

Alice seemed to have no sense of what she was doing. Yes, she was placing Ronnie at Westview Mall, a few hours before Brittany Little disappeared. But she was placing herself there, too.

"Did you see her do anything . . . unusual?"

"No. But I saw Ronnie. I thought you'd want to know she worked there. Did you?"

"Actually," Nancy said, "we did."

"Oh." Alice looked confused. "I thought that's why you came to see me. Because you knew I had seen Ronnie. I thought that's why I was in trouble. I couldn't imagine what else I might have done."

"You can't?"

The girl shook her head.

"Alice—did you go into the mall yesterday?"

"No. I left because I didn't want Ronnie to see me."

"Why did you want to see Ronnie?"

"I didn't want to see her. I just did."

"By accident?"

"Sort of."

"What do you mean, 'sort of.' It was an accident, or it wasn't."

"I knew from my mom that Ronnie had a job at the bagel

place. But I didn't know her hours, or what days she worked. So it's not like I could have planned it."

"But you went there hoping you might see her?"

Her eyes slid away from Nancy's. "Yes," she said in a voice so soft that Nancy needed Alice's nodding head to confirm what she thought she had heard.

"Why?"

"I don't know. I don't know." And then, almost to herself, as if castigating herself. "I thought you didn't know about the bagel shop, that I could help you. I want to help. I'm trying to help."

"You can help us," Nancy said, "by telling the truth."

Fierce, automatic: "I always tell the truth."

"Then tell me this. Do you know anything about Brittany Little, the girl who disappeared? Anything at all, Alice?"

"I don't know Brittany Little. I mean, except from the news. I saw her picture on the news."

"Can I ask you something, Alice?"

Alice gave her an odd look, as if it were late in the game for Nancy to be seeking permission to ask questions. Still, she nodded.

"I mean, it's only because it might give me—give us— an insight. When you took Olivia Barnes, what were you thinking?"

The wounded blue eyes cut right through her, saw the deception in Nancy's question. "How would that give you an insight? I mean, unless Ronnie or I did what happened. And I didn't."

"Still—" Nancy had to know. Even if it proved to have nothing to do with the matter at hand, she had to have the answer to the question that had haunted her for so many years. "What were you thinking?"

"We thought she had been abandoned. We thought we could take care of her until her parents came back."

"And why did you kill her?"

"I didn't," Alice said with a weariness at once disappointed and resigned. "Ronnie did. I wasn't even there when it happened."

"I know that's what you said back then. But you can tell the truth now. It's over. There's no risk now in telling me what happened."

"I am telling the truth. I always told the truth. It's not my fault that no one believed me. Ronnie's a bad girl. You can't know what she'll do. It's almost like there's another girl who lives inside Ronnie and comes out sometimes. That's why people want to believe Ronnie when she says she didn't do things, because she doesn't remember doing them, so she seems really honest. But she's bad, really bad."

"Are you saying she has, like, another personality?"

"Sort of?" Alice's voice was tentative. "I saw this show once, and there was a girl like that. Only with Ronnie, it's not so . . . obvious, you know."

"What do you mean?"

"Her voice doesn't change, and she doesn't tell you to call her by a different name. But it's like there's good Ronnie and bad Ronnie, and bad Ronnie will do anything, and then good Ronnie can't believe she did it, so she's believable when she says she doesn't remember. I don't know why she killed Olivia. If I had been there, maybe I could have stopped her. But I wasn't. I wasn't even there."

Alice's voice rose, petulant after all these years. Yes, she took the baby, yes, she knew where the baby was, yes, she participated in the conspiracy that kept the baby hidden for four days. But she hadn't killed her, and she still didn't understand why the punishments meted out refused to recognize her lesser guilt.

Nancy wasn't sure she did, either. Her odd connection to the Barnes case had not granted her special privileges, despite what everyone believed, but over the years she had indulged her curiosity about the aftermath. Alice had always been adamant about not being with Ronnie when Olivia was killed, and even had a partial alibi—she was home with her mother, reading, if you could call that an alibi. Whose mother wouldn't back up that story, under the circumstances? But the alibi was meaningless because heat and other factors had made it difficult to pinpoint the time of death with any accuracy. The medical examiner had provided a twelve-hour window, adding, as only an M.E. could add: "At least nothing chewed on her after she died." That was an M.E.'s idea of a benediction, not getting chewed postmortem.

"Alice—" There was so much Nancy wanted to ask her, but the sad fact was, it had little to do with Brittany Little and everything to do with Olivia Barnes. Nancy was face-to-face with a girl who had changed her life as surely as anyone. Except, perhaps, Ronnie Fuller. If it were not for the two of them, Nancy wouldn't even be here, in the county. If it weren't for Nancy's freak moment of glory in the Olivia Barnes case, there would have been less to live up to and, consequently, less to live down. She would probably still be in the city, a detective in CID, maybe even a sergeant. She would be who she was supposed to be when she grew up, a third-generation police officer in the Baltimore PD. "County police," her uncle Stan had asked when she decided to come out here. "Do they even have crime in the county?"

You bet they do, she answered her uncle now. The only difference was the ten-to-one ratio. But the detectives worked roughly the same caseloads. And Nancy would have taken fifty never-going-to-be-solved drug shootings over a maybe homicide like this one.

Alice was still holding her plump arms in a prayerful pose. She had a milk-white pallor, almost creepy in its uniformity. Not a nick, not a cut, not even a bruise. It looked as if she never used her hands at all, for anything.

"C'mon, Alice, you say you want to help us. There's one small thing—it would only take a minute—"

There was a light knock on the door. When Nancy opened it, Infante was there, motioning for her to come out. She did, closing the door on Alice, who looked stricken to be left alone.

Helen Manning was standing in the corridor with a fleshy, dark-haired woman with a strange spotted rash on the left side of her face.

"I'm Sharon Kerpelman," she said. "I'm Alice's lawyer. Charge her or release her. At any rate, she's not talking to you anymore tonight."

"Look," Infante said, "I saw your card. You're city PD, you got no jurisdiction here. She's not a juvenile anymore and this isn't a city case."

"I already told you, I'm here on behalf of Rosario Busta-mante, who has agreed to represent Alice. Ms. Bustamante is . . . indisposed and asked that I come here to make arrangements for Alice's release."

"I don't think we can do that."

"Oh, *fuck me*. Alice called and left a message on my machine two hours ago, asking me to accompany her here or find someone who could. I got that message twenty minutes ago. But you know, and I know, she can get up and walk out of here on her own steam. I'm certainly not going to let you talk to her at this late hour, when she's tired and suggestible and would say anything to make you happy."

"We've got her at the scene," Nancy said.

"Really? That's funny because I had dinner with Alice last night, and I don't think she had time to take a child, stash her somewhere, and walk home." Sharon walked over to the door and yanked it open. "Were you at Westview on

Friday, Alice? Don't be afraid to say what really happened, sweetheart."

Alice's voice came back, tentative and sweet: "Well, maybe it was another day. I mean, I did go there once, and see Ronnie. But it was a week or two ago."

Sharon Kerpelman looked triumphant. "See? She hears you're looking for her, and she knows it's all because of what happened in the past, and she can't stop trying to make it right." Maybe it was Sharon, not Helen, who had taught Alice to think of her crime as a past. "And she knows Ronnie's working at the Bagel Barn, and thinks you should know it, too."

"But why lie? Why say it was yesterday if it wasn't yesterday?"

"There's a lot—" Helen began, but Sharon shushed her with a look and an upraised hand. Then, motioning to Nancy and Infante, she led them down the hall, out of Alice's earshot.

"It's hard, being Alice." Sharon was trying to be reasonable in tone, conciliatory and conspiratorial, but she wasn't good at it, and her voice grated on Nancy's nerves. "She got caught up in something that was bigger than she was, and she keeps trying to undo it. Seven years ago, she was too scared of Ronnie Fuller to keep her from doing what she did. Now police come around and she sees a chance for, I don't know, a kind of redemption. She figures if she says what you want to hear, maybe she can balance the scales at last. But Alice didn't have anything to do with this. If Ronnie Fuller did"—she shrugged—"that's *her* lawyer's problem, however."

"Does she have a lawyer?"

"Figure of speech. I wouldn't know."

Without asking permission, Sharon Kerpelman walked into the interview room and came back out with Alice, her arm slung around the girl's shoulder. "We're going to go now. If you want to talk to her again, call me."

"I thought," Infante said, "Rosario Bustamante was her lawyer."

"Right. That's what I mean. Call her."

Infante looked at Nancy, who shook her head sadly. They could fight this bitchy PD, insist that Bustamante herself come down before releasing Alice. But they had lost the moment. Alice wasn't going to talk to them again, not tonight, not with any flow. How odd, to be shrewd enough to call a lawyer, but naive enough to begin speaking without one. Infante turned to Kerpelman and gave a brusque nod, as if it were his decision.

The trio left without another word. But Alice, to Nancy's amazement, turned and flapped her hand at her in a vague, shy wave.

22.

Gloria Potrcurzski had cried the first time she saw her daughter in uniform. Nancy assumed it was because her uncle, her mother's brother, had been injured on patrol in his early years. *Injured* was almost an overstatement—a bullet had grazed his neck, just whistled right by him, requiring nothing more than an emergency room visit. But the incident had brought the family real pain for a few hours while a local radio station broadcast breathless bulletins about a "felled" officer in the 900 block of Hollins. Everyone in Stan Kolchak's family knew his beat and knew his hours, so they had no doubt who the unnamed patrolman was. Yet the story's happy ending just seemed to make the pain more pronounced in Gloria's memory. So when she sobbed at the sight of her twenty-one-year-old daughter in uniform, Nancy had assumed the old fear was washing over her.

"Oh, honey," her mother had said at last, "you look awful in that."

She did, but Nancy had seen that coming. Since entering the academy, she had started noticing that even actresses on the various cop shows looked stocky and awkward in police uniforms. And they had the advantages of wasp waists, tiny butts, and professional wardrobe people. On Nancy, of average height with ample curves, the outfit was spectacularly unflattering—especially the winter one, when she had to wear her sweater tucked in.

But it was the mannish quality that made Gloria Kolchak Potrcurzski cry. Gloria had been the only girl in a family of six, and the world she created for her one daughter had been reactionary in its femininity—pink-and-white room, canopy bed, shelves of dolls, unlimited funds for clothes and hair care. And she was on the verge of success when twenty-year-old Nancy decided she was sick of fighting her own destiny. She changed her major to criminal justice and, nearly two years later, stood before her mother as a freshly minted cadet.

"I never thought my daughter would grow up to be a cop," said the woman who was a daughter to one cop and a sister to two others.

"Don't worry, Mom," Nancy had said. "I'll make detective quick enough, and then I'll wear skirts every day."

She was the kind of daughter who kept such promises. So seven years later, as Saturday eased into Sunday and the fourth of July gave way to the fifth, Nancy was wearing a tailored white blouse, a knee-length khaki skirt, hose, and Easy Spirit pumps. The shoes were more comfortable than regular pumps, but she wouldn't want to play basketball in them, as women had in the old television ads.

Nor did she want to walk along an overgrown path and splash across a polluted stream in a darkness brightened only by the beam of a small flashlight, but that was what she had decided to do.

It was a hot, yeasty night, the kind that made old-timers downtown sniff the breeze and wonder if McCormick Spice Co. had suddenly rematerialized in the harbor. But the smell was all over the metro area, and it was more grain than spice. For Nancy, the hot, scent-laden wind stirred up memories of her Grandmother Potrcurzski's kitchen—homemade rolls rising in a covered bowl, pierogi shells awaiting their fillings, a sweet undercurrent of cabbage. Cabbage could smell sweet if a cook treated it gently. Nancy drove into the past with her windows down, indifferent to the heat, wondering if she could find the right spot after all these years.

Olivia Barnes had been missing for four days going on five before the cadets were sent to this asphalt parking lot on the southwestern corner of Leakin Park. A homeless man had been found pushing Olivia's carriage, using it instead of the usual shopping cart for the odd collection of things he considered valuable. Inevitably, the deranged man was treated as a suspect, but he was adamant in his insistence that he had found the carriage in the creek bed, a narrow stream shrunken by that summer's drought. So a yellow school bus brought the academy students to the southwestern edge of the park. Nancy was among those cadets.

Of course, few classes went through the academy without searching Leakin Park at least once, as a training tool, and such searches usually began with the joking admonition not to grab just any old body, or they'd be there all day. But no one had cracked any jokes on the morning they gathered to look for Olivia Barnes. The only sounds in Leakin Park that day were the slow, measured footsteps of the cadets walking deeper and deeper into the park, trying to keep an even ten feet between them.

Outdoor searches are doomed to imperfection. Nancy knew that even before she went into the academy. People were always stunned when a body turned up in an area the police had already combed, but these second-guessers had never tried to search a forest step-by-step. On a July day, the deep shade of Leakin Park played tricks on the eyes, almost like a jigsaw puzzle, until everything was green, dark green, and gray. It was all too easy to imagine a child's body hidden in a patch of vines that happened to fall in the space between the cadets' dragging feet.

Nancy was partnered with a classmate, Cyrus Hickory, a cocky twenty-three-year-old who couldn't get over the fact that he had a college degree. Cyrus was a study in contrasts, an African-American man with a shaved head and an accent that Nancy would describe as 100 percent redneck because her ear wasn't trained to catch the watered-down imitation of Tidewater that Cyrus was trying out that summer: "When ah was getting my *duh*-gree at Commonwealth. . . ." Nancy reminded him, after every third reference or so to his days at Virginia Commonwealth, that most of the cadets had college degrees now. But Cyrus countered: "I majored in criminology, with a minor in sociology. I chose this career for myself back when I was in sixth grade."

Nancy had assumed he was insulting her, in a roundabout way. With two uncles and a fiancé in the department, she had a triple taint of nepotism. It turned out that Cyrus, from Virginia, didn't know any of this, not on that faraway July day. As a result, he was one of the few people who dared to patronize her, which was oddly refreshing. At least she didn't have to worry if he was playing up to her, the way some others seemed to do.

When they broke for lunch, eating sandwiches and drinking bottled water provided by a group of volunteers with ties to the missing child's family, she told Cyrus that she thought the grid was off-kilter, sending them in the wrong direction.

"You don't know what you're talking about," he scoffed. "The carriage was found in the creek bed. So you gotta figure the kidnapper realized he couldn't push it up the hill, and he dumped it there, then continued up and over the ridge."

"I think he might have been walking along the stream, not trying to cross it, when he decided to get rid of the carriage. What if he was walking *in* the stream?"

"Why would someone do that?"

"Leaves less of a trail, right? No footprints in the dust, no smashed-down undergrowth. It's the kind of stuff they teach you about Indians when you're in the fifth grade."

This information was, in fact, part of the social studies unit on Native Americans taught at St. William of York that year, as it had been in every parish school, even in Nancy's day. But she wasn't thinking about fifth-graders, not then. They were looking for a grown-up, a sociopath capable of carrying a twenty-pound child with ease. It had not occurred to anyone that two little girls had passed the baby back and forth after abandoning the balky baby carriage at the water's edge, or that they walked through the creek bed because their ankles were bare and they knew these woods were full of poison ivy and sumac. Helen Manning had made sure Alice and Ronnie could recognize the leaves the summer before last, after both girls came down with horrible rashes from playing here.

"There used to be a shack, a ways down Franklintown," Nancy said. "My mother has a distant cousin on this side of town, who works at a crab house—" Her tongue flirted with the idea of invoking the name, Kolchak, and seeing if Cyrus recognized it. But she decided against it. She might win Cyrus's deference, but she would lose his respect. "Anyway, we took this shortcut, through the park, so I remember the shack. A little man lived there, with chickens and roosters. We called him the Chicken Man. He was like some . . . vision out of the past. You couldn't figure out how he was allowed to live this way, in a tarpaper shack with an outhouse."

"It's not part of the grid," Cyrus said.

"We're on our lunch break. They can't fault us for going off on our own if we're back in time."

"Chain of command," he said. "You got to respect chain

of command, Nancy. We're not even police yet. You go doing what you want to do, and you'll never be a police."

"I respect chain of command as much as anyone. On their
time, I'll do what they tell me to do. But this is *my* time,
right? You don't have to come with me."

But he did. So they had begun to walk, alongside the creek
and not in it, toward the shack that Nancy remembered. It
was farther away than she had calculated, and she soon realized they had gone so far that they could never get back in
time.

"Great," Cyrus said, glancing at his watch, "now we're in
deep shit."

"I think it's just around the next bend."

But it wasn't. Not around the next bend, or the one after
that, or even the one after that. They must have walked at
least a mile before Nancy saw the place she remembered,
across the creek and up a little hill. It was no longer visible
from the roadway, as it had been when she was a child. The
forest had taken care of that, creating a screen of trees and
vines. Only someone who already knew it was there could
find it.

Funny, she hung back at the sight of the shack, spooked
by the accuracy of her memory. It was Cyrus who splashed
across the creek, heedless of what the water would do to his
shoes and trousers, running up the hill, eager to be done with
this. A trick of sound brought them the whistle call of their
sergeant. They would never make it back in time, no matter
how quickly they moved. There would be hell to pay, double
hell for Nancy, whose insubordination would be assumed to
be evidence of a smugness born of her family connections.
Nancy crossed the creek by jumping from mossy rock to
mossy rock, almost losing her footing on the last leap.

In the doorway of the shack, Cyrus let out a noise that

started as a cry of exultation, then quickly faded into something more strangled and somber. His shoulders sagged as he leaned against the shack, and the structure seemed to vibrate from his weight, rippling like water.

"Stay there," he called out in a choked voice, but Nancy didn't see how she could. She climbed the hill to confront the consequences of her hunch.

The interior of the shack was shockingly cool for such a hot day. How could this little house of sticks, flimsier than anything the three pigs ever built, provide so much protection from the heat? Nancy felt herself shivering as her eyes adjusted, trying to prepare herself to see what she would never be ready to see.

A pile of used diapers was stacked in the corner, the smell almost comforting in its normalcy, although a quick glance revealed that the baby's waste had a sickly green-yellow cast. Plastic cups and spoons—ice cream or yogurt, maybe pudding cups—had been left in another corner and there was a whitish smear next to Olivia Barnes's mouth, as if someone had tried to feed her at some point.

Why feed a baby if you're going to kill her? Nancy thought.

"I don't know," Cyrus said, yet she had not spoken aloud, she was sure she had not. "I just don't know."

The baby's eyes were open, her arms stiff at her sides, as if she had died waiting for someone to hold her one more time. Next to her was an old-fashioned jack-in-the-box, rusted at the corners. It bothered Nancy, that toy. There was something almost obscene about it, with its faded but still garish colors.

She reached into her pocket and put on the gloves they had been given that morning on the bus, like kids on a field trip getting their tickets to the museum or planetarium. The cadets had been instructed not to touch anything if possible, but Nancy chose to ignore this directive, too. She was afraid she might cry if she didn't find something constructive to do. She reached for the box, and although she did not touch the lever on the side, it popped open instantly, as if primed for this moment. She and Cyrus both jumped at its squeak, then laughed weakly at themselves.

The monkey that emerged had a red and yellow costume of cheap sateen, and its plastic face had long ago lost the paint that defined its simian features.

"It's the weasel that's supposed to pop," Nancy said.

"What?" said Cyrus.

"Pop goes the *weasel*. Not the monkey." She closed the lid, turned the little crank, and, sure enough, that was the song it played.

"I guess no one knows what a weasel looks like," Cyrus said.

The fact that this conversation was inane was not lost on either of them. But they were young, and inexperienced. The cynicism that might steer them through such a moment was years away, bodies away, maybe even a lifetime away. Possibly there wasn't a cop in all of Baltimore who was hard enough to save this moment with a smart-ass comment.

Nancy turned the box around and then over. It was then that she saw the piece of masking tape inscribed with the proud, round shapes of a child who has just learned to write in cursive: *Alice Manning*. The name had no meaning to her then, but she could imagine a teacher telling Alice Manning, as teachers had once told Nancy, that her *A* should look like a sailboat going backward, that her *M* should be tall and strong, like an iron fence. A teacher would be proud of the girl who wrote these letters.

Nancy closed the lid, so the toy would be as she found it, and backed out of the house. Cyrus was already running upstream, splashing through the brackish water. He wanted to get there first, she assumed, to hog the credit for her hunch. But she misjudged him, it turned out. He just wanted to get away, to put as much distance as he could between himself and the dead child.

Nancy was thinking about Cyrus as she made her way along that same stream in the dark, her flashlight picking out a path. Again, the trip was longer than she remembered. Again, she rounded bend after bend, expecting to see the house, only to find it wasn't there. What if it was gone? How stupid would she feel, how silly?

The last time she had seen Cyrus was two years ago in Circuit City, when she and Andy were shopping for a new television set. He called himself a sales associate and he said the money was great, better than he had ever imagined. He was good at sales, much to his surprise. "Still a cop?" he asked Nancy. "Yeah," Nancy said, "but out in the county." He nodded, and Nancy detected a world of assumptions in that nod. Everyone thought they knew why she left the city. Everyone was wrong. And even if she told them, they wouldn't believe her. She wouldn't believe it either. Who would ever guess that good luck could be the worst thing that ever happened to a person? Mistakes—everyone made mistakes, and therefore could forgive them. Nancy had been derailed by her own freaky luck.

The shack had slumped over time, sagging as surely as Cyrus's shoulders had. Nancy hesitated at the foot of the hill, just as she had once before. Perhaps her young self had understood, in its dim subconscious way, the consequences of walking up the hill, of finding what she found. Would there be newer, harsher consequences if she walked up to that threshold again? But she had come all this way in the dark. She had to look.

Her flashlight found Ronnie Fuller in a corner of the cabin, knees drawn to her chest, rocking rhythmically. She squinted when the beam from Nancy's flashlight washed over her face, but said nothing. Nancy flicked the light around. No one else was there, alive or dead. There was nothing there at all. Just Ronnie, rocking back and forth, humming a little tune to herself.

23.

"She in there?" Infante asked when he returned to the tenth floor about 2 A.M., summoned by Nancy's page.

"Yeah," she said, drinking a cup of coffee she had just brewed, although she didn't really need the caffeine. Adrenaline was more than doing its job, keeping her alert and sharp, impervious to sleep.

"You talk to her?"

"We chatted, about nothing in particular. But once I got her in there and went down to the machines to get her a soda and a candy bar, she fell asleep."

"And you let her?"

Nancy knew Infante didn't mean his question to land like a rebuke, but it did.

"It's weird, I couldn't wake her for anything," she said, trying not to sound defensive. "I shook her arm, I all but yelled in her ear, but she kept sleeping all along."

"Sleeping all along," Infante repeated. "Well, then, let her sleep. And you, too. Squeeze in a catnap, and I'll keep watch in case she wakes up, and then I'll jump in there. Hey, how'd you know where to find her?"

"Hunch." An honest answer, Nancy told herself, just not a complete one. She would tell Infante the whole story in detail one day. One day, not tonight. Tonight, she found herself saying what she had said to Cyrus, her classmate, all those years ago. "I remembered this shack in Leakin Park from when my family used to go to the Millrace for crabs."

"No sign of the missing girl, though."

"None."

"Did she try to run again?"

"No. She seemed almost happy to be found. It's a scary place at night. It scared me."

The girl had, in fact, lifted her arms to Nancy, taking on a supplicant's posture that confused her. Then she realized: Ronnie was holding her arms out for handcuffs.

Nancy had not given any thought to the challenge of leading someone back along the dark, bumpy trail, much less a person in cuffs. She had assumed she was on a wild-goose chase for Brittany Little's body. Did she have to use the cuffs? The fact that Ronnie was so ready to wear handcuffs should be proof enough that the girl wasn't even thinking about running again. She had decided, after a fashion, to turn herself in.

But what if she did run, once back to the street? What if, once free of the dark, inexact shapes here in the woods, she pushed Nancy down, took her gun, or stole her car? *There's good Ronnie and bad Ronnie,* Alice had warned. *And bad Ronnie will do anything, and then good Ronnie can't believe she did it.* How could Nancy ever explain herself to Lenhardt, or the lieutenant, and all the way up the rest of the chain of command? She hated thinking things through this way, anticipating how she might fail and how others might react. But second-guessing herself was second nature to Nancy.

She had helped Ronnie Fuller stumble down the hill, her arms cuffed behind her, silent until they reached Nancy's car, a Toyota RAV-4.

"Is this a cop car?"

"It's my personal car."

"Oh." And then, as if it were a social situation and she had to say something, anything: "It's nice."

"Thanks."

Ronnie didn't volunteer anything more, allowing Nancy to buckle her into the backseat as if she were a child being put in a car seat. Nancy adjusted the seat belt so Ronnie could lean forward, making space for her bound wrists.

"Where's Brittany Little?" Nancy asked once they were on their way.

"Who?"

"The girl taken from Value City."

"A girl was taken from Value City?"

"C'mon Ronnie. If you didn't know a girl was missing, why did you run away?"

"Because you're a cop, right? You're the cop."

"I'm a detective who's investigating the disappearance of a three-year-old girl not even two hundred yards from where you work."

"No, I mean, you're *the* cop." She waited for Nancy's confirmation. "The one who found the baby. I didn't recognize you at first, but when I thought about it, I knew where I had seen you before. You don't look much different. You wear your hair the same way."

"How did you know what I look like?"

"My mom . . ." The word made Ronnie lose her train of thought. "Well, you were on television, right? Getting some kind of reward? And in the newspaper. Even later, after I was away, I saw you on television a couple of times. Didn't I?"

"Yeah," Nancy confessed. "Yeah."

They rode in silence for a while. Without the opportunity to make eye contact, Nancy didn't want to go too far into the subject of Brittany. But she could ask about Olivia.

"Why pudding, Ronnie?"

"What?"

"You fed Olivia Barnes pudding. We found these little pop-top single servings of pudding all over the shack. But if you bought pudding, you could have bought baby food. Didn't you know you should give her baby food?"

"We didn't *buy* anything. I took those puddings from my house."

"Oh." Nancy thought about this. Until asked and answered, the question had seemed portentous. All these years, she had been thinking about the pudding cups, and the explanation was so simple. Were all the answers as simple as this? If so, she might as well jump ahead, ask the only thing that mattered.

"Why did you kill her?"

"The baby, you mean?" Would Ronnie have to ask for clarification if she hadn't killed more than one child? The simple fact of syntax filled Nancy with hope and dread, for if she was reading it right, Ronnie was all but confessing and Brittany Little was already dead.

"Yes. Olivia Barnes. The baby."

Nancy could see Ronnie's shape in the rearview mirror, but not her face. She was slumped to one side, her cheek pressed against the window glass. She waited so long to reply that Nancy thought she was ignoring the question, or sleeping. But at last she spoke.

"She was sad. She was very, very sad."

Was Ronnie speaking of herself in the third person now? Was this the transition to bad Ronnie from good, or vice versa? Because surely a baby could not be sad, even in an eleven-year-old girl's parlance. Unhappy, yes. Bad or mad. But who would ever describe a baby as sad?

"How did you know the baby was . . . sad?"

Again, a long time passed before there was any sound from the backseat. "It's complicated," Ronnie said at last, sounding like Alice when she had invoked her "past"—

rehearsed, channeling words suggested by someone older. "It's a very *complicated* story."

She did not speak again for the duration of the ride. And now she was sleeping. Infante and Nancy studied her through the glass. In her T-shirt and jeans, she looked younger than she was. Yet she could have looked much older with minimal effort—a short skirt, a little makeup. That was the odd trick of eighteen, Nancy remembered. You could turn the clock forward or backward, be a kid when it suited you, or fool the world into thinking you were a woman. It was a time filled with promises. She had broken up with Andy the summer she was eighteen, taken a chance on the world at large. Then she ran back to him, realizing she shouldn't reject the great luck of meeting her soul mate at age fourteen.

"First she runs, now she sleeps," Infante said. "She's like a textbook example of guilt."

"She's got to be exhausted," Nancy said, a sense of fairness automatic with her. "She has had a pretty long day. And she seemed genuinely baffled when I mentioned Brittany Little."

"You're tired, and you're not sleeping. The only difference between the two of you is she knows what happened to Brittany Little and you don't. You think we should wake her up?"

"I'm telling you, it can't be done. She's dead to the world."

The words hung on, and Nancy wished she had chosen a different way to say it.

Yes, Ronnie Fuller slept, but there was neither innocence nor guilt in her sleep, just a lifelong way of coping with a world that bewildered her. She had always been able to sleep, in almost any circumstances. She had slept through the night at the age of three months. As a toddler, she had dozed in the backseat of the family car, wedged so tightly between her brothers that her father said they didn't need seat belts, not that the old Ford station wagon had any. She had napped in school, leading her teachers to suspect a chaotic home life that didn't allow her to get enough rest, and they were half right. Ronnie had a chaotic home life, but she got plenty of rest, which saved her from much of it. Her bed was her one private place in a most unprivate household.

And when her youngest older brother, Matthew, began trying to get into her bed when she was nine, she used sleep to keep herself safe.

Matthew was twelve at the time, and Ronnie had suspected for several days that he was planning something for her. So far, most of Matthew's plans for her had been cruel but tolerable—pinches, hits, endless "Punch buggies, no punch backs." If she weathered these attacks without comment or reaction, Matthew usually grew bored and found someone or something else to torture. Helen Manning had told Ronnie the story of the Snow Queen, and Ronnie quickly saw the advantage in having a splinter of ice in the heart, as long as you could take it out at will. She thought of herself as the Stone Queen, holding a pose in Freeze Tag. Ronnie had always been good at Freeze Tag.

On an August evening, the year Matthew was twelve and Ronnie was nine, he came into her room when the house was quiet, or as quiet as it ever got, with the living room television blaring into the night, her father's snores rising and falling. Matthew's hands were clutched at the groin of his pajamas, as if he had to pee, and he was holding himself so only the tip peeked out. It was the same way he held the baby field mice he sometimes captured in the Mannings' wild, overgrown backyard. Ronnie could see all this because her eyes were fake-squinched shut, allowing a tiny field of vision through her lashes. She had been lying there, barely breathing, waiting to see what Matthew was going to do when he came for her. She had known, somehow, it would be this night.

"Ronnie," he whispered hoarsely. "Ronnie, are you awake?"

She let out a sigh, the kind of half-murmur, half-talk sound that her father made when he fell asleep on the sofa after dinner, before moving on to an impressive crescendo of snores. She didn't dare try fake-snoring because she knew it would come out like a cartoon character, all whistles and lip-flaps.

"I've got something I want to show you." Matthew reached for her wrist, but Ronnie rolled over as if in a restless dream, pinning her arms in a tight V beneath her stomach, hands crossed at her crotch.

"Ronnie, Ronnie. C'mon, Ronnie, it's a secret, a really cool secret."

It was all she could do not to say, "It's not such a secret, dummo." She knew about sex, if not all its particulars. Her mother had miscarried when Ronnie was four, leading to an early overview of the facts of life. Cable movies and soap operas had filled in the gaps, and Ronnie had a general idea of what went where, what the consequences were, and the odd effect the whole enterprise had on men. She had even seen movies on television that explained why her brother was here, in the middle of the night. These things happened in families, according to the movies, but it was always, always wrong, even when the boy was handsome, which Matthew wasn't, and really loved the girl, which Matthew didn't.

But Ronnie would lose a confrontation with Matthew. He would hit her, she would yell, and her father would come in and dispense slaps all around, indifferent to what had caused the noise. The next night, Matthew would come back, the sequence would be repeated, and eventually, he would take what he wanted from her. As for telling her parents what Matthew was trying to do—well, it was too shameful. Ronnie felt she had to protect her mother from the truth about her youngest son—what he did to neighborhood merchants, not to mention cats, how he behaved at school. She had to protect her mother, in general, from the ugliness of life. Her mother didn't know how awful the world was. Her mother liked to talk about the old shows she had watched on something called *Picture for a Sunday Afternoon,* back when the world had only three channels. Ronnie didn't want her mother to know how things had changed, that children were so dirty now, that there were a hundred channels full of things no one should see.

Helen Manning was clearly sophisticated enough, but Ronnie would be even more ashamed to tell a neighbor about Matthew. This was back when Matthew was the bad one, the one headed for trouble and juvenile hall. Funny, he had turned out okay after it became clear that Ronnie was so awful that no one else in the family could ever be known as the bad one. Ronnie never forgot his face the day they came for her, the stunned, almost joyous look of reprieve. He didn't have to be the bad one anymore.

But this was two years earlier. On her stomach at the age of nine, arms beneath her, hands pressed over her private parts, he was still bad and Ronnie was good, or at least better than him. Smarter, too. She realized she was impenetrable as long as she kept up the pretense of sleeping. Perhaps an older boy, a more vicious one, would have kept going, but Matthew assumed he needed Ronnie's cooperation. The female body was mysterious to him. He would never find his way inside without a little help.

Matthew shook her by the shoulders, hissed her name in ever more ferocious whispers. He poked her hip with the hard novelty of himself, which really grossed her out, but it didn't feel much different from a finger, so she continued to sleep. Soon enough, she wasn't pretending. She drowsed through his whispered come-ons, neither asleep nor awake, until he finally gave up. Later, Ronnie heard that he got a girl in his class to do it, a stupid girl that everyone made fun of, and she was doubly glad she hadn't let him.

Even at Harkness and later, at Shechter, Ronnie never had trouble sleeping. If they hadn't kept her to such a strict schedule, she would have slept ten, eleven, twelve hours every night, and taken naps during the day. But excessive sleep was considered a bad sign at Shechter, so she gave it up. It was part of the price of staying there.

Tonight, she had slept a little bit in the old cabin, leaning against the wall. There had been nothing to do but sleep and wait. She knew she would be found. If anything, she had been surprised at how long she ended up waiting in the shack. The sky was still light when she closed her eyes, and it had been a little frightening to wake to such a deep, complete darkness. Most places in Baltimore were louder than Ronnie remembered, but Leakin Park was quieter and darker.

This was not her first visit back to the shack. She had ended up here, almost by accident, soon after she came home. It had seemed so natural, walking along Franklintown Road, tracing the old paths. She had always felt the park was hers, a secret to share with others. Ronnie had discovered the cabin the summer she was ten, and it had been hard to convince Alice to follow her here. Alice was such a scaredy-cat. But once Alice saw the cabin, she began to take over, making all these silly rules and insisting on her stupid games. "You be the student and I'll be the teacher." "You be the daddy and I'll be the mommy." "You be the fox and I'll be the chicken." "You be the kangaroo and I'll be the koala bear." Alice gave herself the best parts, which she said was only fair because she was the one with the ideas.

Ronnie slept. Ronnie dreamed. Her dreams were in black and white, like her mother's *Picture for a Sunday Afternoon.* She remembered them the way most people remember their dreams the morning after, in vague fragments. She was surprised, come the end of sleep, how hard it was to make a straightforward story out of what had seemed logical and normal in the night. Helen was often there, and Ronnie's mother, and now her doctor. Her dreams were neither scary nor soothing. They just were.

Back on Nottingham Road, Alice was awake, as she usually was at 3 A.M. Either she had inherited Helen's nocturnal tendencies, or she had come to imitate them early on. Even as a child, she had often been awake at 1 A.M., 2 A.M., 3 A.M. The night was full of interesting sounds that got lost in the daytime hours, such as freight trains that rumbled through, miles away.

Helen had never chided Alice about her wakefulness, although she did make a rule that Alice had to stay in bed, except for trips to the bathroom. "*Bedtime* means bed," Helen had decreed. "What you do in bed, and whether the light is on or off, is your own business. As long as you're not tired and cranky during the day, I don't care what you do at night."

Alice did not ask, but she assumed the same rules applied to Helen. What she did in her own bed, with the light off or on, was her own business. Although Helen didn't do things in her bed. When she dated, which was infrequent, she either hired a baby-sitter for overnight or kept the men downstairs. Once Alice was in her room upstairs, Helen took over the living room—smoking in secret, drinking in secret, watching television in secret. That is, they were meant to be secrets. Did she really think that Alice wouldn't figure these things out if she stayed in bed? The little house could not keep a single sound to itself. Ice falling into a glass, a match striking on the flinty strip of a matchbox cover, the muted sounds of late-night television, Helen's muffled laugh, a man's groan—Alice heard everything.

Her grandparents said Helen was permissive. Alice had overheard that, too, but it had required sneaking to the top of the stairs, something she did far more often than Helen suspected. The house was free with its sounds, but not so free with words, and if Alice wanted to hear a conversation or the dialogue from a late-night movie, she slithered out of bed, sliding across the wooden floors as if she were skating, otherwise Helen would hear her footsteps. The porous nature of the house cut both ways. The trick was to wait until the television or the stereo was on, which provided cover for the creak of the floorboards.

The other trick was to wear socks, because the floors were old and splintery. So Alice slid across them, one-two, one-two, one-two, as if skating to a waltz. She imagined herself in the kinds of outfits Helen had worn as a child, a short black skirt with a girl skater appliquéd on it, a woolen helmet that made Helen look like a bald turtle, cursive initials stitched into the side. "I hated that hat," Helen said when Alice paused at that page in the old photo albums.

Tonight, Alice's knees were tented under the yellow- and red-striped sheets on her bed, sheets she had picked out almost a decade ago, when Helen said she could help decorate her room. She had picked these sheets, bold and abstract, because she knew Helen would be disappointed by the ones Alice really wanted, which were pink and covered with rosebuds and little girls with watering cans. She liked these well enough, though, and they were certainly more suitable to an eighteen-year-old than the rosebud sheets would have been.

She examined the two round mountains created by her knees. If she had slept in these sheets every night of her life since she was ten, give or take a trip to her grandparents' house and sleepovers, assuming she was invited to sleepovers, these sheets would probably be worn in spots, beginning to fray at the edges. They had faded, but only because Helen hadn't thought to close the venetian blinds all the way. For seven years, she had let light spill across the bed, the spread folded down as Alice had left it on her last morning here. At night, with just her bedside lamp on, she couldn't see the subtle bands that ran cross-grained with the sheets' stripes, but she knew they were there.

She had a notepad propped up against the slope of her thighs and she was working on a letter, one she knew she would never send, but it was fun to write because it was about her. She had told her mother, who had seen her working on it earlier in the week, that it was a college application, and it could have been, for it was an essay in which she attempted to define herself in the curiously bragging-by-way-of-self-deprecating tone that she instinctively knew such essays required.

But it was not a college application. Alice was drafting a letter to the producers of the reality show on MTV, the one where seven people lived in a house together. She had no desire to be on the other one, which made kids ride around in a Winnebago doing stupid, messy things called missions. Everyone knew that was the show for the also-rans, the losers. She couldn't help noticing that there had never been anyone—how to put it—truly notorious on the show before. One boy had a brother who was murdered, but that was as close as they had come.

Now, it would be better, she knew, if her past were more accidental, if she had been convicted of killing someone, say, while driving drunk and was now in AA. Maybe she should start going to church and talking about God. It would help if she did something creative, too—wrote poetry or rapped.

The real obstacle, Alice knew, was that she was fat. The show sometimes had fat girls, but they were always black. The white girls were thin, thinner each year, so thin they could wear belly shirts and bikinis and navel rings. She wasn't sure why the black girls could be fat and the white girls couldn't, but clearly there was a rule. Come to think of it, not even the black girls were fat anymore.

Still, it felt good to outline her most interesting qualities in a letter, even if she never planned to send it, and no one would ever read it. People were always telling Alice she had so many opportunities, yet the only ones they could come up with were work and school. That didn't seem like so much to Alice. That seemed like what everyone else had. "You have your whole life ahead of you," Helen told Alice, and Sharon Kerpelman had said much the same thing. But Alice knew they were wrong. She had her whole life behind her, a huge, cumbersome weight that she had to drag with her wherever she went, like her own body. Such a life should be good for something.

She studied what she had written. Once enamored of cursive, she had recently discovered she wrote much faster if she printed. Her letters were now squat little capitals instead of the sedate ships that had once skimmed slowly across her pages. The new handwriting was still not fast enough to suit her, however. She would prefer to compose on her mother's computer, but she couldn't bring the computer to bed, and more important, she couldn't trust Helen to respect her privacy. Helen always swore she was the kind of mother who respected others' need for secrets, but, well, Helen was a liar. A big fat liar, and for what? Helen's lies made no sense to Alice.

Even here, in a notepad she can hide beneath her mattress, in a letter she will never send, a letter no one will ever read—even here, she does not dare tell the truth, the whole truth, and nothing but the truth, as they used to say on television. In her real life so far, no one has used that phrase. But then she never got to the point where she was allowed to testify, never put her hand on a book and swore to God. She had wanted to, but no one else wanted her to. In fact, the whole point seemed to be to keep Alice quiet. They kept saying it wouldn't be good for her and Ronnie to go before the judge without everything decided. They needed to reach an agreement outside of court. Alice didn't see how that agreement had helped her at all. The truth was on *her* side, not Ronnie's. And one day, when she was allowed to tell the truth, the whole truth, and nothing but the truth, everyone would finally be helpless before her.

She turned the page over and started a new letter, one that would be sent, when the time was right.

Sunday,
SUNDAY,
July 5
JULY 5

24.

Lenhardt unfurled a regional map across a desk. There were the sisters, Baltimore and Baltimore, city and county, joined but never merged, locked together like two chain-gang escapees in one of those old movies.

"Do you know what this is?"

"A map," Infante said. He was absolutely earnest. The sergeant had asked a question, and by God, the detective had an answer. Nancy started to giggle, only to end up yawning instead. It was 11 A.M., and she had slept for a few hours while Infante kept trying to rouse the sleeping Ronnie, but they were getting punch-drunk from exhaustion. They were also beginning to smell from being in the same clothes for more than twenty-four hours.

"Excellent, Detective Infante. Yes, this is a map," Lenhardt said. "But a map of what?"

"Baltimore?"

"No, my friend. It may look like Baltimore, but this is Fuckedville, U.S.A., our new hometown for the foreseeable future."

"Why . . . are . . . we . . . fucked?" Nancy yawned involuntarily between each word. Lenhardt had cursed in front of her. Things must be bad indeed. She wondered if this meant he could never go back to not-cursing in front of her.

"Don't be crude, Nancy." The sergeant's correction was

automatic and unironic. "The commissioner wants to do a search."

"We can't do a search. We don't have any information on where the child might be."

"No, but we do have a dedicated young detective who pulled a suspect out of Leakin Park late last night." Lenhardt nodded at Nancy. "Good work, by the way, although I wish you had told someone where you were going. And you should have used a car with a radio. Just to be safe."

"Pulled a *suspect* out," Infante said. "But she hasn't told us anything."

"We don't even have a charge on her," Nancy said.

"What's her story for Friday night?"

"Home alone." Nancy had managed to learn that much. "Parents were at a bullroast for dad's union, which matches up with what her mother told us. But she doesn't have any-thing to prove where she was from four, which is when she said she got home from the bagel shop, to eleven, when her parents came home."

"A teenage girl didn't make a phone call? Didn't get on a computer and do that weird talkie-typie thing they do? My kids can't go twenty minutes without making some kind of contact with their friends."

"She doesn't have any friends." Nancy remembered the mother's sad, resigned phrase. *No boyfriend. No friends. Period.*

"What about Alice Manning?"

"The girls claim they haven't connected since they got home. Alice admitted she went by Ronnie's workplace, just to get a look at her, but said Ronnie has no idea."

"That was weird, Sarge," Infante interrupted. "The girl comes in here, on her own steam, to tell us this story that puts her right there a few hours before everything happens. Then this lawyer shows up—a lawyer the girl called and left a message for before she headed in here—and the girl's suddenly saying that it wasn't on Friday, that it was a week or two ago, on a Saturday."

"Yeah, what was that about?" Lenhardt wondered, with no expectation of an answer.

What indeed, Nancy echoed in her head. Her best guess was that Alice, either out of well-intentioned helpfulness or a maliciousness nursed for seven years, wanted to make sure that no one overlooked Ronnie's proximity to the scene. She had lied. Or had she? Sharon Kerpelman said she had picked her up for dinner at eight on Friday evening. Four hours wasn't enough time to abduct a child, disguise her, stash her or kill her, then walk three miles home. But what if Alice wasn't on foot? And what if she wasn't acting alone?

"As long as the girl is missing, the commissioner wants a search," Lenhardt said. "He wants to make sure we look like we're doing everything we can. At the same time—and the commissioner told this to the major, who passed the word to me—he doesn't want anything to get out about how this case may be linked to any other."

He paused, making sure he had both detectives' full eye contact. "You understand what I'm saying? There's no advantage in us talking about Ronnie Fuller or Alice Manning until we get a charge on one of them. And even then, you gotta remember they were juveniles, all those years ago. No one's going to be able to drop their names into a court computer and make a match. If you talk about this, you're talking about stuff that's sealed, that nobody can get. It ain't public record."

"We're not the only ones who know," Infante said, and Nancy nodded. "City police who remember Olivia Barnes won't mind leaking what they know, because it won't come back on them. Hell, the kid's mother can tell anyone she wants that she called us because her kid is a dead ringer for the—for the other kid."

In her head, Nancy finished the sentence the way Infante had intended: *a dead ringer for the dead kid.*

"I hear the state's attorney met with the Barnes family and the father-in-law, Judge Poole, last night," Lenhardt said. "And swallowed a lot of shit, getting them to see it her way. But they were made to understand there's no advantage in allowing a single scenario to dominate. If the public starts thinking this case is solved, they stop noticing stuff that might matter. As long as we've got the damn Amber Alert out, we might as well have people paying attention to it."

"But a search," Nancy said. "It's such a waste of time and money."

"Only if you think of our job as solving cases. If you remember we have to jerk off the media from time to time— well then, the commissioner reckons it's a good show for a Sunday. Tonight, they'll have video of cops searching the woods. They'll report that we're working solid leads, which we are. But that's all they're going to report, right?"

Nancy flushed, aware that Lenhardt was staring at her, not Infante, insisting she make eye contact with him.

"Yes, Sergeant."

"Now, cut her loose, go home, and get some sleep."

"I'd like to have one more go, if you don't mind." Nancy nodded toward the closed door of the interview room. "I know we're heading into double digits, but she's slept for most of it. I just want one more chance."

"She never lawyered up?"

Nancy shook her head. "No. It's weird. She stonewalls like a veteran, but she never asks for a lawyer, never asks to make a phone call, doesn't seem to care if her parents have been notified. When she's not sleeping, all she says is 'I don't know. I don't know.'"

"Then why go in there again?"

"I've been thinking about the T-shirt we found in the

trash. It has blood on it, right? Blood that doesn't match the girl or her mother. It's gotta match someone."

Lenhardt nodded. He was much too smart not to have thought this through before Nancy did.

"See anything on her?"

"No, and I ran my hands over her arms while cuffing her, to see if there was anything there. But she's wearing long pants."

"So, what, you're going in there and hand her a penknife and say, 'Hey, could you poke yourself?' Ask her if she wants to shave her legs? Make a pact with her and become blood sisters?"

"Blood sisters," Infante repeated, but he was too tired to make it into whatever ill-considered joke had occurred to him.

"I don't know. Maybe she'll consent to give us her blood so she can be eliminated as a suspect."

"Except it won't, as you know," Lenhardt said. "It will just eliminate her as the person who bled on the T-shirt. We have to stay open to the possibility that two people were involved in this. In fact, I don't see how one girl does it by herself."

"Look, if the evidence doesn't go with us, even a moron of an attorney is going to know to make an issue of it. But if we can get a match, that's a better use of our time than sending every available body in the county over cold ground."

Lenhardt shrugged. "Go for it. But you gotta go home after, get some sleep."

The sergeant had brought them a bag of bagels that morning. Nancy picked out one of the sweeter ones, a blueberry, and took it into the interview room with an orange soda.

"Here," she said. "Breakfast of champions."

Ronnie was sitting, staring into space. Even awake the girl had an eerie quality about her, almost as if she drifted in and out of a semicatatonic state. Good Ronnie or Bad Ronnie?

"Where's this from?" Ronnie said, poking the bagel, then

pulling a small piece off and chewing it carefully, as if she might decide to spit it out.

"Einstein's, over on Goucher Boulevard."

"Ours are better. I mean, this is okay, but the texture is different. We use a frozen dough from Brooklyn, so it's almost like a New York bagel. Which is what people want, Clarice says. She worked another place where the bagels were too sweet—she called it a Montreal bagel—and that's not what people want in Baltimore."

"Clarice?"

"The manager at the Bagel Barn. You met her."

"Yeah, that's right. We talked to her after you ran away."

"Oh. Yeah." She seemed embarrassed and surprised, as if she had hoped the incident would never be mentioned again.

"Why did you run away, Ronnie?"

"I *told* you." Her voice was weary, but patient. It occurred to Nancy that the girl would never ask to leave, didn't assume she had any rights at all. "I knew you were cops, and I don't get a fair shake with cops. I didn't last time."

"How so?"

Ronnie shrugged. "It doesn't matter."

"Except you're here. So it does matter."

"I mean—no one believed me then, so why would anyone believe me now? People made up their minds what happened, so that's what happened."

Nancy had been sitting, an untouched bagel in front of her, trying to act as if this were an ordinary breakfast between two people who happened to be sharing a table in a crowded diner. Now she hunkered down, her chin barely an inch above the table, and stared into Ronnie's eyes as best she could. They were an unexpected blue beneath all that dark hair. Her brows were wild, her complexion a little spotty. But she could be pretty if she made the smallest effort.

"Ronnie, I can't undo anything you've done, and you can't undo anything someone else has done. But you can keep it from getting worse, you know what I mean?"

"No, I don't," Ronnie said, "because I don't know anything."

"Doesn't it strike you as kind of a coincidence that this happens so near where you work? And that—" Nancy stopped, still not willing to reveal the missing child's resemblance to the sister of Olivia Barnes. She needed the girl to volunteer that piece of information. Sharon Kerpelman had said Alice was suggestible, that she would agree to anything in order to be helpful. But Ronnie seemed far more vulnerable on that score.

Nancy pushed the photograph of Brittany Little across the table.

"She's pretty," Ronnie said.

"Does she look like anyone you know?"

"Yeah, yeah, she does. A little."

"Who does she look like, Ronnie?"

"Like Alice?"

"Like *Alice*? This girl is biracial and has curly hair."

Ronnie looked confused. "You're right. I don't know why I said that. It just popped out. Sometimes I say Alice. I don't know why."

"Ronnie, do you think about Alice a lot?"

"No." She paused. "Not a lot."

"It would be understandable if you did."

"Why?"

The girl seemed genuine in her need for a reply, almost yearning. "Because . . . because of the history you share. I would guess that's something you don't forget."

"Ever?"

"What?"

"Do you think one day I might forget? A man—a doctor—said I might. He said as time went by, I would have other things to think about, other things that would . . . define me."

Stumped for something to say, Nancy picked up the photograph and looked at the smiling girl. *Are you alive? Please tell me you're alive.*

"You know, we found her clothes in the bathroom." She wouldn't mention the hair, not yet. They didn't want that detail out. Not even the girl's mother had been told she had been shorn, in part because her own boyfriend might have done it, just to create the illusion of a stranger abduction. "There was blood on them. And blood on a T-shirt."

Ronnie's eyes were wide. "A lot?"

"Enough to worry us. Also enough to test—and guess what?" She waited a beat to see if Ronnie would volunteer anything. "It wasn't the girl's blood."

"How could you tell?"

"Blood's like a fingerprint. It's unique. It wasn't her blood, and it wasn't her mother's blood. We compared them."

"Huh."

"Yeah, it's amazing what we can do with a little blood. You know, if we took some of your blood and compared it to what we found, and found out it was different, we could let you go home."

"You want me to give you blood?" Ronnie stiffened and jerked her head back.

"You don't have to. But it could speed things up. We can take it from your finger, with just a little prick. You ever make yourself blood sisters with someone when you were a kid?"

Ronnie shook her head both ways, from a tentative yes to an increasingly vehement no. She was almost like one of those bobble-head dolls—once her head started to move, she couldn't seem to regain control of it. Only instead of swaying gently up and down, it continued to swing from side to side. "No, no, no, no, no, no."

"It's just a tiny prick, you wouldn't even notice. And if it's not your blood—and it won't be your blood, right, Ronnie, because you don't know what happened—if it's not your blood, we have to leave you alone."

"*No.*" It wasn't quite a scream, yet something in the girl's tone made Nancy jump. "Nobody cuts me but me."

"What?"

"I mean—I don't want to. I won't, I won't, I won't, I won't."

She began striking her palms on the table now to underscore her words until Nancy finally had to grab her by the wrists to make her stop. For one crazed moment the girl looked as if she wanted to bite her. Her small white teeth snapped near Nancy's face, the way a terrier might.

Then she went limp, and Nancy released her arms, letting her fall to the table. Cradling her head in her hands, the girl began to cry.

"Is Brittany Little still alive, Ronnie? It will make all the difference in the world if we find her and she's still alive. And if she's dead—well, we'll go easier on the one who helps us. I can't make a deal, I'm just a police, but it's always better to be the one who cooperates."

"I don't know. I don't know *anything*. Ask Alice. Take her blood. Ask Alice. Cut Alice." She looked up then, sniffing, and said the magic words. "I want to go home now. Can I go home now? Can I call my mom? Do I need to call a lawyer?"

"Yes," Nancy said. "I mean, yes, you can go, and yes, you can call your mom. You don't really need a lawyer, though."

Not yet.

She escorted the girl from the room to her desk, and let her use the phone there. As she walked, Ronnie was muttering to herself, and Nancy could just barely make out the words.

"Nobody cuts me but me. Nobody cuts me but *me.*"

25.

"You should go to her."

"What?" Cynthia Barnes snapped her head away from the television screen in the kitchen and fumbled without success for the power switch on the remote, as if she had been caught doing something illicit.

"You should go to her," repeated Warren, standing there in bare feet, his golf shoes in his hand so they wouldn't damage the stone floor. She still remembered their consternation when the contractor explained, after the fact, that stone could be damaged.

"I have nothing to say to her." But Maveen Little had finally disappeared, and the face on the television was a child's, beaming over an Esskay hot dog.

"You have something to share. Something in common."

It was all she could do not to snap back: *I will never have anything in common with Maveen Little.*

"I'm worried she's not going to engender a lot of sympathy," Cynthia said, picking her words carefully.

"Because she's unattractive and inarticulate?" Warren was being characteristically generous. Maveen Little was ugly, pale and overweight, with bad skin and a home permanent. "Oh, honey, people aren't that bad."

"They're worse, and you know it."

Warren had no answer for that, so he kissed her on the

temple, more of a father's kiss than a husband's, and eeled out the door, his last look for the television, which he clearly yearned to turn off. When had their kisses migrated from mouth to cheek to temple? Before Rosalind's birth or after? Cynthia couldn't remember. She supposed a day would come when Warren would kiss the top of her head, or settle for a fond shoulder pat, and she still wouldn't care. She loved him, possibly more than ever, but she just couldn't work up the abandon of man-woman love, not while trying to maintain the vigilance required by mother-child love.

This mother's grief was genuine, at least, the kind of grief that distorted face and voice. Not that anyone could really tell. People liked to say, after the fact, that they suspected the South Carolina woman was lying, that they were not surprised when her little boys turned up at the bottom of a lake. But Cynthia knew that people's powers of observation were anything but acute.

"Dear Black Bitch," a concerned citizen had written her seven years ago, divining her address from the numbers on the house, visible in some of the television newscasts, and the newspaper accounts of the crime, which helpfully identified the street. *"Who do you think you are kidding? Everyone knows you killed your baby and are trying to get the Black People to Riot again by saying White Children did this. I will be on my roof with my rifle. Just Like 1968. You have already destroyed the city and now the county is full of Negroes, too. When will you be satisfied?"*

The detached part of her mind, the part that had split away soon after Olivia was taken, marveled at the letter's punctuation and capitalization. Just Like 1968. It was as if the writer thought these words constituted a sentence, or at least a complete thought. Perhaps they did. "Just Like 1968" referred to the riots after King was shot, when white people ran for the city-county line, and the old men of Little Italy really did take their guns to the rooftops, ready to fire if they saw black people crossing Pratt Street.

Maveen Little would get letters, too. The cruelty would be different, more about ignorance than race, although her obvious preference for black men, as evidenced by her café-au-lait child and dark-skinned boyfriend, would draw a few choice comments. No, there would be no shortage of people happy to tell Maveen Little that she was a terrible mother, one who had earned her fate. If the crime proved to be connected to Olivia's death, Cynthia would come up for dissection again, would be drawn into the circle of blame for the sheer sin of continuing to exist. In the end, no one who had been spared by fate could afford to believe it was random.

Was Brittany Little's disappearance connected to Olivia's death? For the first time in years, Cynthia Barnes had read the Sunday paper cover to cover, but she had not expected to find anything she had not known twenty-four hours earlier. Although a civilian for almost seven years now, she had not forgotten the rhythms of the local news operations, the fits and starts with which stories moved forward over a weekend. Only a high-ranking official—the commissioner himself—could confirm that the new case might be linked to an old one, and he wouldn't do that unless someone knew enough to ask. Even then he might not be allowed to tell, because the girls had been juveniles the first time. She knew enough about the law to know that a jury would never be allowed to consider the earlier murder, not unless the girls themselves took the stand.

But eventually, someone would put two and two together, and then the calls would start. Reporters would finally track Cynthia down, and this time she would be happy to tell them exactly how she felt. Angry, betrayed, saddened. She would play up the sad part, although it was the least of her feelings. She would find a subtle way to remind newspaper readers

and television watchers that she was the one who had wanted
to find a way to put these girls away for life, not a mere seven
years. The public defender, the juvenile master, the girls'
parents—they had acted as if they were doing Cynthia a favor, fashioning the seven-year sentence from a trio of
charges. Instead, they had left the entire city vulnerable.

Assuming the cases were connected. She tried to keep her
mind open to the possibility that she was wrong, but Cynthia
could not see how the resemblance between her daughter
and the missing child was a simple coincidence. The hair,
the skin tone, the age—it was too creepily similar. *She*
would not have mistaken Brittany Little for her Rosalind,
but a nonmother, a person who had glimpsed Rosalind only
from afar, could make that error. A person who had studied
her, say, from across the street, or in the Giant on Edmondson Avenue. No, it could not be a coincidence.

But then, Cynthia could not accept the idea that Olivia's
death was coincidental, which everyone else, even Warren,
had been so ready to believe. Cynthia had seen a rebuke, a
conspiracy. "Why do they hate us so?" she had asked her father, all but crawling into his lap as if she were a child again.

The judge had patted her awkwardly, helpless as everyone
else. She had never seen her father without the right answer
before. But he was dumbfounded, incapable of explaining
how two seemingly normal children could do what they had
done. A lifetime of being a judge could not prepare a man
for this. Anyone who spent time in the Clarence Mitchell
Courthouse knew the city's killers were in the end utterly
fathomable. For one thing, they looked like what they
were—hard, soulless, dead inside. And they had come honestly by their status, via childhoods so damaging that one
wondered more at those who didn't kill than those who did.
They even had motives, however twisted. Judge Poole liked
to say that what the drug dealers of Baltimore did wasn't that

different from what the corporations of America did up the road in Delaware, where the federal courts heard cases on takeovers and poison pills. "It's just a little more direct," he said of the city's lethal transactions. "A little more final. But it's still business."

Yet even Judge Poole could not see the death of Olivia as anything other than the worst imaginable luck. Cynthia wondered if some well-meaning friend was holding Maveen Little's hand and trying to comfort her in that inept fashion she could neither forget nor forgive. *You couldn't have done anything. . . . You didn't do anything. . . . Don't second-guess yourself. . . . You must not blame yourself.* In the days after Olivia's body was found, nothing had made Cynthia feel worse than the people who had tried to make her feel better.

Should she go see the missing girl's mother? She wanted to feel something for the woman, but she didn't, and she wasn't sure she could fake it very well. Maveen Little made Cynthia feel shamed, as if there were an unwritten protocol for mothers deranged by grief. This woman was so, well, *sloppy* in her appeals to whatever phantoms held her child. Cynthia had maintained a dignity that some found cold—the "Dear Bitch" letters implied as much—but that was her upbringing. Her parents would not have wanted Cynthia to sob and fling her body about like some ignorant churchwoman. A hard, cynical person—someone like Cynthia's sister, Sylvia, or even the old Cynthia—might have thought, *I'd have snatched Brittany Little, too, to save her from that mama.*

Cynthia could never be that casually cruel again. Yet her sorrow for this woman was generic at best, distant. Part of the problem was that Maveen Little was white. More troubling, she was *poor,* tacky poor. What did Cynthia Barnes have in common with this frizzy-haired woman who shopped at Value City?

Well, black men. But the fact that Maveen Little was the kind of white woman who dated black men only made her more repellent to Cynthia. The boyfriend looked normal enough, and the jailed father had clearly passed some good genes down to the baby. But how could either of them, how could any self-respecting black man think Maveen Little was a prize? Her very name screamed white trash, not to mention the blobby body, the acne-pitted face, the hideous hair. It would be one thing if the Michelle Pfeiffers of the world wanted to go out with brothers, Cynthia could almost abide that scenario, where the black man was so fine that a woman couldn't help herself. But when you saw one of these pale, cheap-looking fat girls with a black man, the only explanation was that the man was looking for someone weak, someone who wouldn't call him on his shit. That was the true insult to black women: not the status that white women conferred, but the fact that black men weren't strong enough. What kind of coward would choose this woman?

And this was the thing about being a victim with a capital *V* that Cynthia could never make peace with. It was such a pathetic class, filled with losers whom she would never know, much less befriend. Cynthia did not wish her fate on anyone, not even the parents of the children who had destroyed her life. But that didn't mean she had to embrace other victims, bond with them, pretend they were related.

She had tried, because everyone said she must. In the early years, she had attempted to join two kinds of groups— one for victims of violent crimes and one for parents who had lost their children. But the first group had been filled with ignorant, uneducated people whose very stupidity had played a role in their circumstances. And the second group—well, the second group hadn't wanted *her*. Oh, no one had been so bold as to say that. The facilitator—apt title— had been ever so gentle when she came to Cynthia and sug-

gested she would be happier in another group, that losing a
child to a disease was profoundly different from losing a
child to a violent act.

Tell me about it, Cynthia had thought. But she was too
proud to go where she wasn't wanted, too proud to be seen
as the tacky one, bringing the whole group down. So she had
stopped going. Stopped going to groups. Stopped going out.
Stopped.

Funny, the one person with whom she had felt a real throb
of empathy was that famous guitarist, the one whose son had
fallen from a window. He was successful, able to provide his
child with the best, yet he had been undone by something as
simple as an open window. The rock star was vulnerable, she
knew, to a certain unspoken criticism. One ran that risk
when living an enviable life. People looked to see how your
very good fortune had caused your downfall.

That had been her sin, that was why God had punished
her. She was guilty of wanting to live an enviable life. It was
one thing to be proud, or vain, but Cynthia had invited the
world to look at her, to confirm her excellent opinion of herself. Toward that end, she had allowed the city magazine to
run photographs of her home, to show her and Warren posed
on their front porch, a power couple in the new city order.
"Barnes Storming," the headline had read. After all, he was
the most successful black plaintiff's attorney in town, turning lead paint into gold. She was the woman who controlled
access to the mayor, the voice in the ear, the gatekeeper.

She had not allowed the magazine to photograph Olivia.
Give her that much. She had not paraded her motherhood.
But she let it be known that she was one of those women who
was juggling, that she had returned to her job at the mayor's
office after a mere three months off—and gotten her figure
back in a remarkable six months. If she hadn't, she would
never have posed for that photograph. Because of the maga-

zine's long lead time, it had run two months later, a month before Olivia was killed. One of her more thoughtful correspondents had enclosed that photograph, scrawling "Pride goeth before a fall" across Cynthia's trim waist, which was emphasized by the fitted coral suit she had chosen.

Cynthia, thanks to her family's churchgoing habits, knew the letter writer had mangled the proverb: Pride goeth before *destruction*. It was a haughty spirit that led to a mere fall.

She turned off the television and went upstairs to dress. She wasn't sure what one wore to pay a call on a grieving mother who was in denial of her grief, couldn't remember what people had worn to call on her. Her outfit should be casual, but not too casual, brightly colored. Nothing black, nothing somber, nothing suggestive of funerals. If Cynthia Barnes could make one wish for Maveen Little's sake, it would be to draw out this limbo. That was something that only she could understand, that the rest of the world got backward. As horrible as this uncertainty was, the days of knowledge would be more horrible still.

26.

Although not much of a reader as a child, Mira Jenkins had never forgotten a children's book in which a girl was given an unexpected gift of a dime. Or was it a quarter? An impossibly small sum of money, at any rate, worthless by today's standards, but capable of purchasing a wealth of things at the dawn of the twentieth century. The girl in the book, dutiful and dull, considered various treats that she could share with her siblings—licorice whips, cookies, penny candy. Instead, she succumbed to temptation and purchased a strawberry ice cream cone, something that could never be shared among four children. The cone—surprise, surprise—proved unsatisfying, and the girl gave it away to another child. There was some moment of redemption, something to do with a kitten, and the girl vowed never again to forget the importance of sharing.

What a sap, Mira had thought at the time. The girl had earned the money. Her siblings didn't have to know she had been given a quarter, much less that she bought ice cream. Hoarding was not wrong, as long as one was discreet. The cruel thing was to enjoy something in front of others, and Mira would never do that.

So she felt no qualms about keeping to herself the maybe-tip from the anonymous caller. If she did the work and it turned into something, she would have earned it. If it proved to be bogus, a dead end, then no one need know she had been duped by a crank caller. The one thing Mira could not afford was being seen as gullible.

Or so she told herself late Sunday afternoon when she decided to drive to Maveen Little's house, having calculated that the reporters who had interviewed her during the day would have finally decamped. A search was on, she knew from WBAL radio. That was today's story. The mother was secondary.

Maveen Little lived in a West Side neighborhood known as Walbrook Junction, in a complex of low-rises built about a decade before Mira Jenkins was born. It was well kept, by the neighborhood's standards, with no broken-down cars or garbage on the grounds. Yet it was its middle-class aspirations that unnerved Mira. Every detail—the abandoned Big Wheel on a patch of dirt in the yard that was neither tended nor completely unkempt, the smell of spices and perspiration in the hall, the bedraggled decorations affixed to the hollow doors—only served to emphasize that the people who lived here wanted something more, and probably weren't going to get it.

"I'm looking for Maveen Little," she told the sullen man who answered the door, the boyfriend. She recognized him from television.

"She busy," he said. The dropped verb seemed to signify his contempt for her.

"I'm from the *Beacon-Light*—"

"Look, she's talked out. She got nothing more to say to the news."

Mira could hear low voices in the apartment, women's voices. One sounded broken and scratchy. The other was pitched lower, her words indistinct, but they sounded like words of comfort. So Maveen was talking, but she was talking to someone else. Another reporter? A cop? Mira conjured up an image of Nostrildamus, nodding and smiling at her, perhaps even handing her one of the fifty-dollar gift certificates that reporters got for going the "extra mile."

"It won't take long," she said. "One quick question—"

"Not today," he said, and closed the door in her face. In that bewildered split second, Mira actually considered sticking her foot between the door and its frame. But she was wearing new light-colored sandals that would show scuff marks. Besides, this guy would probably enjoy crushing someone's toes.

She went outside and sat in her car, the key turned in the ignition so the radio played and the air-conditioning blew. She felt humiliated, despite the fact that no one had witnessed her rebuke. *Failure is not an option, failure is not an option,* she tried to chant to herself, but who was she trying to kid? Failure was always an option. She was beginning to fear it was her only option.

What if she proved to be a failure after all? At this assignment, at this job, at this career—what would it mean to be a failure? For the first time, she dared to wonder if people she considered successful might be failures in disguise. Her father was a stockbroker, the old-fashioned kind who wasn't given to daring speculation or sexy deals, but he had provided his family with a comfortable lifestyle. Was that what he had set out to be? She had never thought about this before. Her father was a stockbroker because his father was a stockbroker.

The motto said: *If at first you don't succeed, try, try again.* But did that mean trying something new, or doing the same thing until you got it right? Did Nostrildamus want to be where he was, or had he coveted a different career path, perhaps at one of the big national newspapers? The world of medium-sized newspapers was not much different from those little Eastern European countries that had appeared after the Cold War ended. No one knew exactly where they were or why they mattered.

Tears pricked the corners of her eyes and she winked them away violently, even though no one was watching. She was trapped. She couldn't leave the *Beacon-Light* until she was perceived as a success, but she was afraid for the first time that she might not be. She had told herself there was nothing she couldn't do if she tried, but the lie was becoming impossible to maintain. There was so much she couldn't do, from physics to the simple act of rolling her tongue in that funny hot-dog-bun shape. She couldn't snap her fingers or whistle. She had been a semitalented dancer as a child, only to hit the wall of physical limitations in her early teens. She simply didn't have the extension she needed, or the right arch. There was no shortage of things that Mira could not do. Why should this job be any different?

She was so distracted by her own thoughts that she almost didn't notice the woman emerging from the vestibule of Maveen Little's apartment, a tall, regal-looking black woman in a killer dress, the casual kind that couldn't be touched for less than four hundred dollars, and that price didn't include the just-right handbag and the matching coral-colored slides. The woman climbed into an SUV, a BMW that looked much too nice for the surroundings, but Mira hadn't zeroed in on it before.

Eyes still moist, Mira reached for her pad and wrote down the license plate. She would ask someone low-level in the library to run it tomorrow, claiming it was connected to a neighborhood story on parking problems, and for all she knew it wasn't much more than that. But she had a feeling it was a lead, and a good one.

27.

Sharon Kerpelman was forever apologizing for her condo, which was difficult to find and not much easier to enter, with codes at the parking gate and the lobby. She also made excuses for its location, deep within the suburbs, and its willful sterility. She apologized because she expected people to expect her to be ashamed of a place that was clean, well kept, and bursting with amenities. She never bothered to explain that she had fled the city because she had suddenly realized she had endured enough charm to last her a lifetime.

That epiphany came while she was looking for an apartment in the Mount Vernon section, just north of downtown. The city had finally begun to develop some high-end rentals, but they were clustered to the east, near the water, or around the hospital complex on the western edge. Neither location appealed to Sharon, who thought her life might make more sense if she could walk to work, given that she never had time to exercise. An agent listened carefully to her wants and proceeded to take her to a series of ever shabbier places that didn't begin to meet her criteria. When she entered the apartment with the bedroom accessible only through the kitchen, Sharon muttered to herself: "Enough." Within a week, using only the classified section of the *Beacon-Light,* she had found her current place, in the Cedars of Owings Mills. Her mother was thrilled, but Sharon liked it anyway, because it was so obviously not what people expected of her.

She had always enjoyed confounding others' expectations. Even when she lived in renovated mill cottages and tacky rowhouses, she had surprised visitors with her taste in furniture, which ran to postmodern collectibles or good imitations. Messy at work, she was neat at home, obsessively so, with no patience for clutter. She loved people's puzzled glances when they came through the door, their attempt to reconcile public Sharon with private Sharon.

So on Sunday evening, as she waited for her visitors, she couldn't help wondering if they would notice how beautiful her apartment was. She sat in a Stickley chair, feet tucked beneath her, staring out the plate-glass doors that led to a tiny patio. The sun had just set, so she could make out her own ghostly image in the window. She liked what she saw, although she knew being a not-beautiful woman was supposed to be a tragedy. Not-beautiful was Sharon's coinage, and it was more or less accurate. Her features were even enough, her hair smooth, her figure pretty good. The only visible defect was the patterned birthmark on her cheek, and it was much less objectionable, in her opinion, than acne-ravaged skin. *Plain* might be the most accurate term, but it sounded a bit self-pitying, and *not ugly* sounded anything but. So—not-beautiful. She was not beautiful, not pretty, not cute. But she got by. In fact, Daniel Kutchner had called yesterday, but she was too busy to see him. Or going to be.

The doorbell rang. She had given both sets of expected visitors the two sets of codes, so she didn't have to buzz them in. She had also given her guests two different arrival times, so she knew who was on the other side of her door. Still, she checked the fisheye, just to be sure.

"Sharon, sweetie," Rosario said, kissing the air and getting a few strands of Sharon's hair caught in her mouth. Something alcoholic was on her breath, which Sharon expected, but still found shocking. Drinking was so *goyish*. Catholic, she amended, for Rosario practiced that form of semialcoholism based on wine and watered-down whiskey.

Even when viewed without a distorting lens, Rosario Bustamante was an odd-looking woman. Short and chunky, with skinny legs and virtually no neck, she was probably in her mid-fifties. No one knew for sure, as Rosario was famously secretive about her age. She was dressed tonight as she dressed on workdays, in a short-skirted suit that suggested she considered herself a knockout, albeit one who had lost interest about halfway through the process of dressing herself. Her blouse had a small rip at the neckline and, Sharon couldn't help noticing when Rosario reached for her, shadowy stains along the armpits.

"Did you have trouble finding the place?" Sharon asked, wondering if etiquette required her to offer Rosario a drink, when common sense dictated that the woman was probably bumping up against the legal limit already. "I know it's a hike from your place in Bolton Hill."

"Well, you tantalized the old cat, didn't you? I am most intrigued. *Most* intrigued. Are they—?" She stopped with uncharacteristic delicacy.

"I told Alice and her mother to come later, about eight-thirty. I thought we should speak privately first."

Rosario settled on the bright crimson sofa, a vintage piece of which Sharon was particularly proud. Yet Rosario seemed oblivious to her surroundings. Sharon wished she had offered her a drink, just to show off her Russell Wright barware.

"So, do you think the police are going to charge your—what should I call her? Your former client, I guess." The directness was typical of Rosario. For all she drank, she was never unfocused. And she seldom spoke of anything except law and politics, and the gossip that connected the two worlds.

"Alice," Sharon said. "Her name is Alice."

Before the juvenile judge, she had always been careful to use the girl's name, to make sure that no one lost sight of the little being at the center of all this. Sharon had figured out quite early that the anonymity designed to protect Alice was a double-edged sword. A specific person, a girl with a face and a name and two yellow pigtails, would have been so much less horrifying than the phantom pair of eleven-year-old girls who flitted across the news pages and danced on the tongues of shocked-looking anchorwomen.

"Alice," Rosario Bustamante repeated, nodding as if she approved of the name and it was key to her decision. "So are they going to charge her? Do they have a case?"

"I'll answer the second question first—no. They have nothing to connect her to this except her own well-intentioned efforts to help them. It's outrageous the way they've jacked her up just because a child has gone missing and the child happens to bear a resemblance to Cynthia Barnes's new daughter. Or so Cynthia Barnes told the cops. She's not beyond making this all up, you know. She's quite vengeful."

Rosario's eyebrows shot up. Her brows had been over-plucked into sideways parentheses. Clearly, she could not have sculpted such symmetrical shapes with her own stubby hands, but it was hard to imagine a woman paying someone to achieve such an odd effect. Rosario's appearance became more and more disturbing the longer one looked at her. There was a slight seediness to her—the odd brows, the misapplied lipstick, and, Sharon couldn't help noticing, the toes peeking out of her sandals. The blood-red paint had been sloppily applied, missing a few nails altogether.

"I don't want to take on Judge Poole's family, even indirectly," Rosario said. "That's a lose-lose for me."

"Agreed. I would never go at them. But I'm not going to sit by and see them try to destroy Alice twice over. They're not the victims *here*. Besides, we kowtowed a bit too much to the family's feelings the first time around."

"How so?"

"We—the other lawyer and I—agreed to a compromise so the girls could get seven years, keeping them inside until they were eighteen. We broke it into three charges—manslaughter, kidnapping, and larceny—and gave them three, three, and one."

"Larceny?"

"Would you believe the Barneses' baby carriage cost seven hundred and fifty dollars? Carriages are like cell phones, I guess. The light ones cost the most."

Rosario's very gaze was a judgment, an assertion that she would never make such a bum deal for a client.

"You have to understand the context." Sharon worked hard to keep her voice slow and measured, anxious not to sound defensive. "Cynthia Barnes was going to make a big stink. She was going to marshal all her father's cronies and lobby the General Assembly to drop the age of juvenile eligibility. She wanted to make it legal for ten-year-olds to be tried as adults, depending on the felonies committed. *Ten!* If she couldn't put Alice Manning and Ronnie Fuller away for life, then she'd make sure the next child who screwed up did serious time. It was a disaster waiting to happen. And the kids who bore the brunt of it would have been poor black kids in Baltimore."

"But your responsibility was to *your* client," Rosario said. "Not to your future clients."

Sharon had been sitting on the edge of the Stickley, bare feet tucked beneath her. Rosario's rebuke was not new to her—she'd had plenty of time to second-guess herself over the years. Hearing the words said out loud made her yearn to fling herself out of the chair and pace in frustration. But her feet were filled with pins and needles, so she stayed where she was.

"Why do you think," she said softly, "that I've asked you here? Why do you think I still care? I know better than anyone what I did. They had the girls' statements, in which each implicated the other, but the physical evidence was ambiguous."

"Ambiguous?"

"Based on the autopsy, Olivia Barnes's death could have been SIDS. Or brought on by shaken baby syndrome."

Rosario smiled. "Sharon, don't shit a shitter. As I recall, there was never any doubt that the girls did the deed. The main question was which one actually picked up the pillow and smothered the child, and whether it was an act of aggression or dumb panic."

Sharon valued Rosario's candor, for she knew how it felt to be misunderstood for speaking one's mind, for not wasting time with artificial niceties and oh-so-careful words.

"Alice was an accessory to one crime, the kidnapping. But whatever happened, the fact remains that she did her time—more time than some grown-ups do for manslaughter. She paid society back, okay, and now society is harassing her, trying to make her a scapegoat because of some freak resemblance and a coincidence of geography."

"Sharon—" Rosario's voice was as calming as a hand on one's sleeve. "Sharon, I would really like a drink."

It was impossible to deny such a straightforward request without asking Rosario straight-out if she was loaded. "Sure," she said, stamping her feet before she stood, to get the feeling back in them. "I have vodka and scotch."

"Scotch with a scooch of ice." Rosario laughed at her own wordplay. She had a gravelly, masculine laugh. Gossip, hardened into legend, maintained she was the illegitimate daughter of one of the city's most beloved mayors, and anyone who had seen his portrait in City Hall had to believe it was true. Daniel Florio in drag would have been a dead ringer for Rosario Bustamante. But Rosario didn't encourage the speculation, because her accomplishments would appear less impressive if there was a powerful patron in the wings, manipulating her rise. Rosario Bustamante's official biography was a Horatio Alger tale of a girl transcending her roots as the daughter of a Mexican cleaning woman to become the city's best criminal defense attorney. But there were tiny hints of connectedness imbedded in her résumé. St. Timothy's for high school, then Vassar and Yale Law. Sure, she could have done it all on scholarship. But how would a cleaning woman have known to aim her clever teenage daughter at the city's private school system? Someone had been whispering in Rosario Bustamante's ear since she was very young.

Sharon brought Rosario her drink, no longer caring if her barware earned her the woman's admiration.

"Rosario—I can't do this without you."

"I'm not sure you can do it *with* me. Pro bono holds less attraction for me as I near retirement age." She bared her teeth in a self-mocking grin. Everyone in the courthouse knew it would be decades before Rosario Bustamante died, probably at her desk, or in a summation. But she wouldn't shuffle off this mortal coil before she sent a few more judges and prosecutors to the edge of apoplexy.

"Helen Manning's parents have money." And Helen would kill herself before asking for it, Sharon knew. That's why a public defender had ended up representing Alice in the first place. But Sharon would persuade Helen of the importance of not being proud this time.

"Sharon, you *know* how I work. I take on cases that I can win, cases with rich clients or ones that are rich in publicity. This lacks the former, and you've told me you want to avoid the latter. I've wanted you to work for me for years, but why should it be on these terms? To put it baldly—what's in it for me?"

"Me. You'd have me, at last."

"How old are you now? Thirty-five? Forty?"

"I'm thirty-four." Sharon couldn't help glancing at her reflection in the plate-glass sliding doors. The sky was completely dark now, so she could see herself more clearly, and what she saw was a woman who, if anything, looked younger than she was.

"Not a comment on your looks, dear, just the sheer number of years I've been bumping into you around the courthouse. You were quite the prodigy when you started out. But for my office, you're long in the tooth. You know that."

Sharon did. Rosario ran a farm team, taking passionate young men and women straight out of law school, then working them to death. She reaped the benefits while most of her associates burned out and crashed, some leaving the law altogether. There was always a ready supply of associates because she was a brilliant lawyer. She had a great instinct for cases that looked open-and-shut for the prosecutor, but could be derailed by a little bare-minimum lawyering. People liked to say that Rosario Bustamante drank to level the playing field, and there had never been a complaint filed against her with the state bar, no matter how many nips she stole in the ladies' room during a trial. If Rosario Bustamante had been Daniel Florio's legitimate son instead of his bastard daughter, she would have been a power broker in the city, rising high in the judicial ranks or winning elective office. Deprived of her birthright, she took great pleasure in kicking the shit out of anyone with power.

"Sharon, you clearly have some family money"—Rosario indicated the surroundings with her chin. "You're one of the few who can afford the dignity of being a public defender without giving up the, um, *niceties* provided by private practice. And everyone knows you're a good lawyer. If you're intent on bailing, find a good firm with a partnership track. You know I'm never going to share the profits of my practice, so why bother?"

"Aren't you going to retire someday?"

Rosario laughed. "Why not just ask me if I plan to die? Yes, I'm going to retire one day, but not for quite some time. What are you planning to do, sit around like a vulture, in the vain hope you can take over my lease and buy my office equipment on the cheap?"

"I could learn enough from you to set up my own practice. Or I could run for public office."

"County council?"

"State delegate, more likely. County council is still a boys' club."

"It's a part-time legislature, dear. The jobs don't pay enough to make it worth your while to spend the three months in Annapolis."

"But *you* would pay me enough. And it wouldn't hurt you to have an associate who was in Annapolis part-time."

"Perhaps." Rosario paused, and Sharon wondered if she

was jealous. "Assuming you got there. But what would you do for me in the meantime?"

Without realizing what she was doing, Sharon knelt before Rosario Bustamante and took her hands. Rosario's knees were splayed—she was always careless about how she sat—and her pantyhose were an off shade of amber that made her legs look jaundiced. From this vantage point, Sharon could see the ladder of a run that had opened on the inside of the right thigh, reaching past the hem of the short skirt. Sharon felt as if she were bowing before a queen, waiting to be knighted.

"I know this doesn't appeal to you, because, if we do it right, there won't be any publicity. The best-case scenario is a case that never happens. The cops find whoever really did it, and leave Alice alone."

Rosario looked at her keenly. "But you don't think that's going to happen, do you?"

"No. I think they're going to find a way to put a charge on her—or at least get a warrant to search her mother's home, which will tip reporters that she's a suspect. If that happens, Alice and her mother are going to need a strong ally, someone who can hold the press at bay, spin the story in their favor. There's stuff about Alice that no one knows, stuff that would blow people's minds if we told. I'll do the work, you can go on mike. But please, please, Rosario, let's do this. I'll sign a personal services contract, give you the next five or ten years of my professional life if you'll just hire me, tonight, and let me work on this case."

Rosario patted Sharon's hair with a gesture that was somehow more fatherly than motherly. "Okay. Let's see where this goes. I hate to say it, but it could be fun. Now"—she shook her glass—"more Scotch, less scooch this time."

"One more thing—"

Rosario scowled, skeptical of being taken.

"The last time around, there was a sort of gentlemen's agreement that the two girls would, um—"

"Hang together?"

"Yes. In a manner of speaking."

"And who were the 'gentlemen' who made this agreement?"

"Me, I guess," Sharon admitted. "Me and the PD for Ronnie Fuller, the other girl. But it was at Helen Manning's behest. She wanted things to be fair."

Sharon slumped on the floor, remembering Helen's bizarre insistence that the legal proceedings must not escalate into a welter of finger-pointing and blame. *I don't care who did what, who thought of what,* Helen kept saying. *The important thing is that they be treated equally. It's only fair.*

"Sharon?" Rosario actually extended her high heel and prodded Sharon's midsection with the toe.

"What?"

"My drink?"

The doorbell rang while Sharon was at the bar. She all but ran to it, eager to introduce Rosario to "their" client. But as always, Sharon needed a moment to reconcile the wide-eyed little girl in her memory with the hulking almost-woman with the impenetrable ice-blue eyes.

She hugged her anyway. "Alice, we've got something wonderful to tell you. Rosario Bustamante is going to be your lawyer, pro bono, and I'm to help her. The Baltimore County Police won't be able to harass you now. They won't dare. You've got the best criminal lawyer in the area working for you for free. For free!"

Helen clapped her hands in delight. Alice looked to Helen, as if she couldn't be sure what to think until Helen

showed her the way. And in that moment, in that lumpy
moon of a face, Sharon saw the child she remembered, the
bewildered little girl who simply could not make sense of
what had happened to her life.

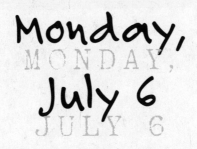

Monday,
July 6

28.

Midnight had barely come and gone when a fourteen-year-old boy in the county due west of Baltimore crept from his bed, took his father's gun from an unlocked drawer in the kitchen, and used it to kill his parents and his older sister. He then lifted the keys to his sister's Jeep Cherokee from the hook next to the kitchen door and managed to drive perhaps thirty miles before he was pulled over on I-70. Thin and small for his age, with large, owlish glasses that gave him a pronounced resemblance to a young actor best known for a series of fantasy films, the boy was still wearing his pajamas. Once the state police made it clear that they did not believe his story about his intrepid escape from a trio of crazed killers who had executed his family—a story taken, more or less, from a cop show he had watched Saturday night—the boy was asked why he had done it.

"I'm not sure," he said with a small sigh. "I didn't really have a plan per se."

"*Per se,*" Lenhardt repeated, after relaying this privileged piece of gossip to Nancy and Infante, who did not look much refreshed despite having devoted their last sixteen hours to attempted sleep. "*Per se.* 'I didn't really have a plan *per se.*' I guess that explains the pajamas. My friend in the state police can't get over it. He shot Mom and Dad while they slept, but big sister heard the shots and made a run for it. They found her in the hallway outside her room."

"Did something set him off?" Nancy asked. "A quarrel, a disagreement, some kind of abuse?"

"His statement at the scene is the only thing he's going to say for quite a while. He's being charged as an adult, and his lawyer is already hinting that he'll have all sorts of fascinating revelations to make, when the time comes. The important thing is, come tomorrow, no one's going to care what we're doing. We're already B-3."

"Be what?" Infante asked on a yawn.

"B-3," Lenhardt said, pointing out the page of that number in that day's *Beacon-Light*. "Eight paragraphs on the search, nothing more. Now we can fly beneath the radar for a couple of days at least, try to do some police work. Kid who kills his family trumps missing-and-presumed-dead kid."

Nancy felt equal parts relief and dismay. "What? The Baltimore metro area can't stay interested in two crimes at once?"

"They can barely stay interested in one," Lenhardt said. "Nobody can, anywhere. The whole country's got attention deficit disorder, but the kids are the ones on Ritalin. You know, I bet this kid was on Ritalin."

"C'mon, Sergeant. You're not suggesting Ritalin made him kill his parents and his sister." Nancy's reproof was simply chatter, something said to keep her end up while her morning-numb brain was still trying to clear. She loved the way cops talked to one another when alone, the certitude, the absolute conviction. In public, they had to speak of suspects, of allegations and beliefs and evidence, then wait for juries and judges to validate their work. Here, among themselves, they could speak the truth as they knew it. This boy had killed his parents. H. Grayson Campbell, the rich guy who had eluded Lenhardt, had managed to arrange his wife's death and disappearance. Alice Manning and Ronnie Fuller were liars. What they were lying about remained to be seen, but they were definitely lying.

"No. I'll let the lawyer who rushed out to the Westminster barracks to offer his services connect those dots. He's got a great case. After all, he can always ask the jury for leniency on the grounds that his client is an orphan."

He popped his eyes, prompting Nancy and Infante to laugh dutifully at the old joke. Chain of command—detectives laughed at the sergeant's jokes.

"Now," the sergeant said, hitching his chair closer to them and lowering his voice. "Let's talk about blood."

"We don't have any," Nancy said, worried that this was her fault. "I couldn't trick Ronnie into giving us a drop, and Alice has that pit bull of a lawyer now." She pushed him the fax that had been waiting for them when they arrived this morning, the announcement that Sharon Kerpelman had resigned from the public defender's office and would be representing Alice Manning in conjunction with Rosario Bustamante.

"Pit bull? You mean bull *dyke*," Lenhardt said.

"I think Bustamante might go that way, but not the young one," Infante said quickly, as if he had spent some time thinking about this.

"Anyway," Nancy said, "we don't have blood samples and we're not going to get them unless we've got probable cause for a warrant. Which we don't."

"These girls were the state's guests for seven years," Lenhardt said.

"Right. So?"

"So, you know anyone who goes seven years without going to the doctor?"

"I haven't been to the doctor for ten years," Infante said.

"I'll rephrase the question: You know anyone *normal* who

doesn't see a doctor? Especially in lockup, where it gets you out of stuff? Let's get the medical records for both of them, see what we find. At the very least we could get a blood type."

"Blood type's only good for eliminating, not verifying," Nancy said.

"I'd be happy to eliminate someone at this point," Lenhardt said. "I've still got Bates from Family Crimes looking into the boyfriend's priors, shaking his tree. The sooner we figure out which road we need to travel, the better off we'll be."

"Will Juvenile Services give us the records just by asking?"

"Maybe. But let's get a subpoena, just to be on the safe side." Lenhardt checked his watch. "It's almost nine. Get the paperwork done, and try to catch Judge Prosser about eleven-thirty. He'll sign anything that's standing between him and lunch."

Mira Jenkins had to stifle a whoop of triumph when she read the e-mail from the library staff: The SUV she had seen outside Maveen Little's apartment was registered to Warren Barnes of Hillside Drive. She knew from reading the clips that Barnes was the name of the girl who had died, that Warren was the father and Cynthia the mother. And although the electronic database didn't provide photographs, how could the woman she saw outside Maveen Little's apartment be anyone but Cynthia Barnes? The two crimes must be connected, just as her caller had promised.

So how to proceed? If she asked the county cop reporter for help, he'd want in on the story, might even steal it from her, only to have downtown take it away from both of them. If she didn't ask him and tried to work the cops herself, the information might circle back to the beat reporter, and then she'd be guilty of breaching protocol.

She studied her e-mail again. The librarian on duty had provided not only the registration, but also a thorough Auto-Track of the car's registered owner. People would be shocked if they knew what computers kicked out about their lives. Here was Warren Barnes's address, his driving record, and even information on his mortgage. The AutoTrack could also find boat ownership, pilot licenses, and years of old addresses and phone numbers. But the Barnes home phone was unlisted, and unlisted numbers were stubbornly elusive. To talk to Cynthia Barnes, Mira would have to drive to her home, an out-of-the-way errand that would be difficult to conceal within the framework of her day. Maybe she could find a feature down there, claim she was going to Woodlawn or Catonsville to chat up neighborhood sources, see what stories she could develop.

Her editor, a short, rotund man who moved too stealthily for Mira's taste, suddenly loomed over her shoulder, thrusting a press release in her face. Reflexively she closed her e-mail, not wanting him to see what was on her screen. Not that it would mean anything to him. Her editor had worked at the paper only three years. The name Warren Barnes wouldn't resonate as anything more than that of a well-known attorney.

"We need some dailies to get downtown off my ass," he said. "See what you can do with this."

This was a press release announcing that the library system had contracted for a special translation program that provided help for patrons in hundreds of languages, via a phone bank in California.

"It could be more than a daily," Mira said, seeing an opportunity to get out of the office, slip the short leash on which he tried to keep her. "Instead of just doing a talking heads piece, why not make it a centerpiece feature? I could go to one of the libraries in northwest, where they have a lot of Russian immigrants, see the system at work. Talk to librarians, see if other library systems have used this program. Plus, we need census figures, don't we? How many foreign-speaking library patrons does Baltimore County have? Or maybe I should try the Catonsville branch—"

"Do whatever you like," the editor said. "Just make sure I have ten to twelve inches by four P.M. My kid has a T-ball game tonight and I need to get out of here by six."

Mira glanced at the clock in the upper right-hand corner of her computer. It was almost eleven. Even if she reached the bare-minimum sources on the first try, she would probably be reporting the story until two, and she would need another two hours to write because she wasn't very fast on bureaucratic stories. Give her a straight narrative line and she could pound it out. Her infamous story on the civil rights park may have been bogus, but no one ever said it wasn't well written. Feature stories flowed out of her. So would the Barnes piece, once she nailed it. Now she would have to resign herself to eating lunch at her desk, knocking out ten to twelve inches by four, then spending another tedious hour answering whatever inane, trivial questions the editors raised. But if her boss really left at six, she could be out of here by six-thirty. A high-powered woman like Cynthia Barnes probably had some big job in the private sector now, and wouldn't be home during the day anyway.

Mira dialed the number to the county library flack and got voicemail. Sighing, she left a message, then flagged down a colleague and asked him to bring her a Greek salad and Diet Pepsi from the deli.

Nancy and Infante caught Judge Prosser before lunch, as Lenhardt had recommended, which made him impatient and grumpy. They could have done it with a state's attorney, but the state's attorney said he'd rather the judge sign off on it,

given that another state agency was involved. Nancy wondered if the state's attorney was setting them up. Prosser, a
short, fat man with a left eye that wandered when he removed his thick glasses, was picking apart their request,
stabbing at typos with the earpiece of his horn-rims.

"*All* their medical records? Why should you get access to
all their medical records when all you want to know is their
blood type?"

"If we specify blood type and it turns out they actually
have DNA samples on file, for whatever reason, God forbid
that a smart attorney says we overstepped," Infante said,
adding a beat late, "Judge."

"Is that the real reason or a glib, cover-your-ass reason
that you just made up on the spot?"

"Can it be both?" Infante asked.

Another judge might have smiled, but Prosser trained his
right eye on the document in front of him while his wandering left rolled toward the window. Nancy, whose stomach
growled when she was standing over a corpse, found herself
mildly ill watching the judge's eye.

"Seems thin," he said. "Mighty thin. Girl disappears,
there's some blood on her jumper and a T-shirt, but it's not
hers and it's not a relative's. You want to see if you can
match the type to these two girls who killed the Barnes child
all these years ago because Cynthia Barnes called you and
made some noise. I can understand why the city cops might
jump when Cynthia Barnes called, but why do you care, Detective?" He directed his question to Nancy, then didn't wait
for an answer. "Isaac Poole is a city judge."

"Eliminating the girls as suspects would be helpful, too,"
Nancy said. "We're going in a lot of different directions on
this case, and we'd like to narrow it down, be more efficient."

"Such as?"

"The boyfriend. It's really irksome—" Oh lord, what a

stupid word. She wished she could take it back, but she couldn't. "It's troubling that not a single security camera in the mall yielded even a frame that shows the girl was there. We're also doing checks on the custodian who claims to have found the clothes."

"You know how many kids get *kidnapped*-kidnapped in Baltimore in a year? I mean, stranger abductions, with ransom notes and everything? One or two, maybe. Most missing children are runaways."

"This child is three years old, judge."

He scowled. "I know that. But why aren't you going after the boyfriend's blood?"

"He provided a sample, and it didn't match," Infante said. "We're continuing to talk to him and the mother, looking for anyplace their stories fall down. I gotta say, though, they're pretty consistent. And city Social Services doesn't have anything on 'em, not even a neglect call."

"You say their stories are consistent. But are they too consistent? Consistency is often the hallmark of something that's been rehearsed. The hobgoblin of little minds, as Emerson would have it."

Nancy, having already risked offending the judge, restrained herself from rolling her eyes. People who quoted other people were show-offs, plain and simple. "The mother seems genuinely grief-stricken. The boyfriend is sorry that his girlfriend is upset, if you get the distinction."

"He's not so unhappy to see the little girl gone?"

Nancy hesitated. The judge, for all his bluster and bullying, had managed to identify the one thing that disturbed her about the boyfriend. He seemed surprised by the profundity of his girlfriend's grief, almost sullen about it. On Saturday, when Nancy and Infante had visited the couple and continued to question them, albeit in the guise of offering them sympathy and support, the boyfriend had held his weeping girlfriend and said: "You still got me, babe. You still got *me*." But that could be because he had, in his heart of hearts, wished the child away and was horrified to realize the consequences of seeing his wish come true.

"He's not the child's father," Nancy said at last. "And given the way things are, I don't think he was planning on being her stepfather. He was living with a woman, the woman happened to have a child. Was the girl a nuisance at times? I'm sure she was. Was she enough of a nuisance that he wanted to get rid of her, or would hurt her in a fit of anger? We can't say. It wouldn't be the first time, though."

Infante leaned in. "The missing girl and the Barnes child really do look alike, judge. It's uncanny. I mean, it could be a coincidence, but it's a hard one to ignore."

Harder to ignore, Nancy thought, that neither Ronnie nor Alice seemed to know about the Barnes child. But maybe that was what they were trying to conceal.

"Especially with Cynthia Barnes and her father breathing down your necks," Judge Prosser replied, putting his glasses back on, which pulled his left eye back to center. "Very well. I'll sign this. Although I'll be surprised if they can even find the records. There are days when the juvenile system can't find the kids in its custody, much less their paperwork. And they may have already forwarded the medical files to the girls' private physicians."

"The girls just left state custody in the past eight weeks. We're counting on the state not being that efficient."

"In my experience, it's only efficient when you don't want it to be," the judge said, chuckling at his own wisdom. He added, almost as an afterthought, "I hope you find the little girl and that she hasn't suffered. Just don't be taken in by the Royal Family."

"The Royal Family?"

"Isaac Poole and his daughter. They think everything is about them. And what's not specifically about them, to their way of thinking, is about their race. You should hear him bitch and moan about his career when he's lucky to have gotten as far as he did. Very paranoid, these people."

Nancy took the signed subpoena and left. But she wanted to ask the judge if the Barnes family had always been this way. It seemed to her that a woman whose child was kidnapped and murdered had come by her paranoia pretty honestly.

Ronnie had shown up for work at the Bagel Barn that morning, trying to act as if nothing had happened. "I clocked you out," Clarice said, and Ronnie nodded her thanks. After that, there was no mention of Saturday's events until the late morning lull.

"So you in trouble?" Clarice asked, her voice casual, as if the answer didn't matter.

"Maybe," Ronnie said. Then: "Yeah, I guess I am. But I didn't do anything. Honest."

Clarice shook her head. She was a black woman living in Baltimore. She knew a lot of people who were in trouble and hadn't done anything. She also knew people who were in trouble and had done something, but maybe not the something for which they were in trouble. And she knew people who were in trouble and had done the very thing of which they were accused, but still had good reason to lie about it. They said confession was good for the soul, and perhaps it was. But it was hell on the body. She had boys in her family, nephews and cousins, who had come out of lockup with lumps and bruises, still halfheartedly denying the charges hanging on them.

Ronnie—well, Ronnie didn't have a mark on her, unless you counted her eyes. Dark, dark blue, they reminded

Clarice of pansies, but not the fresh ones you saw in window boxes, holding their heads up to the sun. Ronnie's eyes looked like flowers after a heavy rain, their little faces pounded flat into the earth.

29.

Cynthia Barnes was no longer interested in food, but she insisted on preparing elaborate dinners for Warren even in the heat of summer. Tonight, it was grilled tuna with a mango-papaya relish and cold tomato-corn soup, served with jalapeño corn muffins. The muffins had been baked in an old pan of her mother's so they came out looking like miniature ears of corn. It was all delicious, all perfect, but the only part of the meal that interested Cynthia was the pinot noir that Warren selected to accompany it.

"This is wonderful," he said, brave and polite. Warren had never outgrown his plebeian palate. He would eat sausage and ham and meatloaf every night, if he could. He would also weigh three hundred pounds and have hypertension and diabetes. But as Cynthia had told him when Rosalind was born, "I'm not planning on raising this child alone. You can choose your vice, but you get only one—workaholism, gluttony, drink. For I am definitely not raising a child alone."

He had not said then what he never said. And perhaps he never thought it, either, but Cynthia did. If she were Warren, she would think it every day. *If only you had raised our first baby instead of leaving the job to some dumb girl.*

She had yearned for this reproach for seven years, only the blow never landed. Yet she could not bring herself to ask the direct questions that would force him to say what he thought of her.

Sometimes she felt it was these unsaid things, not the loss of Olivia, that weighed them down. Other times she wondered if they had made a silent pact to sacrifice their marriage as a tribute to Olivia. It would be wrong, wouldn't it, for them to be happy again? Sometimes, with Rosalind, she had an unguarded moment of happiness and it terrified her. To be happy was to forget. To forget was to risk it all again.

"Did you know," she asked her husband, "that tuna costs as much as steak?"

"Get out."

"More, sometimes. As much as a good cut of New York strip, per pound. Of course, there's no bone, no fat."

"That's true."

She wondered if he slept around. She might, if their roles were reversed. He was, if anything, more handsome than when they met and so much more accomplished. Her parents had been critical of them in their early years together, chastising them for their luxury-filled life and the debts that it carried. But they were rich now, richer than anyone suspected, despite the fact that Warren's victories were a matter of public record. They were actually living below their means, piling up money they no longer had the heart to spend, except on Rosalind and her future.

Olivia had a college fund of five thousand dollars when she died, Cynthia suddenly remembered. Even their accountant had been flummoxed by the tax implications of that. They had left it, gathering figurative dust, thinking it might show up one day in those "unclaimed account" advertisements. When Rosalind was born, they were allowed to roll it over without penalties.

"Do you like this wine?" Warren asked.

"I love it," she said, her fingers tight on the stem of her glass. In fact, she knew no better sensation than the first taste of wine she allowed herself each evening, unless it was the caffeine jolt that started her day. Those were her two mileposts, the signs that she had survived another day, another night. The subsequent sips were never as good, but the first ones were fabulous, like the first bite of an apple.

"Should I get a case? They discount by the case."

"I don't see why not."

A better woman would have set him free, and done it in such a way that no one would think less of him. *She* should have had an affair, or a breakdown, or both. Warren was simply not as damaged—not because he was a man, but because he did not shoulder as much of the blame. Maybe Cynthia should find him a new woman. A few years back, the local paper had run one of those interminably long stories about a woman who had destroyed her own health to give her husband a baby. Ill with cancer that she blamed on the fertility treatments—with no scientific basis, Cynthia couldn't help noticing—she had picked out her husband's next wife. With a supreme arrogance that Cynthia could almost envy, she had looked over her friends and settled on one who had never married, and made it clear that she would consider it an honor to her memory if the friend and the husband hooked up after her death. At the time, Cynthia had read it with her usual dismissive attitude toward any woman who dared to think she had suffered.

"White people are *crazy,*" she kept exclaiming to Warren at intervals, yet she read every installment of the story, fascinated by the dying woman's sly cruelty. It was clear that she had not chosen her best-looking friend, or her most accomplished one, but one who could never upstage her. The woman died before her daughter was two. The husband and the friend married two years later. Cynthia gave them five years, tops. Living with a ghost was tough.

At least Olivia was an undemanding little wraith, so generous with those she had left behind. She never complained, never castigated. She had been colicky as a baby, but she was peaceful now, asking only that they not forget her.

"I love this cornbread," Warren said.

"Guess what—it's low-fat. And that spread you're slathering on isn't margarine, it's yogurt."

"I'll live."

"That's the general idea," Cynthia said. "For you to live."

The joke—that Warren could barely endure Cynthia's attempts to keep him healthy—was an old one, yet they had never expressed it so baldly before, and the starkness of her words made Cynthia want to wince. That had been the general idea for Olivia, too. To live, to grow up, to take advantage of all the things to which she was entitled, by birth and blood and class and education.

She forgot sometimes. For up to an hour at a time, she might forget that she was the mother of a murdered child. But Rosalind changed everything. She could not look at Rosalind without thinking of Olivia. She was the tuna steak to Olivia's New York strip. Just as precious, better for them in some ways, but Cynthia couldn't help preferring one over the other. Warren probably felt the same way, too, but that was another conversation they could never have. They worried more about Rosalind, yes, and their imaginations had been stretched to limits that other parents could not fathom. It was one thing to get your old body back after pregnancy, another to reclaim a mind flabby with fear and anxiety. They could not love Rosalind as much as they loved Olivia because they knew she could be taken from them.

"You okay?" Warren asked.

"I'm fine."

"You're not eating."

"Oh, I don't have much appetite when it's hot like this."

"You keep the A.C. so low that you're wearing a sweater."

She was, a coral-colored silk cardigan.

"But I was running around today, getting things for dinner. You know me, I can't just go one place. The produce stand for the vegetables, Nick's for the fish. They say not to eat fish in restaurants on Mondays, but that doesn't apply to the fish you buy on Mondays, does it?"

"I hope not."

The doorbell rang, and Cynthia was up before Warren could push away from the table. The heavy wooden door had a small square with an iron grille. Between that and the tight mesh of the screen beyond, it wasn't easy to make out the figure on the porch. A white girl, a well-dressed one, whippet-thin and holding a notebook.

Cynthia opened the door only to say: "I can't talk to you." The reporters weren't supposed to come yet. It wasn't time to grieve just yet.

"Mrs. Barnes? My name is Mira Jenkins and I'm a reporter at the *Beacon-Light* and I have information that the disappearance of Brittany Little could be tied to the death of your daughter."

"I can't talk to you," she repeated.

"Not even on background?"

Cynthia was amused in spite of herself. The girl was like a mechanical doll, spewing her limited vocabulary. "Do you even know what that means? On background?"

"Well, sure. It means, you tell me if stuff is true, but you don't put your name to it."

"And can you use it, then? Or do you have to get someone else to confirm it? Or can you use it but attribute the information to a 'source'?"

"I—I don't— Look, you tell me the rules you want to use, and I'll adhere to them. But I don't know why you would call my office and tell us about the investigation if you don't want it in the papers."

The mechanical doll was suddenly a little less adorable. "What makes you think I called? I haven't talked to the press for seven years. When I worked for the mayor, I never spoke to the press for the record. Why would I start now?"

"Well, somebody did. Somebody who knew a lot about your case. And then I saw you at the other woman's apartment yesterday."

Cynthia looked back over her shoulder. Warren had not come out of the dining room. He was moving through the house, but it sounded as if he were cleaning up, clearing the table, starting the dishwasher. A good habit, one instilled by his mother. His footsteps, the running water, provided cover for her voice.

"I'm going to invite you in now," Cynthia said. "We're going to sit in the living room and talk, over iced tea. Well, iced tea for you, wine for me. When my husband comes out to see what's up, we're going to tell him you're a student in the political science department at UB and your teacher recommended you talk to me about city politics. He'll go upstairs to watch television, read his newspaper. Then—and only then—we will talk about *that*."

"On the record?"

Oh, she was a greedy girl. Offered half a loaf, she asked for a whole. Cynthia admired that trait. It was one that had taken her far in life.

"Don't get ahead of yourself," she told the girl, using the warm mentor voice that she knew young women loved, the voice that she had used on her office interns. "But if you do what I tell you, exactly the way I tell you, you'll get your story."

30.

Alice kept her eyes downcast as she walked, studying the ground. The sidewalks in Ten Hills had buckled in places, swollen by the roots of the huge oaks and elms. The uneven pavement made it easy to stumble here, especially in the gray-green twilight, and Alice hated the sensation of stumbling. It was much worse than falling, when people felt obligated to express sympathy or hold out a hand. Tripping just made you look silly and clumsy.

But Alice was staring at the sidewalk because she didn't want to make eye contact with Sharon Kerpelman, who had insisted on accompanying her tonight. Her lawyer had arrived at the Mannings' house at almost the exact moment Alice began scraping the bottom of her bowl with her spoon, chasing the last raspberry drips of what Helen insisted on calling sorbet.

"Just passing by," Sharon insisted, as if Alice didn't know where Sharon lived and worked, as if Helen's guilty bustling with the dishes didn't prove they had arranged this chance encounter. Which meant that Helen and Sharon had talked, outside Alice's hearing. Alice did not approve of this. It was one thing for them to set up the meeting with the other lawyer, that ugly woman. But she didn't want them to get into the habit of talking behind her back. They had done that quite a bit, seven years ago, and Alice still wondered what they said to each other that they would not say to her.

"I usually walk after dinner," Alice said, with a quick glance at Sharon's feet. The lawyer was wearing black sandals with low, chunky heels and a complicated welter of straps. "My mother says it's good for digestion."

"Great," Sharon said. "I'll walk with you."

Alice could not take Sharon on her normal evening route, of course. But she skirted it, leading her through the outer edges of Ten Hills, where big, rambling houses sat back on large lawns. Once, on a summer night such as this, windows would have been open and sounds would have carried—parents calling children in for the evening, the clink and clank of a kitchen being cleaned after dinner, the buzz of a baseball game. But most of the houses had been renovated and now had central air-conditioning, so the only sound was a steady, bland hum.

"It's almost as bad as the seventeen-year locusts," Sharon said. "Worse, because locusts are part of the ecosystem. All these air conditioners are probably making the world warmer."

"You have air-conditioning, right?" Alice kept her voice mild, as if simply making conversation.

"Well, yes, but I live in a condo."

"Oh."

"I mean, these houses were built to take advantage of breezes, to breathe in the summer heat. So you're fighting the architecture when you put in central air. It's very inefficient."

"My mom doesn't believe in air-conditioning, except in bedrooms. And even then, she tries not to use it. She says it makes mold grow in your sinuses."

"Huh," Sharon said. "I suppose it could."

Alice knew Sharon was trying to find a way to talk about

whatever had led to this fake-impromptu encounter. But she wanted it to seem casual, almost an afterthought. *Here we are, walking along, and oh, by the way, where were you Friday night before I came over? Really? Do you know where the little girl is? Between us?*

"I'm never hot," Alice said. "I barely even sweat. Even when I walk at midday, I don't get hot. The secret is not to go fast."

"Do you get enough water?"

"Sure. I guess so." She drank three sixteen-ounce Diet Pepsis every day.

"Because maybe the reason you don't sweat is because you're not getting enough water. Sweating is the body's cooling system. I mean, that's *your* central air-conditioning, in a way."

Alice had thought it was admirable she sweated so little, but now Sharon was making her feel as if this was another failure on her body's part.

"Still, it's great you're walking so much," Sharon said. "You walk at midday and after dinner?"

"Most days."

"All you do is walk?"

"Sometimes I sit for a while. And I've been looking for a job." She had told this lie so often now that it was more automatic and sincere than the true things she sometimes said.

"Your mother says someone brought you home in a car one time. At least once."

"Really?"

"Yes, Alice. Really."

"I don't know why she would say that. All I do is walk."

"She heard a car door slam one night, right before you came up the walk."

"We live on a busy street. There are other people coming and going."

"So you haven't been . . . taking rides from people." A beat. "From men."

It was all Alice could do not to laugh when she realized what was worrying her mother and Sharon. "I wouldn't take a ride from anyone I didn't know. That's really dangerous."

They were at the corner where the big houses petered out and a small business district began, anchored by a storefront church that used to be a dollar movie house. Helen had told Alice that she and Alice's father had gone here on their first date to see *Cocoon,* and then to Mr. G's for soft ice cream afterward, where she had the kind of cone with the chocolate and vanilla swirled together. She had been wearing a 1950s sundress, with tiny black-and-white checks. Helen's stories were always full of details like that—what she saw, what she ate, what she wore.

"We should turn back here," Alice said.

They walked in silence for a block, retracing their steps. It was dark now, and the drone of the air-conditioning seemed even louder.

"Alice, your mom thinks—"

"I know what my mom thinks." Her voice was hard, although she didn't want it to be. "My mom thinks I'm an ugly fat girl who will ride around with strange men and have sex with them because it's the only way I can get their attention."

"No. *No.* But the thing is—the only thing I care about—is that if you were riding with someone, instead of walking, this past Friday night—well, I would need to know that."

"Why?"

"Because that's not what we told the police. And if you tell the police a lie, even a meaningless one, it can cause a lot of problems down the road."

"I was walking."

"Good."

"But it's only three miles, from Westview to our house," Alice said. "Anyone can walk three miles in an hour."

"Yes, but, you couldn't . . . it wouldn't . . . as far as the police are concerned . . ."

Alice stopped and stared directly into Sharon's eyes for the first time. "You're saying it matters where I was, and whether I was in a car or on foot, because the police think I did this."

"Not exactly. You're a suspect. You shouldn't be, but you are."

"Do you want to be my lawyer because you think I'm guilty, or because you think I'm innocent?"

"I want to protect you, to make sure that no one hurts you. Again." Sharon stopped and braced herself against a huge old tree, its craggy bark striped like a tire's tread. She shifted her weight from one foot to another, digging her fingers into the straps to loosen them. The sandals had left deep red marks on her ankles.

"You were supposed to take care of me last time."

"We did our best. We really did, Alice."

"Oh." Alice pretended to think about this. "So that was your *best*."

Letting those words go was like the first bite of something hot and delicious, a liquid warmth that started in her chest and spread into her neck and face. It reminded Alice of the fireworks she had seen Saturday night, as she and Helen drove to the police station—long bright strands of color bursting from a center and then streaming through the sky.

But the feeling disappeared almost as quickly as the Roman candles had.

"Alice—we've been over this before."

"No. Actually, we've *never* gone over it. Why did I have to go away for what Ronnie did?"

"Well, for one thing, they found your toy, the jack-in-the-box—"

"Put there by *Ronnie* after she stole it from *me*."

"And it was hard to be definite about when the baby died. The time frame."

"Ronnie killed her while I wasn't there. Do you think I would have let Ronnie kill the baby in front of me? Do you think I could have stood there while she did what she did?"

"But you were with Ronnie when she took the baby. And you didn't tell anyone where she was, even while there . . . even when there . . ."

"Just say it," Alice said. "She was alive and I could have saved her. But I couldn't see that. All I could see was that whatever happened, we were going to be in trouble. Trouble for taking her, for making people worry. We were in so much trouble. I tried to think of a way to help people find her. I tried to get Ronnie to take the baby home. But she wouldn't, and she wouldn't let me. She just wanted to stay there, pretending it was hers. And then, all of a sudden, she wanted the baby to be dead."

"I know," Sharon said, nodding. "I know."

"Now they think I took this girl and maybe hurt her. Why do the police think I could do that?"

"Because cops can only understand the present by way of the past. It's like the story, you know, about the boy who goes to market for his mother."

"What story? I don't know that story." But suddenly she did. She remembered being nine, in the community room at the Catonsville library for an afternoon program that Helen had deemed worthy. *"John Jacob Jingleheimer Schmidt / His name is my name too / Whenever we go out / The people always shout / There goes John Jacob Jingleheimer Schmidt / la la la la la la la."* They had told that story, too, the one about the boy who never got it right, but it was the song that Alice remembered, the joy of shouting the chorus until she was hoarse.

"He ties a string around a pork chop and drags it behind him, only to have the dogs eat it. His mother says, 'No, you should have put it under your hat.' So he goes to buy butter and puts it under his hat and it melts. And she says—actually, I don't know what she says next. But the point is he keeps applying yesterday's solution to today's problem."

"So I'm yesterday's solution."

"In a sense."

"Which means I was also yesterday's problem."

Sharon shifted her weight back and forth. Alice remembered how her feet felt in the early days of walking, how they burned and ached. Now they were so tough that she could probably go five miles barefoot without feeling it.

"I never thought of you as a problem," Sharon said.

"What about the things that happened to me while I was away? What about the things that were done to me?"

To her horror, Sharon began to cry, a response that Alice didn't crave, and couldn't even use. Whenever a grown-up began to cry, Alice knew she had lost.

"I tried, Alice. I really tried. I did my best and I'm sorry about how things turned out. But no one knew—no one could have known or predicted—I'm so sorry, Alice. All I can do is try to get it right this time. That's all anyone can do."

"You're right," Alice said. "You are absolutely right. All anyone can do is try."

She started walking, indifferent to whether Sharon could keep up. She trained her eyes on the sidewalk, measuring her stride so her foot landed safely in the middle of each square. Not because she worried about stepping on a crack, much less breaking her mother's back, but because the solid, almost jumping movement reminded her of hopscotch. She

had been good at hopscotch, playing kicksies in the Baltimore style, using an old rubber heel as her token. Helen
would go to shoe repair shops and bat her eyes at the old Italian men who worked there, just to make sure that Alice had
an authentic Black Cat Paw heel to fling into the numbered
spaces.

Tuesday,
July 7

31.

"This is how it works in Baltimore," Lenhardt said, perching on the corner of Nancy's desk. "Or how it *doesn't* work. The bureaucracy that wants to help you can't. The bureaucracy that could help you won't."

"Problem with the medical records?" Nancy guessed.

Lenhardt nodded. "Middlebrook, where Alice was held, is finally under renovation, and the nonactive files have been put away in some storehouse for the time being. They're going to try and find them, but I got the feeling they honestly don't know where they are. Shechter, a psychiatric unit at one of the privately run juvenile facilities, is stonewalling us, says they sent the files to a state agency upon Ronnie Fuller's release. But they're not sure if it was Juvenile Services or Health and Mental Hygiene."

"Seems like a lot of work," Infante said, "for information that may not even help us."

"Well, there's blood, and you can't ignore that," Lenhardt said. "Blood is good. But I've been thinking: This is a case about what's *not* there, too. And what's the primary thing that's not there?"

He looked at his two detectives expectantly and Nancy couldn't help wanting to get the answer first. She studied her sergeant's face for a clue, a tell, and saw his eyes slide to the right, toward the stack of videotapes on Infante's desk.

These were tapes from the store's security cameras and the mall security cameras at the various exits. They had watched them several times and caught a glimpse of Maveen Little and her boyfriend, seemingly looking for the girl. But—

"Brittany Little," Nancy said. "Brittany Little is missing. Not a single security camera caught her. Which is possible, but not plausible."

"If a stranger took a kid, he'd have to snatch her fast"— Lenhardt hugged a phone book to his chest to demonstrate—"and even then, she'd probably yell. It's more likely he enticed her out with something."

"We talked to the shift supervisor for mall security," Infante said, "and the security guard from Value City. An off-duty city cop, pretty sharp. He pointed out that if the cameras caught everything, there wouldn't be a shoplifter walking free today."

"The mom came looking for him, and he said she was genuinely distraught," Nancy put in. "She was almost hysterical."

"Well, if your boyfriend killed your daughter, you would be genuinely distraught, too. Why don't you go back to Westview, check out the exits and the placement of the cameras? This lady, this Cynthia Barnes, got us agitated over the resemblance between her girl and our missing one. She was on the phone so fast the night it happened that we barely had time to think this through our ownselves. Granted, the lady's got reason to be antsy. But that doesn't mean we need to be."

She was on the phone so fast the night it happened—but Cynthia Barnes had called Nancy Saturday morning, saying "I just spoke to your sergeant." Nancy's mind jumped back to the Friday evening the child had disappeared, the decision to treat it as a homicide, even with evidence like the hair and the jumper raising the possibility of an abduction. Then there had been Lenhardt's insistence on moving Infante and Nancy up in the rotation. Infante had followed Lenhardt into the bathroom, arguing all the while, coming out furiously resigned.

Coincidences happen, Infante had said. *Look at sarge and the Epstein case.* And Nancy hadn't asked any more questions—not because she was scared to reveal her ignorance of something called the Epstein case, but because she didn't want to find out that her involvement in this case was anything but a coincidence. If Lenhardt was making her work the Brittany Little case because of her old connection to the Barnes case, then he was testing her. If he was testing her, he must not trust her.

"Nancy?"

"What?"

"I'd like to get to Westview sometime this week," Infante said, standing over her. "You want to stare into space, stirring coffee, you can do that in the car."

"Look at my pitcher, Miz Manning. Do you like it?"

"It's beautiful, Gerald."

The boy frowned. He had a perfectly round head, big for his eight-year-old body, with close-cropped hair. He looked like a black Charlie Brown, although he had none of the cartoon character's sheepishness. "My name's Ja-leel."

"Of course. Ja-leel."

"What about mine? You like mine?" A girl held up her painting, heedless of the way the fresher colors sent tracks down the paper. She wore her hair in plump pigtails, trapped by plastic barrettes, three tails in all, with parts so straight and neat the sections might have been partitioned with a ruler. This hairstyle never went away in Baltimore.

"It's exquisite, Bonnie."

"Bon-*ay*, B-O-N-E-T," the little girl corrected. "My name is Bonet."

"That's right, honey." Jesus Christ, Helen thought. Fifteen

kids and maybe two had names that weren't some random array of vowel sounds. She was all for self-expression, but you had to know the rules before you were free to break them. Look at e. e. cummings.

She was teaching arts and crafts at a city-funded day camp, something she had done every summer since Alice went away. If she had it to do over again, she wouldn't have signed up for a session during Alice's first summer at home. But she had made the commitment back in March, forgetting how her life was about to change. Besides, she had gotten used to the extra money, and giving up the job was akin to taking a 5 percent pay cut.

This school was on the city's North Side, in one of the city's richest neighborhoods, but the children were all black. The white families who lived in the huge houses around the school wouldn't dream of sending their children there, not even for day camp. Welcome to apartheid, Baltimore style. People rationalized the city's divisions by speaking of the private school *tradition* in Baltimore, of the strong presence of the Catholic Church, but the bottom line was that it was a segregated city. The whites who couldn't afford even parish schools had fled to the county. When middle-class African-Americans followed them, chasing the same dreams, the whites decamped to counties even farther out.

Alice would have been the only white child in her elementary school if Helen had sent her there. Which was fine by Helen, but not by Alice. The girl's fear of being different was almost pathological. Another child might have gloried in standing out, but all Alice had ever wanted to do was fade in, go along, get along. Helen's mother had defended this characteristic, recognizing it as her own. "Well, dear, perhaps if she had a father—or even knew who her father was—she might not care as much about seeming normal." It was the closest thing to a rebuke that Helen's mother had ever dared to utter.

So Helen had enrolled Alice in the parish school and watched in dismay as she gravitated toward the most ordinary girls, the popular girls, the ones destined to make Alice's life hell once they were adolescents. But it was what Alice wanted. Alice, not Helen.

That's why it had stung to see race become a focal point in the coverage of Alice's crime. That was the one identifying fact, besides their ages and their neighborhood, that had been attached to the "two girls." They were white, their victim was black. One lawmaker had even speculated about trying the two girls for a hate crime. Feelings ran high. For a moment, the city seemed capable of boiling over, all its inequities and grudges and hatreds crammed into this one anomalous incident. It was as if people needed to imbue what happened with meaning. But if Helen was sure of anything in her life, it was the very meaninglessness of what her daughter had done.

"Lookit my house, Miz Manning. That's my house and my mother and my brothers."

Another little boy—Dumas? Dunbar? Ducasse?—was thrusting his picture in her face. The house was clearly *not* his, for it was a detached frame house, white with shutters and a picket fence, a curl of black smoke coming from the chimney. If he had even seen such a house, it was on television. Or walking through this neighborhood that didn't want him, where the local grocery store refused to allow more than four "students" inside at any one time, although the rule didn't seem to apply to the plaid-skirted girls from the private school. In a convenience store last spring, Helen had listened with dismay as the black middle-schoolers taunted the Middle Eastern counterman who tried to shoo them

away. "No mo' stu-dent! No mo' stu-dent in sto!" They gloried in his bigotry, turning it back on him.

Everyone in Baltimore hated everyone else. Whites hated
blacks. Blacks hated whites. The city people hated the suburbanites. The poor hated the rich. These were the true hate
crimes. It was a city where differences ground together, pro-
ducing a sour dust as dangerous as any outlawed substance—
lead paint, asbestos. But only Alice and Ronnie, too young
and bewildered to hate anyone, had been held accountable
for this civic failing.

Mira needed to find a way to make a telephone call without
being overheard. The downtown newsroom had cubicles for
the reporters, which provided a modicum of privacy, but the
suburban offices were large open spaces where everything
was public knowledge. Downtown had Caller ID, too, and a
snazzy cafeteria with a salad bar. She fumed, momentarily
distracted by her automatic resentment at the gap between
what she had and what she deserved. Then she reminded
herself that she would be downtown soon enough, if she did
this right.

The suburban reporters shared their squat, generic office
space with advertising sales reps, who were granted more
privacy because they actually made money for the company.
Mira waited for the ad supervisor to leave for lunch, then
ducked into his office, closing the door behind her. If anyone
asked why she had gone into Gordon's office to use the
phone, she could claim it was to discuss a medical issue with
her doctor. No male editor would pursue that topic with a female reporter. Mira unfolded the piece of paper that Cynthia
Barnes had given her and punched in the beeper number for
the detective on the case. She then entered Gordon's extension and waited.

Cynthia had refused to say anything on the record last

night. She had been willing to confirm that the police thought the disappearance of Brittany Little might be linked to the murder of her own daughter. Asked why, she had said nothing, just raised her eyebrows and tilted her chin in the direction of a photograph on the mantel. Mira saw the resemblance immediately.

"And that is—?"

"My daughter. Rosalind."

"Does she—?"

"No. No, she does not look like her sister." Cynthia seemed to disappear inside herself for a moment, caught up in some private sadness. When she spoke again, her voice was sharp. "That wasn't on the record. This is all background. You can't even say 'a source,' or whatever bullshit word you use now. I will tell you the facts as I know them, but it's up to you to confirm them with someone else."

"How do I do that? You know the county cops are going to no-comment me."

And this was where Cynthia Barnes had told her how to do it, step by step. Mira looked at the piece of paper from her notebook, where Cynthia had written what she dared not say aloud, as if she feared Mira had a tape recorder hidden in her purse. She had torn it out after leaving the Barnes home last night, worried that it could somehow erase itself or get lost if it remained attached to the spiral metal clasp at the top of her steno pad. She had slid it into her pocket, then her billfold, then back into her pocket. Since last evening, she had looked at it at least two dozen times, almost as if it were a magic incantation that must be recited precisely in order to work.

Detective Nancy Porter
Alice Manning
Veronica Fuller

Those last two names alone were gold. Even if this story fell apart, Mira now had information that had eluded other Baltimore reporters for years. She had the names of the two girls who had killed a baby when they were eleven, names that had been protected and withheld. There had to be a story in their release, their return to the very neighborhood where they had done this unspeakable thing. She would prefer them, for the sake of her story, to be unrepentant sociopaths who had killed again. Hands down, that was the sexier story. But she could do a redemption tale, if necessary, although she personally found those a little tiresome. Born again, blah blah. She had read no shortage of stories like that. What people really wanted to know upon meeting a killer was *How did you do it?* Not how as in the method of dispatch, but how as in the sense of breaking that ultimate taboo.

What did it feel like to take another person's life? That was what Mira planned to ask Alice and Veronica. But if they were locked up for Brittany Little's death, which Cynthia had intimated could happen any minute, they would be out of reach. The best-case scenario would be for the investigation to drag on a little bit, so Mira could report that the girls had been questioned, giving her permission to recap their grisly histories, without having to worry about the libel issues raised by the latest case. Also, that would give the Carroll County murders, the one with the deranged fourteen-year-old, time to play out. No one could compete with *that*.

Wasn't it news enough that these two girls had returned to their neighborhood without the community being alerted? If they had been adult sex offenders, they might have fallen under one of those whatchamacallit laws, the one named for yet another little girl victim. But because they were juveniles, they had been granted the right to move anonymously through the world. Was that right? Was that fair? Mira had convinced herself it wasn't.

The phone rang and she grabbed it without thinking, forgetting she was in someone else's office. It didn't occur to her that there could be any other phone call in the world just now except the one for which she waited.

"This is Detective Porter. You paged me and used the emergency code?" Cynthia had told Mira that adding 911 to the phone number written next to the detective's name would get her an automatic response.

"Yes, I'm Mira Jenkins of the *Beacon-Light* and I need to speak to you about the Brittany Little disappearance."

"No comment."

"Wait—" Her voice shrilled, and she struggled to get it under control. "I have information about the case, which I have confirmed from independent sources. I plan to publish this information with or without your cooperation. I'm just giving you the opportunity to correct or contradict my information."

"No comment." She was more tentative this time, less prompt. And she was still on the line.

"I'm going to write that you've interviewed Alice Manning and Veronica Fuller in this matter. Will I be incorrect if I say that?"

"No . . . no comment."

"If you don't tell me I'm wrong, I'm going with it. I also know the missing child bears a marked resemblance to Olivia Barnes's sister. I've seen the photos, so I don't need you to confirm that. But do you think that's why the girls took her? Are they trying to get back at the family? Why are they so obsessed with hurting the Barneses?"

"No comment."

"Do you think it's racial? It's my understanding that the first murder followed a racial outburst by one of the girls."

"You can't print this. You must not print any of this."

"Why, is it wrong?"

"It could be harmful to our investigation."

"But will I be wrong if I publish it?"

"I'm not playing this game."

"I'm going to let five seconds of silence elapse. If you don't say anything, I have to assume it's right."

"But—"

"So I'm wrong?"

"No comment."

"If I'm wrong, you better say straight out I'm wrong."

"You should call our press office. We don't talk directly to reporters."

"I'm not going to quote you. I'm just going to say, 'Police sources confirmed.'"

"I didn't confirm anything and I'm not your source." The detective sounded almost hysterical.

"Didn't you? Look, you have my number if you want to call me back. Meanwhile, I need to talk to my editors about what we're going to print tomorrow."

Mira hung up the phone and let out a little yelp of triumph, wishing she had a colleague to high-five. Then she composed herself before leaving the advertising director's office.

"What were you doing in there?" the cop reporter asked.

"Talking to a doctor about why my hands are so cold all the time. He's going to do some tests."

32.

"Fuck," Nancy said after hanging up the pay phone in a back corridor at Value City. "Jesus, Joseph, and Mary and *fuck* me."

"What's up?" Infante asked, coming out of the bathroom. He had a copy of the *Pennysaver* under his arm, a fact Nancy would have found hilarious in normal circumstances.

"A reporter is chasing the story."

"Well, sure. They been chasing it."

"Only she *knows*. She knows about the girls, has their names. She says I confirmed it by not contradicting it. But I didn't, did I? You heard my end? Did I say anything?"

"I didn't hear anything, Nancy. I was in the can."

"Damn it." It was going to happen again. She was going to be in the paper, and other police would think it was because she was showboating, still desperate for attention. No one would believe she had changed, and she would have to live with it this time. She had run out of room, she had no place else to go, except over the state line to Pennsylvania.

"It might not be so bad," Infante said, which convinced Nancy it was very bad indeed.

She leaned her forehead against the edge of the fake wood partition for the pay phone. They were in a dingy corridor on the top floor of Value City. Nancy remembered when a bakery used to occupy this space, back when Value City was

Hutzler's, the city's grandest department store. Her mother had come here to buy Nancy's first communion dress and then, to reward her for not fidgeting, had brought her to the bakery to pick out any treat she wanted. Nancy had chosen a strawberry cupcake, its pink frosting chunky with pieces of berry. Probably made from jam, she realized now. But at eleven she had believed it was the real thing.

"Let's go do what we came here to do," she said. "I'll worry about this later."

They made a circuit of the store, studying the placement of the cameras. The numbers matched—there were seven cameras in all, and the mall had sent them seven tapes. They left the store, entering a glassed-in corridor of smaller shops. Nancy stopped, did a double take.

"What?" Infante asked as she crouched down.

"Here," she said. Three little bolts, almost impossible to see in the dirty gray carpet, but Nancy's eyes had found them. They looked lost, meaningless, unconnected to this sunny, dusty column of light—until their eyes traveled up the wall, about eight feet. And then it was almost too easy to connect the bolts to the not quite spackled-over holes in the wall.

Infante stood on tiptoe and pressed a finger against the white swirl of Spackle. There was a small freckle of white when he took his finger away.

"Fucking Lenhardt," Infante said. "He's scary sometimes."

"Yeah," Nancy agreed. "This is a case about what's *not* there. But how could he know that the camera was removed?"

The corridor had doors to the parking lot and an enclosed staircase that led to a parking garage below this strange addition, an attempt to create a mall out of what had once been a traditional shopping center. Nancy and Infante walked the corridor once, twice, three times, then began going up and down the stairs. Nancy was walking up the stairs when she saw the glint of something gold. An earring.

"Didn't Brittany Little have pierced ears?" She was thinking of the photo, the curly hair slicked behind two shell-perfect ears. She was pretty sure the girl had been wearing earrings.

"Maybe. But how can you tell one ball stud from another?"

"I don't know. Maybe ears have DNA. Maybe the mom can make an ID." She sealed it in a baggie, just in case. "Let's go talk to the head of security."

The guy was a rent-a-cop, anyone could tell. Fifty-something, short gray hair, a florid face, at least three hundred pounds. Bernard Carnahan.

"You gotta understand," he said, his tone apologetic now that he was caught. "It wasn't my call. Mall management says it's all about liability. The camera malfunctioned. Tape's nothing but snow. We can get sued for that. But we can't get sued for not having a camera. That's how it was explained to me. So we gave you what we had, and didn't give you what we didn't have. No harm, no foul."

Nancy suddenly realized she could raise just one eyebrow, so she did.

"No harm?" Infante sputtered. "If we had known there was a malfunctioning camera at the exit, we would have spent more time in that part of the mall. We just found what could be the girl's earring—which, if it is, confirms the mom's story. She was here and someone took her out. We would have liked to know that four days ago."

Carnahan shrugged. "So, what, now that you got an earring, you got it all figured out?" The detectives had no answer for that. "Look, I'm sorry. I did what my boss told me to do. It didn't seem like a big deal to me. It still doesn't."

The detectives left his office. Everyone lies, Nancy reminded herself. It was a rule of police work. The sheer vol-

ume of lies in the world on any given day was staggering.
The mall management lied about the camera because they
feared a lawsuit. The mother lied about how long she turned
her back on her daughter because she didn't want the cops to
think she was a bad mother. Alice Manning was lying, too.
About what, and to what purpose, Nancy didn't know. But
the girl was definitely lying, and had been from the start.

Ronnie Fuller—Ronnie Fuller, she wasn't so sure about.

"You feel like a bagel?" she asked Infante.

"Yeah," he said, getting it. "I definitely feel like a bagel. I
feel big and round and chewy, and I want someone to slather
me with cream cheese."

The one thing that Ronnie Fuller had known cold the first
day of kindergarten was her alphabet. Other things came
harder—blowing her nose, tying her shoes, playing well
with others—but she had memorized the ABCs because she
had a little board with magnetic letters in various colors,
passed down from her brothers. The arrangement of the colors was mysterious to her, something that hinted at an internal logic that Ronnie could not quite figure out. *A* through *F*
were light, light blue. *G* through *L* were orange. Then came
M through *R,* Christmas red, *S* through *W,* grass green, and
finally *X-Y-Z,* blacker than black.

Ronnie decided the letters were like groups of friends. If
she had known the word *cliques* at six, she might have used
that. The pale blue bunch had the coolness of those who always got to go first, while the middle letters wore bright colors to get attention. She was most troubled by the placement
of her own initial, *R,* at the end of the red group. Because *R*
had to stand next to *Q,* and anyone could see that *Q* was odd,
sort of retarded, a letter that couldn't make a word without *U*
around to help. Yet *Q* stood between *P* and *R,* as if *R* wasn't
good enough to be *P*'s friend. *Q* was like one of those fat

girls who stood next to a pretty girl, shooing everyone else away. But *R* couldn't be with *S, T, U, V, W* because they were green. It was all very disturbing.

She was thinking about her old alphabet board as she picked through the white letters that needed to be arranged on the marquee, announcing the next day's specials. Wednesday was Pizza Bagel day—an open-face bagel with a fountain drink and a bag of chips for $3.99.

"What do you want for the manager's special?" she asked Clarice.

"Turkey," Clarice said. "We're swimming in turkey. They screwed up the order, I guess."

Ronnie laughed a little, entranced by the image—her, Clarice, and O'lene dog-paddling through mounds of pressed white meat.

"Your friends came back today, I see."

"Uh-huh." The detectives had talked to Ronnie on her smoke break, asked the same questions, gotten the same answers.

"Why they keep coming back, Ronnie?"

"I don't know."

Clarice let a minute or two go by before she spoke again.

"You got a boyfriend?"

"No."

"Why you say it like that, like it's a weird question?"

"Because . . . because where would I get one?" There had been boys at Shechter, but there had been strict rules about contact, and Ronnie had never dared to break the rules at Shechter.

Clarice misunderstood. "You're pretty enough. Skinny, but white boys like skinny." She shook her head at the strange preferences of white men.

"I work here, I go home. I haven't met anybody since— well, not since a long time."

"What about when you were in school. You have a boyfriend then?"

Ronnie finally got it: Clarice assumed these visits from the detectives were about someone she dated. It never occurred to her that Ronnie could do anything bad enough, on her own, to get detectives to come around. Clarice thought she was *good*.

The detectives had been indirect, never mentioning the missing girl by name. They had asked Ronnie what she had done since they saw her last. "Slept," she said. "Then I came to work. Then I went home. And I slept again." They asked if she had seen or spoken to Alice, and she shook her head, wondering if Alice was telling them something different. She never knew what Alice might say, what lie she might tell. They asked if she wanted to come talk to them some more, at their office.

"Not really," she said, and waited to see if they would tell her she had to come talk to them anyway.

"There might be some things you'd rather tell us in private."

"What things?"

"Whatever. Anything." The girl detective, the one who looked a little bit like Alice, had something in her hand, a plastic bag.

"I don't have anything to talk about."

It was a relief to see them go, at least for now, to be spared another trip to the police station. When she had seen them in the door, she had thought they were coming to take her blood, and she really could not stand the thought of a doctor's needle pricking her.

She had proposed the blood-sister thing once to Alice, back when they were ten and Ronnie took her to the house in the woods for the first time. Alice had been so scared at first, jumping at the smallest sound. Once there, there was nothing to do, and mingling their blood was just a way to prolong the experience, to avoid the hot walk home. Alice said her

blood was too far below the surface to come out with a needle prick, that she was prone to infections and had been told
specifically by her mother not to prick her finger for any reason. But Ronnie understood: Alice did not want to be her
blood sister. She was saving herself for the other girls in
their class, the ones who didn't say unexpected things or get
into fights.

But Alice grew to like the secret house, almost in spite of
herself. She was the one who began suggesting they go there
all the time—not just in the summertime, but on some weekends as well. She was the one who wanted to fix it up, make
it like a real house, but it was too far a walk to carry anything
heavy. On Saturday night, Ronnie had thought Alice would
be the one to find her, had half expected Alice to come looking for her. Because even when she didn't know why the police wanted her, she knew they would be looking for Alice,
too. They were joined together, whether Alice liked it or not.

She couldn't put it off any longer. She had to talk to Alice.
She had to confront her, remembering to use "good" words.
Conflict resolution, the doctor at Shechter Unit had called it.
*Ask questions. Keep an open mind. Listen to the other per-
son. Focus on finding common ground,* areas of agreement.
Anger is one letter away from danger, Ronnie.

It was time to push fat Q out of the way once and for all
and take her rightful place.

Mira sat in Nostrildamus's office, every fiber of her being
focused on the task of not crying. She could feel the pressure
behind her eyelids, at the base of her nose, in her jawbone,
even at the edge of her rib cage. But she was not going to
cry. She pretended to make eye contact—well, eye-to-nostril
contact—with her boss, but she was really focusing on the
photograph of his wife, which was turned outward, as if her
face were more important to those who visited the office

than to the man who inhabited it. His wife was remarkably normal looking, even pretty. Perhaps that was why he made it face outward, so his employees would know he had managed to snag someone normal.

"I don't see—" she began carefully, making sure her voice didn't shake or throb in any way.

"I admire your initiative," Nostrildamus said, using the fake polite tone that was supposed to show how reasonable and good-natured he was. He was always reasonable and good-natured—until someone contradicted him. "But I just don't think you've got a story. What about the girls? Although I guess they're young women now. Have you talked to them? Have you gotten their side?"

"I just got their names three hours ago," she said, shaving two hours off the time. It was 5 P.M. and she had been summoned downtown after finally confiding in her boss what she was doing. She had been writing furiously, confident that the revelation that the girls had been questioned was a story in its own right. She needed to go daily, lest one of the television stations get it.

But Nostrildamus didn't agree. He had asked her to come talk to him, and she was fearful that the story was going to be taken away. *Because of who she was, because of what she had done.* No one was saying that, of course. Not Nostrildamus or the managing editor, Dominic DiNardo, known as Quasimoto behind *his* back, because he spent his days hunched over his Motorola cell phone, watching the stock market ticker crawling across the text screen. Mira wondered if the bosses had nicknames for the employees. Probably not. They settled for the consolation of winning all the battles.

"A police source confirmed the girls are suspects," she said, for the third or fourth time. "We won't be wrong if we say that."

"I feel we're being used by police here," Nostrildamus said, tilting his head back, so Mira now was staring into the black holes. Sure enough, out came the index finger. "I predict this is a ploy on their part. They're trying to plant a story to shake some information loose. That's not our job."

Mira was stuck. She couldn't tell him that the police were opposed to the story without undercutting herself, revealing the semantic game she had played with the detective to get her second source.

"If it's a good story," she ventured, "why do we care what the police department's objective is?"

Nostrildamus's chin jerked back down and he made eye contact with Mira for the first time—momentary eye contact, to be sure, with his eyes sliding sideways after a brief dead-on gaze, but true eye contact, not eye-to-nostril contact. "This paper does not carry water for law enforcement agencies. They do their job, we do ours."

"The detectives would prefer it if we didn't do a story. They only confirmed the information because I had it solid, from a source."

"Another police source," Nostrildamus said dismissively. "They were playing you, one side against the other."

Mira hesitated, then plunged ahead: "No. My other source is not with the department." She had to concentrate fiercely, lest she drop a pronoun or any other clue. "This source is someone in an unusual position, who has complete knowledge of the investigation, but no ties to the department. Is, if anything, somewhat hostile to it."

"How can that be?" Quasimoto demanded.

"If I tell you more, I'll end up disclosing my source's identity. And that's the one thing I had to promise not to do."

"When you promise to keep a source's identity confidential, you're promising to keep it from the newspaper's readers, not the editors." Nostrildamus probably thought his tone warm and persuasive, but it was merely creepy, the tone of a parent trying to reason with an irrational child. "You can tell us."

"No. My source was adamant that I must not tell anyone."

"If you don't tell us your source, we can't run your story. I want someone on the record—not just a homicide detective saying he won't deny that the police consider these two girls suspects."

"She."

"The source is a woman?" Nostrildamus pounced, proud of himself, thinking he had caught her.

"The *detective* is a woman. The source—I'm not going to tell you anything about my source."

"Then you have no story. And given that you're supposed to be the neighborhood reporter, I can't really allow you to work on such a . . . speculative assignment. Why don't you give your little tip to the county police reporter?"

Mira bit her lip. Cynthia Barnes had convinced her that the price of exposing her would be dire.

"You breathe my name to anyone, I will swear up and down you made this up, that I refused to speak to you. You will not write my name in that notebook, you will not use your little tape recorder. And who do you think will be believed? I have never spoken to a reporter before. Why would I speak to you?"

"Why did you call the newsroom if you didn't want to talk to the press?" Mira had countered.

"Why did I—but I did no such thing. You said yourself you only found me by sitting outside that poor woman's apartment, seeing me drive away."

"Someone called. Someone who sounded like you."

"Black, you mean." Cynthia had sniffed.

No, Mira thought. *Not black, but trying to be someone's idea of black.* She had let it go, agreed to the conditions imposed. What choice did she have? She believed this woman could ruin her. She would say Mira made the story up, and everyone would believe her. Cynthia was the grieving mother, and Mira was the gullible reporter, and would be forever if she couldn't figure out how to get this story in the paper.

"I can't tell you my source," she told Nostrildamus. "I'm sorry, but I can't. I was made to promise explicitly that I wouldn't tell *anyone,* even my editors."

"Just me, then," Nostrildamus said. "Dominic will leave the room."

Quasimoto looked startled by the request, but rose to his feet and shuffled out, eyes on his telephone.

"Okay, Mira," Nostrildamus said, the correct pronunciation of her name always a little threatening in the stingy circle of his mouth. "It's just you and I now. My door is closed. I can keep a secret, so what's the harm in telling me?"

"I made a promise," she said miserably, wondering at a world where a newspaper editor said "just you and I."

"You don't have the authority to make such promises."

"It was the only way to get the story."

Nostrildamus slammed his body against the back of his chair and glared at her. "Well, you don't have a story, so your promise was for nothing."

A question, she had to ask a question. She had to allow him to direct her, to fix her, to find the solution.

"Is there anything I can do—on my own time—that would make it satisfactory?"

He spoke without thinking. But then, Nostrildamus never had to think about what he said because he never listened to what anyone else said.

"You should get the girls."

"What?"

"Interview the girls. Both of them. Then come back to me, and we'll talk about whether you have a story."

Mira left his office, dazed with dread, feeling as if the wizard had asked her to bring back the broomstick of the Witch of the West. She tried to console herself with her usual mantra. *Failure is not an option. Failure is not an option.* But she was worried that even success was risky in this situation, that the only thing worse than failing to do what was demanded of her was actually doing it.

33.

Infante and Nancy arrived back at the office to find dozens of cardboard boxes stacked around their desks, creating partitions where none had been.

"The *M*s," Lenhardt said. "Courtesy of the Department of Juvenile Services. They began arriving about twenty minutes after you left. Naturally. As soon as we decided we could live without them, they found them."

"That's a lot of *M*s," Infante said, going straight to a box and poking its contents with one finger.

"Best I can tell, it's about twenty years' worth of *M*s. I'm not sure if they just didn't understand the subpoena, or if they don't care that they've routinely violated the privacy rights of every *M* and *M* who spent time with them. The grunt I talked to said they just wanted to help, however they could."

"Isn't that supposed to be the scariest sentence in the world?" Infante asked. "We're from the government and we're here to help you."

Nancy did not speak at all, just stood in the middle of the boxes, clutching the baggie with the earring. She had made sure Ronnie Fuller saw the bag in her hand, had even asked her if she knew what it was. "An earring?" Ronnie had asked. There had been something poignant in her voice, as if she didn't get to give right answers very often, but she hadn't offered anything else.

"You want me to take that up to eleven?" Infante asked Nancy now.

"Yeah," Nancy said. "Yeah, that would be great."

"What was that about?" Lenhardt asked once Infante had left.

"An earring. We found it in the stairwell. Turns out that there was a malfunctioning video camera outside one of the Value City exits. Mall management took it down and pretended it wasn't there because they thought the mom might sue them."

"It's a long shot that the lab will recover anything from that."

"I know. And it's so ordinary the mom won't be able to identify it. But we're just covering the bases."

"Good."

Lenhardt went back into his office. Nancy stood among the boxes for almost a full minute before she followed him in. He looked as if he had been waiting for her.

"You got something you want to say to me, Nancy?"

"A reporter—I don't know how she got my pager number—she called and she knew stuff. I kept saying 'no comment,' but she kept twisting it, saying that if I didn't say anything I was confirming it, and if I did say anything I was confirming it. I—I—didn't know what to say."

"What kind of stuff, Nancy?"

"She knew that we were looking at the girls, the ones who killed Olivia Barnes. She had their names. She said she was going to write that we were talking to them."

"Well, there's nothing you can do about that."

"But if a story comes out, people will think I did it. That I talked."

"And?"

"And they won't want to work with me."

"Does Infante think you talked to the media?"

"No, he knows I didn't."

"Well, now I know, too. And I'll make sure the lieutenant and the major know what happened, so why are you so worried?"

Nancy shook her head, afraid her voice would come out thick if she tried to speak right away. Before she had entered the academy, her uncles had sat her down one night and taught her how not to cry. "You're a statue, see?" Stan Kolchak had said. "You can't feel anything. You can't really hear anything," Milton Kolchak had said. "You just stare in the middle distance and pretend you're made out of stone."

She was a statue. She would not cry in front of Lenhardt.

Finally, she said, "You haven't been straight with me, Sergeant."

Lenhardt looked surprised, hurt even. "What do you mean?"

"When you moved us up in the rotation—you told Infante that it was because Jeffries was lame. But Cynthia Barnes had already called you when you made that decision. You made me work this case because you knew."

"Knew what, Nancy? That you found Olivia Barnes? Lots of people know that. After all, you got a lot of attention for that, didn't you?"

"Some."

"Besides, why would that make me move you up in the rotation? What would be the point in that?"

He wasn't denying it, Nancy realized. He was making her think it through. Why did Lenhardt want her to work on this case?

"You were testing me."

"Yeah?"

"You wanted to see if . . . if the things they said about me were true."

"What did they say about you, Nancy?"

She was a statue. She stared into the middle distance, refusing to make eye contact.

"Nancy?"

"They said I liked attention. They said I needed to be a star, all the time. And when I was just a cop like any other, they said I couldn't stand it, so I would do anything to get attention. Anything."

"Anything including making a big stink out of being harassed by a fellow officer?"

"I *didn't.*" Not about that, she amended in her head. Other times, yes, she had sought attention, craved it. Attention, more than food, then, was the thing she desired, and she could not get enough of it. She didn't know why. She even suspected that it was bad for her, an addiction like any other, and she would keep needing more and more and more. Every day that passed without a reporter calling or a television station asking her to come on—every day without attention had seemed flat and gray.

"You tell me you didn't go to the press, I believe you. That's not why I wanted you on this case, Nancy. I don't have the luxury of using this office as a character-building exercise, or to explore the inner psyches of my detectives." Outside his office, a box crashed to the ground, and they could hear Infante swearing a blue streak. "You think I want to spend any time in *those* dark little chambers? No thanks."

"Did Cynthia Barnes ask for me? Or did you have another reason for making me take this case?"

"Cynthia Barnes mentioned you, yes. She remembered you, she knew you were out here. But it was my call. And I asked you to do it for the exact reasons I said—because you're good."

"Oh."

"*Pretty* good. You could be better, Nancy. You're tentative. Yeah, you're great at finding tiny things on the ground—casings, earrings—but you're not so good at talking to people. And I give that eyesight of yours about ten years before it starts to go, so I need you to get good at the other stuff, okay?"

"Why this case?"

"I get a call, a lady says we need to look at these two girls who killed her child. I think—Nancy can do this. She can talk to two eighteen-year-olds because she won't be scared of them, won't be worried that they're going to grab her ass. And Jeffries is a piece of shit."

"You weren't testing me to see if I'd call the press and remind them that I found the Barnes baby?"

"No. But—be honest, Nancy. You did like all the attention back then, didn't you? And you missed it when it went away."

"No. Yes. I don't know. I was scared that I had . . . *peaked* at twenty-two. And I knew I wasn't a good police yet, but suddenly people wanted me to be, like, this prodigy. The more attention I got, the more the other cops hated me, the more I needed the attention to make up for them hating me."

"I remember you on television," Lenhardt said. "You looked like you were twelve."

" 'Heroes for our times.' Except I wasn't a hero. I was an insubordinate cadet. No one liked me, no one wanted to work with me, and then this major, Dolores Dorsey, says, 'Come work for me in Northwest, I'll take care of you.' "

"I knew Dolores when she was on foot patrol in Northern. I could have told you that the only person Dolores ever took care of was herself. And you know what that makes her, Nancy?"

"What?"

"Pretty much like everyone else."

"You're not like that."

"Maybe I am. Maybe I just go about it different. I see value in having detectives who learn to do their job and do it well. Other people want speedier results. The goose that lays the golden egg, right? Dolores brought you out to Northwest to bask in your reflected glory. Only there wasn't any glory forthcoming because you were just a dumb kid who made a lucky find once upon a time. So she cut you open. And—surprise, surprise—no eggs came out."

"She said she had no choice. She said if she didn't report what was going on, I could end up suing later, that it had to go through channels."

"You believe her?"

"Sometimes. Other times, I thought she wanted to embarrass me and humiliate me, and I never knew why."

"She probably doesn't either, Nancy. But it was four years ago, in a different department. Everyone else has forgotten about it. Except you."

A stray comment from Infante, one that hadn't made much of an impression at the time, came back to Nancy.

"Sarge, will you tell me about the Epstein case?"

"No."

"No?" She might have expected "not now" or "over a beer," but it had never occurred to her that Lenhardt would refuse to answer one of his detective's questions.

"No. I put it out of my head, and I'm not going to put it back in. Some things are better forgotten."

Nancy went back to her desk. She wished it worked that way. She wished someone could say, "Get over it," and you did. There should be a pill like that—Oblivital. Four years later, she remembered every detail—the discovery of the graffiti, the workmen coming out to remove the door, the ultimate humiliation of seeing the door loaded into a truck, uncovered, to be taken downtown. "Why can't we just paint it over?" Nancy had asked the major. "There are procedures for these things," the major had said briskly. "It's out of my hands." "I can handle it," Nancy had said. "It's okay, I don't care. Let me show the guys they can't get to me by doing something stupid like that."

But no, the ladies' room door had been carried away and submitted to Internal Affairs, still bearing the legend: "Potr-cuntski." Nancy didn't know if she was supposed to be more offended as a woman or a Polack. Her grandfather would have killed the man who did that to his name. Nancy had to work with him, had to take it with a smile. And when the story made its way into the newspaper, in expurgated form, everyone assumed she had told, that she had tipped the reporter.

Because she had. Old habits die hard. Shamed by her treatment, punished for being a victim, she had tipped a metro columnist who had been good to her, back when she was known for finding Olivia Barnes. But the story had boomeranged, and she became radioactive. The county was the only place she could go, once it got out that she had put in another officer. Her original instinct had been right. She needed to suck it up, take it.

Infante picked up the upended box and started going through the scattered files.

"Holly's looking at the earring," he said. "But she doesn't think there's anything she can pull off it. 'Now if it were a nose ring,' she says, 'I might have a shot.' And a tongue piercing might have a residue of saliva. Or so she says."

"Too much information."

"Yeah," Infante agreed.

"Sort of like the situation we've got here."

"Yeah, but they're here and we're here, so what the fuck. Holly might pull something off that earring. And I can't think of a single thing to do, and I can't bear to go home. Working a case without a body is the worst."

"Yeah." She took a seat at her own desk, dipped into a file box, and began scanning the pages there. But it took a second for her eyes to focus, for her to leave her past behind.

34.

Alice had been a baby when Helen Manning decided, in a matter of minutes, to buy the house on Nottingham Road. "A decision is impulsive only if it's wrong," she liked to say, and no one ever heard her say that she regretted buying the Cotswold-like cottage plunked down on this oversize lot in a sea of brick rowhouses and shabby apartment buildings. For years, she had compared it with the kind of house seen on the painted screens of East Baltimore, usually behind a pond with gliding swans. Lately, people had begun to notice that it bore a marked resemblance to the landscapes in those strangely popular mall paintings, the ones from the man who claimed he was the painter of light. Helen was less than pleased by this observation.

For Ronnie Fuller, who had never seen a painted screen and who had been locked up while the painter of light opened his mall stores and catalog company, the Mannings' house was a fairy tale house, a place so delicious and enticing that she wouldn't have been surprised to bite into a shingle and find it was gingerbread. Indifferent to the signs of neglect and rot that advertised the lack of a full-time man on the premises, Ronnie saw only the things that Helen had done to make the house distinctive—chipped gray-green statues tucked among the wild roses, the back fence heavy with honeysuckle vines, the rose-colored shutters against the sage-green frame. Safe as houses, people said, but the phrase only made sense to Ronnie when she was looking at Helen Manning's cottage.

Tonight, the front door was open, the screen door latched. Ronnie stood on the tiny porch, listening to the whirring of fans throughout the house. As always, there was music playing, fancy music. This was Helen's choice for early evening. It was only when midnight had come and gone that she allowed herself to play the records from her youth, lowering the volume in deference to the neighbors. They were actually records, not CDs, played on an old stereo. "If you take care of your things, they last," Helen had told Ronnie more than once, for Ronnie was careless with possessions. She didn't mean to be, but she was.

Helen had taken care of all her old things. The house on Nottingham was filled with her books, her clothes, and even her toys—tiny stuffed animals from Germany that she said you couldn't buy today for a hundred dollars, old board games like Masterpiece and Life, a red double-decker bus from England, papier-mâché acrobats from Mexico, metal windups, pristine Barbie dolls.

The best toys, by far, were Helen's City Mouse and Country Mouse houses, which she sometimes allowed Ronnie to take from the highest shelf in the living room and set up on the rug. "Which do you like best?" Helen had asked, and Ronnie believed the question was a test. Most little girls would pick the City Mouse, with her red velvet canopy bed, silver-plated mirrors, and outfit of orange satin. Alice loved the City Mouse. So Ronnie said the Country Mouse, who wore a checked apron and carried a broom. "She's my favorite, too," Helen said.

The Helen who came to the door on this evening looked the same to Ronnie as the Helen she had known seven years ago. But then the light was very dim, inside and out. She was wearing bright orange Capris, black ballet flats, and a man's Hawaiian shirt that echoed the orange shades of the Capris. She looked beautiful.

"Vintage," Ronnie said. It wasn't what she had meant to say the first time she saw her, but Helen smiled.

"Hello, Ronnie." She had a little sniff, as if she had allergies.

"Hi, He-Helen." It had always been Helen, never Mrs. or even Ms. Manning, but Ronnie had not said the name out loud for so long. She had never spoken of Helen to anyone, not even her doctor. Just their secret, Helen said, and Ronnie had kept it.

"You grew up so pretty. I always thought you would."

"I'm not pretty," she said automatically.

"Well, you should tweeze your eyebrows in the middle, and wear your hair back. But you're a knockout. Enjoy that body. You won't have it forever, although I know it's hard to imagine. Metabolism always comes to call. Happened to me at thirty, on the dot."

"Oh." The conversation confused Ronnie. She had hoped for something more momentous from Helen. A hug? An apology? Whatever she had expected, it wasn't trying to speak through a screen door, with Helen so oddly detached, talking about eyebrows and hair and Ronnie's body, which was embarrassing. "I was looking for Alice."

"I don't think Alice wants to see you, Ronnie."

She's dying to see me. This thought did not find voice, but it pierced Ronnie's head, as clear and pure a sound as the singer trilling away in Helen's house. Alice wanted to see Ronnie as much as Ronnie wanted to see Alice.

"Is she here? He-Helen?"

"No. I don't know where she is. I don't know where she goes and I don't know what she does."

"Does she have a job?"

"She says she can't find one. But you did, so I have to think it's a lie."

Did Helen mean to be unkind? *If stupid Ronnie can find a job, anyone can.* But Helen had never been cruel to Ronnie on purpose, just careless at times. She probably meant that Ronnie had done well, so Alice could, too.

"What does she do, if she's not working?"

"She says she walks. For weight loss. Although—well, between us, she is bigger than ever. I'm afraid I didn't do well by her when I went wading in her father's gene pool. Between us."

Between us. There was the magic phrase. *Between us, Ronnie, I think you're the one who has the real imagination. Between us, Ronnie, I think you have an artistic temperament. Between us, Ronnie, I sometimes wonder if a bad fairy switched you and Alice at birth. Have you heard about changelings? Because you are so much more like me than she is. Alice is a good girl, a sweet girl, but you're a pistol, Ronnie. You're not scared of anything, are you, Ronnie? Between us, Ronnie, we're two peas in a pod.*

But the words didn't seem to mean anything to Helen.

"Do you think Alice will be home soon? It's almost dark."

"I don't know, Ronnie. But I don't think you should hang around here."

"Don't you—" Her voice tore a little.

"Oh, no, baby, I'm happy to see you. I really am. But a reporter came by here not more than an hour ago. She wants to write a story about you and Alice. Now, Alice has a lawyer, a smart one this time—well, she has the stupid one again, but the stupid one now works with a smart one—and they're going to take care of my baby. They promised me that they'll scare that reporter so badly she won't even think about putting Alice's name in the paper. Have you got a lawyer?"

"I haven't *done* anything." Then, remembering what Helen knew, "Not this time."

"Well, there's doing and there's doing, of course. Sometimes the innocent are more in need of legal protection than the guilty. This reporter, she keeps saying she can write the story even if no one talks to her. Maybe she's bluffing. I don't know. All I know is I didn't talk to her, and I wouldn't, either, if I were you."

"Where does Alice go, He-Helen? When she goes walking?"

"I don't know. I really don't know." The repetition revealed the lie.

"Please, Helen. *Please*." For the first time, the proper name slipped out without a stutter.

Helen leaned close to the screen, to a spot almost directly across from Ronnie's forehead. If Ronnie had tilted her head forward, they would have been touching, more or less.

"She never told me, but I saw her once, when I was coming home from the grocery store. She goes up to the pool. She walks around the swim club, looking at people. Sad, isn't it?"

Ronnie turned to go, then remembered what she had been longing to ask Helen since she came home. "Helen—do you remember the honeysuckle?"

"You mean . . ."

"The time I tried to make honeysuckle soda and sell it from a stand, like lemonade?"

Some strange emotion flooded Helen's face, her voice. "Of course I do, Ronnie. Of course I do. You tried to squeeze the juice from the blossoms into a pitcher of sugar water."

"It tasted awful. And I picked your vines bare. But you didn't mind. You weren't mad at all."

"It was a good idea," Helen said. "There should be a honeysuckle soda. You always had good ideas, Ronnie."

"I did?"

"You did, baby. You absolutely did."

*   *   *

It was past eight, but Infante and Nancy continued to read files, waiting for the moment when inertia turned to exhaustion and they could go home without feeling guilty. Now and then, Nancy forgot what they were looking for and found herself reading about the low-level medical complaints of a Martin or Moore—asthma attacks, chicken pox—as if they were good beach novels. Then she would start skimming again, looking for any trace of Alice Manning.

"I'll give you five to one that Alice Manning's file isn't even in here. Me, I'm just enjoying this tour of our juvenile justice system. A lot of kids get locked up in twenty years. I bet we've already met some of them on this side."

"Charles Maddox sounds familiar."

"They all sound familiar. That's what I'm saying. Hey, here's Metheny."

"That psycho had a juvenile record?"

"No, not the same one. Now, *that* would have been interesting."

"They usually start off with animal torture, those serial killer types. Animal torture or arson."

"Wow, Infante, those two weeks at Quantico are really paying off. You could learn that much from watching the A&E criminal justice files."

"Bite me."

"You wish. Hey, I may owe you five bucks. I just found a Manning."

She opened the file and checked the first name and the DOB. Yes, it was the right girl. "Poison ivy. Urinary tract infection, yeast infection, yeast infection . . ."

"I'm *eating* here." Infante indicated the bag of chips and soda that were his dinner for the night.

Nancy laughed, lost her place on the page, then resumed

reading. "Man, give this poor girl a lifetime prescription of Monistat. She was really prone—shit."

"What?"

"Fuck me. Fuck us."

"What?"

"Alice Manning had a baby. Three years ago."

"How do you have a baby in juvenile detention?"

"How do you get *pregnant* in juvenile detention?"

Lenhardt must have been listening through his open door, because he materialized by Nancy's desk, held out his hand for the folder, and seemed to absorb its contents in one quick glance.

"Even in juvy, it works the same way as it does here in the outside world. The egg goes on a date with the sperm." Lenhardt continued to flip through the file. "Why do you think Middlebrook is closed for renovations? It's a shithole."

"Yeah, but—"

"Where there's a will there's a way. Darwin, survival of the fittest, all that crap." He continued to study the file. "It looks like she managed to hide the pregnancy until she was almost six months gone. They just thought she was a fat girl who was prone to yeast infections. And based on this, she never told them who the father was. That space is blank throughout. A fun fact to know and tell, but does it have anything to do with the case at hand, Detective?"

"She had this baby three years ago. Isn't that what the file says? Alice's child, wherever she is, would be about three now."

"So?" Lenhardt asked, but there was no challenge in his voice, no doubt. He simply wanted to hear where Nancy's mind was going.

"That's the age of the missing girl."

Does she look like anyone? Nancy had asked Ronnie

Fuller, pushing the photograph of Brittany Little across the table.

Alice, Ronnie had said. *She looks like Alice.* Ronnie had corrected herself when Nancy challenged her, but the girl's first instinct had been pure and automatic. Not the daughter of Cynthia and Warren Barnes. *Alice.* She didn't look like the Alice that Nancy knew, but Ronnie had known another Alice, a little girl. Ronnie carried another Alice around in her head.

"We know from DNA testing," Lenhardt said, "that the girl is the biological child of Maveen Little."

"*We* know that," Nancy agreed. "But Alice doesn't. All Alice knows is that she had a baby and she doesn't anymore. Maybe the child was put up for adoption, maybe she died, maybe the grandparents are raising her. But there's no baby in the Manning household."

"Why kidnap Brittany Little?"

"A girl who can't find her own doll might steal another's. And even Alice never denied *taking* Olivia Barnes."

Helen Manning sat in her dark living room. She wished she had some dope, but she wasn't sure she would smoke it even if she did. Alice would know what it was now. Perhaps Alice had always known. Helen had once thought her daughter docile and obedient, unquestioning. But that belief was long gone, seven years gone.

She knew, this time, that Alice was involved in whatever was going on. *Fool me once, shame on you. Fool me twice—* that was the key difference between then and now. Seven years ago, Helen had gone about her life blissfully detached from the tragedy unfolding a few blocks away, allowing herself the rationalizations that made such news bearable. The missing child was a baby, not a grade-schooler like Alice. The missing baby had been left untended. The missing baby was probably taken by a baby-sitter, or someone with a specific grudge against that family. There was even a theory, manufactured from nothing, that the child had been taken to get back at the judge. Even then, Helen understood that people needed to tell themselves such stories in order to go on about their lives.

She thought she had managed the trick of telling Alice what she needed to hear, while remaining honest with herself. *She* had never forgotten that Alice's father was not dead in a car crash, while Alice accepted this information as an article of faith. Sweet Alice had been content not to press Helen on this issue, not to force her to pile too many lies on the initial one. A considerate child, content to settle for a few stories about romantic dates and the proposal that never was.

Then there were the lies Helen had told her parents, after Alice was arrested. Had Alice really been involved in this horrible thing? *Yes, but only because she was weak and impressionable.* Did she understand what she was doing? *Not really.* Why hadn't she stopped the other child? *She says she wasn't there.*

Helen remembered so clearly the night that Olivia Barnes died, not that she knew the poor child was dying at the time. Alice had been particularly sweet at dinner, laughing at everything Helen said, admiring what she wore, asking her questions about her painting, which she had never done before. She had gone through Helen's jewelry box and makeup, asked to play dress-up. Then, almost apologetically, she had asked Helen to read to her.

"Old as you are?"

"I know I can read to myself," Alice had said. "But you do it so much better, with so much expression."

They had piled onto Helen's bed, reading portions of chapter books—*The Search for Delicious, Glinda of Oz,* Helen's favorite of the Oz books. They read baby books like *In the Night Kitchen,* which Helen had always preferred to *Where the Wild Things Are.* Alice knew better than to laugh at the naked boy falling through the sky, although she did place her finger, just once, on his exposed private parts.

"What time is it?" she kept asking her mother. It was eight o'clock, it was eight forty-five, it was nine-twenty, it was ten-fifteen. "What time is it?" *Time for bed,* Helen said as eleven o'clock came and went. She tucked Alice in and went downstairs, feeling pleased with the world and herself. She had done well for a single mother. Alice was a lovely child, even if she did yearn so for everyone's approval. She would grow out of that. Helen would see to it.

It was past twelve when Helen heard a strange snuffling sound coming from the backyard and found Ronnie huddled beneath the overhanging honeysuckle vines. And it was only then that Helen understood why Alice had wanted to read, and why she had been so fixated on time. She had been establishing her alibi. She wanted Helen to be able to tell the police where Alice was, and what Alice was doing, every minute until midnight.

Alice knew she would need an alibi because she knew Ronnie was going to kill Olivia Barnes that night. She knew Ronnie would kill Olivia that particular evening, at that particular time, because Alice had persuaded her to do it. That was the story Ronnie had confided in Helen in choked sobs, as she crouched beneath the honeysuckle seven years ago, and Helen had never doubted it for a minute.

35.

Alice curled her fingers through the gaps of the chain-link fence and pressed her face close enough to feel the metal on her cheek, yet there was very little to see from this vantage point. Here, at the north end of the swim club property, there was a basketball court and an old shuffleboard court, but these areas were deserted after sunset. The pool sat on higher ground, beyond this neglected little valley, and the clubhouse was even farther away. But with nothing to see, there was no risk of being seen, which was why Alice had chosen this spot for her almost nightly visits.

There was plenty to hear, especially on an evening like this, when the pool's teenagers were having a dance party, their monthly reward for all those fifteen-minute increments surrendered to adult swim. Water and concrete combined to send strangely pure sounds to Alice, snatches of conversation and music, the thumping bass lines beneath the songs. "I told you to *stop*." "Diane thinks she's so in demand, but she's so not." "We had to drive to D.C. to find the right ones." The chatter was female, while the bursts of shouts and laughter were male.

"It *stings*!" This seeming objection, voiced by a girl, was clearly a mock complaint, flirtatious and pleased, but it reminded Alice to check the underbrush around her ankles one more time. No, there was nothing to fear here, no leaves of three, no reddish tinge.

Alice had been surprised the first time she realized how close the swim club was to her evening route through Ten Hills. It had seemed so far away when she was young, yet here it was all along, separated by a narrow strip of undergrowth and weedy trees. The sounds had drawn her here, once she figured out how to cut through people's yards and driveways to reach the unclaimed land that buffered the club. That had been nerve-racking at first, but Alice had learned to vary the routes she took each night. She also had a lie at the ready if anyone challenged her. She was looking for a cat or a dog. Nothing more serious than that. After all, if you said you were looking for a little brother or sister, people might actually care. Her fictional cat was black, except for a spot of white on its chest, and wore a blue collar with a round silver tag that identified it as Stella. Her made-up dog was a collie named Max.

So far, however, no one had asked. Sometimes Alice drew a puzzled look from a homeowner watering her garden, or a man stealing a smoke at the edge of his own property. Alice, plain and fat, was as good as invisible. She had resented this once, even after finally finding someone who didn't agree, who praised her eyes, who loved her body. But this quality had come in handy when she was on her quest.

She heard a rustling sound in the wooded no-man's-land behind her and turned, ready to tell her story. *A collie named Max, a cat named Stella. The cat has a blue collar. We call her Stella because my mom says she always wanted to have a cat named Stella, so she could go in the backyard at night and yell "Stella." That makes her laugh. I don't know why.* Helen had, in fact, told Alice she would name a cat Stella, if she had a cat. But she had allergies.

The person coming toward her was thin and not very tall.

Alice didn't need to see the face to figure out it was Ronnie Fuller. No need to make excuses to Ronnie about why she was here. She wouldn't waste a good lie on Ronnie.

"What are you doing here?" Alice asked, her voice soft yet belligerent. It was, in fact, Ronnie's old tone, the one she had used to bluff and bully when they were children, back when Alice was a little scared of her. She wasn't scared of Ronnie anymore, not really, just angry.

"Looking for you."

"We're not supposed to talk to each other."

"It's not a rule." Ronnie's voice scaled up, however, as if she wasn't sure. "It's not"—she groped for a word—"a condition, or anything. It was just, like, advice."

"It's good advice. For me. If I don't have anything to do with you, I won't get into trouble."

"I'm not—I haven't—I didn't do anything."

Something in Ronnie's voice suggested she knew Alice had.

"Really? The police think you did. The police asked me lots of questions about you and the missing girl."

"I didn't *do* anything," Ronnie repeated.

"It happened near where you worked."

"It was near where about a thousand people work, I guess."

The pool area was illuminated at night, but there were no lights here at the edges, so Alice could not make out Ronnie's expression. The old Ronnie had been more likely to hit or pinch when contradicted, blubbering wordlessly. It was disorienting to see her stand her ground. Alice had been prepared to fight the old Ronnie in the old way, using words, piling them on until Ronnie was confused. But Ronnie seemed comfortable with words now.

"There's only one person like you who works near Westview."

"What do you mean?"

"A baby-stealer. A baby-killer."

Ronnie's voice trembled. "You know I never wanted to—"

"But you *did*. You held a pillow over her face until she stopped breathing. That makes you a baby-killer. Not me. I wasn't there. Remember? I wasn't even there."

"It was your idea." But she was growing tentative, betraying her uncertainty. "You told me to do it."

Alice put on a grown-up's prissy, reproving voice. "If Alice told you to jump off a building, would you do that? If Alice told you to play with matches, would you do that? If Alice told you—"

"Shut up."

Ronnie's voice was almost a shriek, loud and sharp enough to carry to the pool. For a second or two, it felt as if everyone was holding their breath, Alice and Ronnie included, waiting to see if something was about to happen. But no footsteps came toward them, and the noise around the pool soon started again.

"I don't want to talk about what happened in the past," Ronnie said, dragging the words out as if they hurt. "It's over, and we can't change it. But what's happening now—if you did it, you have to tell them. You have to take them to the missing girl, and let her mother know where she is. You can't blame me for this."

"Why?"

"Because I didn't have anything to do with it."

"Well, I didn't do anything last time, and I got blamed." Alice put on her bland, obstinate voice, the one she used whenever pressed to give answers she didn't want to provide. *You have to tell us what happened, Alice.* Why? *So we can take steps, punish the man who did this.* But I wanted him to do it. I love him, and I don't want you to punish him. *You can't love him.* Why? *Because he doesn't love you.* But he does, he said so. *Alice, we have to know what happened.* Why?

"It was your idea," Ronnie said.

"Prove it."

"You told me what to do, how to do it. You said it had to be done."

Alice shrugged, her gaze fixed on the pool.

"Look, I don't care about then." Ronnie's voice was increasingly desperate. "I care about now. If you don't tell the truth, the police are going to keep coming to where I work, and I'm going to lose my job. Or the newspaper will write about us—"

"Really?" Alice had thought there would be newspapers and television shows eventually, but not so soon.

"Really. I went to see Helen and she said—"

"Why did you go see my mom?"

"Because I was looking for you. And Helen said—"

She hated to hear her mother's name in Ronnie's mouth. She wanted to yank it from her, scream "Snatch pops, no snatch backs" the way the tough kids did when they stole Popsicles and candy bars. "You shouldn't call her that. Even now. She's my mother. She's a grown-up."

"Helen said—"

"She's my mom. Not yours. You have your own mother and a father, too. All I have is a mother. She's mine. Stay away from her. Can't you just stay away? You don't even live next door anymore. There's no reason for you to be hanging around."

"I just—" Ronnie was stuttering and lost, the way she had been in class, when sister's questions came too fast. When Ronnie began to fall behind, she could never catch up.

"My mom didn't even approve of you."

"Alice—"

"She felt sorry for you. That's why she made me play with you, that's why she let you spend time at our house."

"I don't—"

"Because she felt bad for how awful and nasty your family was, and how you didn't have any real friends. But she never liked you. She made fun of you behind your back."

"No. No, she wouldn't do that."

Alice had thought her final accusation would unhinge Ronnie, but she was suddenly quiet, thoughtful, dangerously close to being in control. "She liked me. She told me all the time how much she liked me. She said I was more like her than you."

Now it was Alice's shriek that cut through the night air. "She didn't, she didn't, she didn't! You're such a liar. You were always a liar and a loser, the girl that no one chose for sides or partners. My mom couldn't possibly like you."

Again, the voices around the pool stilled, waiting. Again, they resumed. Alice lowered her voice.

"Do you know why you did it? Why I told you to do it?"

"You said the baby was sick and unhappy—"

Alice's voice, while low, was triumphant. "I made all that up. Because I knew they would take you away. I thought they would lock you up forever and I wouldn't have to see you anymore. I didn't know you'd be smart enough to steal my jack-in-the-box and leave it there. Otherwise, I could have said I was never there and they would have believed me because it would have been my word against yours."

"I didn't—I never—the jack-in-the-box wasn't what I wanted—"

Flashlight beams suddenly began cutting paths through the woods, playing across the fence, landing only a few feet from where Alice and Ronnie stood.

"Alice? Alice Manning?" a woman's voice called.

"It's the police," Alice hissed, her eyes bright with excitement. "They're coming for you. They know who you are and what you did. They're going to lock you up forever this time. And the newspapers are going to write about you, and everyone will know. Ronnie Fuller killed a baby. Ronnie Fuller, nobody else. Now she's taken another baby, and she'll probably kill her, too."

"I *didn't*."

"I'm going to tell them you told me as much. I'm going to tell them that you said you took the girl and chopped her in little pieces and threw her in the incinerator. I'm going to tell them you did it because she looks half black and you hate black people, always have, just like last time. You told me you hate it when black people and white people have babies together. I'm going to tell them—"

But Ronnie didn't wait to hear the rest of Alice's manufactured history. She turned and ran, away from the lights, indifferent to the twisted vines beneath her feet. She moved with surprising grace through the dark trees, barely making any sound.

"Hurry, she's getting away!" Alice cried out in the direction of the lights. "We're over here, near the fence. Hurry!"

It sounded as if a dozen people were rushing toward her, but it was only two, the police detectives who had talked to her before Sharon said they couldn't anymore.

"Alice Manning?" the female detective asked, as if she didn't already know who she was.

"Ronnie was just here. Ronnie's getting away. Ronnie told me—"

The detectives turned, shining their beams in several directions, but Ronnie had moved so swiftly through the trees that there was nothing to see.

"We'll send a patrol to her house," the woman said. She had her hand on Alice's wrist. Why was she holding on to Alice when she should be chasing Ronnie?

"We want to talk to you," the man said. "We need to ask you about something we found in your file from Middlebrook."

"What file?"

"Your medical records."

"Oh."

"Would you mind coming with us back to headquarters?" The woman made it sound like a question, but Alice had a feeling it wasn't. "You can call your lawyer from there if you need to. But we really need to talk to you."

Alice turned her gaze back to the fence. The teenagers who had been allowed to take over the pool for the evening were standing at the deep end, looking toward the woods, their hands shielding their eyes as they tried to make sense of the light and noise coming from Alice's side of the fence. She did not actually know any of them, but she might have. Her old friends from St. William of York could be among the bikini-clad girls. One of the boys could have been her boyfriend, if she didn't already have one. She imagined confiding in one of these girls: "I have a boyfriend who's six years older than I am. He has a pickup truck, and he takes me out driving, and he wants to marry me." The last was not exactly true, but it was true enough. He would marry her, if she told him that's what he had to do. He would do anything she told him to do. So would Helen, and Sharon, and even her new lawyer, that ugly woman who smelled bad. For once, everyone had to do what she said.

It was nice, being in charge, on the verge of getting the recognition she deserved. Finally, the world was going to know what it had done to her, and she was going to be compensated. She would probably be very rich when this was all over, not to mention famous. She would be on talk shows, where a professional would do her makeup, maybe even pick out her clothes.

Although, if she had a say in it, if she could change who she was and what had happened to her, she'd rather just be eighteen and thin enough to wear a bikini.

"Did you match the blood?" she asked the detectives, curious to know how they had gotten ahead of her, not that it would make much difference. "Is that how you found out? Did you get his blood?"

The man and the woman exchanged a look, but said nothing, just held out their arms to her to help her back through the woods, as if she didn't know the way in and out better than anyone. They climbed the hill to the roadside, a detective on either side of Alice, holding tight to her upper arms. It was like *The Wizard of Oz*, Alice thought, except they didn't skip.

36.

"It's my baby," Alice said. "You can't arrest someone for taking her own baby."

"Sure you can," Nancy said. "Only this isn't your baby. And even if it were, it wouldn't be legal for you to take her, to hurt her, or put her somewhere she isn't safe."

"She's my baby." Alice spoke in a monotone, as if the conversation bored her. "It took me a long time to find her, but now that I have, you can't make me give her back. I never wanted to give her up in the first place."

"Alice . . ." Sharon put a cautionary hand on her shoulder, but Alice shook it off. On Alice's left, Rosario Bustamante rolled her eyes and looked around the interview room, as if hopeful a bar might suddenly materialize. She had arrived on a wave of gin fumes, Nancy couldn't help noticing, but there was nothing to suggest that the older woman was the least bit impaired. She looked rumpled, but no more so than Sharon, who had been getting ready for bed when summoned here.

"She's my baby," Alice said. "I knew it the moment I saw her."

Alice had been repeating this one assertion over and over, her own Baltimore catechism, refusing to elaborate, indifferent to the evidence the detectives offered to the contrary. Told that the DNA evidence had already established Brittany

Little was, in fact, the daughter of Maveen Little, Alice had shrugged and said: "Then you did it wrong. You better double-check." Asked where the child was, she said she wouldn't admit to anything until they conceded the girl was hers.

And so they had gone, around and around, until it was going on eleven o'clock.

"Look, this isn't productive," Sharon said. "Make us an offer. Maybe a misdemeanor."

"What misdemeanor?" Nancy's voice was hoarse from exhaustion, and she sounded a decade older than she had that morning. It was a good effect, actually. She wished she could cultivate it at will. "She's all but confessed that she took the child. There's no turning back from that."

"She's confused, she's suggestible. She doesn't know what she's saying."

"I know exactly what I'm saying," Alice said. "That girl is my baby. They took her away from me so no one would find out what happened to me when I was in Middlebrook. But now everyone is going to know."

Frustrated by the girl's stubborn will, Nancy left the interview room. Helen Manning was sitting with Infante, drinking a soda, as carefree as if she were just passing time in some teachers' lounge. Infante's jowls were blue-black, the bags under his eyes darker still, his hair shiny from being slicked back with his palms over and over again. He looked like the world's most tired werewolf. Nancy tapped him on the shoulder and nodded toward the interview room. They had been taking turns all evening, spelling one another. Lenhardt had come in, but even he conceded he had nothing to bring to the interviews. Nancy and Infante were marathon dancers, obligated to shuffle to the end together or be disqualified.

"What's this about the baby, Mrs. Manning?" Nancy

asked, sliding into the chair Infante had vacated. "Why does Alice think this child is hers?"

"Please—call me Helen. I think of Mrs. Manning as my mother."

She had made this plea before, more than once, but Nancy continued to ignore it. "Why does Alice think this baby is hers?"

"Oh, she doesn't *really*. I mean, she's very fixated on this issue, but she knows her child was put up for adoption. She thinks because she never named the father that the adoption wasn't legal. But given Alice's circumstances, I had the power of attorney. If she hadn't hidden the pregnancy from me into her third trimester, I would have forced her to get an abortion."

Nancy wouldn't be surprised to learn that Alice had concealed her pregnancy for just that reason.

"She got pregnant while in the juvenile facility?"

"Oh, yes. Shocking, isn't it? We begged Alice to tell us who the father was. Because lord knows, he might still be out there, preying on other girls. But she was quite stubborn. She thinks the man loved her. Which I'm sure is what he told her. Don't they always? It was a mess, actually, getting the courts to allow the adoption. But Sharon helped."

"So who adopted the child?"

"Not this Maveen Little woman. This is not Alice's baby."

"We *know* that." It was hard, concealing her exasperation with Helen Manning. But any sign of irritation only wounded the woman, bringing on a pretty fit of weeping that slowed everything down. "But do you know who did? Was it an open adoption?"

"Oh, no, it was confidential. I wanted Alice to move on, to forget about it."

"So why is Alice so convinced that Brittany Little is her child?"

Helen Manning lied so badly, so baldly, that there was al-most a perverse charm to it. Now, for example, her eyes drifted to the acoustic ceiling tiles overhead as if they were the most fascinating bit of decor she had ever seen.

"I haven't the faintest idea."

"You know, we've been very patient with you, Mrs. Manning."

"Helen."

"We've been very patient with you, Mrs. Manning," Nancy repeated. "We have not treated you as an accessory to this crime, or accused you of shielding your daughter or withholding information we need. But that moment is com-ing, sooner rather than later. The time is past where you can keep anything from us, for any reason."

"Alice doesn't confide in anyone, even me." Helen leaned forward and lowered her voice. "She's always been a little secretive. Self-contained. And she's not the most, well, nor-mal young woman. This could be all in her head. She may not have anything to do with the kidnapping. She could think the girl is hers because she saw her on television, and it got all mixed up in her head."

"Why would she even think that?"

Helen sighed, looked away. Now it was a poster on the wall, an admonition to wear seat belts, that demanded her unwavering gaze.

"You have to understand. She had been obsessive on this topic since she came home. *Where was her baby? What had happened to it? How could I give it up? Why hadn't I kept the child and raised it?* She wouldn't leave it alone, and the simple truth—that the child had been put up for adoption and I had no idea where she was—didn't satisfy her. She kept hounding me for answers. I had to tell her something."

"And?"

"I made up a little story that would provide a sense of closure. So I said I had seen her little girl in the Catonsville area—they have such pretty houses over there, lovely old Victorians. I knew Alice would like that. I said the baby had wonderful parents and she was beautiful, with café-au-lait skin and amber hair, which fell in ringlets. Oh—and that she had a birthmark on her left shoulder blade, like a little shadow of her heart."

"And how did you come up with a description of a child who happened to match Rosalind Barnes so closely? Sheer coincidence?"

"Well, yes and no."

Helen Manning was flirtatious in her candor, peering at Nancy with rounded eyes, as if she were a child who was always forgiven for her transgressions.

"You see, I saw the other mother in the grocery store one day, around the time Alice came home."

"The other mother?"

"You know. Cynthia Barnes. The one whose child Alice . . ." Helen Manning's eyes traveled back to the ceiling for a second, but not in search of a lie this time. She was pausing to allow Nancy the chance to finish her thought. "Anyway, she was with this little girl. And I thought to myself: 'That child would not exist if it weren't for Alice.' "

"What?"

"Think about it. The Barnes mother had a baby in her forties, four years after the other girl died. Which isn't to say that what Alice did can be rationalized in any way. But the fact remains. A baby died, and it was my daughter's fault. I never lost sight of that. But another child lives, a beautiful child, and I'm not sure she would if it weren't for Alice. My daughter helped to bring that little life into the world. In a sense. I didn't see the harm in using that child's description to assuage Alice's unhappiness."

"But what about the birthmark? Where did that come

from?" Nancy was thinking of the tips that had come in over the past four days, stories of other curly-headed girls who had disappeared, then reappeared. One, in the Catonsville library, had her shirt on inside-out when she was found. It must have been Alice, looking for the tell-tale heart.

"Oh, I made that up. I told Alice that the mark was like a little shadow of her own heart and she should feel happy, knowing that her daughter would always have this shadow heart."

Helen Manning looked at Nancy with bright, hopeful eyes, as if she expected to be praised for her imagination and tenderness. Nancy said nothing, didn't even bother to excuse herself as she stood up and walked back into the interview room.

In a matter of minutes, a defeated Alice Manning had finally let go of all the secrets she held, the old and the not-so-old. She told them of the man who had seduced her, the man she had protected because she loved him, a man who would now do whatever she told him as long as she didn't give away his name. She told of her long walks through Baltimore, looking for a girl with amber ringlets, a girl with the birthmark her mother had described. Brittany Little did not have a heart-shaped birthmark, but she had an oversized mole on her back. Alice figured it must have changed since her mother saw it last.

Once Alice had found the child she believed to be hers, she hid in the bathroom and waited for the baby's father to come and get them, bringing new clothes. Summoned from his current landscaping job on his cell phone, he had cut his hand badly as he put away his tools, possibly because he could never decide what he feared more, Alice's love or Alice's threats. The wound on his hand opened again as he trimmed the girl's hair with his pruning shears. The blood on the T-shirt was his, and Alice had assumed that DNA testing would show it matched the missing girl's. She believed the police had found the baby's father, and thus found her. She still believed it, even now. He had driven her home in plenty of time to meet Sharon for dinner.

"And then what happened?"

"He took her to where he lives, down south, to wait."

"Wait for what, Alice?" The girl was an endless source of amazement to Nancy. What had she expected, what did she want? A new life, or her old one?

"We were going to prove she was ours, and make them give her back to us. And maybe give us money, too, because it was wrong, what happened to me. Rodrigo was working for the state when we . . . met. They let me get pregnant, then they took my baby away. I didn't say they could. I wanted to keep her."

"Why?"

Alice looked as if she found Nancy stupid beyond belief. "Because she was mine."

"You said they're down south. In Maryland? Virginia? Someplace farther still? We need to know where the girl is, Alice."

She started to answer, but Rosario Bustamante actually placed a hand, loaded with grimy rings, over Alice's mouth.

"Before she tells you that," the old lawyer said, "let's discuss what you're willing to do for my client, now that she's cooperating."

The house in Waldorf was a rental, a shabby one, the kind of place that landlords could foist off on recent immigrants, comfortable in the knowledge they would never complain. Even the legal ones didn't know their rights, didn't understand that broken plumbing and lead paint were not things they had to endure. Rodrigo Benitez was in the country

legally, but some of his roommates were not, and they fled
into the night when the police cars began arriving outside
the shack, running across the same tobacco fields where
some of them had first found work.

The old woman stayed, the child in her lap. She did not
know why Rodrigo had brought her this child and demanded
she care for it. He said it was his daughter, and that the girl's
mother was in trouble. He swore he had done nothing
wrong, despite all signs to the contrary—his nervousness,
his odd comings and goings over the weekend. Then, yesterday evening, Rodrigo had simply disappeared, and she knew
her grandson had lied. He was in trouble, which meant she
was in trouble, and it would be only a matter of time before
police officers came, screaming questions at her. In the
meantime, the child cried for her mother, cried constantly,
but little else she said made sense to the *abuelita*. She tried
to comfort her as best she could.

Yet she had promised Rodrigo she would care for the
child, no matter what. So when the police arrived, she did
just that, holding the girl tightly to her, shaking her head, incapable of making sense even of the halting Spanish spoken
by one of the uniformed men. The girl clung back. She was
three years old and in the course of four days she had been
taken from her mother and brought to a house of strange
smells, and now she saw that someone else was going to take
her yet again. This unknown place suddenly became desirable, an island of certainty, even if people here spoke mysterious words, full of vowels, and she was given soft, mashed
brown food, which looked like pudding but had no sweet-
ness to it. Brittany Little held the old woman, refusing to let
go until a blond woman with a round, tired face held out her
arms and spoke her name.

"It's okay, Brittany. Your mom is outside, waiting for you.
Come to your mother, Brittany."

Maveen Little was reunited with her daughter in a patrol car outside the shack in Waldorf. It was a messy, incoherent moment, with the woman more hysterical than grateful, her emotions out of sync from fatigue and worry. Nancy understood how she felt. The child had been found, Tuesday was now Wednesday, but Nancy still had to process Alice's arrest before she could go home. Still, it had been her decision to drive the fifty-odd miles to Charles County, to see this moment firsthand. She didn't need Lenhardt to tell her that homicide cops had precious few chances to see their victims alive.

Infante must have been thinking the same thing, for he said: "A few more cases like this, and we'll be out of business."

"A few more cases like this," Nancy said, "and I'm going to get a job at Circuit City."

Actually, she had never loved her job more than at that moment.

The media relations office would schedule a press conference in the morning, probably in time for the noon television shows. Nancy was already planning to sleep through it, let the corporal tell the tale. That was how they did it in Baltimore County. Detectives did the work, and the media office relayed the results. The television types would be so focused on the breaking news aspect, they probably wouldn't dig too deep into the whys of it all. The *Beacon-Light* would be left to find an angle that wouldn't be old by the next day.

That would feel good, screwing the paper and that girl who had tried to trick her.

Ronnie Fuller had taken almost two hours to walk home after running away from the flashlights in the woods. She had tried to stick to alleys and side streets, venturing out on Route 40 only when absolutely necessary. Once she arrived at the house on St. Agnes Lane, she had stood across the street, looking for signs that her parents were up and waiting for her, searching the street for a patrol car. But the house was dark, her parents out somewhere, and there was no cop car in sight. She crept up to the front door, only to jump when a small rectangle of paper floated to the ground. It had been stuck between the storm door and the frame.

"Mira Jenkins, *Beacon-Light*," said the front of the card. On the back, in neat block letters, someone had written. "I really, really need to talk to you. Call me!"

Ronnie let herself in, and all but crawled up the stairs to her room. Sleep. She would sleep.

But once on her bed, sleep would not come. All she could think of was Alice, her threats, her taunts. Alice could make a person do horrible things. It would be nothing for Alice to make others believe that Ronnie had taken this child and carved her up. The newspaper knew her name, just as Alice said, they were going to tell people about her. Alice always got her way, in the end.

You be the daddy and I'll be the mommy and this is our baby.

That was how the game had begun, and it was only a game at first. They were going to take care of the baby they had found. She lived in a big house, Alice said. Her parents would probably give them a lot of money for finding her and keeping her safe. But it might take a day or two before a reward was offered, so they had to take good care of her until then.

How much money? Ronnie had wondered.

Oh, a lot, Alice had said with confidence. *Enough so I can go to St. William of York again next year.*

And me, too?

No, Alice had said, looking vague. *You still have to go to public school. But you might be able to buy your mother a new car.*

It was on the second day that the baby had gotten sick and fussy. Alice stopped talking about the reward and started imagining the kind of life that a sick little baby would have in a big house where everything was perfect. Except for her.

No one loves her, Alice had said mournfully over and over. *No one will ever love her.*

Should we take her back? Ronnie had asked. *Should we call someone and tell them where she is?*

They'll only leave her on the porch again, hoping some- one else will take her. They don't want her. She's not pretty, and she cries all the time, so they want her to disappear.

It was so hot tonight, especially in Ronnie's windowless room. Unable to sleep, she decided to run a tepid tub, some- thing she did when she needed to cool off. She locked the bathroom door, even though no one was home. Naked, she slipped into the tub, frowning at her body. She had never liked having such big breasts, which looked silly and out of place on a skinny girl. Clarice had once asked if they were fake. Even her dad sneaked looks at them, although not in a gross way. He seemed dismayed, as if he were scared for Ronnie, as if he knew how other men acted around her.

You be the daddy and I'll be the mommy and this is our baby.

As the daddy, Ronnie had been responsible for bringing food to the cabin and Alice had served it. The baby hadn't liked what they gave her and she cried, and her poo turned green, and that's how they knew she was sick. The only scarier thing than her crying was her *not* crying.

By the third day, she became listless and dull, probably from eating the wrong things, but Alice had insisted they could not take her back. The baby was dying, she an- nounced. It was only a matter of time. She had been sick all along, and her parents had left her outside, hoping someone would take her off their hands. Funny, Ronnie always re-membered the exact phrase: *off their hands*. She had never heard that before.

"You have to take care of this baby," Alice had told Ron-nie. "You have to help her. If you use a pillow and then get rid of it, no one will know. They'll think she died in her sleep. Babies do that all the time. And this baby is going to die anyway. It's cruel to let her suffer."

"Can't we take her back?"

"It's too late," Alice said. "They'll think it's our fault. But it's not. You have to do this, Ronnie."

She hadn't used a pillow, though. She had brought one as Alice had instructed, the one from her bed, still in its Scooby-Doo pillowcase. But in the end, it had seemed wrong to put something so large over the small face. Instead, Ronnie had placed her hand over the baby's mouth and turtlelike nose, counting her own breaths until the baby's stopped. *One one thousand, two one thousand, three one thousand.* This was how they had been taught to count sec-onds back in third grade, and Miss Timothy, a lay teacher, had told them to put their heads on the desk and raise their hands when they thought a minute had passed. *Four one thousand, five one thousand, six one thousand.* Ronnie had not raised her hand until she began to hear small giggles around the classroom. She had forgotten to count, and ninety seconds were gone before she realized she should fake it. *Seven one thousand, eight one thousand, nine one thousand.* It seemed to Ronnie that the little girl's eyes, which had been dull and unfocused for the past two days, met hers with gratitude. She knew she was sick and unloved. She wanted to die. *Ten one thousand, eleven one thousand, twelve one thousand.*

When the body was still and the baby quiet, Ronnie real-

ized the enormity of what she had done and the impossibil-
ity of taking it back. Instead of crawling into her house
through the bedroom window she had been using to come
and go that week, she hid beneath the honeysuckle vines in
Helen's backyard, waiting to be discovered. She knew Helen
would find her somehow. And she did, drawn to the hiding
place by Ronnie's sobs. Once there, she listened to Ronnie's
story without comment or criticism, rocking her in her arms.

It was Helen, not Ronnie, who said they should take the
jack-in-the-box back to the cabin in the woods, so people
would believe Ronnie when she said Alice was there. Helen
understood better than anyone what a good liar Alice was.
But if one of Alice's toys was there, if Ronnie told the part
about the pool, and how they had gone home together—
then, just then, people might believe Alice had done it. Helen had said, Helen had promised.

"I can't undo what you've done," she told Ronnie, holding
her, stroking her hair. "But I can make sure that Alice
doesn't go unpunished. I can make it fair."

Now, Ronnie knew. Alice had gotten what she wanted:
She had made Ronnie go away. But she had to go away, too,
and that was the grudge she carried to this day. Alice would
not rest until she succeeded in banishing Ronnie again. Alice
was the good girl, and Ronnie was the bad girl, and Alice
would keep insisting on those facts. If she knew how Helen
had taken Ronnie's side, she would only become more fierce
in her determination to drive Ronnie out. She would never let
Ronnie be, which was all Ronnie really wanted. Just to be.

Ronnie's hair, which she had piled on top of her head with
a clip, was beginning to slip, and she sat up to rearrange it.
Her elbow caught her father's razor, knocking it from the
ledge of the tub. Her mother must have used it to shave her
legs, which always pissed her father off. Ronnie ran it along
her own legs, which still showed the scars of her long-ago

handiwork. Cutting herself hadn't been a plan, not at first. She loved the sensation of breaking through her own skin, the taste of blood as it gathered beneath her fingernails. Surrendering that lovely habit had been the price of staying in Shechter Unit, but it had been hard. She missed the sensation of drawing blood from herself, of attacking the places that itched and taunted her. She had only stopped because she wanted to stay in Shechter. She could resume if she wanted to. Those rules no longer applied.

It proved to be hard work, opening her veins, but not as hard as it had been all those years ago, when Ronnie had scratched and bitten and clawed through her own flesh. The skin on her wrists reminded her of the almost transparent slices of Parmesan that her mother cut when she was making noodle casseroles. The cheese was so hard on the rind, waxy and hard to remove, yet so fragile once separated.

Finally, the blood began flowing and Ronnie leaned back, arms propped on the ledges of the tub. *No one cuts me but me.* She smiled at the memory of the shocked look on the detective's face, her expression so similar to the one Maddy's mom had worn all those years ago, when Ronnie's fist hit her chin. It had been a good line.

If only Ronnie had more good lines, more words, better words, words that she could put together so people would understand her, know who she really was. If only she could be like Alice, who was never at a loss for what to say—who, in fact, came to believe everything she said so fiercely that her stories might as well be true. Alice would find a way to discount what Ronnie had told her tonight, would decide it was a lie, or that she hadn't heard it right. She might come to accept that Helen had given Ronnie the jack-in-the-box, but not on that particular night or for that particular reason. Alice was so good at sweeping away the facts that didn't fit her version of things. Ronnie saw her back in the cabin, sweeping the floor with a broom she had insisted on lugging there, indifferent to the fact that she was just moving dirt over dirt. And Helen would never admit that the jack-in-the-box was her idea, so—two against one. Even alone with Ronnie, Helen had not spoken directly of the truth that bound them, the secret that only they knew. "Between us" was another way of saying *only* between us.

Besides, nothing, not even Helen's private sympathy, could change the central fact of who Ronnie was. She was the girl who had killed a baby. Ronnie, not Alice. She could say "I'm sorry" a million times over, could go to adult prison for the rest of her life, become a nun, work her way up to manage the Bagel Barn, marry and have her own children. She could do anything and everything, but she could not undo her past, despite the promises her doctor had made. It was what she was, all she was, and all she would ever be.

She was getting woozy, and her hair was trailing in the water again, but she no longer cared. Bit by bit, her upper body followed the strands of her hair. Her bath took on a pinkish hue, as if she had been using rose-scented oils. Ronnie wondered if she would fight the water as it came over her face, if she would change her mind at the last minute.

She didn't.

Thursday,
October 8

37.

"The date is wrong."

"Excuse me?"

"The date. It's wrong."

"I think I know the day my daughter was born—October 8. Today. It's why I'm here. Today is my daughter's birthday."

"No, the day she . . . the day that . . . the second date. July 17. That was the day she *disappeared*. But not—well, it's not exactly right."

Cynthia Barnes followed Nancy Porter's tentative finger: July 17, seven years ago. The girl was right. How could such a mistake have been made? She and Warren had brought so much care to the task of burying their daughter. This, after all, would be the only ritual they would plan for her. There had been seemingly endless decisions—picking out a headstone, planning a service, debating the bas-relief lamb and whether it would be over the top to add William Blake's familiar lines. No poetry, Cynthia had finally decreed. The short span of Olivia's life was more eloquent than any couplet ever written.

So how had this *oversight* happened? Was Olivia dead to her parents from the moment she disappeared? Had Cynthia and Warren lost hope, and in doing so, lost their daughter? Cynthia was still not beyond such bouts of self-recrimination.

Which meant, she understood now, that she never would

be, that she didn't really want to be. Forget and forgive, the old adages advised, although most people switched the order, put the forgiveness cart before the forgetting horse. But if you were determined not to forget something, to remember a deed in all its stark horror, then you would have to be a saint to forgive it. Cynthia had never aspired to sainthood.

"It doesn't really matter," Nancy said. "It's just that, well, I can't help remembering the date."

You remember for you, Cynthia thought, *because it was central to your life.* But she no longer availed herself of the privilege of saying whatever she wished. She might not be a saint, but she also wasn't Sharon Kerpelman, thank God.

"I choose to remember this day."

"That's probably for the best," the detective said, missing Cynthia's tone. She missed a lot of nuances, this girl. "I was touched you agreed to share this visit with me this year."

Actually, Cynthia had done no such thing. She had mentioned her plans in the context of an excuse, a reason not to meet with Nancy at all. Again, a more intuitive person would have picked up on the insincerity of the invitation and turned it down.

"You have done a lot for our family, I suppose. I know my daughter is safe, that those girls were not trying to harm her or get to us. And I needed to know that for my peace of mind."

Nancy nodded. "I can see that. I also can see you usually get what you need, one way or another. Don't you, Mrs. Barnes?"

Perhaps the girl understood more than she let on.

"What are you trying to suggest, Ms. Porter?" Cynthia never called the young woman anything as formal as "detective." It wasn't a real title, like her father's, or something a person earned with a degree.

"Nothing, nothing at all. I've just been thinking about the

fact that what appeared to be a coincidence—the missing girl's resemblance to your daughter—turned out to be anything but."

"That wasn't my fault." Said sharply, swiftly, with the defensiveness of a child. "Helen Manning did that, when she appropriated my child's likeness for the grandbaby she never knew, never wanted to know, if you ask me."

"True," Nancy said. "I don't think Helen Manning had much desire to be a mother, much less a grandmother."

"It was a good thing I called, if you think about it."

"Oh, you're very good with a telephone."

There was nothing to say to that.

"Let's see—" Nancy began ticking off a list on the fingers of her left hand. "You called my sergeant and then you called me, even though I wasn't even the primary on the case. I figure you called the reporter, too, got her stirred up. Because you didn't really care if we found the missing child. You just wanted to make sure that everyone knew who Alice and Ronnie were, what they had done. Brittany Little's disappearance gave you an opportunity you were already looking for."

Cynthia shrugged, as if the matter was of such insignificance that it didn't merit comment.

"You even called me."

"So you said."

"No, I mean *earlier*. Those messages on my cell phone, right after Alice was released—those were your handiwork, right?"

"How would I even know your cell phone number?"

"I don't know. I do know my mom got a call last spring, from a woman organizing a class reunion for Kenwood High School. Potrcurzski, now that's a name you can find in a phone book—and it's the name you knew me by, back in the day. My mom gave the caller my cell and my home phone, but I never did get that invite."

"I was right. In the end, I was right."

"*Half* right," Nancy said, in a bone-dry tone that Cynthia had to admire.

"I'm really sorry about Ronnie Fuller," she said, and the sentiment was as true as she could make it. She did pity the girl's mother, who looked so wrecked on the evening news, the very embodiment of whatever the opposite of closure was. Even Helen Manning had seemed genuinely grief-stricken by the news of Ronnie's death, belying a level of feeling that surprised Cynthia. She hadn't thought the woman was capable of caring for anyone but herself.

Still, Ronnie Fuller would forever be the person who had killed Olivia, and Cynthia just could not be unhappy that the girl had taken leave of this planet.

"If you ask me, what's galling is that the other girl's not even in that much trouble. But the justice system is imperfect. Or so they kept telling me, when it failed me."

"Alice was in a good position to make a deal," Nancy said on a sigh. "Her accomplice is gone, probably out of the country, so he becomes the perfect fall guy. All of a sudden, this guy she was touting as the love of her life is a predator who raped her in the tool shed while she was supposed to be gardening. I can't criticize the state's attorney for not wanting to take it before a jury. A jury might have acquitted. At least she's on probation this way."

"Sharon Kerpelman rides again. She must be very proud of herself."

Nancy allowed herself a wisp of a smile. "She might be, if she hadn't sold her soul to Rosario Bustamante. I just saw her at the courthouse this morning. She's working her ass off, representing real scum now."

"Are you saying Alice Manning wasn't scum?"

"She is to you. In the big picture, she's an amateur. I've been in interview rooms with some truly scary characters.

Alice Manning wasn't one of them." Nancy paused, distracted by her own thoughts.

"What about Helen Manning? If she hadn't told her daughter that stupid story to excuse her own actions . . ." Cynthia might not mourn Ronnie Fuller, but she still had a hard time speaking of the girl's suicide. "She's the one who set everything in motion, with her lies. How does she go on?"

"She goes on because she doesn't see it that way, because she truly believes she was always well intentioned. Helen Manning is a woman inclined to think well of herself."

"Aren't most of us?"

"Not to that extent."

Cynthia noticed that Nancy had placed one hand on her belly, round and full beneath her straight navy blue skirt, a summery polished cotton that was wrong for the season.

"Are you—?" she asked.

Nancy followed Cynthia's gaze. "Oh. No, just indigestion from the pizza I ate for lunch. I'm not pregnant." She smiled. "Not yet."

"Trying?"

"Sort of. No longer *not* trying at any rate."

"Isn't it hard?"

Nancy laughed. "Actually, I like my husband, so I'm enjoying it."

"No, I mean—won't it be difficult to be a homicide detective with a child?"

"Impossible, probably."

"Even if you could work out the day care and the hours—well, I think it would drive you crazy, knowing the things you know about people, then bringing a child into this world. I don't know how you could do it."

"How did you do it," Nancy asked, "knowing what you knew?"

Cynthia wanted to assume that Nancy was alluding to

Olivia's death, the precarious state of happiness, the folly of bringing another child into this world after losing the first. But the detective could just as well have been referring to what Cynthia knew about herself.

"Look, I have a dentist's appointment. Was there something specific you wanted from me?"

"Just to touch base," Nancy said. "I mean, in a weird way I am grateful to you. Given Alice's past, she might have hurt that child once she realized it wasn't hers. I'm glad we found her when we did. It's just too bad that Ronnie Fuller had to be dragged into it."

"Am I supposed to feel guilty?"

Nancy thought about this. "No. Actually—no."

And Cynthia realized that Nancy Porter was one of those odd people who said precisely what she meant most of the time. She had not come here to taunt her, or to punish her, or even to transfer to Cynthia any guilt she might feel over Ronnie's death. She had come here to make clear that no one had fooled her, but also to offer a benediction of sorts. Contemplating motherhood, she understood. Almost.

The girl left, walking on chunky, out-of-style heels with the overcareful tread people used in cemeteries. Once she got pregnant, she was going to be one of those women who just lost it, whose bodies gave in and never found their way back from the world of elastic waistbands. But she wouldn't mind, Cynthia had a feeling. She'd be so happy, she wouldn't mind the extra pounds.

Alone at last, Cynthia said good-bye to her daughter properly, then spent a few minutes talking to God. She started out obedient and humble, but she soon found she was giving him all sorts of instructions, running through a litany of what she would accept and what she would not. Some habits were hard to break. But she promised God that she would trust him, from now on, to figure out what was right and wrong.

God and men such as her father, imperfect as they may be. She had thought that justice was a salve, something she could create and apply to her own wounds. It had only made her rawer.

Later that day, driving home from the dentist, she went by way of Nottingham, another habit she couldn't seem to break. She couldn't help keeping an eye out for Alice Manning. Without even trying, Cynthia had begun to learn bits and pieces of the girl's routine, and she knew Alice could often be seen this time of day, returning from the bus stop on Edmondson Avenue, plodding along with that distinctive, turned-out tread.

Yes, there she was, coming down the street with a knapsack on her back, a blue plastic grocery bag in her hand, swinging it the way a child might swing her lunch box. The girl was fatter than ever and she had dyed her blond hair red, presumably so she wouldn't be recognized at the community college she attended. Yet she had also given an interview to that reporter, Mira Jenkins, just this week, and posed for a big photograph. So anyone who cared knew her hair was red now. Mira had called Cynthia and asked if she had any comment she wanted to make. "I don't talk to reporters," Cynthia reminded the girl, who was too full of her own good fortune to get the sly joke. She was working downtown, she told Cynthia. She was covering juvenile justice, a beat created just for her.

"Juvenile justice." Cynthia had longed to ask Mira, Is that a smaller form of justice, the way a Whopper Jr. is just a smaller version of the Whopper? But she had held her tongue.

At least Alice had the good sense not to smile in the photograph, to look somber and grave, her hands folded on the back of a chair that camouflaged her bulk. She was sorry, she told Mira and her readers. Sorry for everything. But she had always been so easily persuaded by others. First by Ronnie, then by Rodrigo. She would try to be stronger in the future. She would be her own person, not so worried about pleasing others. All she wanted, she said, was to be good and do well in school. She was thinking about a career in nursing, or maybe as a teacher, like her mother. Just like her mother. Lord help her, Cynthia thought, if that wish came true. The last thing the world needed was *two* oblivious Manning women, wreaking havoc on anyone who had the bad luck to get close to them.

"Who that?" Rosalind had asked, coming upon Cynthia as she stared numbly at the paper that autumn morning, poking at Alice Manning's face with her stubby baby finger. "Who that lady?"

Heads together, mother and daughter studied the photograph. Words occurred to Cynthia, factual but inadequate. To speak the girl's name, to tell the story, would give her the power she had always craved, to buy into the very happily-ever-after fairy tale that Helen Manning had used to console herself and her daughter. Does Sleeping Beauty's father ever mention the bad fairy once the spell is broken, much less concede his own hubris? Does the miller's daughter acknowledge that Rumpelstiltskin made her a queen, fair and square, and that she was the one who reneged on the bargain? Say his name and he tears himself in half. Say the name and be done with it.

"Some girl," Cynthia told Rosalind, turning the page. "Just some girl."

A+

AUTHOR INSIGHTS, EXTRAS & MORE...

FROM

LAURA LIPPMAN

AND

wm

WILLIAM MORROW

Here is a preview of
New York Times bestselling author
Laura Lippman's next brilliant and suspenseful novel

the most dangerous thing

available in hardcover from

WILLIAM MORROW

in September 2011.

Chapter 1

They throw him out when he falls off the barstool. Although it wasn't a fall, exactly, he only stumbled a bit coming back from the bathroom and lurched against the bar, yet they said he had to leave because he was drunk. He finds that hilarious. He's too drunk to be in a bar. He makes a joke about a fall from grace. At least, he thinks he does. Maybe the joke was one of those things that stays in his head, for his personal amusement. For a long time, for fucking forever, Gordon's mind has been split by a thick, dark line, a line that divides and defines his life as well. What stays in, what is allowed out. But when he drinks, the line gets a little fuzzy.

Which might be why he drinks. Drank. Drinks. No, drank. He's done. Again. One night, one slip. He didn't even enjoy it that much.

"You driving?" the bartender asks, piloting him to the door, his arm firm yet kind around Gordon's waist.

"No, I live nearby," he says. One lie, one truth. He does live in the area, but not so near that he hasn't driven here in his father's old Buick, good old Shitty Shitty Bang Bang they called it. Well, not this Buick, but the Buick before, or the Buick before that. The old man always drove Buicks, and they were always, always, crap cars, but he kept buying them. That was Timothy Halloran Sr., loyal to the end, even to the crap of the crap of the crap.

Gordon stumbles and the bartender keeps him steady. He realizes he doesn't want the bartender to let go of him. The contact feels good. Shit, did he say *that* out loud? He's not a faggot. "I'm not a faggot," he says. It's just been so long since his wife slipped her hand into the crook of his elbow, so long since his daughters put their sticky little hands around his neck and whispered their sticky little words into his ears, the list of the things they wanted that Mommy wouldn't let them have, but maybe Daddy would see it differently? The bartender's embrace ends abruptly, now that Gordon is out the door. "I love you, man!" he says, for a joke. Only maybe he didn't. Or maybe it isn't funny. At any rate, no one's laughing and Gordon "Go-Go" Halloran always leaves 'em laughing.

He sits on the curb. He really did intend to go to a meeting tonight. It all came down to one turn. If he had gone left—but instead he went straight. Ha! He literally went straight and look where that had gotten him.

It isn't his fault. He wants to be sober. He strung together two years this time, chastened by the incident at his younger daughter's first birthday party. And he managed to stay sober even after Lori kicked him out last month. But the fact is, he has been faking it for months, stalling out where he always stalls out on the twelve steps, undermined by all that poking, poking, poking, that insistence on truth, on coming clean. Making *amends.* Sobriety—real sobriety, as opposed to the collection of sober days Gordon sometimes manages to put together—wants too much from him. Sobriety is trying to breach the line in his head. But Gordon needs that division. Take it away and he'll fall apart, sausage with no casing, crumbling into the frying pan.

Sausage. He'd like some sausage. Is there still an IHOP up on Route 40?

Saturday morning. Sausage and pancakes, his mother never sitting down as she kept flipping and frying, frying and flipping, loving how they all ate, Gordon and his brothers and his father, stoking them like machines. Come Saturday morning, I'm going away. Hey, hey, hey, it's Fat Albert!

When he moved back home six weeks ago, he asked his mother to make him some pancakes and she'd said, "Bisquick's in the cabinet." She thought he was drinking or whoring again, assumed that was why Lori had thrown him out. It was easier to let her think that. Then it turned out it was easier to *be* that, to surrender to drink and bad habits.

When it comes down to it, drunk and sober are just two sides of the same coin, and no matter how you flip it, you are still your fucked-up own self. It sure didn't help that his current AA group meets in his old parish school, now a Korean church. It's too weird, sitting on the metal chairs in an old classroom. Drink and the line gets fuzzy. Get sober and the line comes back into sharp relief, but then everyone starts attacking the line, says he has to let it go, break it down. *Take down the line, Mr. Gorbachev.* Boy, he's all over the place tonight, tripping down memory lane in every sense of the word. Funny, he has a nice memory associated with Reagan, but it feels like he was really young at the time. How old was he when Reagan made that Berlin Wall speech? Sixteen? Seventeen? Still in high school and already a fuck-up.

But to hear everyone tell it, he has always been a fuck-up, came into the world a fuck-up, is going to leave as a fuck-up. Then again, whoever followed Sean was destined to be a disappointment. Sean, the, Perfect. You would think that with three kids in the family, the two imperfect brothers would find a bond, gang up on that prissy middle fuck. But Tim has always taken Sean's side. Everyone gangs up against Go-Go, the nickname Gordon can't quite shake even at age forty. *Go, Go-Go. Go, Go-Go. Go, Go-Go.* That's what the others had chanted when he did his dance, a wild, spastic thing, steel guitar twanging. *Go, Go-Go. Go, Go-Go. Go, Go-Go. GoGoGoGoGoGo.*

Give Sean this: He's the one person who consistently uses Go-Go's full name. Gordon, not even Gordy. Maybe that's because he needs two full syllables to cram all the disappointment in. Actually, he needs four. "Jesus, Gordon, how many times can you move back home?" Or: "Jesus, Gordon, Lori is the best thing that ever happened to you and you've got kids now." Jesus, Gordon. Jesus, Gordon. Maybe he should have been Gee-Go instead of Go-Go.

He thinks about standing up but doesn't, although he could if he wanted to. He isn't that drunk. The beer and the shot hit him fast, after almost two years of sobriety. He was doing so good. He thought he had figured out a way to be in AA while respecting the line. They don't need to know *everything,* he reasoned. No one needs to know everything. There would be a way to tell the story that would allow him to make it through all twelve steps, finally, without breaching any loyalties, without breaking that long-ago promise, without hurting anyone.

He gets up, walks down the once-familiar avenue. As kids, they had been forbidden to ride their bikes on the busy street that essentially bounded their neighborhood, which should have made it impossible to find their way to this little business district, tempting to them because of its pizza parlor and the bakery and the High's Dairy Store. And there was a craft store with an unlikely name, a place owned by the family whose daughters had disappeared. He was little then, not even five, but he remembered a chill had gone through the neighborhood for a while, that all the parents had become strict and supervigilant.

Then they stopped. It was too hard, he guesses, being in their kids' shit all the time and the children slipped back into their free, unfettered ways. Nowadays . . . he doesn't even have the energy to finish the cliché in his head. He thinks of Lori, standing guard at the kitchen window of their "starter" home, a town house that cost $350,000 and to which he is now barred entry. Is that fair? Is anything fair? Sean is still perfect and even Tim does a good imitation of goodness, Mr. State's Attorney, with his three beautiful daughters and his plumpish wife, who was never that hot to begin with, yet Gordon can tell they still genuinely like each other. He's not sure he ever really liked Lori and he has a hunch Sean's in the same boat with his wife, Vivian, who's as frostily perfect as Sean. Tim and Sean, still married to their first wives, such good boys, forever and ever. Hey, he got an annulment, he's technically in the clear. Besides, fuck the church! Where was the church when he needed it? And now it's Korean

Catholic, whatever the fuck that is, probably Kool-Aid and dog on a cracker for communion.

Where was he? Where is he? On Gwynn Oak Avenue, thinking about how Sean, of all people, had figured out that if they rolled their bikes across the bridge to Purnell Drive, they could technically obey the rule never to ride their bikes on Forest Park Avenue and still manage to get over to Woodlawn, where the shops are. Or was it Mickey who had figured it out? Mickey was the one who lived above Purnell Drive, after all. She would have known the route, too. Even when they were kids, Mickey had been smart that way. She should have become the lawyer, not Tim. She was the real brains.

He walks for ten, twenty, thirty minutes, willing his head to clear. He walks down to the stream, where there once were swans and ducks, then to the public park, the site of an amusement park that closed before Go-Go was old enough to go there. It survived integration, his father always said, but it couldn't beat back Hurricane Agnes. Still one roller coaster remained standing for years, long enough for Go-Go to feel thwarted, denied. Sean and Tim claimed to have gone many, many times, but they weren't that much older. Sean would have been seven or eight when the park closed. Maybe they had lied? It makes Gordon feel better, catching perfect Sean in a potential lie.

Soon enough, the hypothetical becomes real to him, and he has worked up a nice fury. He gets out his cell phone and punches his brother's name on his contact list, ready to fight with him. But his hands aren't steady and he fumbles the phone as Sean's voice comes on, cool and reserved. The phone ends up on the ground, where the black turtle shape is hard to find in the dark. As Go-Go crawls around on his hands and knees, he hears Sean's voice, disgust evident. "Gordon? Gordon? Jesus, Gordon—"

I shoulda been Gee-Go. Does he say that out loud? His hand closes over the cell phone, but Sean has hung up. Okay, it isn't exactly the first time he has drunk-dialed his brother. But he's had a good run of sobriety, so Sean shouldn't have been all pissy and judgmental. Sean has no way of knowing he took a drink. No, Sean expects him to fail. That's unfair. And what kind of brother is that, anyway, expecting—rooting—for his younger sibling to fail? But that's Sean's dirty little secret. His perfection is relative, dependent upon the fuck-ups of Go-Go and Tim, and Tim isn't giving him much breathing room these days. In another family, Sean wouldn't even be all that. In another family, Sean might be the problem child, the loser. Especially if he had been treated like a loser from jump, the way Gordon was. They set him up. Of course he did whatever he was asked. He was just a little boy. Any little boy would have done what he did. Right?

His head clearer, he walks to the convenience store, buys a cup of scorched coffee, and drinks it in his car, his father's old Buick, the last iteration of Shitty Shitty Bang Bang, which has survived his father by almost fifteen years now. He is less than two miles from his mother's house. He has to make exactly four turns—two lefts, two rights. There are—he counts—one, two, three lights? The first one is there, right in front of him, complicated because there are actually five points at this intersection—five points, like a star. He sees Mickey making the drawing in the dirt, the stick slashing down and up, across and down, then up.

He makes it through, heads up the long steep hill. *I think I can I think I can I think I can.* Past the cemetery, through the second light. Almost home. Almost home. Only it isn't his home.

At the next light, he turns right instead of left. *Go, Go-Go, Go, Go-Go. Go, Go-Go.* Climbs the freeway entrance ramp just before the Strawberry Hill apartments. Mickey's family had moved here right before high school and Mickey's mother was hot. Sean and Tim swore they saw her sunbathing topless once, but they probably lied about that, too. Roller coasters, topless girls—they lied about everything.

Gordon heads west on the highway, then makes a U-turn before the Beltway cloverleaf, aiming his car back home along the infamous highway that ends, stops dead. As teenagers, they treated this two-mile stretch as their own little drag strip, but now the secret is out and others race here. He wonders how fast his father's old Buick can go. Ninety, one hundred? *Go, Go-Go. Go, Go-Go. Go, Go-Go.* The steel guitar twangs in his ears, in his memory, sharp and awful. Guy could not play for shit, much as he loved that damn, stupid guitar. *Go, Go-Go. Go, Go-Go. Go, Go-Go.* He is dancing, wild and free, his little arms moving so quickly it's almost like he's lashing himself, self-flagellation, and everyone loves him and everyone is laughing and everyone loves him and everyone is laughing and he is splashing through the stream, heedless of the poisonous water, no matter what Gwen's father says about tetanus and lockjaw, desperate to get away, to escape what he's done. *Go, Go-Go. Go, Go-Go.*

By the time he hits the Jersey wall, even the needle on the old Buick's speedometer has abandoned him.

Chapter 2

Clement Robison's house is wildly impractical for almost anyone, but especially so for an eighty-eight-year-old man living alone, even if he happens to be the one who designed it. Forty years ago, when Clem began the drawings for his dream house, he could not imagine being eighty-eight. Who can? Eighty-eight is hard to imagine at eighty-seven. His youngest daughter, now forty-five, summoned home—or so she's telling everyone—by her father's accident, doesn't really believe she'll ever be as old as he is. Oh, she expects, hopes, to enjoy the genetic advantage of his longevity. But the number itself, eighty-eight, is like some monstrous old coat discovered in the hall closet, scratchy and smelling of mothballs. *Who left this here? Is this yours? Not mine! I've never seen it before.*

The Robison house was modern once and people still describe it that way, although its appliances and fixtures are frozen like the clocks in a fairy tale, set circa 1985, the last remodel. A mix of milled stone, lumber and glass, it nestles into the side of the hill on a stone base, a door leading into the above ground basement, but the family custom was to use that door only in the most inclement weather, and Clem is not one to break long-standing habits. He has continued to mount the long, stone staircase, which creates the illusion that one is climbing a natural path up the hillside. The steps are charming, but there is something off about them. Too low or too high, they fool the foot, and over the years almost everyone in the family has taken a tumble or near-tumble down. Gwen's turn came when she was thirteen, rushing outside and neglecting to consider that the sheen on the steps might be ice, not mere moisture. She traveled the entire flight on her butt, boom, boom, boom, her friends laughing at the bottom. At thirteen, the end result was a bruised coccyx and ego, nothing more.

Her father, coming outside to get the paper on a cool but dry March morning, missed a step, tumbled almost to the street and broke his left hip.

"Do you know how many people die within a year of breaking a hip?" Gwen asks her father, still in University Hospital.

"Gwen, I taught geriatric medicine for years. I think I'm up on the facts. *Most* people don't die."

"But a lot do. Almost a third."

"Still, most don't. And I'm in good health otherwise. I just have to be disciplined about recovery and therapy."

"Miller and Fee want you to sell the house, move into assisted living."

"*That* again. And you?"

"I'm holding them off. For now. I told them I would assess your situation."

They smile at each other, coconspirators. Gwen believes herself to be her father's favorite, although he would never say such a thing. His denials are sincere when her much older siblings, Miller and Fiona, bring up the contentious matter. "I was just more available when Gwen was little," their father says. "Less career obsessed." "Daddy doesn't have favorites," Gwen says. But she knows the seven-year gap between Fiona and Gwen is not enough to explain their father's clear preference for her. There is her remarkable resemblance to their mother, dead for almost twenty-five years. And there is the bond of the house and the neighborhood, Dickeyville, which Gwen and her father love more fiercely than anyone else in the family. As a child, she used to take long walks with him in the hills behind the house, never letting on that she traveled farther and deeper into them when she was with her friends. Miller and Fee, living thousands of miles away, have been trying to get their father out of the house for years, decades, ever since their mother's death. Gwen, who remains in Baltimore, has done whatever she can to allow her father to stay in the family home. Should the day come that he really can't live there, it has always been their unspoken understanding that Gwen will take over the house for her own family.

"How are things at home?" her father asks.

It's an open question, applicable to the physical status of her house and a much larger, if vaguer problem. Gwen chooses to address the physical.

"Not great. The county came out and pushed the ruins of the retaining wall back on our property, but says it's our job to re-build it. And even when we do, it won't necessarily address our foundation issues. The ground could shift again."

"Why—never mind."

"Why did we buy out there when our inspector warned us of this very problem? I ask myself that every day. For me, I think it was because Relay reminded me of Dickeyville. Isolated, yet not. A little slice of country so close to the city, the idiosyncratic houses. And for Karl, it was all about convenience—the com-muter train station within walking distance, BWI and Amtrak ten minutes away. Go figure—for once, my dreamy nostalgia and his pragmatism aligned and the result is utter disaster. There's probably a lesson to be learned there."

"The lesson," her father says, "is that you have a five-year-old daughter."

"Don't worry," Gwen says, pretending not to understand. "We've figured out how to make it work once you come home. I'm going to get up at six A.M. and drive over there, do the break-fast and getting-her-off-to-school thing. And I'll reverse it at day's end, be there for dinner and bedtime. But I'm going to spend the nights at your house, so we don't have to have a nighttime aide."

"Gwen, I can easily afford—"

"It's not about affording. And it's just for a few weeks. Anyone can tolerate anything for a few weeks." Months, years, her mind amends. It is amazing what one can tolerate, what she has tolerated. "Also, it's not the worst thing in the world, making Karl curtail his travel, to learn that he's part of a household, not a guest star who jets in and out as it suits him."

"He is who he is, Gwen. You went into this with eyes wide open. I told you all about cardiac surgeons. And Karl was already a star. It's not like this sneaked up on you. Not like the chicken."

"What?"

"The chicken. That's why I fell. There was a chicken on the steps, trying to peck at my ankles, and all I wanted to do was avoid stepping on it. I twisted my ankle and went over."

Gwen tries not to show how alarming she finds this. *A chicken?* There haven't been chickens in their neighborhood, ever. Except for—but those birds were far away and far in the past. No, that couldn't be. Her father must have imagined the chicken. But if her father was imagining chickens, what else was breaking down inside his mind? She would almost prefer there was a chicken. Maybe there was. The past few years have seen a flurry of stories about animals showing up in places where they shouldn't be— wild cats in suburbs, a deer crashing through the window of a dental practice, and, come to think of it, a chicken in one of the New York boroughs. And Dickeyville is the kind of place that has always attracted crunchy granola types. It is easy to imagine some earnest, incompetent locavore trying to raise chickens only to have them escape from his ineptly constructed coop. Gwen will ask around when she goes by the house this afternoon, to begin preparing for her father's return.

The Robison house is isolated, even by Dickeyville's standards, which in turn feels cut off from much of Baltimore. It is officially the last house on Wetheredsville Road, only a few feet from where the Jersey wall now blocks the street, marking the start of a "nature trail" that one can follow all the way to downtown. The blocked street means Gwen can't use the old shortcut, through what is properly called a park, but which she and her childhood friends always referred to as the woods. Their term was more accurate. Leakin Park is a forest, vast and dense, difficult to navigate. Gwen and her friends covered more of it than almost anyone, and even they missed large swaths.

Traffic is surprisingly heavy, the journey longer than anticipated, giving the lie to her blithe words about dashing back and forth between here and the house in Relay. Still, the chance to move to Dickeyville, even temporarily, is providential. Maryland law requires a separation of at least one year to file for an uncontested divorce. She learned this during her first divorce, a sad bit of knowledge she had never planned to use again. Does anyone plan to divorce twice? Then again, after that first failed marriage, the fact is always there, incontrovertible. You're not going to go the distance with one person, your chance at perfection is lost. For someone like Gwen, who is professionally perfect—she edits a city magazine that instructs others how to have the perfect house, children, wardrobe—this is particularly irksome.

Yet even if she can manage to extend her time in her father's house for a year, it won't be enough. It is the spouse who *stays* who can file after one year, on the grounds of abandonment. As the spouse who is leaving, Gwen will have to wait two years if Karl doesn't agree, and he has made it clear that he won't, ever. She can't spend that much time away from Annabelle, but nor can she afford her own place in their current school district. They aren't upside down in their mortgage, but they have virtually no equity, and home equity loans are hard to get now, anyway. Karl has lots of money, but, again, he isn't going to use it to let her leave him. And if she spends even a single night back in the Relay house, the clock resets on the separation. Maybe Annabelle will move into the Dickeyville house and they can keep this information from the school?

But the Dickeyville house will be chaotic, once her father returns. A geriatric specialist should have designed a home that would be friendlier to old age, but his house is downright hostile to the idea. There is the first level, the stonewalled basement, with the laundry room and various systems. Then the large glass-

and-timber first floor, built to take advantage of the site, but with only a powder room. Yet the top two floors, with the full baths, have narrow halls and tight corners. Her father, appalled at the spiraling costs and delays, skimped on his dream house's bedrooms. She will have to set him up in the first-floor "great room," where he will have nice views and space in which to move, if no bath. But then her father will dominate the first floor, and privacy will be found only in the cramped, dark bedrooms above. And how will he bathe? Besides, Annabelle would be lonely, as Gwen once was, and she won't even have the freedom to roam the woods. What was considered safe in Gwen's childhood is unthinkable for Annabelle's.

Her head hurts. It's all too complicated. *Dial it back,* as she tells her writers when they are in over their heads on a story. Concentrate on one thing, one task. Get to the house, make sure it's clean, do laundry, call a nursing service, let the nursing service figure out the best place for her father to convalesce.

Once there, she finds three newspapers in yellow wrappers, several catalogs, but almost no real mail. Her father doesn't recycle—on principle, he believes it's a ruse, an empty, feel-good gesture—so she tosses everything, leaving only the bills on the kitchen counter. The kitchen is small, another victim of the house's cost overruns, but her mother made it a marvel of efficiency. The light at this time of the day, year, is breathtaking, gold and rose streaks above the hill. Even with the old appliances, the yellowing Formica counters and white metal cabinets, it is a warm, welcoming room.

Gwen goes upstairs. Everything is in order, there is no evidence of a man in decline. Widowed at sixty-three, her father quickly learned to take excellent care of himself. His closet and drawers are neater than Gwen's, there is an admirable lack of clutter. A single page from the *Times,* dated the day before his fall, is on his nightstand—the Wednesday crossword puzzle, filled out in ink, without a single error. The puzzle, the tidy house, it all indicates he's of sound mind and should back up his version of events. So why does she keep thinking of it that way, as a *version*? She's still troubled about that chicken.

Glancing out the narrow casement window toward the street, Gwen sees a black-haired man walking two dogs as black as his hair. She knows him instantly by the part in his hair, impossibly straight and perfect, visible even from this distance.

"Sean," Gwen calls out through the window. Seconds later, she is running heedlessly down the stone steps that undid her father.

"Gwennie," he says. Then: "I'm sorry. Old habits. *Gwen*."

"What are you doing here?"

"Well—my brother, of course."

"Tim? Or Go-Go?"

"Gordon," he says. Perhaps Sean has sworn off nicknames. Funny, Gwen liked hearing Gwennie, even if it always carries the reminder that she was once fat. Gwennie the Whale. She was only fat until age thirteen. They say people are forever fat inside, but Gwen's not. Inside, she's the sylph she became. If anything, she has trouble remembering that she's growing older, that she can no longer rely on being the prettiest girl in the room.

"What's the incorrigible Go-Go—excuse me, *Gordon*—done now?"

Sean looks offended, then confused. "I'm sorry, I assumed you knew."

"My father fell three days ago, broke his hip. I don't know much of anything."

"Three days ago?"

"In the morning. Coming down the steps to fetch his paper."

"Three days ago—that's when Go-Go . . ." His voice catches. Sean is the middle brother, the handsomest, the smartest, the best all-around. Gwen's mother used to say that Tim was the practice son, Sean the platonic ideal, and Go-Go a bridge too far. Gwen's mother could be cutting in her observations, yet there was no real meanness in her. And her voice was so delicate, her manner so light, that no one took offense.

"What, Sean?"

"He crashed his car into the concrete barrier where the high-way ends. Probably going eighty, ninety miles per hour. We think the accelerator got stuck, or he miscalculated where it ended. I mean, we've all played with our speedometers up there."

Yes, when they were teenagers, learning to drive. But Go-Go was—she calculates, subtracting four, no, five years from her age—forty, much too old to be testing his car's power.

"He's—"

"Dead, Gwen. At the scene, instantly."

"I'm so sorry, Sean."

Go-Go, dead. Although she has seen him periodically over the years, he remained forever eight or nine in her mind, wild and uninhibited. The risk taker in the group, although it was possible that Go-Go simply didn't understand the concept of danger, didn't know he was taking risks. She flashes back to an image of him on this very street, dashing across the road in pursuit of a ball, indifferent to the large truck bearing down on him, the others screaming for him to stop.

"Thank you."

"How's your mom holding up?" She remembers that Mr. Halloran died years ago, although she didn't go to the funeral, just wrote proper notes to the boys and their mother. It was a busy time in her life, as she recalls.

"Not well. I came home for the funeral—I live in St. Petersburg now."

"Russia?"

A tight smile. "Florida."

Gwen tries not to make a face. Not because of Florida, but because the Sean she remembers would have been in Russia, a dashing foreign correspondent or diplomat. He's still pretty dashing. Close up, she can see a few flecks of white in his hair, but the very dignity that bordered on priggish in a teenage boy suits him now. He has finally grown into his gravitas.

"I feel awful that I didn't know. When is the funeral?"

"Tomorrow. Visitation is tonight."

Gwen calculates, even as she knows she must find a way to attend both. She will have to ask for another half day at work, make arrangements for Annabelle tonight. There is already so much to be done. But this is Go-Go—and Sean, her first boyfriend, even if she seldom thinks of him in that context. Gwen is not the kind of woman who thinks longingly of her past, who tracks down old boyfriends on the Internet. The Hallorans, along with Mickey Wyckoff, are more like the old foundations and footings they sometimes found in the woods, abandoned and overgrown, impossible to reclaim. They had been a tight-knit group of five for a summer or two, but it couldn't be sustained. Such coed groups didn't last long, probably. Funny, it has never occurred to Gwen until now that she and Mickey could disengage thoroughly from the group, but the Halloran brothers had to remain a set, mismatched as they were. Crass Tim, Serious Sean, Wild Go-Go.

"I'll be there." She considers placing a hand on Sean's forearm, but worries it will seem flirtatious. Instead, she strokes the dogs, who are old, with grizzled jowls and labored breathing, so ancient and tired that they don't object to this long interlude in the middle of their walk. Yet old as they obviously are, they can't be more than, what? Fifteen? Sixteen? Which is still older than her marriage to Karl.

"Mom will appreciate that," Sean says and heads back up the hill. She knows the route, knows the house at which he will arrive after going up Wetheredsville, then turning left on "New" Pickwick, a street of what once seemed like modern houses, small and symmetrical relative to the shambling antiquities for which Dickeyville was known, following it to the shortest street in the neighborhood, Sekots, just four houses. The Halloran house always smelled of strong foods—onions, cabbage, hamburger—and it was always a mess. Sometimes, the chaos could be comforting; no child need worry about disturbing or breaking anything in such a household. It could be terrifying, too, though, a place where the adults yelled horrible things at one another and

Mrs. Halloran was often heard sobbing, off in the distance. The boys never seemed to notice, and even Mickey was nonchalant about it. But the Halloran house scared Gwen, and she made sure their activities centered on her house, or the woods beyond.

Go-Go, dead. The only surprise was that she was surprised at all.

Most thought he was called Go-Go because it was a bastard-ization of Gordon, but it really derived from his manic nature, ev-ident from toddlerhood, his insistence on following his brothers wherever they went. "I go-go," he would say, as if the second syl-lable, the repetition, would clinch the argument. "I go-go." And he did. He ran into walls, splashed into the polluted waters of the stream, jumped from branches and balconies. Once, Go-Go spent much of an afternoon running head-on into an old mattress they had found in the woods, laughing all the while.

Now he has run head-on into the barrier at the end of the high-way. Gwen can't help wondering if he was drunk. Although she hasn't seen the Halloran boys for years, she knows, the way that everyone knows things in Dickeyville, that Go-Go has a prob-lem. It is implied, if never stated outright, in the lost jobs, the broken first marriage, the rocky second one, the fact that he re-turns to the roost for open-ended stays.

Then again, who is she to judge Go-Go? Isn't she pulling the same trick, running home, a two-time loser in matrimony, taking comfort in a parent's unconditional love? Mr. Halloran may have been hard as nails, but Mrs. Halloran, when she wasn't screaming at her sons and wondering why they had been born, spoiled them to the best of her ability, especially Go-Go. And while most people will assume Gwen is nothing more than a devoted daughter, some will see through her. Her brother and sister, certainly. And Karl.

That is, Karl would see through her if it ever occurred to him to look, really look at her. But if Karl looked at her that way, they wouldn't be in this fix. At least, that's how she likes to see it.

Laura Lippman

Jan Cobb

LAURA LIPPMAN grew up in Baltimore and returned to her hometown in 1989 to work as a journalist. After writing seven books while still a full-time reporter, she left the Baltimore *Sun* to focus on fiction. She is the author of eleven Tess Monaghan novels, including *Baltimore Blues, The Sugar House, Another Thing to Fall,* and *The Girl in the Green Raincoat;* seven stand-alone novels, including *Every Secret Thing, To the Power of Three, What the Dead Know, Life Sentences, I'd Know You Anywhere,* and *The Most Dangerous Thing;* and one short story collection, *Hardly Knew Her.* She is also the editor of another story collection, *Baltimore Noir.* Lippman has won numerous awards for her work, including the Edgar, Quill, Anthony, Nero Wolfe, Agatha, Gumshoe, Barry, and Macavity. She lives in Baltimore, Maryland, with her husband, David Simon; their daughter; and her stepson.

NEW IN HARDCOVER

NEW YORK TIMES BESTSELLER

LAURA LIPPMAN

the most dangerous thing

Some skeletons refuse to stay buried . . .

Years ago, they were all the best of friends. But as time passed and circumstances changed, they grew apart, became adults with families of their own, and began to forget about the past and one another. With each passing year, the memory of the terrible lie they shared faded as well.

Now, though, when Gordon, the ne'er-do-well of their little gang, dies, these long-ago friends are suddenly thrown together again. And then the revelations start. Could their long-ago lie be the reason for their troubles today? Each one of these old friends has to wonder if their secret has been discovered—and if someone within the circle is out to destroy them.

 Follow Laura on Facebook!
www.LauraLippman.com

WILLIAM MORROW
An Imprint of HarperCollinsPublishers

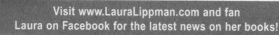